Omnibus

A SERIES OF MURDERS
and

CORPORATE BODIES

Simon Brett

Back-In-Print Books Ltd

Published by Back-In-Print Books Ltd 2004
ISBN 1 903552 49 4
Previously published in Great Britain by
Victor Gollancz under ISBN 0 575 04466 7 and 0 575 05152 3

Printed and bound on demand by
Lightning Source.

Back-In-Print Books Ltd
P.O. Box 47057
London SW18 1YW
020 8637 0975

www.backinprint.co.uk
info@backinprint.co.uk

When Simon Brett studied at Oxford he became President of the OUDS, appeared in cabarets and directed the Oxford Theatre Group at the Edinburgh Festival Fringe in 1967.

Later he worked as a light entertainment producer for BBC radio and television before taking up writing full time in 1979.

Simon created the Charles Paris and Mrs Pargeter detective series and, to his fans' relief, he is still writing more. He also made a name as the author of the radio and TV series *After Henry*. The radio series *No Commitments*, the best-selling *How to be a Little Sod* and the novel *Shock to the System*, filmed starring Michael Caine, are other fruits of his imaginative mind. He is married, has three children and lives in a village on the South Downs.

This is a Back-In-Print Book.

- This title was out of print for some time but Back-In-Print Books has brought it back in to print because of demand from Simon Brett fans.
- This re-print was produced on demand using digital printing technology.
- Paper and print quality are higher than most conventionally printed paperback novels.
- Digital printing may cost somewhat more but ensures that book titles need not go out of print as long as there are readers who want them.

What other titles are available from **BiP**?

Check out our web site at www.backinprint.co.uk for other titles released by Back-In-Print Books Ltd and news about forthcoming titles.

Do you want any other titles?

If you know of a title which is out of print and you think there might be a reasonable demand please contact us.

Back-In-Print Books Ltd
P.O. Box 47057
London SW18 1YW
020 8637 0975

www.backinprint.co.uk
info@backinprint.co.uk

A SERIES OF MURDERS

*To Alan and Peta
(not forgetting Petra)*

Chapter One

'NOW LISTEN, LADS, we're dealing with a cold-blooded murderer who will stop at nothing.'

Sergeant Clump stared belligerently over the counter of Little Breckington Police Station at the dozen constables facing him. 'And that is why you've been gathered here from all corners of the county to see that his evil plans are foiled.' He leaned forward as he warmed to his task. 'Now, there's only one thing that's going to defeat a criminal of such cunning, and that is –'

'Superior cunning,' a voice from the doorway coolly interrupted.

The thirteen policemen turned as one to look at the newcomer. They saw a tall figure in a dark floppy hat and cloak. A monocle graced one eye; from it a dark cord snaked down to the buttonhole of an immaculately tailored suit. A pale cravat frothed at the stranger's neck; white spats gleamed above the shine of his black shoes.

'Mr. Braid,' said Sergeant Clump in a voice that combined admiration and resentment in equal parts. 'I wondered when you was going to turn up. But don't you worry, sir. Everything's in hand. We shall catch this devil without needing your assistance.'

'Really?' Stanislas Braid wafted across the room and came to rest in a chair by the counter. He looked up at the sergeant; his expression was quizzical, challenging, almost insolent. 'Well, I suppose there has to be a first time for everything.'

The sergeant's face contorted into frustration. He looked, as the police always should when faced by the coruscating brilliance of an amateur sleuth, baffled.

They held each other's gaze for a long time. Much longer, indeed, than would have been expected in the normal course of events. Then, mercifully, a new voice released them. 'Okay, we've got that.'

At the Floor Manager's words the assembled policemen on the set relaxed, broke their formal stances, and turned to chatter and giggle with each other. Charles Paris eased his finger around the neck of Sergeant Clump's jacket. Uncomfortable, those pre-war high-collared uniforms. And hot under the television lights.

Russell Bentley, the actor playing Stanislas Braid, shook his head with dissatisfaction. There was clearly something in the scene he hadn't felt happy with.

The Floor Manager held up a finger, indicating that the cast should stay in position, while he listened to his earpiece for instructions from the gallery. He nodded as he took in his orders, no doubt already tactfully rephrasing the Director's words.

One final vigorous nod. 'Yes, we're okay on that. Got the scene. Extras won't be wanted again till after lunch. Russell, you've got a costume change.'

At this signal, the dozen policemen broke ranks. Though they would rather have been called background artistes than extras, they weren't going to argue. Their more immediate priority was to get to the canteen before the rush. They were a docile breed, content to spend long days over endless cups of coffee waiting for their two minutes of anonymous performance.

Charles Paris looked at where his watch should be and remembered with annoyance that the one provided by Wardrobe didn't work. His own had been thought too modern for the vaguely thirties setting of the *Stanislas Braid* series. Still, Charles reckoned the West End Television bar must be open by now. Time for a quick one, surely.

Russell Bentley, however, was set to frustrate such intentions. 'Oh, come on,' he complained. 'We can't take that scene like that.'

Everyone on the set froze truculently. The star, with the instincts of long experience in television, addressed his remarks to the one camera on whose top a red light glowed, knowing that its output could be seen in the gallery. 'It was terrible.'

Though he was speaking to the camera, the reply from the Director was relayed through the floor manager's earpiece. 'Rick said it was fine, Russell.'

'But it wasn't. Camera three certainly wasn't tight enough on me at the end.'

'It was fine, and we are rather pushed for time,' the floor manager assured him, bowdlerising the words that burned in his earpiece.

'That's not the point,' Russell Bentley objected. 'Look, if the schedule's too tight, that's not my problem. All I know is that I've got a professional reputation and I'm not going to have it destroyed by slapdash direction.'

The Floor Manager's long training in keeping a straight face could not totally suppress a wince at the gallery's reaction to that. He smothered it in a conciliatory smile. 'Rick says it was really great, and we must move on.'

'Just take a cutaway of my reaction,' Russell Bentley bargained, knowing that his suggestion should be quicker than retaking the whole scene. The cutaway would mean recording just the one shot and slotting it in when the scene was edited.

The Floor Manager's smile was diluted by more vitriol in his earpiece. 'Rick said it really did look fine,' he paraphrased inadequately.

'No, I'm sorry. I refuse to do the costume change until we get this right.'

The background artistes stirred with uneasy fascination as Russell Bentley became more 'difficult'.

'Look, this is the first episode of the series. Already some of the filming has been pretty unsatisfactory, though perhaps it can be tidied up in editing.

But you've got to understand, the performances we lay down now are the ones we're going to be stuck with for five more episodes – more, if we go to a second series. So I'm afraid no bloody schedule is going to get in the way of my playing Stanislas Braid as I think he should be played!'

To Charles this sounded a bit rich. If there was one thing Russell Bentley was known for throughout the business, it was the fact that he played every part in exactly the same way – as Russell Bentley. He had started to play Russell Bentley when he was developed as a film star by the Rank 'Charm School' and had seen no reason to change the formula when his career developed into television. The idea that it took him time to home in on a new characterisation was incongruous.

But at the same time Charles knew that what was going on was not really a discussion of the character of Stanislas Braid. It was a power struggle between Russell Bentley and the Director, Rick Landor. The star wanted the guidelines for his treatment during the series to be established early on and was prepared to use his considerable experience in manipulation to get his own way. Rick Landor was a relatively new Director, and Russell was determined to break the young man in. They'd already had a set-to on Monday, the first day of filming, and now, on Wednesday, Russell was trying to assert his authority over the studio part of the production, too.

Still, Charles thought, mustn't complain, just take anything that comes along. After all, he was working, actually contracted till the end of June for a whole television series of six programmes, three months' highly paid work – when was the last time that had happened to Charles Paris?

Russell Bentley won this round of the struggle. Rick Landor, no doubt deciding that the loss of time promised by further argument was greater than the loss of time involved in taking the single shot, capitulated.

'Okay, we'll do the cutaway,' the Floor Manager relayed, failing to disguise his relief at the end of the skirmish.

As always, such things take longer than they should. The continuity of the characters' positions and eyelines had to be checked on the recorded tape and the background artists regrouped exactly as they had been on the first take. Charles Paris had to be moved by millimetres back and forth along his counter. Then Russell Bentley was not happy with his expression in the first two takes of the cutaway. By the time the shot was finally in the can, it would have been quicker to retake the whole scene.

'Okay, break for coffee there,' the Floor Manager shouted. He consulted his watch. 'Back at twenty past eleven.'

Oh, damn, thought Charles, it's earlier than I thought. Have to wait a while for that drink.

He grinned across to a girl standing at the edge of the set. She, too, was dressed in thirties style: a pastel summer dress, a neat little hat perched on the back of her head, hair corrugated by a perm. But the girlish costume seemed at odds with her dark, almost Italian colouring and the thick sensuality of her lips.

'Going for a coffee?' asked Charles, who hadn't had the opportunity to talk to her much during the previous week of rehearsal and two days of filming and thought he might make up for lost time.

'Maybe in a while,' Sippy Stokes replied diffidently.

So Charles went off to the canteen on his own.

The scene in the W.E.T. canteen might have looked bizarre to an outsider, but the people there were used to seeing tables filled with thirties policemen and bright young things in striped blazers from the *Stanislas Braid* set, exotically crested and mini-skirted dancers from a pop programme in Studio B, along with the usual makeup girls in nylon tabards, PAs in designer leisurewear, shirt-sleeved cameramen, T-shirted scene shifters, and the occasional sharp executive suit.

Charles bought his subsidised cup of coffee and Eccles cake and reflected, not for the first time, on how much he always found himself eating when working in television. It's all those breaks, he thought, all those oh-so-available subsidised canteens. Even worse when doing the filming – location caterers providing lavish spreads, people who would never normally eat between meals cramming every spare moment with a bacon sandwich. He sometimes wondered whether Wardrobe had problems with long series, constantly having to let out the stars' waistbands. Though the stars were probably working so hard that they burned it all off. It was the supporting artistes who faced the real hazard of obesity, he concluded as his stomach strained against Sergeant Clump's belt.

The table he joined was, predictably enough, a theatrical one. A couple of the policeman-extras, who still thought of themselves as actors and were not yet reconciled to a lifetime of 'background' work, were sitting there.

Also in uniform, though in his case a grey chauffeur's uniform, was Jimmy Sheet, who played Stanislas Braid's faithful driver, Blodd. Though Sheet was now concentrating on acting, the admiring glances of a few secretaries in the canteen reminded Charles that the young man had only recently given up his career as a pop singer.

The others at the table were Will Parton, Mort Verdon, and Tony Rees, the last two Stage Manager and Assistant Stage Manager, respectively. Charles had worked with Mort on a previous W.E.T. series, *The Strutters*, and appreciated the willowy man's outrageously camp humour. Tony Rees he didn't know well, but he had a lot of time for Will Parton, the writer who had adapted most of the *Stanislas Braid* scripts from the crime novels of W. T. Wintergreen. Will had a good line in cynical repartee, which was responding well to Mort's contrasting style as Charles joined them.

'Right, tell me, who's this an impression of?' Mort demanded, suddenly erasing all expression from his face and freezing.

'A zombie?' Will hazarded.

'Close, close.' Mort relaxed. 'No, that was Russell Bentley looking happy.'

'Ah, of course.'

'And this one?' Mort recomposed his face into exactly the same anonymous pose.

This time Will caught on. 'Russell Bentley looking sad!'

'Exactly, boofle,' Mort agreed. 'And this morning, of course, we saw Russell Bentley stamping her little foot, didn't we?'

'Missed that,' said Will. 'I wasn't in the studio.'

With relish in the telling, Mort supplied the details of the recent conflict.

'I don't blame him,' Will said at the end of the narration, 'if he's having problems finding the character. I've read every one of the bloody books of W. T. Wintergreen, and dear Stanislas Braid still seems completely cardboard to me.'

'But then dear Russell is a completely cardboard actor,' Mort observed judiciously, 'so it's actually very good casting.'

'Which is more than can be said for some of the other casting,' Jimmy Sheet announced.

Mort cocked a quizzical eyebrow at him. 'Now who *could* you mean?'

'Are you not feeling at home in the role of Blodd yet?' asked Will.

'What?' Jimmy Sheet was instantly on the defensive. 'Don't you worry, I can manage it fine. All right, I know I done the singing for a few years, but I started out as an actor. Italia Conti School, all that.'

'That wasn't what I meant,' Will reassured Jimmy. But Charles wondered. Will was very good at needling people in an ambiguous way; he had an infallible knack of homing in on someone's insecurities.

'All I was saying,' Will continued soothingly, 'is that the lovely W. T. Wintergreen has put almost exactly as much reality into the character of Blodd as she has into dear old Stanislas himself. I don't envy you playing the part.'

'Oh, I reckon it's all right,' said Jimmy. 'Not too hard. Way I see him, Blodd's a sort of fairly chirpy cockney type, you know, good to have around, keeps everyone cheerful. Bit of an eye for the girls, too.'

Will Parton nodded gravely. 'I'm glad you see it that way. Because that's exactly how I've written the part.'

Charles caught Will's eye, and both of them had to look away to avoid giggling. Jimmy Sheet didn't realise he was being sent up. The character he had described had very little to do with the character of Blodd as written, but it was a very good portrait of how Jimmy Sheet saw himself. Just as Russell Bentley was playing Russell Bentley, so Jimmy Sheet clearly intended to play Jimmy Sheet.

'Has W.T.W. herself been around today?' asked Charles diffidently, shifting the subject.

'She was in the gallery this morning,' Mort confirmed. 'With her dear loopy sister.'

'And they were both poking round the set first thing,' added Tony Rees in his truculent Welsh voice. 'Disapproving of all the props and that.'

Will laughed bitterly. 'How's Rick bearing up to them?'

'With difficulty.'

'I can imagine. I make a solemn vow' – the writer laid his hand on his heart – 'that in future I will only adapt the works of dead authors. I cannot stand any more of the genteel interference of people like W.T.W. and Louisa. Why can't they do what all other writers involved in television do – just take the money, do as they're told, and shut up?'

The deep cynicism of this reminded Charles of Will's unsuccessful attempts to be an original playwright and the contempt in which he held his lucrative television contracts.

'Anyway, I think there'll be tears before bedtime,' said Mort Verdon piously. 'Poor young Rick is not finding life easy between the demands of his ageing star and his extremely aged crime writer.'

'Not to mention his rather less aged starlet,' Will threw in casually.

'Who do you mean?' asked Charles.

But Jimmy Sheet knew straightaway. With a smile of complicity to Will, he said, 'That was what I meant about casting.'

'Ah.'

'Not the greatest little actress in the world, I'd say.'

'As an actress, Sippy Stokes is absolute death.' Then Will added mischievously, 'And she hasn't even got the excuse of having been a pop star for the last five years.'

''Ere, what do you think you're –?'

'I was joking, Jimmy. Just joking.'

Jimmy Sheet subsided with a grin, but he didn't look totally reassured. Once again, Will's attack – if attack it was – had been ambiguous.

Sippy Stokes, the object of their bitchery, had been cast for the series in the role of Stanislas Braid's beloved daughter, Christina. This was another character who worked better for enthusiasts of the crime novels of W. T. Wintergreen than for Will Parton. He had had considerable difficulties in making the part even vaguely playable, though he was quite pleased with the lines he had eventually come up with. Played by an actress of real skill and energy, he reckoned they would just about work.

On the evidence of the rehearsal of the previous week and of that week's filming, Sippy Stokes was not such an actress. Even Russell Bentley, usually far too absorbed in giving his performance as Russell Bentley to notice what any of the rest of the cast did, had been heard to comment on her incompetence.

'No, some people are born actresses,' Will Parton mused aloud, 'some achieve actressness, but I'm afraid you could thrust everything you liked upon Sippy Stokes and you'd never make her into one.'

'She speaks well of you, too,' said Mort.

'Well, quite honestly,' Will persisted, 'I would have thought the basic minimum requirement for an actress is the ability to act.'

'Don't you believe it, boofle. Lots of actresses have made very good careers from completely different "minimum requirements".'

'Nell Gwynne, for example,' Charles suggested.

'Yes, very good example. I mean, she did all right. Now there was a girl who knew her onions.'

'Or her oranges.'

'Thank you, Charles – always rely on you for a cheap line, can't we? Point I'm making, boofle, is that you never hear much about what old Nellie was like as an actress, do you. Never read any notices... "Nell Gwynne made an enchanting Ophelia..."'

'Or even "I would have enjoyed the evening more without Nell Gwynne's Juliet".'

'Yes. Mind you, Charles, I don't think any critic would be quite that vicious.'

'Ah.' Charles grimaced apologetically.

'Oh, really? Who?'

'*Surrey Advertiser*. And I'm afraid the actual line was "I would have enjoyed the evening more without Charles Paris's Romeo".'

'Oh, bad luck. Anyway, point I'm making, boofle, is –'

But Mort Verdon never got on to the point he was making, for they were interrupted at that moment by the arrival of Ben Docherty, the Producer, and Dilly Muirfield, the script editor, of *Stanislas Braid*. Will Parton greeted their appearance with a groan. He knew it would be him they wanted to see, and he knew it would be about more rewrites that they wanted to see him. 'As someone once said,' he had growled at Charles a few evenings before, 'you don't write for television, you rewrite for television.'

Sure enough, there were 'a couple of points' on the next week's script that Ben and Dilly wanted to 'just have another look at,' so Will allowed himself to be dragged away, protesting that he was sure Shakespeare didn't have this trouble.

Though the coffee break had another five minutes to run, the taciturn A.S.M., Tony Rees, also reckoned it was time he was getting back to the studio, and Jimmy Sheet wanted to check some lines in his dressing room.

Mort Verdon regaled Charles with a few scurrilous stories about Ben Docherty's drinking, mostly along the lines of 'My dear, he was once so pissed he contracted a whole cast for a series one afternoon, completely forgot he'd done it, and contracted a completely different lot the next morning,' but then he, too, had to return to check through some props for the next scene.

That left Charles with his two policemen, the background artistes.

'This is the first episode, isn't it?' asked one of them. Charles confirmed that that was indeed the case.

'And that police station is a regular set?'

'Oh, yes.'

'And you're a running character?'

'Yes,' said Charles, still having a bit of difficulty in accepting his unusual good fortune. 'In every episode.'

'Ah.' The background artiste nodded with satisfaction. 'That's good.'

Charles was curious. Why?'

'Well, you're always going to need policemen on a police-station set, aren't you?'

'Um.'

The background artiste winked at his companion. 'And got to keep familiar faces, haven't you? Can't keep changing the personnel in a village police station, can you? I think we could be in for a series here, Bob.'

They both looked so pleased at the idea that Charles hadn't the heart to disillusion them, to tell them that the whole point of Little Breckington Police Station, as created by the inimitable W. T. Wintergreen, was that it only had one policeman. Sergeant Clump was the village bobby; he did everything on his own; it was only in this one episode that he enlisted the help of police from other areas.

But there was no need to tell the two background artistes that. Charles knew too much about theatrical dreams and hopes to crush them so gratuitously.

Chapter Two

HE WANDERED BACK to the studio shortly after half past eleven. Better just check what they were moving on to next. He still quite fancied a drink, but he didn't want to look desperate. Of course, there was the half bottle of Bell's back in his dressing room, but no, he should resist that. Drinking in secret always made him feel a bit like a secret drinker. Whereas having a drink in the W.E.T. bar had a more open, honest – almost virtuous – feel to it.

The rehearsal light rather than the recording light showed outside the double doors of Studio A, so Charles was not worried about slipping inside. He looked out across the five sets cunningly angled by the designer to fit into the studio space. Cameras and mobile sound booms on long cables prowled between the different locations.

Apart from the Little Breckington Police Station set, there were the hall, sitting room, and billiard room of Breckington Manor, the stately home of Stanislas Braid (who of course had aristocratic parentage and for whom money had never been a problem).

There was also the set of the great man's study, whose bookshelves were meant to reflect his polymathic knowledge. The ornaments in the room attested to his extensive travels and the gratitude of wealthy – in many cases, regal – clients all over the world. No doubt the silver elephants expressed the thanks of some maharaja whose daughter's kidnapping Stanislas Braid had solved when the entire police force of India had been baffled. The fine decanter and glasses were no doubt the gift of a Viennese countess whose husband's murderer Stanislas Braid had unmasked when the entire police force of Austria had been baffled. The fine brass candlesticks on the mantelpiece probably bore witness to the relief of a Greek shipping magnate after Stanislas Braid had defused the bomb whose whereabouts had had the police of twelve nations baffled.

And so on, and so on. At least, thought Charles Paris, whose role as Sergeant Clump was to express the continuing bafflement of the police on a weekly basis, W.E.T. hasn't stinted on the set dressing. Everything looked very solid and real. The prop buyers must have had their work cut out to find that lot. Charles didn't think he'd ever been in a television production with so many props.

No, *Stanislas Braid* would look good. But, as so often in television, Charles worried about the difference between the look of the product and the product itself. With no discredit to Will Parton, who had worked miracles with what he had been given, the scripts did have a dated feel. Not a period feel, which, Charles suspected, was what W.E.T. was really striving for, but a dated feel. There is all the difference in the world between a loving re-creation of a past period and something that just looks old-fashioned. And though it was early on in the series to form judgements, Charles had a nasty suspicion that *Stanislas Braid* would achieve the second effect.

Nothing was actually being rehearsed when Charles came into the studio, but there was a huddle of activity over in front of the sitting-room set. He moved toward it, but as he drew closer, he realised that the activity was just another argument between Russell Bentley and his Director. This time it must have been more serious, because Rick Landor had actually come down on to the studio floor and was speaking to his star without the mediation of a floor manager. Also on the scene were the thin, faded figures of W. T. Wintergreen and her sister, Louisa, no doubt contributing their own objections to the argument.

It was clearly going to be some time before anything got rehearsed, let alone recorded. And Charles wasn't even in that scene. Definitely be time for a drink. Just so long as he told someone where he was.

He moved away quietly. No need to draw attention to himself; someone might think of something he was needed for. He went around the edge of the study set into the corridor between the studio wall and the backs of the flats. The smell of canvas warmed by strong lights was achingly familiar from the backstages of a thousand theatres. Ahead of him he saw a familiar back view kneeling down at the foot of a flat. Good, someone he could tell where he was going.

'Tony.'

The A.S.M. whirled around at the sound of Charles's voice. He looked flushed. 'Goodness, you startled me.'

'Sorry. Just wanted to say, nothing seems to be happening on the set. I'm going to nip to the bar for a quick drink, okay? Get me paged up there if I'm needed.'

'Yes, fine, okay,' said Tony Rees.

One of the advantages of having worked for the company a few times was that Charles knew the quickest way to the bar from almost every part of W.E.T. House. From this end of Studio A the best route was out through a dark little storage room used for props, into the scenery dock, up the stairs to the first floor, and through the Casting Department.

Cheered by the anticipation of soon having a large Bell's in his hand, Charles started on his way.

The scene that met his eyes in the murky props room was one of total chaos.

The room, probably not more than ten feet wide, was flanked with tall shelves to store props, and because of the large number required to give period flavour to *Stanislas Braid*, these were loaded. Unfortunately, no doubt because of the weight of their burden, one set of shelves must have become top-heavy and fallen forward.

The result was an amazing pile of debris, as if a bomb had gone off in a junk shop. Old cash registers lay on the floor beside elephant's foot umbrella stands; the shards of chamber pots mingled with crushed cigar boxes; billiard balls dotted their colours over a heap of smashed crockery and dented tankards.

Charles briefly contemplated telling someone about the accident. On the other hand, a selfish instinct urged, it wasn't really his job. Someone else, whose job it might well be, would soon come through. And now the idea of an imminent drink had taken hold in his mind, Charles Paris didn't want to put it off that much longer. No, probably better all around if he just went straight to the bar.

And that is where he would have gone if he hadn't seen, protruding from the bottom of the pile of debris, something that couldn't, by the wildest stretch of the imagination, be a prop for the *Stanislas Braid* series.

It was a human hand.

A human hand that Charles had a horrible feeling he recognised.

A human hand attached to a human arm that, when Charles tried to move it from beneath the weight of the shelves, appeared to be very firmly attached to a human body.

A human hand, what's more, that was still warm. Warm but very still.

He scrabbled away at the pile of debris, and each object he moved revealed to him more of what he somehow already knew. When he saw the dress, it confirmed the message given by the hand. And the glistening blood on the dress confirmed the message of the body's stillness.

When he uncovered the head, it was, though crushed and battered, still easily recognisable as that of Sippy Stokes.

Chapter Three

CHARLES COMMUNICATED the news of Sippy's death as discreetly as he could. He reckoned that since the producer is the person with overall responsibility for a production, Ben Docherty should be informed first. Fortunately, because it was still before lunch, Ben was able to take the news with appropriate sobriety. He informed the W.E.T. in-house security, who sealed off the props room and called the police.

The Producer urged Charles to keep quiet about his discovery and decreed that recording should continue for as long as possible. This was avowedly to avoid panic and anxiety among the cast, but Charles knew it was also Ben fulfilling his professional role. The producer is responsible for the budgeting of a television series, and even a half day of studio time wasted is ruinously expensive. Already, so early into production, thanks to Russell Bentley's difficulties in homing in on the character of Russell Bentley and W. T. Wintergreen's objections that Russell Bentley was nothing like the character of Stanislas Braid that she had created, the show was slipping behind schedule. The thought of that kind of time slippage escalating through a series is the stuff of which producers' nightmares are made.

The decision to continue recording, however, did not get the production much further advanced. As Charles discovered when he got back to the studio, trying to hide the state of shock he was in (and without even having had his promised large Bell's to alleviate that shock), the argument he had witnessed between star and producer had arisen because Russell Bentley still wasn't happy with the way the scene in Little Breckington Police station had gone. Retaking the cutaway shot had cleared up one problem, but now he had a new cavil with something that had happened at the beginning of the recording.

Rick Landor had fought hard against the proposed retake and had enlisted Ben Docherty's support in his argument but been let down by the Producer's instant capitulation. Ben Docherty, Charles was beginning to realise, was a vacillating character, and Russell Bentley was quickly getting the Producer exactly where he wanted him. This did not augur well for the series. For Rick Landor to give in to the star was one thing; he was only going to be directing two of the episodes. But Ben Docherty was Producer for the whole series. If he started caving in to Russell Bentley at such an early stage, it was going to be very difficult for him ever to reassert his authority.

These, however, were not Charles's problems, and he was in no condition to worry about anything except his reaction to the discovery of Sippy Stokes's body. Like most shocks, it came in little waves, suddenly weakening and unnerving him. And the words of Will Parton circled, with uncomfortable irony, around his head. 'As an actress, Sippy Stokes was absolute death.'

Once the production team had conceded that the police-station scene would be retaken, there was further delay, because Russell Bentley had by now changed out of the relevant costume and would have to change back again. Charles Paris waited nervously behind his counter, his mind a mess of ugly thoughts. He was hardly aware of the two policemen with whom he had had coffee jostling for position with their fellow background artistes so that they would be prominently in shot, thus staking their doomed claims to be rebooked for the rest of the series.

However much discretion Ben Docherty and the W.E.T. security men had deployed, it all went for nothing when the real police arrived. Two uniformed men and two in plain clothes marched into the studio before Russell Bentley had completed his costume change, and loudly demanded to speak to the Producer. As the plainclothesmen went into a huddle with Ben Docherty, the two in uniform looked on contemptuously at the proceedings.

'Who're those two, Bob?' whispered the first background artiste with whom Charles had had coffee.

'Don't know,' his friend whispered back. 'Never seen them before.'

'No.' The first one sounded thoughtful. 'I thought I knew practically everyone in the "background" business.'

'There's a new agency started up. Perhaps they're from there.'

'Well, they'd better be Equity, that's all I can say.'

'Yes, and why is Rick putting more in this scene, anyway? More than twelve aren't going to register in the shot, are they?'

'No. Well, just watch it when those two come in. See they don't push to the front.'

'Don't worry. I'm not going to lose my position.'

'Nor me.' The first background artiste looked across at the two newcomers in disparagement. 'Must say, I don't think they're very good.'

'No. I mean, at least we look like policemen. Those two –'

'Could be postmen.'

'Traffic wardens...'

'Anything. They look so out of place in those uniforms, don't they?'

'People just don't think when they're casting these days, do they?'

'No.'

Charles was prevented from hearing further background artiste bitchery by a gesture from Ben Docherty, who beckoned him over. He obeyed and was met by the hard stare of one of the plainclothesmen. 'You're the one who found the body?'

Charles nodded.

'We'll be needing to talk to you in a minute. Stay around.'

'Yes.'

'Just going to have a look for ourselves. Then we'll call you.'

'Okay.'

At that moment, Russell Bentley appeared on the scene, once again dressed in his floppy hat, cloak, and monocle. He swept up toward the group surrounding Ben Docherty.

'Here I am,' he announced with a flamboyant flourish of his hat, 'ready once again to prove that the plodding British policeman is no match for the gifted amateur.'

'Oh, really?' said the plainclothesman in a voice as dry as a water biscuit.

The Little Breckington Police Station scene was retaken twice more, and at the end of the proceedings, when he went off once again to make his costume change, Russell Bentley had the gall to say that he thought perhaps the original take had been best, after all. The two background artistes, who lived in hope of a series booking, looked confused as they tried to remember how prominent they had been in the original take.

Charles still hadn't mentioned what lay in the props room to anyone other than Ben Docherty, but the arrival of the policemen alerted everyone on the set to the fact that something was going on. There was much whispering and curious conjecture in Studio A, but though people tried to draw him out, Charles kept his knowledge to himself.

More real policemen arrived in the studio. There was a confusion of constables as the background artistes milled and gossiped around the fringes of the set. One of the plainclothesmen bustled across to Charles. 'We'll be wanting to speak to you in just a minute,' he said in passing.

Charles nodded and drifted across toward the props-room door. It was dark behind the flats in this corner of the set. The outline of a uniformed policeman standing guard on the door nodded to Charles. 'Hello, Sarge,' it said, seeing the gleam of the stripes and unaware in the dim light of the anachronism of Sergeant Clump's uniform.

'Hello there,' said Charles, seeing no reason to disillusion the constable. His actor's instinct stopped him from using his own voice. If people were going to think he was a policeman, then it was a point of honour for him to sound like a policeman. He automatically homed in on the unimpressed voice he had used as the inspector arriving in Act Three of any number of dire stage thrillers, including the one he had once played in at Colchester, whose title he had mercifully forgotten, though its review from the local paper was burned ineradicably into his memory: 'I have been more thrilled by an attack of shingles than I was at any point during last night's performance.'

At that moment, the props-room door opened, and a harassed-looking face peered out. 'Could you give me a hand?' it appealed.

'Sorry, Doctor. Got to stay on guard,' said the constable.

'What about you, Sergeant?'

'Oh, all right,' said Charles Paris equably, and followed the doctor to the scene of the crime.

'Just need some help moving the shelves out of the way.'

Amid the debris, the heavy shelves still pinioned the late Sippy Stokes to the ground. Charles tried not to look at the crumpled body, but even if he'd closed his eyes, he knew its disturbing imprint would still be on his mind.

'Should we be moving anything, though?' he asked, mindful of the minimal knowledge he had of scene-of-the-crime procedure.

'It's all right. The photographers have been,' said the doctor.

They took one side each and heaved the wooden frame back up into position with difficulty.

'God, no one would stand much chance with this lot landing on top of them, would they?'

'No,' the doctor agreed grimly. 'Mind you, I don't think it was the shelves that did the damage.'

'What, you mean she was dead before they fell?' In his excitement Charles used his own voice, but fortunately the doctor did not seem to notice the lapse.

'Seconds before, maybe,' he replied. 'It looks as if it was a blow to the back of the head that killed her. The weight of the shelves just made sure.'

'So...you reckon someone hit her?' the sergeant asked, safely back in his sergeant's voice.

The doctor gave Charles a sardonic look. 'I wouldn't say that, no. Sorry to puncture your fantasies of a nice juicy murder, Sergeant. No, I think it's more likely that some *thing* hit her.'

'What kind of thing?'

The doctor gave a shrug that encompassed all the confusion of props that lay around. 'Take your pick. A lot of these items would have been heavy enough. Look, there's blood on the corner of that cash register...and on that fire screen...and on those kitchen scales...Just a matter of finding the piece whose outline matches the dent in the poor kid's head.'

'So what you're saying is that you reckon something fell off the shelves before the shelves themselves fell down?'

'As I said, seconds before. No, I should think the shelves were loaded so as to be top-heavy. They started to topple...As they did so, various items slipped off...and it was one of those items that hit her on the head a split second before she got the full weight of the shelves on her.'

'But what would have made the shelves fall down?'

This prompted another shrug from the doctor. 'Who can say? Maybe they were just badly stacked. Maybe the girl was fingering something, trying to pull something out...I don't know. All I do know is that West End Television is going to face a very big claim for compensation.'

'And you really don't think there's any suspicion of foul play?'

'Come on, Sergeant. Accidents happen. I don't know, I haven't done a detailed examination yet, but I'd have thought foul play was extremely unlikely.'

'Oh,' said Charles, and the disappointment must have showed in his voice, because the doctor went on: 'For heaven's sake, man, stop being so ridiculous. You sound as if you wish there *was* a murder. You don't sound like a professional policeman at all.'

'Good heavens. Don't I?' asked Sergeant Clump of the Little Breckington Police Station.

Chapter Four

WHEN, ON THE DOT of six, the plugs were pulled in Studio A, everyone felt that it had been a long day. During the lunch break, the news of Sippy Stokes's death had spread throughout the *Stanislas Braid* production team, then throughout W.E.T. House, and finally, through the medium of the press and radio, to the outside world.

Ben Docherty, having had his customary alcoholic top-up at lunch-time, insisted belligerently on continuing recording through the afternoon, though it might have been more appropriate to cancel out of respect for the dead. Or respect for the living, come to that. Everyone on the set was upset by the fact of a death in the studio, though some seemed to be taking it worse than others. Rick Landor, in particular, looked shattered when he heard the news, and though he struggled gamely through the afternoon's recording, he went through the motions like an automaton.

It wasn't an easy afternoon's recording, anyway. They kept starting to rehearse scenes, only to grind to a halt when someone realised that Stanislas Braid's daughter, Christina, should have made an appearance in them. And Russell Bentley kept averring that there was no point in recording any more, anyway, because everything they'd already done would have to be scrapped when Sippy's part was recast. Charles couldn't help noticing that the star made these pronouncements with considerable relish. For Russell Bentley, Sippy Stokes's death was unadulterated good news.

In fact, it was striking how, throughout all the ranks of the production team, though everyone was suffering from shock, no one showed much sign of grief or regret. In her brief time working on *Stanislas Braid*, Sippy Stokes had not made many friends.

Charles Paris's name would never appear in *The Guinness Book of Records*, but that was only because there is no section in that work for the event called 'Getting out of Costume and into the Nearest Bar'. At the end of that studio day, however, he performed another Personal Best and was draped over a large Bell's before most of his fellow artistes had even made it to their dressing rooms.

Of course, he couldn't expect to compete with the production crew, who did not have the handicap of costumes and were halfway down their first pints of lager before he arrived in the W. E.T. bar.

Nor could he compete with a writer. Will Parton had already downed his first glass of dry white and willingly accepted Charles's offer of a refill.

'So,' said Will, raising his glass, 'farewell, then, Sippy Stokes.'

'Farewell indeed,' Charles responded, shuddering slightly as the image of her body once again flashed up on the screen of his mind.

'One more unwanted person vanished into the Great Void. Prompting once again the Universal Question: What does it all mean?'

'Hmm.'

'I'll tell you what it means, Charles. It means what it always means in television – more bloody rewrites!'

'Oh, but surely they won't need to change the scripts?'

'They *always* need to change the scripts – first rule of television. At least they don't always need to change the scripts, but they always insist on changing the scripts. Producers and script editors would feel they were failing in their God-given mission if they accepted a script in its original form. I tell you, if I delivered *Hamlet* to this lot, they'd come back to me with a great pile of notes. 'Wouldn't it be better if he was a bit more decisive? And there aren't really many laughs, are there? And couldn't you combine the parts of Rosencrantz and Guildenstern? Seems rather a waste to have two of them, doesn't it, because they both serve the same function? And could we cut the scene in the graveyard? Well, you know how expensive film is, and it doesn't really seem to *add* much. And as for that ending – well, talk about downbeat. Can't you liven it up a bit?'

Charles chuckled. 'I take your point. Was that the sort of meeting you had this morning?' Will looked at him, uncomprehending. 'This morning, when Ben and Dilly dragged you out of the canteen?'

'Oh, then. No, actually that one didn't materialise. Soon as we got outside the canteen, Ben, with typical resolution, remembered there was something else he should be doing. But don't worry, the meeting is only postponed. More rewrites will still be wanted.'

'I still don't see why you'll have to rewrite just because someone new's taking over the part of Christina.'

'I'm sure I will have to, though. The new person they get will be totally different from Sippy, that I can guarantee.'

'Why?'

'Well, this time I should think they'd get an actress.'

'God, I set that up for you perfectly, didn't I?'

'Yes, Charles. Thank you very much – feed lines always appreciated.'

Charles grinned. But he felt uncomfortable. He had some atavistic inhibition about speaking ill of the dead. Though his opinion of Sippy Stokes's acting abilities hadn't changed from that morning, it seemed somehow wrong to be making such comments now.

'Anyway,' Will went on moodily, 'even if they don't want the later scripts totally rewritten – which they almost definitely will – I've still got a lot to do on the first one, particularly now.'

'What, the one we've been doing today?'

'Yes. "The Brass Candlestick Murder".' The writer put a world of contempt into his enunciation of W. T. Wintergreen's title.

'But surely we'll just scrap everything that Sippy recorded and redo those scenes with a new actress?'

'Don't you believe it. Oh, no, if Ben Docherty can see a way of saving a few bob, then who cares how much extra work the mere writer has to do?'

'You mean he's intending to use the scenes with Sippy in them?'

'Yes. Not a business famous for its sentimentality, television. No, dear warm-hearted Ben will salvage every last inch of tape he can. Anything rather than retaking the lot. So my latest directive this afternoon is to assemble a new jigsaw from the scenes we've already recorded and find some "really plausible explanation" – I quote Dilly Muirfield's words – for the fact that Stanislas Braid's adored and irreproachable daughter, Christina, suddenly vanishes out of the second half of the story.'

'But that'll cock up the continuity into the next episode, surely? I mean, you can't have a completely different actress suddenly appearing as the same character.'

'Don't worry, the superbrains of the *Stanislas Braid* production team have come up with a way round that. In episode two, "The Italian Stiletto Murder", because Christina is still away, Stanislas Braid's *other* daughter, Elvira, suddenly returns from her finishing school in Switzerland.'

'That's ridiculous.'

'Not really. Not by the standards of the medium. Remember, Charles, we are working in television.'

'But what would W. T. Wintergreen say to her precious hero suddenly developing another daughter?'

'She has not as yet been consulted on this point. And when she is, scream and kick though she may – and scream and kick though her loopy sister Louisa may – W.E.T. will have their way with them. Stanislas Braid will sprout a second daughter.'

'Writers must have more control of what happens to their books than that.'

'Depends what it says in the contract. And knowing W.E.T.'s Contracts Department, I should think they've sewn up the *Stanislas Braid* property in every way, right down to the merchandising of *Stanislas Braid* "His 'n' Her" Bath Mats.'

Charles shook his head in what he would have liked to be disbelief. But it wasn't – oh no, he found Will's words all too believable.

'Charles, in television and film the concept of writers having "control" just does not exist. Never forget the old Hollywood story of the starlet who was so dumb she slept with the writer.'

Charles laughed and accepted Will's offer of another drink. He felt like quite a few drinks that evening. He wanted to go to bed with a mind anaesthetised to images of crushed and crumpled bodies.

After a long swallow of Bell's, he asked, 'And is that really for real? The business about Elvira? They really want you to do it?'

'Cross my heart and hope to end up writing one-liners for David Frost. Yes, it really is true.'

'But how on earth can you do it?'

'I'm a television writer,' Will asserted with a deep cynicism. 'They pay me, I do it.'

'Well, I don't envy you that task.'

'Introducing Elvira in ep. two?'

'Yes.'

'Oh, don't worry about that. I've already done it.'

'Done it? But Sippy only died this morning. You couldn't have had time.'

'I may not be the greatest writer on earth,' said Will Parton, affecting an American Drawl, 'but I sure is the quickest.' Then, in response to Charles's continuing expression of puzzlement, he went on: 'No, actually, I did those rewrites a few days back.'

'But what...? Why?' Charles was at a loss. 'I don't understand.'

'Then I will explain it to you. I was sworn to secrecy over this, but quite honestly, now that Sippy's dead, I don't see that any harm can be done by telling you. The fact is, as we have all observed, to call Sippy Stokes an actress was an offence under the Trades Description Act.'

Once again Charles winced inwardly at this attack on the dead girl.

'Well, even Ben Docherty, through his post-meridian alcoholic haze, couldn't help noticing that she had about as much talent as a bar of soap. In fact, when he saw the rushes of the first few days' filming, he knew a monumental blunder had been made. It was then that he made the decision she would have to be replaced, so Dilly Muirfield summoned me to a meeting, which witnessed the birth of Elvira and her wonderful finishing school.'

'But just a minute – if Sippy was that bad, why didn't Ben just sack her and recast for the first episode?'

'What, and waste three days' filming? Anyway, all the rest of the cast were contracted. It'd be an expensive write-off. And then they'd have to find dates to make another episode, and Russell Bentley's availability gets sticky after the end of this contract.'

'Ah...So did Sippy know she was about to be dumped?'

'Oh, no. Ben's thinking was that if she knew, there was a danger she might think, Stuff this lot, and not turn up for the remaining studio days.'

'No professional actress would do that. She might be seething with fury, but she'd still turn up.'

'Well, that was Ben Docherty's estimate of the situation.'

'So when was she going to be told?'

'Ah, this was to be the masterpiece of television diplomacy. At the end of the final studio day on this episode.'

'The day after tomorrow?'

'Right. At the end of the day, when Sippy fell, utterly knackered, into her dressing room, she would be confronted by the show's CastingDirector.'

'Ben not even doing his own dirty work?'

'Good heavens, no. Anyway, the Casting Director would then tell the poor kid that in spite of the fact that she'd been contracted for all six episodes, she was being paid off then and there.'

'Quite a substantial payoff. She'd get everything she'd been contracted for, wouldn't she?'

'Yes, it'd be a decent lump sum. Still peanuts, though, from Ben's point of view, compared with writing off the whole episode.'

'Yes,' Charles mused aloud. Then a new thought struck him. 'But lots of people round the production must've known. I mean, the read-through for the next episode's on Monday. They must have cast the part of Elvira by now.'

'Oh, yes. They have.'

'So that poor kid would have been busting a gut, trying to act for three whole days, without knowing that she'd already been written off?'

'That would have been the situation, yes. Oh, indeed, if it's humanity you're after, why not join the wacky world of television?'

'Shit. Well, at least she was spared the interview with the Casting Director.'

'Yes, I should think the Casting Director's feeling pretty relieved, too.'

'Hmm. And you're sure she didn't have an inkling of what was going on?'

'Positive.'

'What about Rick? Did he know?'

'I'm fairly sure he didn't, either.'

'But he must have got a copy of the new script for episode two, mustn't he?'

'No. Different director for that one. Remember, Rick's only directing alternate episodes so that he can catch up on post-production.'

'Yes, of course.' Charles was silent for a moment before saying thoughtfully, 'The one question all this does raise is how on earth Sippy was ever given the part in the first place.'

'Ah,' said Will Parton. 'Now that's something I think Rick Landor *might* know.'

Her voice was guarded when she answered the phone; even more guarded when she heard who was speaking.

'Charles, how are you?'

'Oh, well, you know, Frances, not so bad.'

'Meaning quite bad, from your tone of voice.'

'Well…perhaps a bit shaken.'

'And perhaps a bit drunk?'

'Perhaps a bit.'

'So what's shaken you? Has something devastatingly unlikely happened…like your getting a job, for example?'

'I have got a job, actually. Surely I told you?'

'Charles, it's over three months since you last rang me. On that occasion, too, you chose to make your call just before midnight...presumably on your arrival back at Hereford Road from some bar that closed at eleven.'

'I'm sorry, Frances. I didn't realise it was that late.'

'Well, it is. And the last words you said to me at the end of our previous conversation three months ago were "I'll call you before the weekend".'

'Oh, were they?'

But Frances couldn't stay peevish for long; it wasn't in her nature. 'What is it that's shaken you?' she asked in a gentler tone.

'Oh, it's – I don't know. Somebody died.'

'Somebody you were close to?'

Was he being hypersensitive to hear a hint of jealousy in her voice? Though they hadn't lived together regularly for many years, Charles liked to feel that his wife still cared for him.

'No, not anyone I was close to,' he replied.

'This isn't another of your murder investigations, is it, Charles?'

'No, no. At least I'm fairly sure it isn't.'

'Oh, so you rang up just before midnight to tell me that someone you weren't particularly close to has died?'

'Well, yes, but...I wanted to hear your voice.'

'This is my voice. This is what it sounds like. I think you'll find it hasn't changed a great deal in three months.'

'And I want to see you.' Suddenly he did, desperately. 'I really want to see you, Frances.'

'Ah, do you?'

'You want to see me, don't you?'

The pause that greeted this question was longer than he would have wished.

'You know, Charles,' said Frances finally, 'in many ways my life is much more restful when I *don't* see you.'

'Yes, but then who wants their life to be restful?' he joked.

'At midnight, Charles, let me tell you, restfulness is pretty high on my list of priorities.'

'I know. I'm sorry. It's unforgivably late. But look, let's make a plan to meet.'

'I don't feel up to making plans now, thank you, Charles.'

'But when might you feel up to making plans?'

'When you're sober,' said Frances, and put the phone down.

Chapter Five

CHARLES HAD drunk more heavily than someone in work should have done. The trouble was that throughout his theatrical career work had been such an intermittent visitor and stayed for such short times that his regular habits were those of someone out of work rather than those of an employed person. And his usual method of dealing with a skinful the night before – a gradual rising punctuated by black coffee, aspirins, and retreats back to bed until the blessed relief of a pint around eleven-thirty – was unsuitable for someone who had a nine o'clock makeup call at W.E.T. House.

He did make it, but his head pounded, his skin felt very tight, as though he had had face-lifts all over his body, and the makeup girl's job was made more difficult by the fact that he had the shakes. He quipped that she might do better not to try rubbing the makeup into his face but simply to hold the sponge out and let him tremble against it. She didn't appear to be amused by the idea.

No one seemed to know what the day's studio schedule would be. Normally reliable sources of all information, like Mort Verdon and the Floor Manager, could offer no help. Everything was disorganised. The sudden departure of Sippy Stokes had made a bigger hole in the production than anyone had realised the previous day.

Eventually some sort of running order was concocted. Basically they were going to pick up any scenes they could that didn't involve Christina Braid. Will Parton – also somewhat the worse for wear – was on hand for necessary script carpentry, sawing the beginnings and ends off scenes and making the stumps look as tidy as possible.

But there was a kind of lethargy about everything. Russell Bentley walked through his scenes in a muted way, already determined that the whole episode should be remade from the start. And the absence of W. T. Wintergreen and her sister added to the sense that the proceedings weren't really important.

The Producer and Director did their best. Ben Docherty, full of the positive aggression that characterised all of his actions before lunch-time, urged the cast on to greater efforts. And Rick Landor, still looking ghastly, did all the right things with a kind of nerveless deliberation. Deep down, though, both of them seemed to have lost the will to continue.

Charles was only involved in a couple of scenes on the set of Stanislas Braid's study. Both followed the usual pattern of their encounters, in which the gifted amateur ran circles around the ponderous professional. The second scene seemed only to have been inserted in the script to plant the pair of candlesticks on Stanislas Braid's mantelpiece, the candlesticks that he was to use so brilliantly to re-enact the murderer's crime at the episode's denouement. The denouement itself they could not record. The character of Christina was so integral to that scene that it would require from Will not a quick bit of carpentry but a major act of cabinet-making.

Charles went listlessly through the motions, vowing throughout the morning that he would never touch another drop of alcohol and, after a couple of drinks at lunch-time, thinking throughout the afternoon that his morning's vows had been perhaps a little rash. He dutifully did all that he was instructed to do, lifting and putting down the candlesticks endlessly while Rick Landor tried to frame his shots against the bored barracking of Russell Bentley.

By five o'clock they had run out of scenes that they could even pretend were worth doing, and Will made it clear in no uncertain terms that there was no chance of his having done the monumental rewriting required by the following morning. So Ben Docherty, whose customary early-afternoon belligerence had by now given way to a sleepy acquiescence, was forced to recognise the inevitable. The following day's studio would have to be scrapped. Reluctantly, knowing the effect it would have on his budget, he told the assembled company that they would not be called for Friday and instructed Mort Verdon to ring round the remainder of the cast and give them the news.

Charles Paris changed more slowly this time. He was not after a Personal Best now, merely trying to eke out the time until the bar opened at half past five. His morning headache had returned; he was determined not to drink as much that evening. But then Charles Paris's life was a long catalogue of such determinations.

Changing out of costume and punctiliously scouring the last speck of makeup off his face only lasted him till twenty past five, so he took an atypically long route to the bar. He went through the Studio A control gallery, vaguely looking for Rick Landor, but the only person he found there was Mort Verdon, pressing down the buttons of the telephone after another of his calls to the cast.

'Rick around, Mort?'

'No, boofle. Editing. Suite three. He was booked from six, but he managed to move it since we broke early.'

'Hmm. He seemed quite cut up about Sippy dying,' Charles hazarded.

'Yes, well, he would be. I think he and Miss Wooden might have been rather close.'

'How close?'

'Close enough to get splinters,' said Mort Verdon archly. 'And close enough for Rick to get the teeniest bit tetchy when Jimmy Sheet started switching on the charm.'

'When did that happen? I didn't notice anything.'

'No, takes a trained eye.'

'What happened? What did your trained eye see?'

'Well, didn't really see anything while we were in rehearsal or filming. But I happened to see them together in Stringfellow's on Tuesday night.'

'Stringfellow's? I didn't know that was your scene, Mort.'

'Lot of things you don't know about me, Charles Paris.' The stage manager winked at him slyly. 'Mind you, anytime you want to find out more...you have only to ask.'

Charles had one large Bell's in the bar before setting off to find Rick. As he approached the editing suites, he was once again struck by the unequal distribution of work load in television. Every production was surrounded by an enormous team of people, but the only ones who really had to work hard were the designer, the director, and the director's production assistant. And of those the director had to work hardest. It was typical that after a long day in the studio Rick Landor would be faced by an evening's videotape editing. Or an evening's film editing. Or an evening preparing a camera script. It was a stressful job.

And a job that could be made even more stressful if one had a girlfriend who had died.

Through the glass panel of the door of suite 3, Charles could see Rick lounging back in a chair. The Director appeared to be on his own, and with no audience to hold himself together for, he had allowed his face to show the strains of the last few days. He looked up at the discreet tap on the door and composed his expression into something more purposeful and energetic.

He gestured Charles to enter. 'What can I do for you?' he asked.

Charles hadn't really planned what the excuse for his visit would be but homed in on something safe. 'Just wondered if you might be down for a drink in the bar later?'

It wasn't that strange a suggestion. The Director and actor had met for the occasional quick drink over the last week. And though Charles's coming all the way to the editing suite to make his invitation might have seemed unusual, Rick did not appear to notice any incongruity.

'I doubt it, actually, Charles. I'm pretty bushed. And I'm booked in here till nine – well, half past eight, cause we started early – but I think after that I'll head straight back home. Thanks for the idea, though.'

'Oh, well, plenty of other opportunities.'

'Sure.'

Charles looked around the suite. Videotape is not edited like film. The tape is not actually cut; different takes are joined together by a process of dubbing from one machine to another. Digital displays show the position of the various tapes. At that moment, the large machines, with their giant spools, stood idle. On the monitor in front of Rick, Stanislas Braid was frozen in his study, caught in mid-gesture.

Answering Charles's unspoken question, the Director said, 'P.A.'s getting coffee, and the editor's gone to get another tape. Library didn't send up all we needed. Another cock-up.'

Charles nodded. 'Bit of a chapter of cock-ups the last few days have been,' he said, trying to open out the conversation.

'You can say that again.'

'I didn't know Sippy very well.'

'No. I did.'

There was no ambiguity in Rick's tone. He made no attempt to hide the relationship. In fact, he seemed more than ready to expand on it. 'My marriage broke up three years ago.'

Of course, Charles remembered, a broken marriage was virtually an essential qualification for a young director in television. Mind you, he reminded himself with a little shiver at the recollection of Frances's coldness on the telephone, I'm a fine one to criticise.

'Sippy was the first girl I'd got even vaguely involved with since. Not that it was that serious, but ...'

'I'm sorry. It must have been hell for you the last couple of days.'

'Not great, but...the show must go on,' said Rick grimly. 'Can't think about that sort of thing too much when you're working. And I seem to be working every hour God sends at the moment.'

'Yes, I was just thinking that as I came along here.'

'Still, can't complain. At least the work's there,' said the Director brusquely. 'And I do love television.'

'Really?' said Charles, for whom the only really attractive thing about television was the money.

'Yes, I love it. Even though it broke up my marriage – Well, I suppose it wasn't all television's fault. The fact that my wife was a promiscuous little bitch might have had something to do with it, too...And now television has broken up another relationship for me.'

'You blame television for Sippy's death?' asked Charles, eager to pounce on any stray clue that might be about.

'No, not really. I just mean that she died in a television studio, that's all.'

There seemed something evasive about the way Rick spoke, as if he had started to say something else and then decided to backtrack.

'You heard that I actually found her body, did you?'

'Yes. Must've been nasty.'

'Was.' There was a silence. 'I had to talk to the police.'

'Me, too.'

'Didn't elicit much from them about what they thought had happened.'

'Nor did I,' said Rick unhelpfully.

Charles looked at the picture on the monitor screen. Something in it caught his attention. Masking his excitement in casualness, he asked, 'When did you record that scene?'

'That? Oh, immediately after the break yesterday morning. It's hardly a scene, really. It's just one of those moments of Russell sitting in his study with a cigar and looking thoughtful.'

'The Great Mind at work. Stanislas Braid's Mighty Intellect solves another case.'

'That's it. There'll be a good few of those shots through the series.'

'Hard to tell how it's going at this stage,' Charles prompted diffidently.

Rick Landor looked up at him with a cynical smile. 'Well, I don't think it's going to be *Miss Marple*.'

'What do you mean?'

'That's W.E.T.'s idea. Look at the sales round the world of the BBC's *Miss Marple* series – that's the bandwagon they're trying to hitch on to. They think, Let's get something of the same kind...detective stories...lots of period detail...We'll clean up. Hmm, well, I think they may have miscalculated.'

'Why?'

'For a start, W. T. Wintergreen is no Agatha Christie.'

'And Russell Bentley is no Joan Hickson.'

'No. And then again, the way they're making it is all wrong. W.E.T.'s trying to do it on the cheap, as usual. I mean, that half-on-film and half-in-studio stuff just looks so old-fashioned nowadays. The international market wants series that're all on film.'

'And you'd much rather be directing something that's all on film?'

'Need you ask?'

No, Charles needn't have, really. All television directors think they're film directors manqué. And most of them nurse secret fantasies of one day single-handedly reviving the British feature-film industry.

'About Sippy...' Charles began again.

'Hmm?' Rick responded wearily.

'Your relationship was still happening...you know, when she died?'

The director's eyes narrowed. For the first time he showed signs of resenting Charles's probing. 'What makes you ask that?'

'I don't know. You just didn't seem to take much notice of each other round the studio.'

'There is such a thing as professionalism, Charles.'

'Yes, yes, of course. I know.' There is also such a thing, he reflected, as not wishing to draw attention to the operations of the casting couch. Particularly if the person cast did not show such exceptional abilities on a television set as she presumably did on the couch.

'No,' he went on, taking a calculated risk. 'I mean, if I'd been asked to say who – if anyone – in the company Sippy was tied up with, I'd probably have plumped for Jimmy Sheet.'

That one hit home. Rick Landor's eyes blazed. 'Well, you would have been wrong, then, wouldn't you, Charles?'

But the vehemence of the denial meant that the matter was at least worthy of further investigation.

Not at that moment, though. The editor had just returned with the right tape, and at the same time Rick's P.A. appeared with a tray of coffee and packets of biscuits. Charles made his good-byes.

He may not have got much information out of Rick Landor, but the visit to the editing suite had filled him with a bubble of excitement. Something he had seen there had brought bursting to the surface an idea that he had vigorously suppressed since his discovery of Sippy's body.

The frozen picture of Stanislas Braid's study on the editing monitor had differed in one particular from the set on which Charles had worked that afternoon. Differed indeed from the set that he had seen when he returned from his coffee break the previous morning.

On the later occasions there had been two candlesticks on Stanislas Braid's mantelpiece. In the scene that had been recorded about the time of Sippy Stokes's death, only one candlestick was in evidence.

Where was the other one?

Was it fanciful to imagine that the base of a candlestick might fit the dent in the young actress's head?

Or fanciful to imagine that Sippy Stokes had been murdered?

Chapter Six

IT WAS A NOVEL experience for Charles to ring his agent when he was working. Usually, such calls were made during those long sags in his career when it looked as if nobody would ever employ Charles Paris again in the history of the universe. At such times, though ringing his agent didn't actually help – Maurice Skellern was so incompetent that he never knew of any jobs coming up – it did at least spread the misery.

But for that Friday morning's call the circumstances were totally different. Charles was at the beginning of a three-month contract for W.E.T. For once in his life he had a guaranteed income; he could see some way ahead financially – not very far ahead, it was true, but three months further ahead than he usually could. So it was almost with an air of condescension that he dialled his agent's number.

'Maurice Skellern Artistes,' the voice at the other end of the line grudgingly conceded.

'Maurice, it's Charles.'

'Oh, Charles, I nearly rang you yesterday.'

'Really?' For Maurice to have rung him would have been almost unprecedented.

'Had a couple of availability checks.'

'On me?' That, too, was an event of sufficient rarity to be included in one of Arthur C. Clarke's collections of astounding phenomena.

'Yes, it was some feature-film company and...oh, er, yes, the National Theatre.'

'What? Why on earth didn't you contact me?'

'Well, you're not available, are you, Charles? You're tied up with W.E.T. for the next three months.'

'Yes, but...' It was true, though. Wasn't that typical of his life, Charles thought bitterly. For nearly two years his phone had been so silent he had kept considering getting British Telecom to check whether it was still working; for two years the producers, directors, and casting directors of every theatre, film, and television company in the world had been clinically immune to the magnetism of his talent; and then suddenly, once he was working, the interest started flooding in.

Or did it? He had no proof that the calls had actually happened. And inventing them was an excellent way for Maurice to make it look as if he were being a punctilious agent. Though Charles was not basically a suspicious person, he took much of what his agent told him with a cautionary pinch of salt.

'Did they really call, Maurice?'

'Who?' came the innocent reply.

'These people from the film company and the National.'

'Charles, would I lie to you?'

Yes, of course you would, you old bastard. And often have. But he didn't voice the thought. What was the point?

Maurice moved hastily on, not giving his client time for second thoughts about answering his question. 'Nasty business you had in the studio the other day.'

'What?'

'That actress. Slippy...'

'Sippy. Mind you, that's no less silly than Slippy. Yes, she had chosen to call herself Sippy Stokes. At least I assume she had chosen it. No one's actually christened "Sippy", are they?'

'Wouldn't have thought so. At least she'd have been safe with Equity. No likelihood of a clash with someone else of the same name.'

'True.'

'Nasty business, though. Getting crushed by all those props falling on top of her.'

'Maurice, how is it that you know all this?'

'Like to keep my ear to the ground.'

'Yes, but how is it that you keep your ear to the ground to pick up all the gossip but never know who's doing any casting or where there are any jobs going?'

'Ah, now, come on, Charles, be fair. Who was it who tickled up the interest from this feature-film company and the National Theatre?'

It was wonderful, Charles reflected, how these two – probably fictitious – calls out of the blue to check availability had now metamorphosed into opportunities that Maurice had painstakingly engineered on his client's behalf. But once again it wasn't worth pointing out the anomaly.

'Anyway,' his agent went on, 'be a big compensation bill for W.E.T.'

This seemed to be a universal first reaction to the news of Sippy Stokes's death.

'Yes, I guess so. Incidentally, since you seem to know everything about it,' Charles went on with heavy but wasted irony, 'you haven't heard any suggestions that the death was not an accident, have you?'

'What, murder or something like that, you mean?'

'Well, it's a thought. She wasn't the most popular person round the production.'

'No, haven't heard anything like that. Isn't the buzz I'm getting from my sources, anyway.'

Not for the first time in their relationship, Charles wondered who on earth Maurice's 'sources' might be. Whoever they were, they were pretty good. For relaying gossip, that is. Not for the business of finding out where the jobs were. In that they were as hopeless as Maurice Skellern himself.

'Mind you,' the agent continued, 'I gather the police are still investigating, so maybe something'll come out at the inquest.'

'Well, if you do hear anything, Maurice…'

'I'll let you know. And anytime, anything you want found out, so long as it's in "the business", you know you have only to ask.'

'Sure.'

'But,' said Maurice, moving on with enthusiasm, 'have you heard who's taking over Sippy Stokes's part?'

There was a particular note of glee that always came into his voice when he was imparting information he felt confident his audience didn't know, and it was there as he asked this question.

'No. No, I knew they'd recast, but I haven't heard who it's going to be.'

'Name "Joanne Rhymer" mean anything to you?'

'The "Rhymer" bit does, obviously. Any relation to Gwen Rhymer?'

'Daughter.'

'Ah.' The name brought back not wholly unpleasant memories for Charles. 'I wonder if she shares her mother's well-known proclivities?'

'Which proclivities?'

'I was only thinking of the promiscuity, actually. I mean, in the old days Gwen Rhymer used to be called the Blue Nun.'

'Blue Nun?'

'Yes, like the wine.'

'Eh?' Maurice was being more than usually obtuse.

'Blue Nun is recommended as the ideal accompaniment to all meals,' Charles spelled out, 'and Gwen Rhymer used to be called the Blue Nun because she…went with everything.'

'Ah, with you. Nice one, Charles, nice.'

'So her daughter's getting the part…hmm. Big advantage that can be for a young actress, having a parent in the business.'

'Yes, well, if you think of the number of producers who probably still fancy getting inside the lovely Gwen's pants, the daughter could pick up quite a few favours, I'd imagine.'

'And of course if she does carry on the family tradition, she could pick up a good few in her own right. Oh, well, I will look forward to meeting her on Monday. That's when we've got the read-through for ep. two, "The Italian Stiletto Murder".'

'Still having read-throughs, are you?'

'What do you mean?'

'Well, most series like this, once you get up and running, they dispense with the read-through. Go straight into rehearsal.'

'I think to call the *Stanislas Braid* series "up and running" would be a gross distortion of the truth, Maurice. Apart from the problems raised by the recasting, Russell Bentley's making very heavy weather of the whole thing.

He's not going to give up the read-throughs in a hurry. They give him his first opportunity to cut new directors down to size.'

'Dear, oh, dear,' said Maurice with fond nostalgia. 'Russell Bentley. He's been around forever. I remember all those dreadful movies in the fifties – *The Hawk's Prey*, was that one of them? They were all stinkers, anyway, that's all I remember. Ah, well, there's always been a strong spirit of forgiveness in the British public.' He chuckled. 'Anyway, have fun, Charles. Keep smiling.'

'Incidentally, Maurice, I'm intrigued. How is it you manage to know more about the production I'm working on than I do myself?'

'My job, isn't it? Someone's got to have their finger on the pulse of this business, haven't they? I mean, where do you think you'd be if you hadn't got me looking after your interests?'

The possible answers to this question were so varied and the options they offered so attractive that Charles didn't bother to say anything.

Charles put down the receiver of the pay phone on the landing and went slowly back to his room. He filled the kettle and switched it on for coffee, then moved a couple of shirts spread out over his armchair in lieu of ironing and sat down.

He looked around the bed-sitter and saw it as a stranger might. Tatty, tacky, and untidy. The bed lumpy under its crumpled yellow candlewick. The furniture, which had been painted grey so long ago that it might even have been at a time when grey was trendy. The discoloured, dead gas fire. The dusty plastic curtain that hid the sink and gas ring, and beside it, as if to mock his infirmity of purpose, the equally dusty but more attractive curtain he had bought some months previously to replace it.

But that sort of activity required so much effort. Well, perhaps not effort. After all, it was simply a matter of transferring the hooks from the old curtain to the new one and hanging it up. No, the problem was more one of will. He had to want to do it, had to want to make his environment attractive, to turn the anonymous room into a home.

It was something he had never been good at. Frances had been good, very good. She turned everywhere they lived into a home, and while they were living together, he had liked the warmth of that feeling. But after he had walked out on the marriage in pursuit of some unattainable concept of freedom, he had reverted to type. Reverted to the sense that everything was temporary, that he was just camping until he sorted his life out. But his life remained resolutely unsorted-out; his bed-sitter, resolutely unimproved and anonymous.

For a moment, as he looked around the room, he contemplated moving. Why not? Buy somewhere, put a foot back on the bottom rung of the property ladder he had formerly climbed with Frances. After all, at the moment he could afford it. W.E.T.'s fees were very generous. And, in spite of Rick Landor's gloomy prognostications for its success, there had been talk of a second series of *Stanislas Braid*. According to Will Parton, there were enough W. T. Wintergreen titles to do at least six more. And then they could move on to new story lines, 'opening the writing out,' as Dilly Muirfield put it (or 'wheeling in the massed hacks,' as Will put it).

Yes, this one could run and run. And having his face seen in the country's living rooms on a weekly basis might bring Charles Paris the actor back into fashion. (Well, into fashion – he had to admit he'd never really been there before.) Yes, it might all be all right. He probably could risk the commitment of buying somewhere.

But even as he had the thought, he knew he'd never do it. It wasn't really lack of money, it wasn't his environment either that was at fault. It was him. Wherever he was, he would still be Charles Paris. And Charles Paris would always feel transitory, never quite committing himself to an environment, a community, perhaps even an identity. That was the reason he was an actor. So much easier to channel yourself into other personalities than to stand up and be counted on your own.

Anyway, he felt more at ease – or if not more at ease, at least less challenged – living in anonymous surroundings, seeing as little of them as possible, and then ideally through a permanent haze of Bell's whisky. That was just the way he was.

Having dispelled from his mind the idea of moving, Charles found it quickly filled with thoughts of Sippy Stokes's death, or as he preferred to think of it, Sippy Stokes's murder.

Maurice's words about the police still investigating encouraged this conjecture. Yes, it could have been an accident, but why should the shelves suddenly have toppled over when Sippy was in the props room? Why should she have been in the props room, anyway? And why should she have had the bad luck to be hit by a randomly falling object?

The idea of her having been hit by a carefully aimed object was much more attractive. And the idea that that object was the temporarily removed candlestick was even more appealing.

Charles thought back forty-eight hours and tried to remember the exact sequence of events.

On the Wednesday morning, when the studio broke for coffee after recording Russell Bentley's cutaway shot, Charles remembered seeing Sippy Stokes alive and well. She had turned down his casual invitation to join him in the canteen. It was only about half an hour later that he had found her body, still warm and bleeding, in the props room.

The actual coffee break had only been twenty minutes, but Charles thought it reasonable to assume that that was when the murder had taken place. Then the studio and its environs would have been almost deserted; to commit a murder once the cast and crew had returned would be much more risky.

But who could have been in the studio during the break to do the deed?

Charles focused his memory, trying to re-envision who had been in the canteen and for how long.

Rick Landor hadn't been there at all. Nor had Russell Bentley. Nor, come to that, had W. T. Wintergreen and her sister. Any of them could have been anywhere during the break.

Will Parton had been in the canteen but been dragged away before the end of the break by Ben Docherty and Dilly Muirfield. However, their proposed script discussion hadn't taken place, so any of those three could in theory have gone back to the studio to dispose of Sippy Stokes.

Jimmy Sheet had left at the same time as Will, claiming he was going to look through some lines in his dressing room. But then, if he was planning a murder, he wouldn't have balked at lying about his intentions.

Mort Verdon had stayed chatting with Charles until after the end of the break, so he seemed to be in the clear, but the quiet A.S.M., Tony Rees, had left at the same time as Jimmy Sheet. And, Charles suddenly remembered, Tony Rees had looked very guilty when surprised around the back of the set, just before the discovery of Sippy's body. Yes, that young man certainly merited investigation.

But what motive might he have had to kill the actress?

What motive might any of them have had, come to that?

Charles scanned the possibilities:

Rick Landor was having an affair with Sippy Stokes and seemed angry that Jimmy Sheet was trying to ace him out.

If Jimmy Sheet was involved with her, maybe he had some motive of jealousy or anger.

Ben Docherty had already made the decision to sack the actress, which surely ruled out any reason for trying to get rid of her prematurely.

Russell Bentley was unhappy with the recording that they'd done so far, but even for someone with an ego as big as his, it was a little fanciful to imagine that he'd resort to murder to get the episode remade.

Dilly Muirfield and Will Parton appeared to have no possible motive for killing Sippy Stokes, unless they felt extremely strongly about the effect her dire performance was having on their series. And surely, though television people were notorious for how seriously they took television, that was going a bit far.

Oh, and then presumably W. T. Wintergreen and her sister might also have been snooping around the set during the coffee break. But again, except for the benefit of ridding the world of a dreadful actress, they didn't seem to have an obvious motive.

Insufficient information, Charles concluded. I'm going to have to find out a great deal more before I can start coming to any conclusions about the case. And do a lot more thinking.

But fortunately he was prevented from doing any more thinking at that moment by the ringing of the phone on the landing.

* * *

'Hello?'

'Oh, good morning. Is that Charles Paris?'

'Yes.'

'This is Winifred Railton speaking.'

'Oh.'

His monosyllable must have revealed how little the name meant to him, because the elderly, cultured voice explained, 'You probably know me better as W. T. Wintergreen.'

'Oh, yes. Funny, I was just thinking about you.'

'Nothing bad, I hope?'

'Ah. Well…um…' He couldn't really say that he'd been assessing her suitability as a murder suspect, could he? 'No, no, of course not.'

'Look, Mr. Paris, I was wondering if it would be possible for us to meet.'

'Yes, I'm sure it would. But we'll be meeting on Monday at the read-through, anyway, won't we?'

'Oh, yes, I'll certainly be there. But I was meaning meet in a more private way. It's so impossible to talk on those occasions.'

'Yes. Well, perhaps a drink after rehearsal…'

'I wondered if you would like to come to tea with me and my sister on Tuesday afternoon,' W. T. Wintergreen said firmly.

'Oh. Um…Well, I'm not quite sure what the schedule –'

'I've checked. You won't be required for rehearsal on Tuesday afternoon.'

'Well, then, what can I say? Yes, of course I'd be delighted. Where would you like to meet?'

W. T. Wintergreen had it all worked out. 'If you come to our cottage at half past three, that will be fine.'

'And where is your cottage?'

'Ham Common.'

'Oh.' Sounded to Charles a hell of a way to go for tea. Still, he'd said yes. And it could be rather interesting.

'I'll give you the precise address on Monday. Louisa and I will look forward to seeing you then. I trust you have a pleasant weekend. Good-bye, Mr. Paris.'

Well, thought Charles as he put the phone down, what on earth was all that about?

On Saturday morning Charles rose late, more or less reassembled himself with coffee, and by half past eleven was feeling ready to go out to his local for a few pints and maybe even one of their range of Designer Ploughman's Lunches. What would it be today? A Brie Ploughman's? A Boursin Ploughman's? A Terrine de Canard Ploughman's? A Bratwurst and Sauerkraut Ploughman's?

He sometimes wondered what had happened to pub food in the last few years. In the old days, when you ordered a Ploughman's Lunch, you got a chunk of dry bread, a slab of hard cheese, a gold-wrapped packet of butter, with a tomato and maybe a pickled onion by way of garnish. Whereas now the Ploughmen really seemed to have moved up the social scale to become at least Gentlemen Farmers.

Charles blamed the Common Market. Most totally inexplicable developments in modern Britain had something to do with the Common Agricultural Policy.

It was while he was indulging these thoughts that he realised he was at that moment uniquely qualified to ring his wife. 'When you're sober,' Frances had said, and not a drop of alcohol had passed his lips for nearly twelve hours.

He rang her Highgate flat and was gratified to find her in. He felt suddenly very close to her. Yes, he had decided while the phone was ringing, they should meet up the next day for lunch. Sunday lunch, just like the old days. He could take her out somewhere on his W.E.T. loot. Or, better still, she might offer to cook lunch for him. Now that really would be like old times.

'See, Frances, here I am, ringing you at a reasonable time of day and stone-cold sober. What more could you ask?'

'A divorce?' she suggested, but her tone was not as hard as her words.

'You don't want one really, Frances. You love being unmarried to me.'

'Ha. Ha. Anyway, tell me about this job you've got.'

He told her. She was impressed. 'Three-month contract – running character. You realise you're in danger of becoming a success, Charles Paris?'

'Oh, I don't think that'd ever happen,' he said in mock self-deprecation.

'No, nor do I,' Frances agreed dryly. 'Still, I'm glad they're doing W. T. Wintergreen. I used to like her books.'

'I have to confess I'd never heard of them until the job came up.'

'They're good, if you like that sort of thing.'

'Having read the scripts, I'm not sure that I do. They're totally unrealistic.'

'That's part of their charm. Stanislas Braid is one of those completely unbelievable superman-sleuths who know everything about everything. School of Lord Peter Wimsey. And he has these wonderful and totally unrealistic relationships with everyone around him. Blodd, the chauffeur... the delightfully innocent and deeply loved Christina. Yes, totally unbelievable, but comforting.'

'Hmm. I think I prefer my detective heroes a bit more realistic.'

'No, no. Couldn't disagree more. The last thing I want is reality muscling in and spoiling a good detective story. I'm a great believer in the "Warm Bath" school of crime fiction – you know, books that are all snug and soothing and reassuring, books in which the Goodies are Good and the Baddies are Bad and you need never have a moment's anxiety about the fact that Good Will Triumph.'

'I find some of them a bit arch and mimsy-pimsy.'

'Wimsey – mimsy-pimsy?' asked Frances in mock horror.

'Oh, shut up. When did W. T. Wintergreen write her books?'

'I don't know exactly. Maybe she still *is* writing them?'

'Surely not still about Stanislas Braid? Not still set back in the thirties? In that old country-house time warp?'

'No, perhaps not. I'm not sure. I know she published a few before the war, and at that time apparently they were spoken of in the same breath as Dorothy Sayers and Margery Allingham. Then I think she went on till…late fifties, maybe? I certainly haven't been aware of any new titles since then. But I'm really not up-to-date. Ages since I've read one. Mind you, they were very important during my adolescence. Read all of them then; it felt like dozens. I had these fantasies of marrying someone as suave and debonair and brilliant as Stanislas Braid.'

'Good heavens. Did you really?'

'Yes, I did. And look what I ended up with.'

'Thank you, Frances, for those few kind words. Anyway, you will no doubt be impressed to hear that I am going to have tea with W. T. Wintergreen herself on Tuesday.'

'Are you really?'

'Mm. Shall I tell her my wife's a fan?'

'Yes, by all means.'

'Right, I will.' A silence hung between them. 'Frances, I was actually ringing to see if we could meet up.'

'Ah.' She didn't sound one hundred percent welcoming to the idea.

'We did talk about it.'

'*You* talked about it.'

'Yes. Well?'

'When do you want to meet?'

'Soon. Sooner the better.'

'Well, I'm leaving this afternoon to go and stay with some friends for the weekend.'

'Oh.' He felt a stab of disappointment.

'School as usual next week, and at the moment I find I'm too tired really to enjoy going out weekday evenings. Next weekend, perhaps?'

'Yes.' Now he was near to clinching the date, Charles felt unaccountably gauche and unwilling to firm it up. Almost as nervous as he had felt in such circumstances during his teens. And this was with his own wife, for God's sake. 'Well, look, I'm not absolutely certain of the schedule on the series for this week. They add odd days of filming and things. I think next weekend'd be all right, but can I get back to you on it?'

'Yes, fine,' said Frances. But she made it sound as if it didn't really matter to her a great deal whether he did or not.

He had his designer lunch in the pub. Dutch Rollmop Ploughman's. That really was taking the Common Agricultural Policy too far, he reckoned. Still, it gave him a good thirst for the beer.

He felt pretty good, really. Almost content. There was no one in the pub he knew more than to nod at, but that suited him fine. And of course no one recognised him as an actor. He wondered idly if that situation would change once *Stanislas Braid* was being funnelled into the nation's sitting rooms. Six months thence, if he sat on the same chair, would he be aware of people on the fringes of his vision nudging each other and whispering, 'Isn't that...?' The idea seemed ridiculous. But the extrovert in Charles Paris, the part that made him an actor, wasn't wholly repelled by it.

He picked up a tabloid newspaper that someone had left on the table and glanced through it. World news didn't seem to get any less depressing. In fact, now it seemed to him that the bits that weren't depressing or horrifying were just boring. He tried to remember when he'd last read something in a newspaper that had *interested* him. A very long time ago. Dear, oh, dear, he was becoming a cynical, desiccated old stick.

His eye was caught by a familiar name on the gossip-column page, and he read the snide little paragraph with fascination.

'Everyone knows there's nothing wrong with gilded warbler Jimmy Sheet's marriage. He keeps telling us that after the threatened earthquakes of last year it's as solid as a rock. So no doubt loveable cockney Jim has told his wife all about the mystery brunette he squired to Stringfellow's on Tuesday night. Otherwise one might say that Jimmy, now turning his attentions from music to acting, is in danger of being caught in the act!'

It was a typical piece of nudging copy, but it confirmed what Mort Verdon had told Charles. And confirmed Sippy Stokes's fairly lowly profile in the entertainment industry. The columnist had presumably tried without success to identify her. Just as well, from Jimmy Sheet's point of view, that no one had made the connection between the mystery girl at Stringfellow's and the dead actress whose photograph was all over Thursday's newspapers.

Still, the paragraph offered an intriguing new sidelight on the character of Jimmy Sheet. Hmm, thought Charles, maybe newspapers do sometimes contain news that's interesting.

Chapter Seven

CHARLES sometimes wondered who found television rehearsal rooms. Was there an elite band of dedicated men whose sole mission was to scour London for boys' clubs and rugby clubs and church halls and drill halls that passed the stringent tests of suitability for their purpose? How many potential venues were rejected on the grounds of being too comfortable or insufficiently dispiriting? How many were rejected for being too convenient for public transport or because they had adequate parking? How many failed selection because they were actually congenial places in which to spend one's time?

The conjectural band of searchers had clearly excelled themselves when they found the St. John Chrysostom Mission for Vagrants Lesser Hall, in which the rehearsals for *Stanislas Braid* took place. This was the apotheosis of the television rehearsal room, the one for which every other hall in London must have been rejected.

Situated a good twenty minutes' walk from the nearest tube station, jammed in an alley between a cement works and a timber yard, whose lorries were a perpetual hazard to anyone foolish enough to risk leaving their car outside, the Lesser Hall's high windows were so begrimed that what light did filter through had an unhealthy, diluted pallor about it. The lights inside, kept constantly switched on, apologetically illuminated walls the colour of baby shit. As Charles looked around the room on the Monday morning of the second read-through, he realised with delight that he had finally found a context in which to use one of his favourite words: 'fuscous'.

The only bright colours in the room, apart from the clothes of the cast and production team, were the strips of variously coloured tape with which the outlines of the different sets had been marked on the floor by assiduous stage managers. But these were largely covered by the long chain of tables, surrounded by chairs, at which the read-through was to take place.

W. T. Wintergreen – or Winifred Railton – had acknowledged Charles with an inclination of her head but made no reference to their conversation of the previous Friday. She had a script open on her lap and, with her sister, Louisa, as ever, close beside her, was deep in conversation with Dilly Muirfield. From the expression on the script editor's face, she was getting yet more complaints that the script of this episode, 'The Italian Stiletto Murder,' had diverged too far from the original book and that, as Louisa Railton recurrently complained in fierce whispers to her sister, 'Stanislas Braid just wouldn't do that.'

Charles spared a few moments of sympathy for Dilly Muirfield's role. She was the mediator; it was she who had to listen to the endless cavils of the writer of the books, the writers of the scripts, the stars, the producer, and the director. She then, rather as the floor manager did in the studio, had to translate the complaints into acceptable demands for the people against whom they were made.

Charles had heard this process in action more than once. He had heard Russell Bentley denouncing the script to Dilly with the words 'It's a load of shit – the work of an absolute incompetent. I mean, the character of Stanislas Braid virtually disappears for the whole middle of the episode.'

And he had heard Dilly relaying the message to Will Parton in conciliatory tones: 'I was just wondering whether it might be better if we inserted a little extra scene for Stanislas Braid in the middle here, you know, just to remind the audience how he's proceeding with his investigation?'

He had also heard Will Parton's response to this suggestion, and though the object of the writer's vilification had been Russell Bentley, it was Dilly Muirfield who had to listen to all the foul language. She really was in a no-win situation.

Working for a producer like Ben Docherty, whose daily Jekyll and Hyde act made him quite capable of spending the whole afternoon reversing all the decisions he had made in the morning, can't have made the script editor's job any easier.

What was striking about that morning in the St. John Chrysostom Mission for Vagrants Lesser Hall was how little impact the death of Sippy Stokes had made on the production. Rick Landor, the one person who might have been personally affected, was not there, and for the new Director it was ancient history, something that had happened the week before, nothing to do with him.

The new Director was only in his late twenties. This was his first major production, and he was very much on his dignity, determined to impose his authority on the proceedings. His mind was too full of the professional challenges of the coming fortnight to have any room for thoughts of the previous week's death.

But the rest of the cast and production team, those who had been working with the dead girl only a few days before, seemed equally unaffected. The ripples caused by her death had quickly smoothed themselves out, and the surface of the production was just as it had been before.

Or, to be truthful, it was rather better than it had been before. Previously, the knowledge of what a bad actress Sippy Stokes was had infected everyone with a kind of unease, the feeling that her incompetence might be sabotaging the chances of their series.

The new girl, Joanne Rhymer, it was immediately evident, would be a very different proposition. For a start, she looked much better for the part. Sippy

Stokes, though an attractive girl, had had a gypsy, almost tarty quality about her. Her dark hair and sensuous lips had seemed too knowing for the innocent Christina, and the woodenness of her performance had given some of her lines an unwanted air of innuendo, as if she were sending up their naiveté.

But Joanne Rhymer, although dressed as fashionably as befitted a twenty-year-old actress, had about her a timeless quality. Her face was heart-shaped, and her blond hair showed off flashes of auburn even in the muted lighting of the St. John Chrysostom Mission for Vagrants Lesser Hall. She had a trim figure that would suit the range of thirties dresses so painstakingly assembled by Wardrobe.

Above all, she had about her an air of credible innocence. The potentially twee lines of Christina, the cloying relationship between her and her father, might become almost believable when expressed by this child-woman.

Charles couldn't help speculating about how much her character reflected the innocence of her appearance. His conversation with Maurice had reminded him of Gwen Rhymer's fabled nymphomania. Was it by any chance a characteristic that the daughter had inherited? Was he looking at another Blue Nun in the making?

You're a disgusting, prurient old sod, he told himself. Real classic dirty old man. But this self-administered admonition didn't stop his speculations. The trouble was, you see, he had once been the beneficiary of Gwen Rhymer's 'proclivities', and while not approving of her behaviour or reputation, he couldn't help remembering that he had enjoyed the experience enormously. So he felt justified in having more than a passing interest in her daughter's character.

As soon as the read-through started, it was clear that Joanne Rhymer's talent was equal to her looks. She brought a kind of resilience to the character's naiveté. Lines that looked hopelessly sentimental on the page managed, through her delivery, to become charming.

Everyone in the rehearsal room was aware of the contrast from the first read-through. At that stage they had suspected that Sippy Stokes was, like a lot of actresses, just a bad reader. The full deficiency of her talent had not then been exposed. But it had still made for an edgy atmosphere.

With Joanne Rhymer in the part, though, everyone could relax. Charles watched as she read her first scene and saw the relief growing on various faces around the table.

Will Parton looked positively triumphant, finally vindicated in the knowledge that his lines would work if played in the right way. W. T. Wintergreen and Louisa also beamed; for the first time they seemed to be happy about the way one of the *Stanislas Braid* characters was being portrayed. Russell Bentley seemed at ease, too. He probably wasn't aware of why he felt better; the habit of not noticing what the rest of the cast did prevented him from realising how well his lines were being fed to him; but at last he seemed able to play the part of Russell Bentley.

And Ben Docherty's face glowed with benevolence, as if he were a proud father watching the performance of his favourite daughter.

Yes, there was no doubt about it. Joanne Rhymer's performance worked. She *was* Christina Braid.

Except, of course, she wasn't. She was Elvira Braid, just back from finishing school in Switzerland. Her sister, Christina, thanks to the inspired invention of Will Parton, had 'gone to Paris to nurse an old school friend recovering from a nasty bout of influenza'.

They got through the whole of the first Stanislas Braid/Christina scene before Russell Bentley interrupted the reading. 'Look, there's something wrong here.'

'Sorry, could we read straight through?' said the new Director. 'We're doing this on the watch. We'll pick up any notes afterward.'

'No, this is important. We've got to sort it out before we go on.'

'I'm sorry. Read-through first,' insisted the director, unaware that he was entering his first battle of wills with his star.

'No,' said Russell Bentley firmly.

The P.A. gave a short-tempered sigh and clicked off her stopwatch.

'Look, I'm the Director,' said the new Director, 'and if I say we continue the read-through, then we continue the read-through.'

'No,' Russell Bentley repeated.

'Come on, you're a professional actor. Surely you know how to behave at a rehearsal?'

This was dangerous ground. The worst insult that can be thrown at an actor is the accusation that he's unprofessional. And for a new director to throw it at his star on a first read-through showed a lack of diplomacy that verged on the suicidal.

Russell Bentley's face flushed with anger. 'Are you saying that I'm not –'

Ben Docherty realised the gravity of the situation and fulfilled his producer's role by interrupting. 'Now just a minute. Don't let's get heated about this. I think Russell may have a point.'

'I'm the Director,' the new Director insisted doggedly, 'and I say we should get on with the read-through.'

'Well, I'm the Producer,' said Ben Docherty, 'and I say we should hear what Russell has to say first.'

'All right.' The new Director flung his script petulantly down on the table. 'If you're one of those producers who constantly undermines his director's authority...'

Ben Docherty didn't rise to this bait. Instead, he turned to his star in a conciliatory manner and said, 'Now, what was your point, Russell?'

'Simply this, Ben. This lovely young girl – what was your name again, dear?'

'Joanne.'

'Yes, Joanne...is playing a part just like that of Christina, my daughter, and yet –' Russell continued, repeating for emphasis '– and yet we keep referring to the character as "Elvira".'

'Yes, Russell, and you know the reasons for that. Look, I agree, the characters are virtually interchangeable, but that makes things even simpler. All you have to do is to say the different name.'

'It's not just that. I also have a bit of meaningless drivel about finishing schools in Switzerland and friends with influenza. Why can't I just cut all that and call the character Christina?'

'You know why. Because we've already got two-thirds of an episode in the can with a different actress playing Christina.'

'A rather dreadful actress, I may say.'

'That, Russell, is a matter of opinion. All I know is that W.E.T. can't afford to write off what we've already done on the first episode.'

'Well, I think they should.'

Charles had been aware of considerable muttering between the two Railton sisters during this exchange but was surprised when W. T. Wintergreen's voice was suddenly heard, firmly announcing, 'I couldn't agree more.'

The Producer turned wearily to the crime writer.

'Look, W.T....Miss Wintergreen...Miss Railton.' He was always at a loss as to how to address her. 'I know it would be very nice if we could just scrap the last two weeks' work, but I'm afraid it's a matter of economics.'

'No, it's not. It's a matter of what the public expect from a series called *Stanislas Braid*. My readers are already going to be deeply distressed and disappointed by the number of gratuitous changes which have been made to my books, but when it comes to changing the names of one of the major characters, one of the best-loved characters indeed, the character of Christina...well, I just don't think they'll stand for it.'

'Think yourself lucky they haven't changed her sex and made her black,' Will Parton muttered to no one in particular.

'Miss Railton,' Ben Docherty began, homing in on the name with infinite patience, 'I'm rather afraid you may flatter yourself about the power of your readers. You say they won't stand for it....Well, how do you suppose they're going to express the fact that they don't stand for it? Anyway, Miss Railton, we're not talking about books. As I've told you many times before, we're talking about television. A whole different ball game. Do you realise that *one* showing of *one* of the episodes of this series will be seen by more people than all the readers of all your books put together? Most of the viewers, I'm afraid, will never have heard of W. T. Wintergreen. A large number of them probably never read books, anyway. So, for them, whether a character is called Christina or Elvira will not make the blindest bit of difference.'

'But it makes all the difference in the world!' This outburst came from Louisa Railton, so incensed by what was being said that she forgot her customary shyness.

Russell Bentley renewed his attack on the beleaguered Producer. 'Listen, Ben, I have a reputation in television. When members of the public see my name on a credit in the *T.V. Times* or whatever, they know what kind of thing to expect.'

Yes, your inimitable impersonation of Russell Bentley, thought Charles mischievously.

'In other words, what I'm saying is, I've got my own standards. And I don't feel that anything we recorded last week was up to those standards.'

'But we did all that filming,' Ben Docherty wailed. 'I mean, the costs if we do write it off are just terrifying.'

'Not as terrifying as putting that rubbish out. I mean, since when has W.E.T. been in the business of putting out substandard productions?'

'Since the company was formed,' Will Parton mouthed silently to Charles, who tried not to giggle.

'Anyway, we didn't get the whole episode recorded,' Russell Bentley continued. 'You're going to have to extend the schedule to pick up the extra scenes, and since you've got to rebook everyone for that, you might as well just remake the episode.'

'Not necessarily.'

'What do you mean?'

'He means,' Will Parton suddenly interposed, 'that he might not have to *rebook* everyone.'

Russell Bentley looked at the Producer, who was gazing with hatred at the writer. 'That was a private conversation we had, Will.'

'Well, we may as well make it public, because I'm afraid your little idea isn't going to work, Ben. I'm prepared to go through quite a few contortions as a writer, but this time you're just asking too much.'

'What "little idea" is this we're talking about?' asked Russell Bentley quietly.

'There's no need to tell him,' the Producer snapped. 'Come on, we should be getting on with this read-through.'

But Will Parton, having decided on his course, was not going to be deflected from it. 'Ben's idea,' he said coolly, 'was that I should do a major rewrite on the episode – a major salvage operation – a major evisceration, if you like. That I should somehow incorporate the scenes that are in the can and rewrite the rest of the story in a way that only involved rebooking two artistes.'

'Only two!' said Russell Bentley.

'But that would make nonsense of my story,' objected W. T. Wintergreen, appalled by the perfidy of the suggestion.

'Oh, yes,' said Will ironically, 'it'd make nonsense of the story. It'd make a dreadful television programme that I'd be ashamed to have my credit on…that all of us would be ashamed to have our credits on. Oh, yes, but think of the money it'd save.'

There was a silence. All eyes were fixed on Ben Docherty.

But the Producer's eyes were fixed on Will Parton. Fixed with an expression of deep loathing.

Chapter Eight

AFTER THIS confrontation the read-through continued, but the 'atmosphere' it had engendered remained in the St. John Chrysostom Mission for Vagrants Lesser Hall. As soon as they had reached the end of the script, Russell Bentley turned straight back to Ben Docherty and reiterated, 'It's going to make a lot more sense if we do just change the girl's name back to Christina. Cut all that heavy-handed garbage in the first scene about finishing schools. It'll make the whole thing flow much more smoothly.'

'But that will mean committing myself to scrapping last week's work. So long as we change the name, we have at least got the option. See what kind of magic Will can work on the script.'

'I can't do magic,' the writer announced flatly. 'I can manage the occasional conjuring trick, but magic – forget it.'

'Well...'

'Mr. Docherty,' said W. T. Wintergreen, 'you really must call the character Christina. You've just no idea how important it is. So much depends on the characters having the right names.'

'A lot may depend from your *readers'* point of view,' the Producer conceded, deciding that W. T. Wintergreen was an easier target to hit back at than Russell Bentley, 'but so far as I'm concerned, a name is just a name.'

'Then you've clearly never written anything,' the old girl responded spiritedly.

'He's *re*written a good few things,' Will Parton muttered.

'If you had,' W. T. Wintergreen continued, 'you would know the care that must go into the selection of the proper name for a character. Sometimes I spend whole weeks before I start a book getting the names right.'

'I don't think the viewing public are as hypersensitive about it as you are.'

'I'm not concerned with the viewing public.'

'Well, I am. In fact, it's my sole concern. It's my job to be concerned about the viewing public.'

'The fact remains that the character of Christina is a "Christina" and not an "Elvira".'

'Yes, come on, let's just call her Christina and be done with it,' said Russell Bentley.

'No, I'm sorry, Russell. I'll have to give this some thought.'

'Look, Ben, if you were reckoning just to pick up the odd scene over the next two and a half months so that you can cobble together a first episode, forget it.'

'But we can't afford to extend the schedule.'

'I'm afraid I can never take it that seriously when a commercial television company pleads poverty, Ben.'

'It's true. Then there are problems with booking studios. And you're not available after the end of this contract.'

'I will make myself available,' Russell Bentley announced grandly. 'If that is the only problem in the way of remaking the first episode, I will guarantee to make myself available.'

'Oh, well...' For the first time Ben Docherty's resolve appeared to weaken. 'I'll have to check the feasibility of it with Contracts and studio and Outside Broadcast facilities.'

Russell Bentley beamed. Once again he appeared to be achieving what gave him the greatest satisfaction in life – getting his own way. 'Everything's possible, Ben, even in television.'

The Producer chewed his lip unhappily. Then the new Director chipped in, demonstrating once again that whatever his skills in framing artistic camera shots, he had a few things to learn in the diplomacy department. 'But you're going to have to give us a decision very soon. I mean, I'm the Director of this show, and I can't fart around with script changes at this point.'

'I'll have to check a lot of things out,' said Ben Docherty, too dispirited even to notice the insubordination.

'Well, you'd better do it bloody quickly. If we're going to cut the finishing-school crap, we may have to add something to make up the time.'

'Oh, I'm sure you won't need to,' Will Parton drawled. 'Most directors can easily make up time with a few artistic shots that slow down the pace and add nothing to the story.'

He spoke with the bitter experience of a writer who had seen too many of his favourite lines cut to make way for directorial self-indulgence, but the new director's keenness to get on with rehearsal prevented the outbreak of another argument.

'As I say, I'll think about it,' Ben Docherty confirmed. Then he looked at his watch. 'I'd better get back to the office.'

Charles Paris felt certain that the producer's route back to his office would take in some convenient pub.

'Right.' Russell Bentley turned to the new director the minute Ben Docherty was out of the room. 'Let's take that as read then. We cut all the finishing-school garbage, and you, my dear – What was your name again?'

'Joanne.'

'Of course, Joanne. Well, you, Joanne, will be referred to as Christina throughout.'

Everyone in the St. John Chrysostom Mission for Vagrants Lesser Hall seemed very happy with this hijacking of their producer's authority. For some, like W. T. Wintergreen and Louisa Railton, the satisfaction derived from artistic considerations. For others, like Charles Paris, its roots were more basic. If the schedule for making the *Stanislas Braid* series was to be extended, that meant not only that unemployment would be staved off by another couple of weeks but also that he would receive yet another healthy W.E.T. fee.

Yes, it was very satisfactory all around. The production could continue as if Sippy Stokes had never existed. And it would be a much better production for her absence. So everyone, with the possible exception of Ben Docherty, had benefited from her death.

But had anyone actually benefited enough to justify their murdering her?

'Here we are, boofle. Schedules.' Mort Verdon bustled up to him, a sheaf of photocopied sheets draped over his arm. 'Going on your travels, Charles.'

'What do you mean?'

'Filming for the next episode. Actually going away.'

'What – you mean locations farther than half a mile from W.E.T. House?'

His question only slightly exaggerated the situation. Like most television companies, W.E.T. had its little repertoire of favourite locations, and the reason for their popularity was their proximity to the company headquarters. Because W.E.T. House was situated in Lisson Avenue, NW1, a disproportionate amount of the action in W.E.T. series seemed to be located in that area. Television car chases took place on the Westway. Television crooks lived in Maida Vale mansion blocks. Television drug pushers haunted Church Street Market. Television lovers entwined at London Zoo or on the towpath of Regent's Park Canal. And Regent's Park itself was transformed into an incredible variety of television exteriors, from the Dust Bowl of the American Midwest to the steaming jungles of Borneo.

Mort Verdon nodded in reply to Charles's question. 'Oh, yes, boofle. And you'd better pack your bucket and spade. You're going to the seaside.'

'How exciting. Where to? How long for?'

'You're going to the Isle of Purbeck.'

'Oh.' Charles looked blank. 'Remind me.'

'Dorset. It's not a real island. At least not for a few millennia. More sort of *pen*insula than insular these days.'

'Name some towns.'

'Swanage, Studland, Corfe Castle.'

'Oh, right. I know where you mean. Just didn't know it was called the Isle of Purbeck.'

'Learn a little something every day, boofle.'

'I certainly try to. When is this?'

'Ep. three. Rick's next production. Week's rehearsal starting fortnight today and travel down the following Sunday to start filming Monday morning. Travel back Tuesday evening, rest day Wednesday, studio Thurs and Fri.'

'Terrific.' Though he found the actual process of filming deeply boring, the prospect of forty-eight hours of hotels and location catering was very appealing. 'W.E.T. really pushing the boat out.'

'Hard to avoid it with an episode called "The Seashore Murder",' said Mort Verdon dryly.

'Hmm. Why is it I never get involved in episodes called "The Barbados Murder" or "The Acapulco Murder" or "The Seychelles Murder"?'

'Don't be greedy, Charles. You'll have a lovely time in Swanage.'

'Oh, I'm sure I will. Nice hotel?'

'Of course.'

'Great.'

'All the facilities you might require – bar, restaurant, another bar, sauna, yet another bar. Ideal bed-hopping territory.'

'Oh, I think I'm a bit old for that sort of thing.'

'Not what I've heard, Charles Paris.'

Charles chuckled, as if to dismiss the idea. Mind you, he was rather flattered by it. Even slightly excited.

'Anyway, boofle...' Mort Verdon leaned forward in mock-seriousness and laid his hand on Charles's. 'If you want to hop into my bed, all I can advise is, book early to avoid the crowds.'

'Okay.' Charles grinned back. 'Thanks. I'll bear that in mind.'

The rehearsal schedule for the next three days was confirmed, and Charles was not called again till Wednesday morning. So, as W. T. Wintergreen had told him, he would be free on Tuesday afternoon.

Before the new Director started blocking Russell Bentley and Joanne Rhymer's first scene, there was a break, during which the girls from Wardrobe went around, checking measurements with the cast members only appearing in that episode and discussing choice of costumes with the regular performers. Since Sergeant Clump never appeared in anything other than his uniform – though Will Parton had threatened to get a wacky scene of the village bobby in his underwear into the last episode – Charles was free to do whatever he wanted to do.

What he did want to do was, unsurprisingly, to go and have a drink, and he looked around the St. John Chrysostom Mission for Vagrants Lesser Hall for a suitable accomplice in this enterprise. If there wasn't anyone around, Charles would not revise his plans in any major way; but drinking with someone else always did give him a spurious feeling of righteousness.

Jimmy Sheet had also been released from rehearsal for the rest of the day, and since Blodd, like Sergeant Clump, was rarely seen in anything other than his uniform, he did not need any discussions with Wardrobe either.

'Fancy a drink?' Charles asked diffidently.

'Where?' asked the former pop star.

'There's a pub just down the road. Pretty grotty, but the beer's okay.'

Jimmy Sheet grimaced. 'Don't like pubs, really, these days. Don't get no privacy; people keep recognising me.'

'Oh.' This was one of the hazards of show business that Charles's career had not yet had to negotiate. Still, maybe when Sergeant Clump was a familiar face in the nation's living rooms, all that would change. Somehow he doubted it.

'Tell you what, though,' said Jimmy Sheet. 'We could go to this club I know. Have a quick snifter there.'

'Well, fine, if that's all right. Where is it?'

'Not far. We'll go in the motor.' His cockney glottal stop completely removed the 't' from the word. He pronounced it 'mo-ah.'

The 'mo-ah' turned out to be a two-seater silver Mercedes. It had a personalised 'JS' number plate. Not for the first time, Charles reflected on the contradiction he had encountered in the personality of many 'celebrities', who, while constantly asserting their desperate desire for privacy, drove everywhere in vehicles that advertised their presence.

The car was parked athwart double yellow lines opposite the St. John Chrysostom Mission for Vagrants. Jimmy Sheet wasn't going to put his 'mo-ah' at risk from the swinging lorries of the cement works or the timber yard. And the risk of traffic wardens clearly didn't worry him. Without comment, he removed the ticket from the windscreen and shoved it into the glove compartment to join a pile of others.

As soon as they were under way, Jimmy Sheet picked up the car phone and punched out a number from the memory. 'Won't be a sec., Charles. Oh, hello, love, it's me. How's things? Yeah, great. No, I'm not called again till tomorrow. Sure. Yes, well, I'll be back round four, I reckon. Four, half past. No, just going off for a drink at the club with one of the cast. No, love, of course not. He's a bloke. Charles Paris. No, well, he – You might recognise the face. Of course I am. Say hello, Charles.'

Charles looked in amazement at the telephone thrust in front of him.

'It's the wife,' Jimmy Sheet said, as if that explained everything. 'Sharon. Go on, say hello.'

'Oh, hello, Sharon,' Charles obeyed, though he felt somewhat bewildered.

Jimmy Sheet took the phone back. 'See? Told you. Okay, then, see you later, love. Love you. 'Bye.'

He returned the phone to its rest and made no comment on the bizarre incident that had just taken place.

Jimmy Sheet's club was on a small street not far from Grosvenor Square. Once again he pulled the Mercedes to a halt on double yellow lines directly outside the entrance and, pausing only to don dark glasses, got out, clearly intending to leave it there.

'Aren't you worried about getting clamped?' asked Charles tentatively.

'Nah. There's this service that sorts it out for you. And I've got an account with this limo company what'll send one round pronto to take me home.'

Money, it seemed, was not a problem for Mr. Sheet.

His club looked expensive, too. But whereas Charles had been expecting something rather glitzy and American, a place full of girls with variegated hair where no drink was served without a cluster of umbrellas in it, the reception into which Jimmy Sheet ushered him was very restrained and patrician. Panelled walls and marble pillars, much nearer the Athenaeum than the Groucho.

The porter, who would have been well cast as a minor retainer in an episode of *Stanislas Braid*, goodafternoon-Mr.-Sheeted him, and Jimmy magnanimously asked after the porter's family while signing Charles in. It was interesting to see how quickly new money absorbed the habits of old money.

In the dark wood-and-leather peace of the bar, Jimmy Sheet greeted a few pinstriped gentlemen who showed no resentment of his open-necked shirt and oyster-grey leather jacket. They were too much gentlemen even to show resentment of Charles's neolithic sports jacket.

A waiter, so discreet as to be almost invisible, took their orders for a large Bell's and a spritzer. Jimmy Sheet popped a stuffed olive in his mouth, chewed it, and asked, 'How'd you think it's going, then?'

'Not too bad,' said Charles cautiously. 'Rather better as of this morning than it was last week.'

'Yeah.' Jimmy Sheet nodded reflectively but did not pick up the cue to talk about Sippy Stokes. 'Hope it'll be all right. The agent said it'd be a good series for me to do. Don't want to end up in a bummer.'

Charles tried to imagine what it must be like to move in a world where your agent recommends shows that would be 'good for you to do' rather than one where you grabbed anything that was offered.

'I'm sure it'll be all right,' he said automatically. 'Because actually this is your first big acting break, isn't it?'

'Could say that,' Jimmy Sheet agreed. 'Mind you, "break" makes it sound like it was accidental. I mean, this was a calculated career move.'

'Ah.'

'Well, I mean, I could've kept on with the singing, but, you know, last couple of singles didn't get as high up the charts as the ones before, and I always reckoned to get out of that while I was still on top. It's all only means to an end, isn't it?'

'Is it?' asked Charles.

'Oh, sure. I done the singing because, you know, gives you a good international profile, but I never was going to stay with it. I mean, the money's there if you want to. Go into cabaret, you know, keep recycling the old hits – you can do that till the cows come home. But that was never how I wanted my career to pan out.'

'No?'

'Nah. Anyway, all that travelling. You know, I reckon I done my bit on the touring front. Need something that doesn't take me away from home so much. Like to spend more time with Sharon and the kids.'

'Actors do a lot of touring and location stuff.'

'Oh, sure. But in the music business, you got to do it to keep up your profile. In acting, you know, you can choose your work.'

Can you? thought Charles. First I've heard of it.

'And the acting, you know, you can keep it going, fit it round other things, business commitments and that.'

'Really?'

'Yeah. I mean, again television's only another kind of staging post.'

'Is it?'

'I'm just doing this series to, you know, like remind the public I'm not just a singer, I'm a good actor, and all. Kind of re-establish me in the public's mind in a different role.'

'I see.'

'Not going to stay with the television.'

'Why not?'

'Well, it's not sort of international.'

'I thought it could be. I thought it was becoming increasingly international.'

'Yeah, but not at the same level as the music business or feature films.'

'Well...'

'Apart from anything else, the money's peanuts, isn't it?'

Since the three months of the *Stanislas Braid* contract would be the best-paid three months of his life, Charles didn't feel qualified to reply to this.

'No, as I say,' Jimmy Sheet went on, 'it's feature films I'm going into in the long term.'

'Oh, really?'

'Might do some theatre as well...You know, if the right part comes up on Broadway, that kind of number.'

Charles kept wondering why all this didn't sound unconvincing. He had heard similar dreams expressed by any number of actors, and his normal reaction was, all sounds great; you just wait till you get out into the real world, sonny. But Jimmy Sheet spoke with such assurance that he made his plans sound more like business decisions than pipe dreams. He seemed to be in no doubt that he would be able to follow his proposed career path, and Charles found himself equally convinced.

'What do you put your money in?' Jimmy Sheet asked suddenly.

'I beg your pardon?' said Charles.

'Your money – what's it in?'

'Erm ...' Difficult question to answer, really. The truth – I haven't got any – sounded just too pathetic and self-pitying. 'Oh, this and that.'

'Mm. Spread the investment – something to be said for that, certainly. I got most of my dosh in property.'

'Have you?'

'Yeah. Don't think you can ultimately lose with property.'

'No. No, I suppose not. As Mark Twain said, "Buy land, my son, they are not making any more".'

'Who?'

'Mark Twain.'

'Don't know him.' Jimmy Sheet restlessly picked up another olive and flicked it into his mouth. 'Got some property in the States, bit in Australia, quite a lot here in England.'

'Ah.'

'Well, you got to do something with it, haven't you?'

'Yes, yes.'

Jimmy Sheet winked at the waiter, who ghosted up with more drinks. Charles decided it might be timely to move the conversation away from money, about which he'd never had the opportunity to know anything, to what he was really interested in.

'Terrible business last week, wasn't it?'

'What's that, then?' asked Jimmy.

'Sippy Stokes.'

'Oh, yeah, yeah.'

'Dreadful when something like that happens. You know, you feel you should have done more.'

'Done more like what?'

'Got to know her better, perhaps.'

'Why?'

'Well, when someone dies –'

'People die all the time.'

'Yes, but when it's someone you know –'

'You just said you didn't know her.'

Jimmy Sheet certainly wasn't making the conversation easy. 'No, I mean...' Charles floundered on. 'What I mean is, you just feel it's kind of a waste.'

'Not a waste of an actress, certainly.'

'Perhaps not. But a waste of a person.'

'Maybe to the people who were close to her.'

'Do you know who was close to her?'

Jimmy Sheet's eyes narrowed. 'Well, I gather Rick Landor wasn't averse to giving her one every now and then.'

'I suppose that's how she got the part.'

'Can't think of any other reason. No, old Ben nearly bust a gut when he heard about it. They'd done most of the major casting, and he was still dithering about who was going to play Christina – mind you, I think he'd got that Joanne bird in mind from the start. Then suddenly he hears Rick's pulled a fast one and put through the booking for his little bit on the side.'

'Couldn't Ben have put a stop to it?'

'Contract had gone out. He'd have had to pay her off for the series. And we saw this morning just how keen he is on writing things off.'

'Yes. Mind you, he had decided to pay her off after the first episode, anyway.'

'Had he?'

Quickly, Charles filled Jimmy in on what Will had told him in the bar after Sippy's death.

'Shit,' said the singer at the end of the account. 'That Ben Docherty can be a really nasty operator.'

'Yes. It's amazing that Sippy didn't hear from someone what he was planning.'

'Well, she didn't. She didn't have a clue on the Tuesday night, anyway.'

Jimmy Sheet had given something away there, and Charles pounced on it. 'Oh, really? Did you see her on the Tuesday night?'

'What? No. No. Just at the end of the filming, you know, just had a chat.'

Charles would have recognised that the man was lying even if he hadn't known of his visit with the 'mystery brunette' to Stringfellow's.

'So you weren't one of the people who was close to her?'

'No. No, course I wasn't.' Jimmy Sheet was becoming heated. 'Shit, just because you've worked in the pop business, everybody thinks you're bloody bonking everything in sight. Look, all right, in what I do, things I've done, there's always been girls around. But I'm a happily married man. I got Sharon and the kids. Okay, in the past there may have been the odd flutter, but that's all finished – got it?'

It didn't take a very advanced student of psychology to recognise that the vehemence of this defence was totally disproportionate to the hint of an accusation that Charles had made. Nor to identify it as the operation of a guilty conscience.

As if to reinforce that impression – which hardly needed reinforcing – the ectoplasmic waiter suddenly materialised at Jimmy's side and murmured discreetly that Mr. Sheet's wife was on the telephone.

Checking up on him, Charles thought as the harassed husband went off to take the call. There was something amiss with Jimmy Sheet's marriage. His wife was a neurotically jealous woman, and she didn't trust him. As the newspaper gossip column had hinted, she could well be the sort to divorce him and take away his beloved children if she caught a whiff of any other extramarital excursions.

Taking Sippy Stokes out to Stringfellow's on the night before her death might well qualify under that heading.

Fine, so long as it remained secret. But it was a risky thing to do. Mort Verdon had seen them there. Any number of other people might have seen them there. It was only luck that the newspaper columnist hadn't been able to identify the 'mystery brunette'.

Anyway, suppose Sippy Stokes didn't want it to remain secret? Suppose she had threatened to tell the lovely Sharon what had happened?

Then Jimmy Sheet might well feel that Sippy Stokes needed to be silenced.

Chapter Nine

'OH, HELLO, Charles. It's Maurice.'

'*You* ringing *me*? Good heavens, what's happened?'

'Availability check.'

'Good God, there's no stopping them at the moment. Is it the National Theatre again? I don't know, that lot just won't take no for an answer. Oh, well, I suppose if they *insist* on my giving my Lear, I can't really say no, can I?'

'Ha. Ha. You're in a very chirpy mood this bright Tuesday morning, aren't you? What's got into you?'

'I think it must be employment. I had forgotten how it felt to have things to do in the gaps between sleeping. And now my agent being flooded with availability checks...'

'One's hardly a flood, Charles.'

'What about the two you had last Thursday?'

'What? Oh, yes. Yes, of course, I'd forgotten those.'

But the pause between the 'What?' and the 'Oh, yes' had been too long. Maurice had given himself away. As Charles had suspected, the availability checks of the previous week had been pure fabrication.

'Anyway, who wants to know my availability?'

'W.E.T.'

'Hey, how about that? Success breeds success. What is it? Supporting artiste given his own series? New spin-off called *Sergeant Clump Investigates*? Or are they asking me to appear as a well-loved W.E.T. personality on some wacky, tacky game show?'

He offered these suggestions as jokes, but only partly as jokes. No actor can suppress that secret hope that one day, it really is all going to happen for him.

'It's none of that, Charles. It's still *Stanislas Braid*.'

'Are they committing themselves to the second series already?'

'No, they're adding some extra dates to this series to pick up the episode they lost last week.'

'Ah, yes. Yes, of course.' So Ben Docherty had finally given in to the pressures around him. Sippy Stokes was to be erased completely from the series of *Stanislas Braid*. Russell Bentley had had his own way yet again.

'That's good news, Maurice. When is it? How're they doing it?'

'Just tacking a fortnight on to the end of this series. I mean, that's assuming everyone can make the dates. As I say, it's only an availability check at the moment. Presumably, if any regulars are committed elsewhere, they'll have to rethink. I mean, Russell Bentley's never out of work, so he might be a problem.'

'He said he'd definitely make himself available for this. It came up at the read-through yesterday.'

'Oh, well, it should be all right, then. He's the one who's likely to be difficult. I can't think anyone else is going to have much coming up.'

Charles cleared his throat. Then he cleared his throat again.

'What's up, Charles? Touch of the old laryngitis?'

'No, Maurice' came the dignified reply. 'But isn't there something you've forgotten?'

'What's that? Not your birthday, is it?'

'No.'

'Wedding anniversary? But I thought since you and Frances weren't living together anymore, you didn't –'

'No, Maurice. Just think. W.E.T. rang you to check my availability?'

'Yes.'

'Well, isn't there something you haven't done?'

The agent was still at a loss. 'What's that, then?'

'Come on, Maurice. You haven't checked my bloody availability, have you!'

'What – you mean, I haven't asked whether you'll be free for a fortnight at the end of this contract?'

'Exactly.'

There was a silence from the other end of the phone. Then it was interrupted by a sound that could have been an asthmatic having an orgasm. Charles recognised that Maurice was laughing.

'Oh, I'm sorry,' said the agent when he was sufficiently recovered to speak. 'I am so sorry, Charles. Aren't we being grand?' This idea sent him off into another burst of hysterical gasping. 'Oh, dear. Oh, dear. All right, Charles. Here we go. Ready?'

'Yes,' Charles replied primly.

'Right. Charles Paris, is it possible that you might be available to record an extra episode of the *Stanislas Braid* series for West End TV in the two weeks immediately following the cessation of your current contract with the company?'

'Hang on a minute,' said Charles. 'I'll check.' Then, after a pause during which someone who possessed an engagements diary would have had time to consult it, he returned to the phone. 'I think it might be possible. There are one or two things in the air but nothing firmed up yet.'

'I see,' said Maurice soberly, playing out the game to its conclusion.

'Yes, I think so long as W.E.T. issues their contract pretty sharpish, we should be all right.'

'Oh, good, Charles. That is a weight off my mind.'

'Mine, too, Maurice,' said Charles, and then spoiled the whole effect by giggling. 'Good news, though, isn't it?'

'Excellent. How'd the Rhymer girl shape up at the read-through?'

'Great. She's really good. No, I'm afraid the whole show will be immeasurably better without the services of Sippy Stokes.'

'Ah, well...Incidentally, did you hear about the inquest?'

'What?' Once again Charles was taken aback by the efficiency of his agent's information service.

'Inquest on Sippy Stokes. Yesterday morning.'

'No, I haven't heard anything. What happened?'

'Not a lot. Police asked for an adjournment while they made further investigations.'

'Oh.'

'Well, you know what that usually means, don't you?'

'What?'

'Means the police think the death's suspicious, doesn't it?'

'Oh,' said Charles. 'Does it?'

He thought he might need a few drinks at lunch-time to get him through his encounter with the Railton sisters, but he drank whisky rather than beer. There was a danger that two or three pints diluted with tea would keep him running back and forth to the lavatory all afternoon.

As it did for most people living in central London, the thought of a journey all the way out to Ham Common took on the dimensions of a search for the source of the Nile. That people commuted daily from that kind of distance (it took about half an hour by car) was a constant source of amazement to him.

He caught the tube to Waterloo and a train to Richmond. From there he took a cab to the address W. T. Wintergreen had given him at the read-through. (What is all this with cabs, Charles Paris? he found himself wondering. Honestly, one three-month contract with W.E.T. and you start behaving like a bloody plutocrat.)

Because of the Nilotic proportions of his imagined expedition, he had left far too much time for the journey, and it was only a quarter to three when he approached his destination. Hastily, so that his early arrival would not be an embarrassment, he managed to stop the cab just before it turned off to Ham Common and spent three-quarters of an hour walking away from the Railtons' cottage toward Ham Gate of Richmond Park.

It was a pleasant April afternoon, and Charles Paris felt as if he were in the depths of the country. Amazing to think all this lay such a comparatively short distance from central London. He really ought to get out more. There were any number of lovely places he could get to without great effort. And being out in the open air must be better than just mooching around his bed-sitter or spending too long in the pub.

But even as he formed these pious intentions, he knew that he would never put them into practice. Like moving out of Hereford Road, organised expeditions into the countryside somehow weren't Charles Paris.

There was an ancient black Volkswagen Beetle parked outside the cottage on whose door Charles knocked at precisely three-thirty. W. T. Wintergreen admitted him with old-fashioned formality.

The cottage that Winifred and Louisa Railton shared was so small it felt like a doll's house, and entering it was like stepping back thirty years. The decor, the furniture, everything about the place had a fifties feel to it.

So did the spread laid out on the table in the tiny sitting room. Charles didn't realise that people still had 'tea' on that kind of scale. It was a meal that had never particularly appealed to him, but he couldn't help being impressed by the serried ranks of sandwiches, the plates of rock buns and almond slices on doilies, the – yes, they really were *fairy cakes* (goodness, when had he last seen a fairy cake?) – the sugar-dusted Victoria sponge, the ginger cake, the meringues, the Dundee cake. It had an air of excess about it, as if a television designer had been determined to show every aspect of his research into the period and piled on too much detail.

Yet the two Railton sisters seemed to find nothing unusual about the scene. It did not appear that they had pushed the boat out particularly in Charles's honour. The feeling was that they had a tea like this every afternoon of their lives.

And why not? Everything about the cottage bespoke an orderliness, a life of neat predictability, in which untidy emotions were controlled by an unshakeable daily timetable. In a television studio or in the St. John Chrysostom Mission for Vagrants Lesser Hall, the Railtons looked anachronistically out of place, whereas in their own environment they fitted in. But then, of course, it was a deeply old-fashioned environment.

Charles looked at the sisters while Winifred went through an elaborate tea-pouring ritual of jugs and strainers and sugar tongs and spoons and tried to estimate how old they were. Louisa was clearly the younger, perhaps by as much as seven years, though it was difficult to tell with women of their age.

Both had salt-and-pepper hair cut in straight lines across the napes of their necks and clipped back with slides on either sides of their heads. Their skins were freckled, but with sun spots rather than the blotches of age. They were thin, both above average height, with Winifred a couple of inches taller than her sister. Winifred wore glasses with almost transparent frames. Both had on flowered print dresses that buttoned all the way up the front and stout buckled sandals at the end of bare, thin freckled legs.

They could really have been any age between sixty and eighty. Charles tried to work it out. If the first W. T. Wintergreen books had come out before the Second World War, even given exceptional literary precocity, Winifred must have been at least twenty in 1935. Which would put her in her late seventies. With Louisa around the seventy mark. Yes, that'd be about right.

The thought of Winifred's books reminded him of the message he had to pass on.

'My wife is a great admirer of your detective stories, er...' Like Ben Docherty, he had difficulty in knowing how to address the writer. He settled on '...Miss Railton.'

She didn't offer any informality of the 'Please call me Winifred' variety but simply acknowledged the compliment. 'That's very nice to hear, Mr. Paris. I don't think any writer can tire of hearing that people enjoy his or her books. Not, I hasten to add, that it's something which I hear often enough to be in any danger of tiring of it.'

'Oh, I'm sure...' Charles shrugged ineffectually.

'I was not actually aware that you were married, Mr. Paris.'

'Well, I...'

'No, I'm sorry. Something someone said around the television company led me to suppose that you were not married.'

'I am...sort of...technically married.'

'Ah.'

'But we don't live together all of the time.'

Any of the time, actually, he thought with a sudden access of misery. He really must ring Frances. See if there was any chance of their getting back together. Yes, he'd make that his number-one priority. Ring her that evening.

'No, my wife was saying,' he moved on, 'that your books really got her through her adolescence.'

'How nice.'

'She said the first ones came out in the late thirties.'

'Yes. *The Spanish Rapier Murder* was published in 1937.' Winifred Railton flashed a modest smile. 'I did begin rather young.'

'And then you continued till – when, the late fifties, was it?'

'Yes, excepting the war years. Sixteen titles in all.'

'Very impressive. Why did you stop? Was it that styles were changing in crime fiction?'

'No, not really.' She cleared her throat. 'We had domestic problems. Our father was ill. I found I had my time cut out looking after him.'

'That's our father,' Louisa Railton said suddenly.

She pointed to a framed photograph on the mantelpiece. The clothes dated it as having been taken in the late twenties. A large fair-haired man sat at a garden table. Behind him, with an arm around his shoulder, stood a tall, bespectacled girl in a tennis dress. On his knee sat a smaller girl without glasses who looked up adoringly into her father's eyes. Both children were strikingly pretty, and there was no doubt that they were the originals of the two old women with whom Charles sat over that lavish tea in Ham Common.

The house in front of which the group had been photographed was a huge Edwardian pile. Clearly, though a cottage in Ham Common was a very desirable property, the Railton sisters had come down in the world since their childhood.

Louisa Railton was looking at him with such naked appeal in her eyes that Charles felt he had to make some comment on the photograph. 'A very fine looking man,' he said.

'Oh, yes,' Louisa agreed.

Winifred seemed unwilling to get side-tracked into a conversation about her late father. 'Mr. Paris, you may have wondered why we invited you here this afternoon.'

'The thought did cross my mind, yes.'

'The fact is, Mr. Paris, we are not at all happy with certain aspects of the way West End Television is making the *Stanislas Braid* series.'

'No. Well, I'm afraid television is a difficult medium. I mean, often it's hard for a writer of a book to see why certain changes have been made to a –'

Winifred Railton cut through his flannel. 'The fact is, Mr. Paris, that the W. T. Wintergreen books are very dear to us.'

'I'm sure they are.'

'We have lived through the creation of each and every word of those books.'

'I can understand how –'

'Have you ever done any creative writing, Mr. Paris?'

'Yes, I have. I've written a few plays. Never quite had the nerve or the energy to tackle a novel.'

'No, but you will know from writing your plays how deeply involved one gets with the characters one creates.'

'Certainly.'

'And how distressing it is to see one's characters incorrectly portrayed.'

'I'm sure it is, Miss Railton. I think, with television, what you have to do is just take the money and forget about it.'

'That seems an extremely spineless approach, Mr. Paris.'

'Maybe, but it's one that will save you a great deal of heartache. Television is a medium notorious for making changes. Goodness, you should get Will Parton on the subject of things that've been done to his scripts over the years. You wouldn't believe it.'

'I don't think Mr. Parton's experiences are really relevant, Mr. Paris. It is not as if he is a creator of characters; he is merely a journeyman, an interpreter of other people's original work.'

'I think you may be underestimating the skill that he brings to what he does.'

'Mr. Paris, he clearly doesn't care about it. He sees his work on the *Stanislas Braid* series as just another job of work.'

'Well, yes, but –'

'Do you know, before he started adapting them, he had not even read one of the W. T. Wintergreen books?'

Charles found it interesting to note how Winifred constantly used the pronoun 'we' when describing the writing of the books and yet could speak of 'the W. T. Wintergreen books' as if they were somehow detached from her.

She allowed a pause for him to appreciate the full enormity of Will Parton's ignorance, and Charles had a horrible fear that he was about to be asked how many of the books *he* had read.

But the danger passed. 'As I say, Mr. Paris, there are far too many things in the production which the West End Television people have got completely wrong.'

'Yes, I am sure there are a few *details* that –'

'We are not talking about details, Mr. Paris. We are talking about major points in the tone of voice and the characterisation in the books which have been wantonly altered.'

'Ah.' There seemed little point in making further attempts to describe how television worked; better just to sit out their objections and mutter occasional condolences. They had dragged him out all this way just to have a moan, and a moan they were going to have, whether he liked it or not.

'For a start,' Winifred Railton began her catalogue, 'they have got the character of Stanislas Braid completely wrong.'

Charles said nothing.

'He is meant to be an intellectual, and yet it is clear that that actor, Russell Whateveritis...'

'Bentley.'

'...Russell Bentley has probably never read a book in his life.'

'Miss Railton, the whole point about acting is that actors *take on* characters. Just as you don't have to be a murderer to play the part of a murderer, so you don't have to be an intellectual to play the part of an intellectual. You act. You become another personality. You think yourself into the way that personality would react and behave.'

'That Russell Bentley doesn't. He makes no effort to think himself into anything. He is exactly the same when he's playing the part as when he's not.'

This observation was so unanswerably true that Charles could think of no response to it.

'What's more,' Louisa Railton suddenly burst out, 'that actor's got dark brown hair, and anyone who's read even a couple of pages of any of the W. T. Wintergreen books knows that Stanislas Braid didn't have dark brown hair!'

There was a childlike petulance in the outburst, and when her sister calmed her, Charles realised that Winifred did treat Louisa almost like a child. She was protective, overprotective, as if she wanted to keep from her younger sister the truth of what the world was really like.

'While one regrets,' Winifred conceded, 'that the physical appearance of the characters is wrong, that worries me less than the fact that their *souls* are wrong.'

'Their souls?' Charles echoed weakly. He sneaked a look at his watch. Dear God, it was only twenty past four. He'd asked the cab to pick him up at five-thirty, reckoning that two hours was probably an appropriately genteel time to spend over tea. The thought of over an hour more of this catalogue of complaints was deeply depressing. While he could feel sympathy with the Railton sisters' objections, he knew that there was nothing he could do to help them. They had been involved with the characters of the W. T. Wintergreen books for over fifty years. They knew nothing of the workings of television. There was no level at which his explanations would make any sense to them.

'Yes, their *souls*,' Winifred confirmed. 'Russell Bentley is nowhere near the soul of Stanislas Braid. And that other young man is hopelessly wrong for Blodd. Blodd is not meant to be a cockney. It is stated quite clearly in all the books that Blodd was brought up in Cornwall.'

'Surely that's a relatively minor point?'

'It would be a relatively minor point if the soul of the character were right. But it isn't. No one reading the W. T. Wintergreen books could doubt that Blodd is a lugubrious character – positively melancholic at times. And yet this young man plays him as if he were running a side-show at a funfair.'

'Don't any of the characters seem right to you?' Charles pleaded.

'Well, now, the new girl who started yesterday, she seemed right for Christina.'

'Yes,' Louisa agreed softly. 'The colouring's right, apart from anything else.'

'Except, of course, they're destroying everything by not calling her Christina. They've got this dreadful idea about introducing someone called Elvira. I mean, the idea that Stanislas Braid could have two favourite daughters is just so ridiculous and incongruous.'

'And the idea that he would call one of them Elvira...'

'....almost defies belief,' W. T. Wintergreen concluded bitterly.

'Well, I think, Miss Railton, that I can set your mind at rest on that matter.' Thank goodness there was at least one detail on which he could bring the two poor old dears comfort. He related the conversation he had had with Maurice Skellern about his availability for an extra fortnight, and they were forced to concede that that was encouraging news.

'But,' he concluded, 'with regard to the other things W.E.T. is doing, I'm afraid I can't be of much help to you. I can't make them change their policies.'

'Oh, no, we know that,' said Winifred. 'You don't think that was why we invited you down here, do you?'

'Well, I hadn't really thought...I don't know...'

'We invited you down here,' she continued firmly, 'to give you some tips on how you should play the part of Sergeant Clump.'

'Oh, did you?' said Charles weakly.

'Yes. Now tell us – how do you see the character of Sergeant Clump?'

'Well,' he began cautiously, 'I'd seen him rather as a not very intelligent village policeman.'

'Yes, he *is* a not very intelligent village policeman...'

'Oh, good,' said Charles with considerable relief.

'...but there's so much more to him than that. Isn't there, Louisa?'

'Oh, yes, Winifred. So much more.'

'I mean, when you get into his *soul*...'

'Yes, when you get into his *soul*....'

And for the remaining hour of his stay the two Railton sisters proceeded to fill Charles Paris in on the hidden depths of the soul of Sergeant Clump.

It was the most exhausting hour of his life. He greeted the arrival of his cab as if it were a food lorry in a refugee camp.

When he finally got back to Hereford Road, Charles Paris drank two inches of Bell's whisky and fell fast asleep before he even had time to take his clothes off.

He completely forgot about his intention to ring Frances.

Chapter Ten

TWO PLAINCLOTHES policemen arrived at the St. John Chrysostom Mission for Vagrants to interrupt rehearsals on Wednesday morning. They were making some inquiries into the death of Sippy Stokes, 'just checking out,' as they put it, 'how exactly she met her end.' The word *murder* was not mentioned, but its shadow immediately loomed in the minds of everyone present.

The new Director was furious at this disruption in his schedule. 'I am the Director of this show,' he kept saying, 'and it's my job to see that it gets made.'

The policemen were impassively firm; they knew he had a job to do, but they also had a job to do. Could they please talk to the members of the cast and production crew who had been in the studio on the previous Wednesday morning? Grudgingly, the new Director gave way, and the relevant members of his team were trooped away to be questioned in the St. John Chrysostom Mission for Vagrants Great Hall.

The police said that they had no reason to believe that the death of Sippy Stokes had been anything other than accidental, but in cases like this they did feel an obligation to find out as much about the background as possible.

Charles wondered what new evidence they had uncovered. As he had many times before in his detective career, he envied the police their research facilities. There's nothing like an encounter with a professional criminal investigation to make an amateur sleuth profoundly aware of his amateur status. Why couldn't Charles Paris have been blessed with a convenient brother-in-law on the force, like Lord Peter Wimsey's Inspector Parker? Even Stanislas Braid was not above picking Sergeant Clump's so-called brains when he needed a little privileged information.

But Charles had no such handy informant. He could only guess the stage of investigation that the police had reached. Perhaps something had come up at the post-mortem. Maybe the doctor's bland conviction that all he had to do was find the relevant fallen object to fit the dent in Sippy Stokes's skull had proved inadequate. None of the objects had fitted? They were now looking for a murder weapon? An anonymous letter had been sent to the police announcing that Sippy had been murdered? Charles could only conjecture.

The policemen didn't give the impression that their inquiry was particularly urgent, though. They seemed to be going through the motions rather than conducting a life-or-death investigation. Their manner was that of men who had been given a directive from above to make certain inquiries; they were doing as they were told but didn't have much faith in the value of what they were doing. Whether that was actually the case, or whether their apparent diffidence masked an uncompromising determination to get at the truth, was another question at whose answer Charles could only guess.

They asked the assembled crowd of actors and production staff what they had been doing between eleven and twelve the previous Wednesday morning, and all the answers conformed with what Charles had witnessed in the canteen and Studio A during that period.

All the answers except one. Tony Rees, the quiet A.S.M. who seemed content to live in the shadow of the more flamboyant Mort Verdon, produced a different version of events from what Charles remembered.

'I went to the canteen for coffee as soon as the break was called,' the young man told the police. His voice was so rarely heard that it was quite a shock to hear how thick the Welsh accent was. 'I was going back to the studio when I remembered I had to pick up a props list from Design Department. So I went up there.'

'And what time did you get back into Studio A?'

'I don't remember exactly.'

'Well, was it before twelve o'clock or after?'

'Definitely after,' said Tony Rees.

The police did not question this answer, but Charles Paris knew it was a lie. He clearly remembered seeing the A.S.M. behind the set at about a quarter to twelve, only moments before his unpleasant discovery in the props room.

He also remembered that at the moment Tony Rees had looked extremely guilty.

Immediately on his return from the St. John Chrysostom Mission for Vagrants Great Hall to the St. John Chrysostom Mission for Vagrants Lesser Hall, Charles was swept up into rehearsal by the new Director. ('I'm Director of this show, and already far too much of my time has been wasted this morning.') When he next had a break, Charles noticed with dismay Tony Rees had left the rehearsal room.

The following day he wasn't there, either. According to Mort Verdon, the A.S.M. was laid up with the flu. So Charles couldn't pursue his most intriguing line of investigation.

In fact, the only constructive thing he did the rest of that week was to pluck up courage and ring Frances. She agreed to have dinner with him on Saturday night. She didn't sound over the moon about the idea, but at least she agreed.

'Dear, oh, dear, Charles Paris, are you becoming a theatrical smoothie?'

'Hardly, Frances.'

'Well, I mean, taking me out to dinner at Joe Allen's.' She looked around the dark wood-panelled basement, with its long noisy bar, its red checked tablecloths, its blackboard menus, its swooping waiters in long white aprons.

'Oh, come on. We're only here because the food's good. And it's cheap.'

'Nothing to do with the fact that it's a favoured haunt of stars of stage and TV?'

'No, of course not. I'm not like that.'

'No?'

'No. Anyway, they didn't give us a table by the wall where they put the stars.'

'They didn't, did they, the rotters? Perhaps you have a little way to go before you're really a big telly name.'

'Shut up, Frances.'

'But it's true, Charles. You are different. Subtly different. Being in lucrative employment has wrought a mysterious change in you.'

'No, it hasn't.'

'You wouldn't have taken me to Joe Allen's a year or so ago. You'd have made some disparaging remark about theatrical trendies if the place had even been mentioned. Now you think it's just possible that you might be becoming a theatrical trendy.'

'No, I don't.' But the idea she had planted did, for the first time in his life, have a little sneaking appeal. Why, after all, shouldn't he be successful? He'd waited long enough, in all conscience. He'd served his time. Why shouldn't Charles Paris become famous in his declining years?

And if he could be a success in his professional life, why couldn't he get his private life sorted out, too? Time for decisive action.

'Frances...' he began.

'Yes?'

'I wanted just to talk for a moment about us.'

'Us? That sounds ominous.'

'Where we stand.'

'We're sitting down,' she said, evasively flippant.

'No, I meant –'

'I know what you meant, Charles. All right.' She laid her hands, almost as if she were laying her cards, on the red-and-white-checked tablecloth in front of her. 'Where do we *stand*? Well, my *stance* is that of a headmistress of a girls' school, living in a flat in Highgate. Your *stance* is that of an intermittently employed actor living in a bed-sitter I'd rather not think about in Bayswater. My job is extremely time-consuming and uses up most of my energy. Your job is intermittently time-consuming, and I don't think I really want to know how you use up the rest of your energy. We are neither of us in the first flush of youth.' She lifted her hands up in a 'That's about it' gesture. 'Yes, Charles, I'd say that's where we stand.'

'You have forgotten to mention one thing, Frances.'

'Really? What's that?'

'That we're married to each other.'

'Oh, Charles, I wouldn't put it as strongly as that.'

'How strongly would you put it, then?'

'Well, I think I'd go as far as to say that we're not divorced.'

'Oh, thank you.'

She wasn't making it easy for him. On the other hand, why should she? There was too much history between them. Too many promising starts at repairing their relationship had come unstuck for her to be anything other than wary in her dealings with her husband.

'Am I to gather that this is another attempt at a *rapprochement*, Charles?'

'Yes. Yes, Frances, it is.'

'I see. And how far are you proposing to *rapproche* this time?'

'As far as possible.'

'All the way? I say. Dramatic stuff. Do you mean you want to *rapproche* your way back into my bed?'

'No. Well, yes, I do. But not just that.'

'What, you mean *rapproche* your way back into living together? Even *rapproche* your way back into' – her voice dropped to an awe-struck whisper – 'being *married* to each other?'

He nodded. 'That's what I mean.' She looked bewildered. 'What do you say?'

'What do I say?' She mused for a moment, as if considering a plethora of possibilities. 'Well, I think the first thing I'd say is Why?'

'Why?'

'Yes, why should we go back to being married? It didn't work first time.'

'No, I agree. But if we tried harder –'

'I tried extremely hard the first time, Charles,' she said with some asperity.

'All right. If I tried harder.'

'I have seen a few of your attempts at trying harder. Not always very impressive. No, I don't think that's a very good argument as to *why* we should get back together.'

'But, Frances, I'm not getting any younger.'

'And that is an even worse argument. You are offering me the unique opportunity of sharing your arthritis and incontinence, are you?'

'No, I'm just saying that, I don't know, we do have a lot of things in common.'

'Name one.'

'Well...' The pause was longer than it should have been. 'Juliet.'

'Yes, we have a daughter in common, but she is now grown up, with a family of her own. We no longer need to "stay together for the sake of the children", particularly since we didn't stay together at the time when that argument might have been relevant.'

No, she certainly wasn't making it easy. He tried another, more sentimental tack. 'Even after all this time, Frances, and after everything that's happened, still, even now, in a strange way, we were made for each other.'

'I blame the manufacturer,' said Frances.

'But it's true. We do still love each other.'

She was silent. She looked away from him. When she looked back, her eyes were glazed with unshed tears. 'Yes,' she sighed, 'it's true. But it's not relevant.'

'Of course it's relevant. If two people love each other –'

'Then what? It doesn't mean they can live together. Good God, Charles, we're living proof that it doesn't mean that.'

'Love is important.'

'I don't deny it. But a lot of other things are important, too. And though I don't question the quality of your love, I have less faith in your ability to deal with the other things in life.'

'Well...'

'Come on, you have absolutely no interest in domesticity. And by domesticity I don't mean housework or anything like that. I just mean living in a house with someone else.'

'No, but...'

'You can't deny it, can you, Charles?'

'No.' He sighed and gazed into the middle distance. 'There are some things I'm interested in, though. Even good at. I often think if life were all making love and getting drunk, I could cope with it better.'

'Yes, I think most of us could. But I'm afraid it isn't. And even if it were, some people could be forgiven for wishing that the love-making was always directed towards the same person.'

The bitterness of her final words reminded him of how much he had hurt her in the past. At that moment he felt infinite regret for his behaviour toward her. At that moment he vowed he would never again make love to any woman other than Frances. At that moment he vowed that if Frances wouldn't have him, he would never make love to anyone ever again. At that moment...

'Well, Frances, it sounds as if you don't really want to *rapproche* that far.'

'No.'

'So won't we see each other again?'

She let out a huge exasperated sigh of frustration. 'Yes, of course we'll bloody see each other again, Charles Paris! God, I know you're an actor, but why do you have to make everything so dramatic all the time? Like it or not – and most of the time I don't think I do like it – we are involved with each other. I can't just shake you off and pretend you don't exist – much as I would often like to. No, you're part of me. I've *got* Charles Paris in the same way that some people have *got* colour blindness...or hay fever...or eczema."

Charles grinned. 'Do you know, Frances, I think that was a compliment.'

She grinned, too. Unwillingly. 'Nearest you're going to bloody get to one,' she said, and leaned across the table to ruffle his hair.

They had a second bottle of wine and finished the meal in high good spirits. Charles put his arm around his wife as they left the restaurant.

They were just at the door when he caught sight of two familiar figures at a table in the far corner. A man and a woman, heads bowed together, deep in intimate conversation.

The man was Ben Docherty, Producer of *Stanislas Braid*. But it was the woman he was with who interested Charles.

She was the Blue Nun. Gwen Rhymer. Mother of Joanne Rhymer.

So maybe Ben Docherty had had a vested interest in the recasting of the part of Christina Braid?

Chapter Eleven

THE FILMING for the second episode of *Stanislas Braid* was standard W.E.T. filming; in other words, no location was more than half a mile away from W.E.T. House. But the production team did not have the freedom of selection that some other series enjoyed. *Stanislas Braid* was set in the thirties – or at least in that cloud-cuckoo Golden-Age-of-Detective-Fiction Country-House-Murder time that approximates the thirties – and so the usual moody shots of urban decay at the tail-end of the twentieth century could not be indulged.

As a result, the location managers had their work cut out finding suitable venues for the Great Detective's investigations. It wasn't that there weren't plenty of buildings of the right period – London is full of them – but tracking down buildings unmarred by television aerials, entryphones, or an adjacent McDonald's was not so easy. Double yellow lines had to be painted out, parking meters disguised as lampposts, and glass-sided telephone boxes dressed up as red ones. There were many interruptions to the schedule as traffic of far too contemporary a design was diverted and the five expensively hired vintage vehicles were repositioned to give an illusion of metropolitan bustle.

(The authentic 1930s bus had cost so much to hire that Ben Docherty insisted it should earn its keep by appearing in almost every shot. Its destination board was constantly changed to give the impression that the whole bus network of London was on the screen.)

Anachronistic passers-by also had to be kept out of shot, and as filming always attracts crowds – particularly when the setting is historical – this was a major problem. The limited number of background artistes that Ben Docherty's budget allowed stood around in their thirties garb as city gents, ladies of leisure, policemen, barrow boys, nurses, newspaper boys, and flower sellers (it is an unalterable rule of British television that any London daytime exterior set before the war shall include at least one newspaper boy and one flower seller), but there was always the threat of the irruption of a track-suited jogger, a leather-clad motorbike messenger, or a wandering Rastafarian with a ghetto blaster. The location managers were kept busy fielding such invasions.

The result of all these restrictions was that the shooting tended to be very intimate – a lot of close-ups against authentically ancient backgrounds. Opening the shots out always ran the risk of including glimpses of an Indian takeaway, a distant billboard advertising computers, or an errant punk listening to a Walkman.

These difficulties added to the problems of a schedule that was already tight. *Stanislas Braid* was being made on a fortnightly turnaround – a week's rehearsal, two days' filming, three days in the studio, to produce fifty-two minutes of television – so there wasn't much room for finesse in the production. The new Director, who, needless to say, saw himself as the latest messiah of the British film industry, was constantly frustrated in his attempts to 'make every frame a Rembrandt' by Ben Docherty's urgings that they were slipping behind schedule. The Producer was terrified of losing time so early in the production. Most of the later episodes involved filming outside London, and what with the amount of travelling and local difficulties likely to be encountered, the threat of slippage would be much greater then.

Charles Paris did not have a great deal to do in that week's filming. Sergeant Clump was rarely off his home patch of Little Breckington, so his involvement in the London scenes was limited. This gave Charles plenty of opportunity to observe the other people around the set and, particularly, to think about the death of Sippy Stokes.

Most of the potential suspects were there. Jimmy Sheet, to whose shaky marriage an indiscreet Sippy Stokes might have posed a threat, acted his scenes efficiently and spent a lot of time signing autographs for the crowds that gathered.

Russell Bentley, when not showing resentment that more people asked for Jimmy Sheet's autograph than for his own, spent most of his time paraphrasing his lines, much to the fury of Will Parton. It also infuriated W. T. Wintergreen and Louisa Railton, who insisted on watching everything that went on.

Filming offered great opportunities for paraphrase to an actor like Russell Bentley. Since the scenes were mostly done in very short takes, the lines were not really learned, simply mugged up seconds before each take. And if the lighting, the sound, the background action, and the framing of the shot had worked, the Director was unlikely to worry about how approximate the lines might have been. So Russell Bentley had wonderful opportunities to say fewer and fewer lines as Stanislas Braid might have said them and more and more as Russell Bentley would say them. None of these opportunities did he waste.

The star seemed to have developed a very good working relationship with his new daughter. Joanne Rhymer, as well as being attractive, really was a very good little actress, and though Russell Bentley kept complaining that the relationship was a bit too good to be true, they played their scenes together well. So her appearance on the set was good news for him.

Presumably, it was also good news for Ben Docherty, since it advanced his campaign with the girl's mother.

But surely neither of them would have resorted to murder to make that good news happen? Would they?

What about the Railtons? What about Will Parton, come to that? They were all better off without Sippy Stokes. But, again, murder seemed an extreme way of defending the integrity of one's writing.

No, there was only one person who Charles thought could help his investigations in any meaningful way. Tony Rees. And the Assistant Stage Manager was still off work with the flu.

The first studio day of that episode, Wednesday, began with another row between the new Director and W. T. Wintergreen. It was about a set that had made its first appearance that day. Christina Braid's bedroom.

'I'm sorry,' the crime writer said. 'It just shouldn't be like that. It's too bright. The blue is too bright.'

'It shouldn't be blue, anyway,' her sister contributed. 'In the books it's made quite clear that Christina's room is done in the subtlest of pastel shades. Almost white wallpaper, with a tiny motif of a pale yellow flower. And bedclothes of the palest pink.'

'I'm sorry,' said the new Director, 'but this is how the designer sees it.'

'Well, then, I'm afraid he sees it wrong,' W. T. Wintergreen objected calmly. 'Has the designer actually read any of the books?'

'I don't know. I expect he read one or two before the series started.'

Oh, yes? thought Charles. I bet he didn't.

W. T. Wintergreen was implacable. 'It's wrong. It'll have to be changed.'

'It will not be changed,' said the new Director. 'It has just been built, and we have a very busy schedule for the next three days. There is no way it could be changed even if anyone wanted it changed.'

'I want it changed,' said W. T. Wintergreen.

'So do I,' Louisa Railton agreed.

'Well, you can both forget it. Look, I am the Director of this show, and it's my job to see that the show gets made. And if you keep wasting my time, it won't be.'

'I am not wasting your time. I am merely trying to get things right.'

'Listen, if you two continue to disrupt my production, I will have you banned from the studio.'

'You can't do that. I am W. T. Wintergreen. I wrote the books.'

'And I am the Director, and I am making a television programme! Or trying to!'

The argument was clearly going to run for some little while yet. Charles Paris drifted over to the set of Stanislas Braid's study. There was no one about. He moved toward the mantelpiece and picked up the candlestick that had been missing at the time of Sippy Stokes's death.

He lifted it up and turned it over. He didn't quite know what he was expecting – dried blood, a lingering dark hair? – but whatever it was, he was disappointed. Just the discoloured base of a brass candlestick with the name of the hire firm painted on it in blue.

He put it back. Then he remembered that the set had been completely dismantled and rebuilt during the last fortnight. It was quite possible that the candlesticks had been put back the other way around.

With a burst of excitement, he picked up the second candlestick and upturned it.

Nothing except the name of the hire company. Or at least nothing the naked eye could discern. Maybe a police forensic examination could find some minuscule traces for incrimination. Once again he wondered what the police were up to. Had they written off the death as an accident? Or was their investigation still proceeding?

'What are you doing?'

Charles turned at the voice to face Mort Verdon. The stage manager was looking at him suspiciously.

'Just interested in where these things were hired from.'

'Uh-huh.' Mort didn't sound convinced. 'Sorry, we have to be careful. You'd be amazed how much stuff disappears off television studio sets.'

'Really?'

'Oh, yes, boofle. Lots of light-fingered people about, you know. Whenever it's something historical, when you've got a few antiques littered round the place, you'd be surprised how little of it finds its way back to the hire companies. There's a great deal of, what shall we say, natural wastage?'

'Oh, well, Mort, I can assure you that I wouldn't dream of –'

'No, never really thought you would, boofle. Just…as I say, we have to keep an eye on things.'

'Of course.'

'Series like this is an absolute field day for those of kleptomaniac tendencies. All this stuff…'

'Yes. Has a lot gone missing already?'

'Oh, yes. Those candlesticks, for a start.'

'What do you mean?'

'Those aren't the ones we had on the first episode.'

'Really?'

'No. The first pair…disappeared at the end of the week.'

'Where do you think they went?'

The Stage Manager shrugged. 'Some member of the production team sneaked them out under his anorak, I suppose. Expect they're on a stall in Church Street Market by now. We had to hire some more.'

'Oh.'

'Never mind. W.E.T. can afford it.'

'Ben Docherty keeps saying the budget's very tight on this show.'

'The budget may be tight, but W.E.T. can still afford it.' Mort Verdon's wry smile suggested that, like Russell Bentley, he hadn't much time for commercial television companies pleading poverty.

'Hmm. Well, look, Mort, I'm sorry you suspected that I –'

'No, I didn't, really. Not when I saw it was you. Anyway, actors very rarely walk off with things from the set.'

'Oh, good. I'm glad that my profession has a reputation for honesty.'

'No, actors usually walk off with their costumes.'

'Ah.'

'Be surprised at the end of a series how many leather jackets and tailor-made suits somehow don't find their way back to Wardrobe.'

'Well, Mort, I really don't think you have to worry about that happening with me on *Stanislas Braid*, do you?'

The stage manager looked appraisingly at Sergeant Clump's ancient blue serge and grinned. 'No, Charles, I think we'll be all right there.' A thought struck him. 'Unless of course you're one of those fetishists who gets his kicks in bed from dressing up as a policeman.'

'Oh, no!' Charles's face took on a horrified expression. 'Mort, how on earth did you find out?'

The break for lunch was announced, and Charles was about to make another bid for a Personal Best to the bar when he noticed Tony Rees.

The Assistant Stage Manager might well have been around the studio all morning, but Charles hadn't seen him. He looked pale and wretched, so the flu that had laid him low for a week appeared to have been genuine. But what interested Charles more was that Tony Rees also looked furtive. He was hanging around the fringes of the set as if waiting for all the rest of the production team to leave.

Charles decided that he, too, would linger. He wanted to talk to the A.S.M., but first he wanted to see what the young man was up to. Charles called a loud 'See you later' to no one in particular and then made for the props-room exit. He opened the double doors and let them close with a soft thump, like an intake of breath. He remained inside the studio and moved to a vantage point behind the window of Christina Braid's bedroom. Gauzy print curtains ('far too strident' in W. T. Wintergreen's estimation) hid him from the rest of the studio but did not impede his view of Tony Rees.

The A.S.M. stood immobile for a long couple of minutes, testing the silence of the studio. It was complete; after the bustle of the morning, the stillness was absolute.

Satisfied that he was alone, he moved briskly into action and started straight toward the bedroom set. Charles pushed himself back into the angle between two flats but realised with horror that Tony Rees was coming around the edge of the set toward him. The actor dropped to an uncomfortable crouch behind a loudspeaker.

Tony Rees was too preoccupied to be vigilant. Having made the decision that he was alone, he had no suspicions of surveillance. He walked quickly past Charles, who was close enough to have touched his trouser leg, and continued around the back of the set.

But only ten or fifteen yards farther on he stopped. There was a sound of something being moved, fabric at first, then maybe metal. Charles wished he could see what was going on. He craned around as far as he dared from his uncomfortable crouch but still couldn't see enough. He leaned forward on all fours.

This was a foolish position for someone dressed as Sergeant Clump to take up. One of the features of the sergeant in the W. T. Wintergreen books – and one of the few that had been carried over into the television series – was that he always had in his breast pocket a row of pencils with which to scribble laboriously in a notebook his criminal theories (all of them doomed to be proved wrong by the quicksilver intellect of Stanislas Braid).

Now it is a simple fact of gravity that pencils do not stay in the breast pocket of someone leaning forward on all fours, and sure enough, a cascade of them fell to the floor in front of Charles.

The sounds around the back of the set ceased instantly. Charles, scrabbling to pick up his pencils, saw Tony Rees's feet appear in front of him. Using the innocent expression that had got him such a big laugh in *See How They Run* in Chester ('about as funny as being woken up in the middle of the night by a motorbike' – *Liverpool Daily Post*), he said, 'I seem to have dropped my pencils.'

'Oh?' said Tony Rees, and he stood unmoving in front of the prostrate policeman.

Charles gathered together the last of the pencils and stood up. 'That's all of them,' he said fatuously.

'Yes,' said Tony Rees, still immobile.

'Well, I was just about to leave the studio,' Charles babbled on.

'So was I,' said Tony Rees.

They walked out silently, side by side. Whatever it was the A.S.M. had been doing around the back of the set, he had no intention of continuing it now that he knew he had been observed. Equally, he did not intend to leave Charles alone in the studio to check on his activities.

'I wondered if we could talk?' said Charles diffidently as they walked up toward the bar.

'I'm busy this lunch hour,' said Tony Rees, sullenly Welsh.

'Well, maybe some other time?'

'Maybe.'

Whatever the nature of Tony Rees's 'busyness,' it seemed to take second place to keeping an eye on Charles. As he commiserated with Will Parton in the bar over the latest sequence of rewrites Ben Docherty and Dilly Muirfield had demanded, Charles was aware of the A.S.M. sitting alone at a table in the corner, making one Perrier last a long time. And when Charles and Will decided to nip down to canteen for a W.E.T. subsidised steak, Tony Rees coincidentally also decided that it was time he had something to eat.

Whatever the secret he kept behind the set was, the A.S.M. didn't want Charles to sneak into the studio and investigate it.

Charles Paris was kept busy at the beginning of the afternoon with another

Little Breckington Police Station scene. Though this involved three policemen from other forces, Charles did not recognise any of the background artistes involved. He felt a momentary pang for the dashed hopes of the two who had seen *Stanislas Braid* as a prospect of long-term employment.

The scene involved, as usual, Sergeant Clump putting forward his thesis about the solution of the current crime, which this week was 'The Italian Stiletto Murder,' and Stanislas Braid, with a few deft thrusts of logic, cutting it to shreds. All of these scenes were so similar that Charles envisaged problems with lines before the end of the series; even after two recordings, he was worried about which speeches fitted in which episode.

And Russell Bentley, whose skill with paraphrase during the filming seemed to have gone to his head, now regarded every line as merely an idea around which he could embroider. This led to conflicts with the new Director, who insisted, 'I'm the Director of this show, and I have to hear the lines as printed if I'm going to know when to cut my shots.' It also made life difficult for Charles, since he never knew when his cue had come. The only indication he received was a quizzical silence coupled with a mildly reproachful look from Russell Bentley.

But these were mere ripples compared to Studio A's major storm of the afternoon, which occurred in a scene involving Stanislas Braid, his daughter, Christina, and Sergeant Clump. The action was simple enough. Because of the danger of the mission he was about to undertake, Stanislas entrusted his precious daughter to the care of the trustworthy British bobby. Rehearsal for the scene the week before had been slightly sticky, because Russell Bentley kept objecting to the extravagant terms in which Stanislas Braid referred to his daughter.

'I mean, it is over the top, love,' he said at one point to the new director, whose name he never attempted to master. 'You know, okay, they love each other as father and daughter should, but lines like "I want this, my most precious jewel, kept in the strongest casket in Christendom" sound a bit much to me. I mean, can't he just say, "She means a lot to me. I want you to guard her with your life, Clump"? Something along those lines'd be better, wouldn't you agree, er, old man?' He appealed to Charles, of whose name he remained equally ignorant.

The discussions had rumbled on through rehearsal without any final decisions being made about changing the lines. Charles thought Russell Bentley had a good point, for once. The Stanislas/Christina relationship was potentially cloying, and though the casting of Joanne Rhymer made the lines possible, they did still seem excessive. Will Parton also thought the relationship was a bit much, but he was pleased with the way he had adapted it from the books and reckoned he had 'taken the curse off it' sufficiently.

So he didn't want changes to his carefully wrought dialogue. And, needless to say, W. T. Wintergreen and Louisa wanted the relationship more sugary rather than less. As usual, they couldn't understand why a single word had been changed from the original book.

The new Director didn't seem too concerned about the issue. Like all directors, he regarded words as just things that got in the way of his pictures. But because it was easier for him to work from a fixed text than one that kept changing, he recommended leaving the lines as they were.

When they rehearsed the scene that afternoon in the studio, Russell Bentley spoke his speeches more or less as written. 'Sergeant Clump, I am handing into your care a jewel of inestimable price. She is the star who from her birth has shone over my life.'

'Nice bit of twinkling,' Charles murmured to Joanne Rhymer when they broke after this line.

She grinned at him, a rather intimate grin. She looked very like her notorious mother when she did that. Charles felt a little illicit flicker of interest.

When they came to shoot the scene, however, Russell Bentley, as he so often did, produced completely different lines. 'Sergeant Clump,' he said, 'my daughter's a good kid. You look after her properly, or I'll have your guts for garters.'

Remarkably, at the end of the short recording, the floor manager said, 'That was fine. Okay, just wait for a "clear" on it and we'll move on.'

So the change of lines couldn't have affected the new director's camera angles. Probably so busy watching the pictures that he hadn't even heard what was said.

But before the floor manager had time to move them on to the next scene, the studio was suddenly invaded.

'Stop! Stop!' shouted an elderly but authoritative voice.

It was W. T. Wintergreen, sailing magnificently in with Louisa in tow, determined to save her dialogue.

'We've got to go on,' said the floor manager gently.

'No! We will not go on until that last scene has been done right!'

The floor manager was silent for a moment, receiving instructions in his earpiece. No doubt having filtered out the obscenities, he announced diplomatically, 'The Director says he's the Director of the show and we've got to get on with the next scene.'

'I am the writer of the W. T. Wintergreen books, and I say we don't go on until we get it right. I will not have actors massacring my characters.'

'Hardly massacring the characters, old girl,' protested Russell Bentley, as oblivious of W. T. Wintergreen's name as he was of anyone else's, 'just making the characters a bit more realistic.'

'I wrote them realistically.'

'Yes, they are completely real!' Louisa chipped in.

'Well, I'm afraid the kind of reality people expect nowadays is a bit different. Listen, I have a reputation in television. If the public see that a show's got Russell Bentley in it, then they –'

The star's thousandth reiteration of this routine was surprisingly interrupted. By Ben Docherty. And, even more remarkably, by Ben Docherty being decisive.

He burst into the studio like a whirlwind. No doubt he was well fuelled by his lunch, but whatever its cause, his performance was impressive.

'Right,' he roared. 'That's enough!'

The entire studio was silent.

'We've wasted quite enough time on this sort of discussion! We're slipping behind schedule, and we can't risk doing that. Miss Wintergreen, the directors and I have been very patient. We have listened to your suggestions and followed many of them. But now I'm afraid you are just becoming disruptive. I must ask you and your sister to leave the studio and to keep away from W.E.T. premises until the production of *Stanislas Braid* is finished!'

'What?'

'You heard what I said.'

'But I wrote the books. I created Stanislas Braid.'

'That is neither here nor there. You must leave!'

W. T. Wintergreen stood her ground, preparing to defend herself. But then Louisa Railton began to cry, weakly, feebly, like a child. Winifred put her arm around her sister's shoulder and said quietly, 'Very well.'

'Tony.' Ben Docherty summoned the Assistant Stage Manager. 'Will you please escort Miss Wintergreen and her sister out of the building.'

Tony did as he was told. The three of them, a small funeral cortege, trooped out of Studio A in total silence.

Charles realised it was his chance. He was not needed in the next scene. He moved surreptitiously to the edge of the set, then slipped behind, just as he had seen Tony Rees do earlier in the day.

There was no one in sight, no one to interfere with this search. He gauged how far along Tony had gone and dropped to his knees.

At the bottom of the flats there was a roll of excess canvas. Charles probed along its length, feeling for some unexpected shape.

He found it. Through the canvas it felt thin, hard, and metallic.

He unwound it from its hiding place.

It was an Italian stiletto. The point felt wickedly sharp.

He thought back a fortnight. Once again he saw Tony Rees rising guiltily from something he had hidden at this very spot.

While they were recording 'The Brass Candlestick Murder,' Sippy Stokes had been killed with a candlestick.

Now they were recording 'The Italian Stiletto Murder.' Who was *its* victim intended to be?

Chapter Twelve

'IS THERE another murder on your mind, Charles?'

'Well, there might be, Frances. Why do you ask?'

'You sound preoccupied. You sound like you do when you're investigating a murder. Is it that actress whose death was in the papers a week or so back?'

'Mm.'

'And do you reckon you know who killed her?'

'Yes.'

'Then go to the police.'

'I haven't got any evidence. In my experience, when I go to the police with no evidence, they laugh at me.'

'Yes. Well, one can see their point. Anyway, be careful, Charles.'

'The fact that you say that must mean you care, Frances.'

'Stop fishing for compliments. Of course I care.'

'Good.'

'But don't assume that I'm particularly happy about the situation.'

'No.' A little, prickly silence on the telephone line. 'I did mean what I said, Frances. I really would like us to get back together again on a permanent basis.'

'Huh. No other women?'

'No other women.'

'Suggest it again when you've gone a whole year without making love to any other women and maybe I'll listen more seriously.'

'A year from today?'

'Yes. You know you'll never manage it, Charles.'

'Of course I will. Easy-peasy.'

'We'll see. Is it tomorrow you're off to Dorset?'

'Late afternoon, yes.'

'And is your murder suspect going with you?'

'Yes.'

'Well, don't do anything stupid.'

'You see, you *do* care.'

'Don't push your luck, Charles Paris,' Frances growled.

Why was it, he reflected, that coach journeys took adults straight back to infantile behavior? As soon as the *Stanislas Braid* team entered the coaches chartered by W.E.T. to take them to Swanage, the silliness began, and it continued all the way to Dorset. Songs, party games, impressions of members of the production team, paper darts, all helped along by the bottle of wine someone had thoughtfully provided. They were weak with laughter by the time they arrived.

He certainly had no chance to talk to Tony Rees. Just as he had had no chance to talk to Tony Rees for the last week. The A.S.M. avoided him deliberately. For the journey to Dorset, he waited to see which coach Charles got into and deliberately got into the other.

Still... 'The Italian Stiletto Murder' had been safely recorded, and no real-life murder had marred the proceedings. Charles was beginning to doubt the strength of the chain of logic that had seemed so strong when he had found the hidden weapon. At times he even questioned his conviction that Sippy Stokes had been murdered. Time blurred things. The more days went by and the less new evidence came to light, the lazier his interest grew.

And even if she had been murdered, did it actually matter that much? Everyone was happier for her death. Even Rick Landor, back in charge as Director of this episode, seemed restored to his normal good humor.

Charles did not believe in absolutes of right and wrong, the necessity that for every crime there must be a matching retribution. As he travelled down in the coach to Swanage, diverted by the silliness around him, and particularly by the chatter of Joanne Rhymer, he could entertain the possibility of Sippy Stokes's death slipping quietly out of his mind. Never to return.

The W.E.T. contingent arrived in Swanage about five and checked into their various accommodations. Charles was delighted to find that his new-found status as a regular character in a television series entitled him to a room in an AA three-star hotel, along with Russell Bentley, Jimmy Sheet, Will Parton, Joanne Rhymer, and Rick Landor. Other members of the cast were scattered in various two-star hotels. The W.E.T. staff members, following many years' experience in the management of expenses, had mostly opted for hotels cheap enough to ensure that they made a profit on their overnight allowances.

Charles checked into his room, which commanded what would presumably be a good view of Swanage Bay when the weather wasn't so dull. The sky had gotten darker and damper the farther west the coach went, and by the time they arrived in Swanage, everything was shrouded in a thick sea mist. The limited visibility did not augur well for the next two days' filming.

Still, that was Rick Landor and Ben Docherty's problem, not his. At times, the passivity of being an actor almost drove Charles Paris to distraction, but there were also times, like this one, of gleeful irresponsibility in his chosen profession. And, as ever, being in a strange hotel room gave him a lift. It seemed to recharge his identity, give him a feeling of starting afresh, the sensation that nobody had any expectations of him and he could behave in any way he chose.

The way he chose initially was not very different from the way he might have chosen at any other point in his life. He decided to take advantage of his 'resident' status and go down to the hotel bar for an out-of-hours drink.

On the way he met Will Parton, in a towelling dressing gown. The writer was going down to the hotel swimming pool. So were most of the others, except for Jimmy Sheet, who was going to work out in the hotel gym. Did Charles fancy joining them?

Well, no, actually. He had swum in his time and quite enjoyed it, but the effort of all that changing and getting wet and getting dry and changing back again always seemed to Charles disproportionate to the amount of pleasure involved. And when the charms of diving into a swimming pool were set against those of diving into a large Bell's...well, there was no contest.

He had a couple of large Bell's and, having agreed with the barman in about half a dozen different formulae of words that it was very foggy, decided, since none of the rest of the *Stanislas Braid* team had reappeared, that he would go out for a walk before dinner.

He hadn't bothered to go up to his room for his coat and was surprised at how wet the mist was when he got outside. In fact, rain was driving with some persistence through the murk. By the time Charles had gone a couple of hundred yards down toward the front, he had decided that he must either curtail his walk or risk the final disintegration of his sodden sports jacket, so the sight of a pub was a welcome one. A quick drink, he reckoned, and the rain might have eased off a bit before he went back up the hill to the hotel for dinner.

Inside the pub, the light seemed as murky and steamy as it did outside. A few people stood around in raincoats and anoraks. It was only just after seven, so the pub was not yet very full.

But sitting facing him in an alcove at the far end of the room, Charles saw a figure he recognised: Tony Rees.

On the evidence of the last week, Charles fully expected the A.S.M. to walk straight out of the pub and was amazed to see Tony rising with a half of lager in his hand and coming to intercept him with an expression on his face that could almost be described as genial.

'Charles, good evening. Can I get you a drink?'

'Well, why don't I get you one, Tony?'

Charles made for the bar but was diverted by the A.S.M., who took him firmly by the arm and led him to a seat in the alcove adjacent to the one from which Tony had just risen. 'Now, what's it to be?'

'Large Bell's'd be good.'

'Fine. Large Bell's it shall be, Charles Paris,' said the A.S.M. loudly and bonhomously.

While Tony was at the bar, Charles puzzled over what could have brought on this sudden affability but had reached no conclusions by the time his drink arrived.

Tony Rees sat down opposite him, still with the same half of lager. 'Cheers.'

'Cheers.'

'You said you wanted to talk to me, Charles.'

'Yes. Yes, I did.' He was again taken aback by the ease with which he was being offered the interview, which had been evaded all week.

'Well, what was it about?'

'Candlesticks...for a start.'

'Oh,' said Tony Rees, and his face fell. 'How much do you know?'

'I know that a candlestick was moved off the set of Stanislas Braid's study on the Wednesday of the first episode, just before Sippy Stokes died.'

'I see.'

'And I know what happened to it subsequently.'

'Do you?'

'Yes. You also know what happened to it subsequently, don't you?'

'Well...'

'Yes, you do, Tony. You know exactly what happened.' The A.S.M. looked horror-struck. He reached forward for his drink, but his hand was shaking too much to hold it. The half-pint leaped from his hand onto the table, cannoning its contents out into Charles's lap.

'I'm so terribly sorry.' Tony Rees was instantly at his side with a handkerchief, making ineffectual efforts to mop up the mess.

'Don't worry, Tony. Hasn't made me much wetter than I was already.' Charles indicated two heavily anoraked figures who were just leaving the pub. 'Don't envy anyone who's going back out there at the moment. Come on, let me get you another drink.'

It was a pleasure to stand up. The lager-drenched trousers didn't cling to his legs quite so clammily in a vertical position. He bought another half and, since his own drink seemed mysteriously to have emptied itself, another large Bell's.

When he sat down again, he continued in a businesslike fashion. 'I haven't forgotten what we were talking about.'

'No.'

'Candlesticks...and stilettos.'

'Yes. You saw me going to get the stiletto that lunch break when I didn't realise there was anyone in the studio.'

Charles nodded.

'Well, what are you proposing to do about it, then?'

'I don't know, Tony. It depends really on how much you are prepared to tell me. Then maybe I suppose we go to the police.'

'The police! Over something like that? But everyone does it.'

If Tony Rees's speech had sounded flabbergasted, then Charles's reaction to it sounded even more so. 'Everyone does it!'

'Yes.'

'What are we talking about, Tony?'

'Nicking stuff from the studio.'

'Oh, are we?'

'It's like a perk of the job, Charles. And it's not as if W.E.T. can't afford it,' said Tony Rees, echoing Mort Verdon's words.

'So you nick stuff on a regular basis?'

'If you put it like that, yes. Not big stuff. And stuff I know I can get rid of without too much bother.'

'Stuff like candlesticks and stilettos?'

'Yes. Got a dealer down Church Street Market I know'll give a good price and not ask too many questions.'

'So you just pick things up off the set?'

'Well, carefully, like. I mean, if you do it too obviously, people're going to notice, aren't they? I tend to do it sort of gradual.' As he knew more confidential, the thickness of Tony Rees's Welsh accent increased.

'So you take something and hide it round the back of the set?'

'That's it. Then wait till it's quiet.'

'Lunch break or some time like that?'

'Uh-huh. And slip it out at my leisure.'

'I see.'

'Oh, now come on,' Tony Rees pleaded. 'We needn't be talking about going to the police over something like that. I mean, that stiletto – I only got twenty quid for it. Hardly talking about the crown jewels, are we?'

'And the candlesticks?'

'Got a bit more for them, certainly. But, you know, I reckon the company owes me a favour or two. I mean, all this rationalisation and what-have-you they're doing…cutting down the overtime and the amount of jobs there are.'

'So you reckon you've got to make it up somehow?'

'That's about the size of it, yes. Pick up what you can where you can.'

'Do anything for money, you mean?'

'Why not? Don't look so bloody pious, Charles. Listen, commercial television's taking the public for a bit of a ride. I don't reckon it does any harm for them to be taken for a bit of a ride themselves. In a small way.'

'You don't feel any guilt about stealing from them?'

'Course not. They don't notice it one way or the other.'

It all sounded very plausible. Charles thought he probably had found the full extent of Tony Rees's criminal activity. But there were still details he wanted to check. 'The candlesticks, Tony…'

'What about them?'

'When did you take them?'

'End of the last studio day that week. You know, the Thursday, because the Friday was cancelled, wasn't it? There was such chaos in the studio at the end of that day, nobody knowing whether the set was going to stay up or be taken down, you could have walked away with anything.'

'But that wasn't the first time you'd taken the candlesticks – or at least one of them – was it?'

The A.S.M. blushed.

'You took one on the Wednesday, didn't you?'

'Yes, but I put it back.'

'Why? What actually happened?'

'Well, tell you what…Just after we broke for coffee, we'd done a scene of Stanislas Braid in his study. You know, sitting there and thinking, like –'

'I remember.' It was the scene that had been frozen on the monitor when Charles had visited Rick Landor in the editing suite.

'Now, at the end of that scene, I was just clearing the set, and I noticed there's only one candlestick there.'

Just as Charles had noticed on the monitor.

'So I thought, what the hell, some other bugger's nicked one. They'll have to get another pair, anyway. I may as well have that one.'

'So you took it and hid it in your usual hiding place behind the set?'

'That's right.'

'Then why did you put it back?'

'Well, bugger me if ten minutes later I don't go back on to that study set and suddenly notice that the missing one's been returned. I reckon they're more likely to look for one than two, so I pop mine back. Felt bloody relieved I did, too, actually, since the whole studio was swarming with police half an hour later.'

'Yes.' Charles nodded slowly. 'And it was because you'd moved the candlesticks that you lied to the police about when you'd gone back into the studio…You know, later, when they questioned us at the rehearsal room?'

'Yes, well, don't want to draw attention to yourself, do you?'

'No.' Charles was silent. Then he asked, 'Tony, you didn't see anyone either taking the first candlestick or putting it back, did you?'

'No, I didn't see anyone.'

Someone had done it, though. Charles now had proof that someone other than Tony Rees had taken a candlestick during the break and replaced it shortly afterward.

He also felt fairly sure that while it was in his or her possession, someone had used the candlestick to kill Sippy Stokes.

Back at the hotel he was going to change his lager-stained trousers, but he met Will Parton and the others in the bar and, after a couple more large Bell's, went through with them to the restaurant. They were a large party and commandeered two tables, which they insisted the hotel staff put together. While they didn't actually behave badly, no one in the restaurant was left with any doubt that these were media people, who saw it as part of their mission to liven up Sunday night in Swanage – not, in the estimation of Will Parton, the most difficult thing in the world to do. 'I've seen more get-up-and-go in a mortuary,' he murmured at one point in the evening.

The group around the tables included Charles, Will, Rick Landor, Russell Bentley, Jimmy Sheet, Joanne Rhymer, and surprisingly, Ben Docherty. The

Producer had said at the end of the previous week that he intended to stay in London, but either the need to see how his budget was being spent or the realisation that he was missing a lot of W.E.T.-subsidised drinking made him change his mind, and he had driven down to Swanage on his own.

If it was the drinking that had drawn him, he was not destined to be disappointed. The 'school treat' atmosphere of the jaunt encouraged them all to order a great deal of wine, and as they relaxed, their conversation became increasingly indiscreet.

'Here's to *Stanislas Braid*,' said Will Parton, raising his glass, 'the show that stands a chance now it's got rid of most of the dead wood!'

'What dead wood do you mean?' asked Charles.

'Oh, take your pick. W. T. Wintergreen? The bizarre Louisa? Sippy Stokes? Mind you' – Will leaned close to him for a moment and whispered – 'there are a few other bits of pruning that wouldn't hurt.'

'Like who, for instance?'

The writer looked across at the show's star. 'Wouldn't do any harm to have Stanislas Braid played as Stanislas Braid rather than as Russell Bentley, would it?'

Charles grinned.

'How're the rest of the scripts going, Will?' asked Joanne Rhymer, who was sitting next to Charles (a state of affairs of which, incidentally, he heartily approved).

'All written months ago. But all no doubt to be rewritten right up to the moment of transmission.' He smiled sweetly at his Producer. 'Isn't that right, Ben?'

Ben Docherty beamed benignly. He was at the stage of his alcoholic cycle when the drink mellowed him. 'No, not a lot more. Nearly all done. Just those few tinkerings with the last episode.'

'It shall be done, *Mein Führer!*' Will Parton barked with a cod Nazi salute. 'I haff brought here ze book off ze famous Double-Vee Tee Vintergreen to achieve ze tinkerings zat vill be ze Final Solution of ze script.'

Ben Docherty smiled paternally at his writer's excesses.

'Which book is the last one based on?' asked Charles.

'*The Transvestite Hermaphrodite Murder*,' Will Parton replied, 'in which Stanislas Braid is dragged kicking and screaming into the twentieth century.'

'Ha. Ha. No, what is it really?'

'*The Medieval Crossbow Murder*.'

'Oh, well, I wonder which one of us will be killed by a crossbow bolt from the blue?' Charles mused aloud.

'Why do you say that?' asked Jimmy Sheet, suddenly alert.

Charles didn't actually know why he was embarking on this particular tack, but having started, he saw no reason not to continue.

'Well, think about it…We try to record *The Brass Candlestick Murder*, and we get stopped by an actual death.'

'Not by a murder,' said Jimmy Sheet firmly.

'We don't know that,' said Charles, cavalier in his lack of caution.

'And certainly not a murder committed with a brass candlestick.' Ben Docherty had now joined in the conversation.

'We don't know that either,' Charles asserted. He was vaguely aware that he was being reckless, but his inhibitions were down, and he thought he might achieve some useful results by making his suspicions public. 'I mean, suppose someone had decided they wanted to kill Sippy Stokes.'

'I don't think this is in the best of taste,' Rick Landor objected quietly.

No, it wasn't. Charles knew it wasn't. He was fully prepared to stop there, but Jimmy Sheet insisted, 'Go on, Charles. This is interesting.'

'Well, suppose someone decided to do away with the poor kid, took a brass candlestick off the set during the coffee break, lured her into the props room, hit her over the head with it, and then pushed the shelves of props on top of her.'

After their recent rowdiness, the tables had gone very quiet. Charles knew he was a bit drunk and being rather stupid, but he had got to a point where he couldn't go back. His investigation into Sippy Stokes's death wasn't progressing. It needed a kick to get it moving again, and maybe what he was doing was providing that kick.

'You've been reading too many of the works of W. T. Wintergreen,' said Ben Docherty flatly.

'Yeah, it's a load of cobblers, what you're saying,' Jimmy Sheet agreed. 'I mean, that could never have happened, anyway. And even if it had happened, it's the kind of thing you could never prove.'

'You could prove it if there had been an eyewitness.'

'But there wasn't no eyewitness,' Jimmy Sheet persisted. 'Which is just as well, because there wasn't anything for an eyewitness to see.

'How do you know?' asked Charles.

There was a new coldness in the former pop star's eyes as he enunciated, 'Because Sippy Stokes died by an accident. And if anyone had witnessed an accident, they'd have bloody well come forward and told the police.'

'They might not have done.' Charles knew he was becoming irritatingly tenacious to his idea but reckoned an irritation factor might be useful in drawing reactions out of the assembled group.

'Are you saying,' asked Ben Docherty, 'that you witnessed Sippy Stokes being murdered?'

'No, I'm not saying that. I'm just saying that if she was murdered, then someone – not me but someone else – could have witnessed her being murdered.'

'Any suggestions who?' asked Jimmy Sheet.

It was around then that Charles realised just how drunk he was. He also realised the insane risk that he was taking. If, as was possible, Sippy Stokes's murderer was sitting in that restaurant, then he was issuing a challenge. Almost, it could be said, issuing an invitation to the killer to see that Charles Paris was somehow prevented from making comparable suggestions again.

'No, none at all,' he replied, caving in and trying to cover up his indiscretion. 'No, I was only joking. Of course it was an accident, and of course no one saw it happen.'

The conversation moved on smoothly to the prospects for the next day's filming, given the atrocious weather conditions. Charles felt foolish. He also felt uncomfortable and, for the rest of the meal, conscious that Jimmy Sheet, Rick Landor, and Ben Docherty were all looking at him with more than usual interest.

So, partly to dispel his unnerving awareness of their scrutiny, he went on drinking. And continued when the W.E.T. party moved into the bar at the end of the meal.

The rest of the evening passed in something of a haze. Charles remembered being, to his way of thinking, rather scintillating in conversation with Joanne Rhymer in the bar. He remembered how achingly like her mother she looked at close range.

He couldn't quite remember the sequence of words that led to her telling him her room number and asking him to give her ten minutes. He could remember the excitement of anticipation and the unwise decision to have another drink to steel himself for the encounter ahead.

Then he remembered being awakened sometime later by Joanne and finding himself lying fully clothed on her bed. And he remembered all too well the dialogue that followed.

'I think you'd better be going back to your room, Charles.'

'Yes. Yes, of course. Um...did anything happen?'

'No. No, nothing happened, Granddad.'

And as the bed in his own room did aerobics beneath him, he remembered wondering whether Frances would consider that impotence made him technically innocent of the charge of making love to another woman.

And he remembered feeling fairly certain that she wouldn't see it that way.

And feeling that it wasn't a very good record, really. He'd promised Frances a year's abstinence from another woman. And – unless she'd excuse him on a doubtful technicality – he'd so far failed to achieve forty-eight hours.

Chapter Thirteen

CORFE CASTLE is very properly a favourite spot for tourists. Apart from the castle itself – or rather its remains – which dominate the area from its hilltop setting, the village itself has a charm that has changed little from the beginning of the century. This obviously made it an ideal location for filming in the *Stanislas Braid* series. The cottages, built of fudge-like local stone and topped with slates of similar colour, looked perfect with the Great Detective's vintage Lagonda drawn up in front of them. The sight of figures in thirties costumes pottering along the narrow streets struck no note of incongruity. True, double yellow lines had to be covered and shop fronts dressed up a bit, but the problems, compared to those presented by a London location, were minimal.

At last Rick Landor, as Director, had the opportunity to take a few long shots, confident that his perspective would not be marred by anachronisms.

Or at least he would have had the opportunity if the weather had not been so atrocious.

Though the visibility was slightly better than the evening before, rain still fell with a dispiriting evenness, and at times the cloud cover dropped low enough to obliterate the huge outline of the castle from the horizon. Cameramen and sound operators, wardrobe and makeup girls, cast and design staff, all clustered under bright umbrellas. The location caterers, whose van was stationed in a nearby car park, were kept busy producing bacon sandwiches to warm up sodden members of the production team. There were a lot of wet anoraks about.

And not just among the W.E.T. contingent. Even on a damp Monday morning in April a good few visitors had made the pilgrimage to Corfe Castle. Perhaps because the weather denied them the spectacular views they had hoped for or simply because they were mesmerised by anything to do with television, they seemed more than happy to regard the filming as a bonus tourist attraction. They clustered, unrecognisable and shapeless in anoraks of blue, yellow, and orange, behind the barrier that the location managers had erected, and followed the proceedings with great interest.

Charles Paris was not feeling at his best. He had been too preoccupied the previous evening to order a room-service continental breakfast and that morning had resisted the lavish spread offered in the hotel dining room. Anyway, all he really wanted was coffee, which he got from the caterers' van as soon as the brain-jolting coach trip from Swanage to Corfe Castle was over. He also, optimistically, asked for a bacon sandwich, but its salty smell and the greasy tentacles of fat creeping out of the bread made him shove it hastily into a litter bin before he threw up.

He felt wretched and awful, and his wretchedness and awfulness were compounded by the fact that he knew he had no one to blame but himself for feeling wretched and awful. Joanne Rhymer was on the set, but he kept clear of her, unwilling to confront that mock-innocent, sardonic smile.

What he really felt like was a hair of the dog. But he knew that was the way of disaster. He shouldn't. Better to punish himself by abstinence. Mind you, he couldn't erase from his mind the recollection that he had noticed an off-licence just up the road.

The dreadful weather and the sepulchral light couldn't be allowed to stop the filming. Ben Docherty was footing the bill for a large number of people to spend two days on the Isle of Purbeck, and he was determined to get his money's worth, so Rick Landor started to galvanise his sodden team into action.

The set-up of 'The Seashore Murder' was that Stanislas Braid and his beloved daughter, Christina, together with Blodd, of course, were spending a few days' holiday in a quiet seaside town (whose calm was soon to be disturbed by a series of inexplicable murders along the seashore). The Braids had rented a small cottage in the seaside town (impersonated, needless to say, by the inland village of Corfe Castle), and by one of those coincidences beloved of W. T. Wintergreen, dear old Sergeant Clump was also taking his annual leave in a nearby boarding house, thus enabling him, even off his home patch of Little Breckington, to be appropriately baffled.

Charles had hoped the fact that the sergeant was on holiday might open out the possibilities of his wardrobe a bit, but no. One of W. T. Wintergreen's little jokes about the character was that his pride in his uniform meant that he took it off only to sleep (and in one of the books Stanislas Braid was even waggish enough to express his doubts over that).

The first scene to be filmed that morning was the detective's farewell to his daughter outside their rented cottage. Three of the seashore murders had already taken place, and Stanislas Braid's intuition told him that he now had to go to Limehouse and consult what, with the insouciant anti-Semitism of the thirties, W. T. Wintergreen's original book had described as 'a slimy Jewboy of a moneylender'. (This had been cleaned up in Will Parton's script to 'a rather dubious moneylender'.)

The detective was therefore to be driven off to London by the faithful Blodd, leaving Christina to 'enjoy the beauties of this wonderful summer, my dearest angel' (and, incidentally, to be put at risk of becoming the seashore murderer's fourth victim – a fate only averted by the timely return of Stanislas Braid with the solution to the crimes and an exciting cliff-top rescue).

They rehearsed the scene in the disheartening mizzle. The film cameraman fiddled with his lenses and lights but eventually told Rick Landor there was no way he could make it look like a nice day.

'Will! Will!' theDirector shouted. 'We're going to have to adjust the lines here.'

'Why?' asked the writer belligerently as he emerged from under an umbrella. He looked nearly as wrung out as Charles felt.

'We can't talk about "enjoying the beauties of this wonderful summer" on a day like this, can we?'

'Don't see why not. It's no less realistic than everything else in the series.' Will was evidently in a truculent mood.

'Oh, come on. You've got to think of something.'

'Um…'

Russell Bentley got out of the Lagonda and scurried for the shelter of an umbrella. 'God, what a shitty, piss-awful day,' he muttered.

'Rick, how's about Stanislas tells Christina to "enjoy the beauties of this shitty, piss-awful day"?' Will suggested innocently.

'Don't be bloody stupid!'

'Why not? In every other speech Stanislas Braid says what Russell feels like saying rather than what I wrote.'

'Will, we're wasting time,' Rick complained.

'Yes, come on, for Christ's sake!' said Ben Docherty, converting the bile of his hangover into professional anger. 'We're slipping behind schedule. Think of a line for the bugger to say.'

'Which bugger's this?' asked Russell Bentley, who Ben Docherty hadn't realised was in earshot.

'Er, um, Stanislas Braid,' the producer replied hopefully.

'Oh, him.' Russell Bentley was satisfied. The insult had nothing to do with Russell Bentley.

'How about' – Will Parton winced at the crassness of the cliché he was about to bring out – '"Enjoy yourself, Christina, my angel. Never mind the weather. Every cloud has a silver lining, and soon the sun will shine again for you, my precious one"?'

'Terrific,' said Ben Docherty.

'Like it,' said Rick Landor.

'Could you give me that exact text?' said the P.A., standing with pencil poised over her script. 'What was it? "Enjoy yourself, Christina, my…?"'

'I'm not sure.' Russell Bentley decided it was time to make his contribution to the discussion. 'I think there are a few too many of these "my angels" and "my precious ones". I mean, she is his daughter, after all. It's not as if they were lovers.'

'You never know,' murmured Mort Verdon, as ever magically materialising when sexual innuendo entered the conversation. 'Might be a smutty old cow, that W. T. Wintergreen. Maybe we should play up the soft-porn element in this series. Do wonders for the video sales.'

'Anyway, we certainly don't want any hint of that,' Russell Bentley continued. 'I mean, I have a reputation in television, and let me tell you, any suggestion that I was involved in anything incestuous would –'

'There is no suggestion of that,' Will Parton snapped. 'It's just the way they talk. It's an idealised relationship. Honestly, in the period setting, nobody's going to think it sounds at all odd.'

'I'm not so sure,' Russell Bentley niggled on. 'And I think it's something we should be very careful about. It's even worse in that scene we're scheduled to be doing tomorrow. You know, the one when I come back, the cliff-top one. The affection between father and daughter in that does seem a bit over the top to me.'

'Look, if you're finding the lines too difficult to play –' Will Parton began.

'Not a matter of that, dear boy.' Russell Bentley as ever avoided using people's names. Which was just as well since he didn't know any of them. 'I can play them fine, and dear, young' – he indicated Joanne Rhymer with a vague gesture – 'is playing them fine, too. It's just, I think they're a bit too much.'

'So what are you suggesting?' asked Will with withering irony. 'That I should do a complete rewrite on tomorrow's scene?'

'Yes, that's it exactly,' replied Russell Bentley, glad to have got his point across.

'I am not going to do any more bloody rewrites on this script!' shouted the writer.

'Well, I'm not going to do that scene tomorrow unless it's rewritten!' shouted the star.

Ben Docherty stepped between them. He was faced with a common producer's dilemma – a conflict of interest between the writer and the star. He had to take sides. But then he was a producer, so there was never any question about which side he would take.

'Actually, Will, I think Russell's got a point. Could you do us a rewrite on that scene by the end of today, please?'

The weather limited the amount of filming they could do in the village. Some lines could be adjusted to make reference to the rain, but scenes like the one in which Christina Braid was meant to set off from the cottage wearing a sun hat and carrying a deck chair just had to be postponed. *The Stanislas Braid* production team could only pray for better weather the next day.

Rick Landor did have one good time-saving idea, though. The script called for a lot of action on the cliffs overlooking the seashore where the murders had taken place. These were scheduled to be shot the following day on the nearby promontory of Durlston Head. But, given the misty conditions, Rick realised that some of them could be shot on the Corfe Castle hill. Over the far side of the ruins the land dropped away very steeply, and filming against that outline in a swirling mist would give a satisfactory illusion of the sea below. W.E.T. had already got permission to shoot a couple of other short scenes inside the National Trust property of the castle's grounds, so there would be no problem about doing a little extra. And it would save the time-consuming business of moving to another location that afternoon.

This was the kind of budget-saving thinking of which Ben Docherty heartily approved. As the Director announced that they'd done all they could in the village that morning and they'd have an early lunch break before picking up again on the hill, the Producer went across to congratulate Rick on his prudent housekeeping.

Charles could put it off no longer. He went to the off-licence to buy a half bottle of Bell's. But once it was safely installed in his raincoat pocket, he decided that his fragile condition required something less ferocious than whisky. A pint of bitter would be more gentle therapy; that'd sort him out.

Walking across to the pub, Charles saw Tony Rees chatting to some of the anorak-shrouded tourists who had been watching the morning's activities. The A.S.M. moved away as he saw Charles approach and called out to the crowd, 'No more excitement here today, I'm afraid. Fun's over. We'll be filming up at the castle this afternoon, but you'll have to pay your entrance fee to see that.'

The tourists walked quickly away, and Tony gave Charles a slightly anxious grin. 'Not still thinking of going to the police, are you?'

Charles shook his head, an unwise thing to do to a head in its condition.

Two pints later there seemed to be a possibility of life continuing. As often happened, the beer had rediluted the residue of the previous night's alcohol, and he felt drunker than two pints should justify. Still, he did also feel better. It really was dreadful how another drink always made him feel better.

And he was suddenly ravenously hungry. He hurried across to the car park and loaded a plate up with sausages, eggs, and chips from the location caterers van. Then, rather than having his lunch diluted by the rain, he took it into one of the coaches. A sheepish look around as he got in confirmed, to his relief, that Joanne Rhymer wasn't there. He sat in a vacant seat next to Mort Verdon.

'How're things, boofle?'

'Better for a drink.'

The Stage Manager nodded. 'Rumour has it you were up to the old bed-hopping again last night.'

'Untrustworthy source of information, rumour.'

'Oh, yes.' They were silent for a moment. 'Nice, was it?'

'Not one of my greatest triumphs.'

'Dear, oh, dear.' Mort Verdon shook his head in pity. 'Perhaps you'd do better with a man, you know.'

'Who can say?' said Charles. 'Trouble is, I'm afraid it's never appealed that much.'

'Ah, well…Don't know what you're missing, boofle.'

'So I'm told.'

At that moment Tony Rees's face appeared over the top of the seat in front. 'Mort, have you got the schedule for the next episode?'

'Yes, it's in my little duffel bag. Front of the coach.'

'Do you mind if I have a look at it? Something I want to check.'

'Be my guest.'

The A.S.M. moved down to the front of the coach.

Mort Verdon's eyes narrowed. 'Wonder what he's up to?'

'Why should he be up to anything?' asked Charles innocently.

'Because he always is, that's why.'

'What kind of things?'

'Fiddles, little deals, anything that gives his W.E.T. salary a bit of a lift.'

'Helping himself to props and what-have-you?'

'Well, let's just say if Corfe Castle is found mysteriously to have gone missing at the end of this afternoon's filming, I think we'll know in whose knicker drawer to start looking for it.'

The solidity of what remains of Corfe Castle after the demolition efforts of parliamentarian sappers and explosives in 1646 is a testament to the strength of its medieval structure, but the castle is only a skeleton of what it once was. Parts of the old keep stand upright, a landmark above the town, but around them there is a rubble of toppled towers and broken masonry. It has the air of a folly built by a crazed aristocrat, an ideal setting for some tale of Gothic horror.

This quality was enhanced that April afternoon by the drizzling mist that kept lifting and descending over the castle's remains. Rick Landor and his cameraman did their best but kept having to break off when the visibility would suddenly drop to about ten yards. At such times there seemed a real danger of losing members of the *Stanislas Braid* team. Figures loomed eerily out of the mist, and it was impossible to see until they came close whether they were actors, production staff, or the few sodden tourists who resolutely continued sight-seeing, even when there were no sights to see.

But slow progress was made in the filming. When the clouds lifted, the outline at the edge of the hill looked very convincingly like a cliff above an unseen sea, and at those moments Rick Landor and Ben Docherty urged their cast into action, fearful of wasting a second of the precious light.

The scenes were fortunately short ones, without too much dialogue. Stanislas Braid, Blodd, and Sergeant Clump were tracing the footsteps of the murderer, looking for the clues that would once and for all convict him and send him to the gallows. Sergeant Clump would point to footprints that the Great Detective instantly identified as being weeks old; only Stanislas Braid himself was allowed to find 'the mark of a size seven-and-a-half riding boot that has been recently repaired by an apprentice cobbler and whose scuffed heel tells us that its wearer is afflicted by a slight deformity of the right leg…probably the legacy of a childhood attack of rickets.'

Slowly, as the afternoon progressed, one by one these scenes were immortalised on film, but the weather was deteriorating fast. The clouds seemed to descend more frequently, and each time they lifted, the cameraman winced more when he checked his light meter. Eventually, at about a quarter to four, he shook his head firmly and said, 'No point in doing any more. The quality just won't be good enough.'

'Oh, I'm sure it will,' cajoled Ben Docherty, as ever more concerned about his programme's budget than its quality.

'No way.'

'Well, look, let's not call it a "wrap" yet,' the producer pleaded. 'Keep everything set up, give people a twenty-minute tea break, and then see if the light's improved after that?'

The cameraman shrugged. 'All right, you can if you like. But it's a waste of time. The light won't get any better today.'

'Can't we put more artificial light on it?'

'I'm using all the lights I've got.'

'Oh, well, look, let's take the break, anyway, and see. What do you say, Rick?'

'Okay. You're the Producer, Ben,' said the Director in a way that left no doubt that he was in complete agreement with his cameraman.

The tea break was announced. Russell Bentley complained that there wasn't time to get back down to the car park and the caterers' van, so Mort Verdon was unwillingly dispatched down the castle hill to fetch up thermoses of coffee and tea. The production team dispersed, wandering off into the mist – some, like the few remaining tourists, to indulge in a little abortive sightseeing, others to check whether there were any parts of the castle where Cromwell's army had left enough roof to provide a little shelter from the constant soft but saturating rain.

Charles Paris was feeling bad again. Under the weather, he thought to himself with a grim little smile. The lift given by the lunch-time beer had worn off, and his headache was back with temple-stretching ferocity. With it, the headache brought remorse, the knowledge of how deeply he had humiliated himself the night before. And how thoroughly he had betrayed his intentions toward Frances.

He knew he had no alternative now. The half bottle of Bell's from the off-license still thumped reassuringly against his thigh in the pocket of the raincoat he had put on over Sergeant Clump's damp blue uniform. A quick slurp might pick him up again. Just the one. Really. Then a quick bite to eat when they got back to the hotel. Nothing to drink and a very early night.

What else could he do to make himself feel virtuous? Ring Frances? But no, he decided on consideration. The memory of the previous evening was too raw for him to risk speaking to his wife. In his current abject state he'd probably confess everything. And that was hardly going to advance the cause of their *rapprochement*, was it?

He didn't want anyone on the production team to see him drinking. It wasn't that he was a secret drinker, he told himself – the circumstances were exceptional. He just needed this one drink to get him through the rest of the day's filming. (He conveniently forgot that there was unlikely to be any more filming that day.) Then, after that one drink, no more. Nothing that evening. Maybe have a few days on the wagon. No booze at all for a while. Good idea, yes.

He walked away through the remains of the keep, along the ruins of the new bulwark and down toward the south-west gatehouse. Around the corner of that, at the foot of the old bastion, he would be sufficiently out of sight to have his quick medicinal drink. (Guilt made his planning so elaborate; given the heavy mist, he could in fact have nipped around the corner of any outcrop of masonry and felt pretty confident of being unobserved.)

As he sloshed through the long, wet grass at the foot of the keep, he thought he heard something. Hard to tell through the deadening mist where it came from or exactly what the sound was. A cry, perhaps an animal's cry, and a heavy thump.

He thought nothing of it as he moved forward. He took the half bottle out of his pocket and heard the reassuring click as he broke the seal on its golden top. He raised the bottle to his lips and was about to take a long, restorative swallow when he saw an indistinct shape on the ground ahead of him.

He walked toward it, feeling suddenly cold.

The shape had a human form. But it looked foreshortened, the head unnaturally folded under the body.

He recognised the clothes but turned the dead weight over to confirm his worst fears.

It was Tony Rees. Still warm. He had only just landed. The thump Charles had heard had been the impact that had so immediately and thoroughly broken the A.S.M.'s neck.

The mist suddenly swirled and lifted, and Charles could see up to the window in the broken wall of the keep some thirty feet above him.

No one was visible in the dark frame of the window. But a few minutes earlier, Charles felt certain, someone had been there.

The person who had pushed Tony Rees to his death. Who was also, Charles would have risked a substantial bet, the person who had murdered Sippy Stokes.

Chapter Fourteen

'OF COURSE it was murder,' said Charles, looking moodily out of the window of Will Parton's room at the foggy darkness of Swanage Bay.

'You have no reason for saying that,' the writer argued. 'In those conditions, with the wind and the fog and the stones all slippery, anyone could have lost their balance and fallen off that windowsill.'

'Yes, but why would anyone *be* on that windowsill in the first place? Tony'd have had to climb all the way up there. Why would he do that – unless he had arranged to meet someone?'

'I've no idea, Charles. It seems to me that playing Sergeant Clump is going to your head. You're seeing murders everywhere.'

'Doesn't it have that effect on you – working on the series? Don't you start to see murders everywhere?'

'No. All I start seeing everywhere is more bloody *rewrites*! Like this one.' Will Parton gestured at the screen of his lap-top computer. 'Just because Russell Bloody Bentley doesn't want his screen image tarnished by a whiff of incest. Personally I think that'd do it a lot of good – first interesting characteristic he's shown in his entire film or television career.'

There was a silence. Will Parton tapped away at his keyboard.

'You don't suppose Russell could have killed him, do you, Will?'

'Oh, for Christ's sake, Charles, shut up! I can't imagine Russell killing anyone...or doing anything else that requires any exercise of the imagination, come to that. And what possible motive could Russell have had for killing Tony Rees?'

'I don't know. Blackmail, maybe? Tony was into everything...anything he could use to screw a bit of money out of people. I wouldn't be surprised if he was into blackmail. If Russell had some dark secret –'

'Russell's only dark secret is that he's as thick as two short planks. And it's not much of a secret; it's self-evident to everyone who meets him.'

'I do like this blackmail idea, though. Maybe not Russell. Jimmy Sheet, perhaps? He's scared witless his wife's going to find out about his dalliances with other women.'

'He doesn't appear to have any dalliances with other women at the moment.'

'No, but it seems he did with Sippy Stokes.'

'Certainly looked that way, yes.' Will Parton stared at Charles in sudden alarm. 'Oh, my God! Sergeant Clump doesn't think that Sippy Stokes was murdered, too, does he?'

'Yes, I do.'

'Charles, why do you have to get into all this? Why pretend you're as good as Stanislas Braid? Why not be content to remain as Sergeant Clump and be baffled?'

'I have good reasons for thinking Sippy Stokes was murdered.'

'Do you? Well, I have good reasons for wanting to get this bloody rewrite finished. The main one being that as soon as I have finished it, I am going down to the bar to treat myself to a very large drink. Look, why don't you just go down there, get yourself one in, and wait for me? If I can get a run at this *without interruptions*, I'll be through in about twenty minutes.'

'No, I've decided I'm not going to drink anything this evening.'

'Oh, Goody Two Shoes. Afraid of getting into more inappropriate beds, are you?'

Charles blushed. Will Parton grinned and returned to his keyboard.

'Of course,' Charles mused after a time, 'Tony Rees might have had something on Rick Landor.'

Will Parton slammed his fist down on the table. 'Charles, will you please shut up!'

'No, but listen, I've had a thought. Suppose Tony Rees actually witnessed the murder of Sippy Stokes.'

'Assuming that such an event ever took place.'

'And then he tried to blackmail the person who had done the murder?'

Will Parton yawned.

'Which was why he got killed.'

'Yes, well, thank you,' said Will in the tone of someone ending a conversation. 'I don't promise anything, but I'll see if I can get that into ep. five as a subplot.'

'Oh, my God!' said Charles suddenly.

'What the hell is it now?'

'I've just thought – You remember how I was behaving last night?'

'Hard to ignore it, I'm afraid, old man. Hard for Joanne to ignore it, either, I would imagine.'

Charles ignored the gibe. 'You know, I was talking at dinner about Sippy Stokes possibly having been murdered.'

'Yes.'

'And I did sort of imply that someone might have witnessed the killing.'

'Hmm.'

'You don't suppose the murderer then got suspicious of Tony Rees and that's why Tony got murdered?' The enormity of the idea that Charles might have inadvertently caused someone's death turned him cold.

'No, I don't, Charles,' said Will in the last stages of exasperation. 'All I suppose is that if you don't shut up, there'll be another murder. You will be the victim, and *I* will be the perpetrator. Got that?'

'Yes. Sorry.'

'Now will you please leave me alone to finish this bloody script! You've got your own room, haven't you?'

'Yes.'

'Well, go to it. Give me twenty minutes; then we'll go and have a drink.'

'But I –'

'You can have Perrier.'

'Well, I –'

'Go to your own room, sit down, read a good book. Failing that' – Will picked up an old hardback from the table and flung it across to Charles – 'read *this*.'

It was a copy of *The Seashore Murder* by W. T. Wintergreen.

'Thanks very much,' said Charles without enthusiasm.

His lack of enthusiasm proved justified. W. T. Wintergreen may have seen Frances through her romantic teens, but she wasn't really Charles's sort of writer. He found the style distinctly arch, or perhaps 'twee' was a better word?

But the extracts he read considerably raised his estimation of Will Parton's technique. The adaptations had filleted their originals with great skill, stylising the old-fashioned elements in a way that made them much more acceptable to modern tastes.

He could also understand Russell Bentley's objections better from the book than he could from the scripts. Once again Will had done a good job in diluting the W. T. Wintergreen text. In the book the Stanislas Braid/Christina Braid relationship was nauseatingly sugary.

He threw *The Seashore Murder* down onto his bed – it had only taken ten minutes for him to get bored with it – and focused his mind on Tony Rees's death.

The blackmail idea did appeal. It conformed with what he knew of the A.S.M.'s character, and it also provided an obvious link between the two deaths.

If Tony had witnessed Sippy Stokes's murder and then started to blackmail its perpetrator, that would provide a perfect reason for him to be silenced.

But it needn't have been the murder. Tony Rees might have known another secret about someone involved in *Stanislas Braid*. Who could say what indiscretions the various suspects might have committed in their pasts?

There was of course one person who probably *could* say. Charles shuffled through the back of an old out-of-date diary from which he had never bothered to transfer his address list, found a London number, and dialled it.

'Hello?'

'Maurice, it's me, Charles.'

'What on earth are you ringing me at home for? There's nothing in this business so urgent that it won't wait till the morning.'

'It's not about business.'

'Oh? What is it, then?' Maurice sounded suspicious.

'I want some information.'

'What kind of information?'

'A bit of show-biz gossip.'

'Dirt?' Maurice's tone had changed. Now he sounded very alert, almost enthusiastic.

'Dirt,' Charles confirmed.

'Dirt on who?'

'There are four people I'd like you to check out.'

'And what sort of stuff do you want?'

'Oh, any indiscretions in their past. Criminal...or personal...The sort of stuff they'd want kept quiet, anyway.'

'I get you.'

'Do you think you can do it?'

'Charles,' his agent said reproachfully, 'need you ask?'

'No, of course not. Sorry.'

'Right,' said Maurice Skellern gleefully. 'Give me the names.'

With that line of inquiry launched, Charles once again brought his mind to bear on Tony Rees. He tried to recall everything he had seen the A.S.M. do over the previous twenty-four hours and think if there was anything that struck a discordant note.

The first strangeness was the young man's unexpected affability in the pub the night before. After nearly a fortnight of avoiding Charles, suddenly Tony was grasping him by the arm and buying him drinks. There must have been some explanation for the change.

The other thing that hadn't seemed odd at the time but might, in posthumous retrospect, appear slightly strange was Tony's request that lunch-time for Mort Verdon's production schedule. Why should the A.S.M. suddenly want to know what was happening in the next episode when they were in the middle of filming on this one?

Of course, there were any number of innocent answers to that question, but Charles thought it just might be worth checking out. He reached for the phone again and dialled the number of a room in the hotel.

'Hello?' The voice was not suspicious but guarded.

'Mort, it's Charles Paris.'

'Oh, hell*o*.' The voice opened out. 'Seen the error of your ways at last, have you, boofle? Thought you would. Well, just give me a moment to slip into something casual and then' – the stage manager dropped into a Mae West impersonation – 'come up and see me.'

'Ah, sorry to disappoint you.'

'Story of my life, boofle,' said Mort, and dropped instantly out of their customary masquerade. 'What *can* I do for you, then, Charles?'

'It's about schedules.'

'Hang on a moment while I just control my excitement. *Schedules*, did you say?'

'Yes.'

'*Production* schedules?' asked Mort, as if the world could hold no topic more exciting.

'Yup.'

Mort's voice subsided into flatness. 'What about them?'

'You remember that Tony – the late Tony – borrowed your schedule for the next episode at lunch-time today?'

'I do remember.'

'Did he give it back to you?'

'No. No, he didn't. But, quite honestly, I'm not going to hold it against him. I mean, the poor boy's dead, and I'm hardly going to go and get stroppy with his next of kin and demand my schedule back at a moment like this, am I? Mind you, I can't think the details of the next episode's filming and studio are going to be much use to poor Tony where he's gone.'

'No,' said Charles. 'It's strange…'

'What?'

'Well, you know I found his body.'

'Yes. I'm sorry. Seem to be making rather a habit of that at the moment, don't you?'

'Mm. Mort, I shouldn't have done this, but before I went to get help, I checked through Tony's pockets.'

'Macabre thing to do.'

'Yes, I suppose it was a bit. Anyway, your schedule wasn't there.'

'Oh, well, as I say, I'm not about to make a great fuss.'

'No. I also looked through Tony's bag on the coach…You know, before the police came to take it away.'

'Quite the little Sergeant Clump, aren't we?' murmured Mort, echoing Will's words.

'Yes. Thing is, your schedule wasn't in his bag either.'

'Well, Charles, boofle, I don't think we have to alert Interpol straightaway, do we? It is, after all, only a few photocopied sheets we're talking about. Tony might have dropped it, he might have shoved it in a litter bin, could be anywhere. Don't worry, I'll get another one before we start rehearsing that episode.'

'Yes, yes, fine. Well, thanks, Mort.'

'No problem. And don't forget, Charles, if you wake up in the night feeling a little queer, you've got my room number.'

'Thanks. I'll bear it in mind.'

Charles put the phone down and looked out pensively into the murk beyond the windowpane.

The telephone trilled, and he picked it up again.

'It's Will. I've finished the sodding thing. Let's have that drink. Pick me up on the way.'

* * *

'Come in. It's on the latch.'

Charles obeyed Will's instructions and went into his room. The writer was scribbling a note on a blank sheet of paper. His portable printer was rattling out the rewritten scene. It stopped. With practised ease, Will Parton tore off the perforated strips on the sheets and shuffled them neatly into order.

'This one's for Russell, since he's the one who, in theory, has to learn the stuff. I'll do copies for Ben and Rick later. I'm parched.'

With satisfaction he put the note on top of the pile of sheets.

'DEAR RUSSELL,' Charles read, 'HERE'S THE REWRITE. YOU CANT COMPLAIN NOW. ALL CLEANED UP. NO ONE COULD IMAGINE IN THEIR WILDEST FANTASIES THAT THERE WAS ANYTHING OUT OF THE ORDINARY IN THE RELATIONSHIP BETWEEN STANISLAS BRAID AND CHRISTINA. YOURS, WILL.'

'Are you going to give it to him now?'

'No,' said Will. 'I'll drop it into his room later. Don't want to get involved in discussions about how the part of Russell Bentley should be played at this precise moment. My first priority is a drink. Come on.' At the door he asked, 'And you're certain you're not going to be drinking tonight?'

'Certain,' said Charles.

They stayed in the bar most of the evening. Charles survived one round on Perrier, but then he reasoned that he really did need a large Bell's. That afternoon a sudden death had once again stopped him when he was about to have a drink. And he was in a serious state of shock after finding Tony Rees's body.

There was only one interruption in his evening's drinking. After they had been in the bar for about an hour, he was paged by Reception. There was a telephone call for him.

It was Maurice. Calling back with the dirt. Charles spent ten minutes in the phone booth by Reception scribbling furiously in a notebook. All interesting stuff. Then he went back to continue drinking.

'Really must get that script to Russell,' said Will at the end of the evening as they tottered toward his room.

He fumbled with the key, but as he leaned against the door, it gave and opened inward. 'Stupid twit. Must have forgotten to lock it.'

They stumbled into the room. Will looked at the empty table with an expression of puzzlement.

'That's funny,' he said. 'Someone's taken my rewrite.'

Chapter Fifteen

THE NEXT MORNING the weather seemed little improved, so there was no chance of picking up the summery scenes in Corfe Castle. But since the precedent of a misty seascape had already been established the previous afternoon, the decision was made to shoot as much of the seashore stuff as possible on Durlston Head. The W.E.T. coaches therefore drove through Swanage and up out of the town to the location. Tony Rees's death had put a damper on everyone's spirits; there was no sign of the hilarity of previous coach trips.

The location caterers were already set up in the car park when the coaches arrived, and many of the crew, who had only half an hour before finished large hotel breakfasts, immediately tucked into their first bacon sandwiches of the day.

By this time the weather did look rather more promising. Every now and then the clouds parted to admit a few frames of watery sunshine. The cameraman began to look as optimistic as the lugubrious traditions of his trade allowed.

Ben Docherty urged Rick Landor on to get the morning's filming finished as quickly as possible. If they could have all the Durlston Head stuff in the can before lunch and if the weather continued its promising trend, there would be a reasonable chance of getting the outstanding Corfe Castle scenes done in the afternoon. In spite of deaths and climatic disasters, the Producer was still determined to get his series made in time. The thought of having to spend another day in Dorset was too awful to contemplate. The next day's rest day was obligatory by union rules, so if that got moved on, all the studio bookings would have to be shifted. The cumulative effects over the series didn't bear thinking of. Even overrunning on that day's schedule offered the direful prospect of overtime payments. The Producer tried, unsuccessfully, to disguise his panic as efficiency.

The disappearing rewrite of the night before had not been explained, but fortunately the text was on the memory of Will's lap-top, and he had been just sober enough to get it to print up other copies. Everyone seemed happy with the changes. Russell Bentley, in particular, was effusive in his praise of the writer's efforts. He still couldn't remember Will's name, but he did enthuse, 'You've done frightfully well, old boy. Must get you writing something else for me.'

The scene that had caused all the fuss was a tense little moment of drama in which Stanislas Braid and Christina appeared to be trapped on a cliff-top ledge with no hope of escape. In the W. T. Wintergreen version they took this as an opportunity to tell the depth of their feelings for each other. Will Parton's rewrite had changed it to something altogether more jokey. The affection was still there, but masked in a kind of flippant bravado.

The new scene, however, was not scheduled for shooting till later in the morning. First, a few laborious moments of Sergeant Clump and Blodd had to be filmed as they wandered in panic along the cliff path, looking for the missing detective and his daughter. These scenes were very short – Blodd rushing into shot and saying something like 'No sign of them,' then rushing out of shot, to be followed seconds later by a ponderously puffing Sergeant Clump – but there were long pauses between them as Rick Landor and the cameraman tried to find new vantage points and angles along the cliff path.

In one of these breaks Charles took the opportunity of checking Jimmy Sheet's reaction to the death of Tony Rees. 'Dreadful business yesterday, wasn't it?'

'What's that, then?' asked the former pop star.

'Tony.'

'Oh, yeah.' Jimmy Sheet grinned unpleasantly. 'Don't think anyone'll miss him.'

'No, I gather he had his less pleasant qualities,' Charles prompted.

'Huh. You can say that again. Nasty bit of work. No secret was safe when you got someone like that around.'

'Oh?'

'Still, he isn't around, so that's no longer a problem, is it?'

'Did you find it a problem?'

Jimmy Sheet gave Charles a hard look. 'What's that to you?'

'Just wondered.'

'Well, I'd advise you to stop wondering. Tony Rees is dead, and from my point of view that's the best thing that could have happened to him.'

'How do you think it did happen?'

Jimmy Sheet looked Charles straight in the eyes with insolent self-assurance. 'He fell, didn't he?'

They got the searching of the cliff path filmed, and Charles's scenes were finished. Needless to say, Sergeant Clump was not bright enough actually to find the missing detective. No, as ever, he was baffled. It was Stanislas Braid's own ingenuity that got him out of this particular fix. As it did out of every other fix in which he found himself.

But although his work was done, Charles had no alternative but to stay around the location. No transport would be going back into Swanage until the Durlston Head scenes were finished, and he didn't fancy walking five miles.

So he sat on one of the stone benches thoughtfully placed for sightseers to look out over Durlston Bay. The weather was continuing to improve and, although leaden clouds hung like a Roman blind over the horizon, he could get some impression of the beauties of the Isle of Purbeck's coastline.

He looked up to see Ben Docherty approaching. The Producer sat down beside him and said with a nervous grin, 'All done?'

Charles nodded. He reached into his raincoat pocket and pulled out the half bottle of Bell's. Though its seal had been broken, the contents were still intact. 'Fancy a drop?'

'Wouldn't say no,' said Ben. 'Bit nippy.'

Charles wondered how he could broach the subject of Tony Rees's death but was saved the trouble, because Ben Docherty did it for him. 'That business yesterday, Charles…'

'What?'

'The A.S.M..'

'Oh, yes.'

'You found him, didn't you?'

'Uh-huh.'

'I mean, you *found* him? He was there when you got there? You didn't see him fall?'

'No, I didn't.'

The answer seemed to please Ben Docherty, who nodded slowly. 'The police talked to you?'

'Yes.'

'You didn't gather from them what they thought had happened?'

'Police never give much away, do they?'

'No, no,' the Producer agreed slowly. But his mind was still not at rest. 'And there's no talk round the cast?' he asked diffidently.

'Talk about what?'

'Well, about Tony's death.'

'Obviously everyone's *talking* about it, but' – time for a bit of tactical obtuseness – 'I'm sorry, I don't quite understand what you mean.'

'I just mean, Charles, nobody's sort of suggesting, you know, like maybe the death wasn't an accident?'

'I haven't heard anyone say that,' said Charles. Which was true enough. Present company, of course, excepted.

'Good,' said Ben Docherty. 'Good.'

Thermoses of coffee were brought from the caterers' van. 'Can we make it a short break?' Rick Landor pleaded. 'Just ten minutes. We're doing well, but we've still got a lot to do.'

Charles, feeling rather dozy after his whisky with Ben Docherty, accepted a cup of coffee. Rick also had one, which he downed in three nervous gulps. 'Getting there, getting there,' the Director said.

'The studio stuff's relatively straightforward this week, isn't it?' asked Charles.

'Not too bad. Should be simpler than the last one I did, anyway.'

'What do you mean?'

'Come on, Charles, you remember what it was like. I'm glad I wasn't the one to have to do the dirty deed, but it's a great relief to have had W. T. Wintergreen banned from the premises. She didn't make that week easy for me.'

'And then, of course,' said Charles casually, 'there was Sippy Stokes.'

'Yes, yes, there was.' The director was silent for a moment. 'Sounds dreadful to say it, but I'm afraid this episode'll be a lot easier without her around.'

'Oh, but I thought she was your casting.'

'Yes, I suppose she was. I mean, I put through the booking, but I was under pressure.'

'Who from?'

'Sippy herself. Doesn't do to speak ill of the dead, but I'm afraid she was a nasty bit of work.'

'Weren't you lovers, though?'

'Yes, we were. But I'd tried to break it off many times. She wouldn't let me. The trouble was, she knew things about me which – well, things that could have got me into quite a bit of bother.'

Yes, thought Charles, remembering the information that Maurice had supplied him with the night before. Something to do with your cocaine habit, perhaps?

But he said nothing as Rick Landor continued, 'Anyway, giving Sippy the part of Christina was a kind of once-and-for-all payoff.'

'She blackmailed you into casting her?'

'That's what it amounted to, yes. It was a habit she had, one of her less endearing habits.'

'Hmm. Do you think she tried the same trick with Jimmy Sheet? You know, threatened to tell his wife after they'd been out together?'

'Let's say it wouldn't have been out of character if she had.'

'I see.'

They gazed out over the sea. It was almost blue. The dark clouds were moving away to the west. It looked as though they would get all the Corfe Castle summer scenes safely done that afternoon.

'Bad luck, really,' said Charles, 'having two blackmailers in the same production.'

'What do you mean?'

'It was a bit of a sideline for Tony Rees, too, I gather.'

Rick Landor abruptly looked at his watch. 'Got to get on,' he mumbled. 'Check out the eyelines we've got on the next set-up.' And he moved away.

Charles stayed looking out over the sea. He didn't seem to have progressed far in his search for the killer of Sippy Stokes. Or the killer of Tony Rees, come to that. He felt certain that the two deaths were linked, almost certain that the same person had perpetrated both.

Jimmy Sheet...Ben Docherty...Rick Landor...Each one of them had a secret to hide. A secret Tony Rees might easily have found out about. Each one of them was a potential suspect.

And of course there was one other potential suspect involved in that morning's filming on Durlston Head.

He found Russell Bentley sitting in a folding chair, a white towel tucked bib-like around his neck, while a makeup girl tried to make him look like a man who has just fallen off a cliff and clawed his way back up to it to find his beloved daughter stranded on a ledge.

The makeup girl's job was not an easy one. While Russell wanted to look authentically battered, he didn't want any marks on him that might be deemed disfiguring. A discreet scratch along the temple was fine, so was a bruise on the cheekbone, but he wouldn't tolerate anything that spoiled the shape of his nose or the outline of his jaw.

The makeup girl did her best to meet these exacting conditions. She had the tools of her trade on a little tray propped up on a stand beside her. Bottles and cakes of various flesh tones. Liner pencils. Spirit gum. Brushes and sponges. A bottle of Arterial Blood to authenticate the scratches. She did not look up from her task as Charles approached.

'Russell...' he began.

The star squinted up into the sun. 'Oh, hello, er...' Once again the name escaped him.

'Pity about Tony Rees, wasn't it?'

'Who?' But the star knew; Charles could see it in his eyes. Russell Bentley was just using his notorious amnesia for names to play for time.

'You know. The one who died up at the castle yesterday.'

'Oh, yes. Tragic business.' The sentiment was automatic; there was no hint of real emotion in his voice.

'I suppose so,' said Charles. 'It seems he was a nasty piece of work, though.'

'Really? I didn't know him at all.'

'Apparently he was the kind of person who would find out secrets about people, secrets they very definitely wanted kept quiet, and then he would make the people pay for his silence.'

'Would he? I don't really see what this has to do with me.'

'No.' Charles allowed a few seconds' silence. 'You got your way over the rewrite, then?'

'Sorry?'

'The scene with Christina. The one you're about to film.'

'Yes. Well, it does make the whole relationship much more relaxed. And less emotionally charged. I mean, they are father and daughter, after all.'

'Yes, and you have your reputation in television to consider.'

'Exactly.'

'Wouldn't do for the public to think Russell Bentley was the kind of man to be involved in incest.'

'No.' The star held up a cautionary hand to the makeup girl, who was poised with her brush and bottle of Arterial Blood at the ready. 'Not too much of that stuff. Don't want to look like Rocky IV.'

'Or,' Charles persisted, 'the kind of man to be involved with underage girls.'

A new light came into Russell Bentley's eyes. 'What are you talking about?'

'Some parties back in the early sixties. Involving people working on a film called *The Hawk's Prey*.'

From the expression on Russell Bentley's face Charles knew that, as ever, Maurice Skellern's information had been correct.

'I don't know what you're talking about,' the star lied, trying to bluster his way out.

'Oh, I think you do. And I think Tony Rees also knew what I was talking about.'

'Nonsense. I'm certainly not going to –'

But the star never said what he was certainly not going to do. There was the sound of a gunshot from somewhere behind Charles. He saw the shock on Russell Bentley's face at the sight of the red stain spreading over the towel that covered his throat; there was more expression there at the moment than the star had ever shown in his portrayal of Stanislas Braid.

As Russell Bentley slumped back in his chair and the makeup girl screamed, Charles turned and started up the hillside toward the clump of trees where the gunshot had come from. Brambles snatched at the blue serge of Sergeant Clump's uniform; branches of shrubs slashed at him as he thundered forward. He pushed aside the branches of a tree and suddenly stopped dead.

In front of him stood someone with a bewildered look and a gun.

It was W. T. Wintergreen.

Chapter Sixteen

SHE looked at him for a moment, her face still puzzled. Neither of them spoke. Then, suddenly, she fled.

She showed a surprising turn of speed for a septuagenarian, and given Charles's surprise and the fact that he was out of breath from his dash up the hillside, she had twenty yards' start on him before he got his legs moving.

He pulled after her and might have caught up to her over a longer distance, but W. T. Wintergreen had not far to go. She burst out of the clump of trees from which the shot had been fired and raced across the hillocks of long grass to a rough track, where her old black Beetle was parked.

The driver's door was open. She leaped in and slammed it. By the time Charles was close enough to do anything, the engine had sputtered into life. He just had time to catch a glimpse of the tear-stained face of Louisa Railton in the passenger seat as the car screeched away, sounding like a demented lawn mower.

He stood still, sweating and breathless, as the Beetle diminished into the distance.

Then, attempting to reorganise in his mind everything he had ever thought about the murders, he moved slowly back down the hill.

Russell Bentley was not dead. When Charles came to think of it, he couldn't imagine Russell Bentley ever dying – just going on being Russell Bentley for all eternity.

He wasn't even injured. Nor, though she was in a state of hysterics, was the makeup girl. The bullet fired from the hillside had missed both of them. By remarkable good fortune, though certainly aimed at Russell Bentley, what it had hit had been the bottle of Arterial Blood in the makeup girl's hand. The ghastly stain on the star's towel was courtesy of Leichner rather than of his own arteries.

In fact, except for the makeup girl's hysterics, the incident had had little effect on the *Stanislas Braid* production team. Russell Bentley was of the opinion that it hadn't been a gunshot, anyway; he thought the bottle of Arterial Blood must have been flawed and have broken spontaneously. The makeup girl swore she had heard something, but she was in too emotional a state for anyone to take what she said very seriously.

And Charles Paris, the one person who knew that a shot had been fired, for reasons of his own kept that knowledge to himself.

The filming continued, and the Durlston Head scenes were finished before lunch, much to the delight of Ben Docherty. The weather had cleared completely, and there was every prospect of getting the Corfe Castle scenes shot within the time allotted. His precious budget looked as if it had survived another threat.

Charles Paris went in the W.E.T. coach back to the hotel in Swanage. There was no point in his returning to Corfe Castle, and he told Mort Verdon that he would make his own way back to London.

He packed quickly and at the hotel Reception organised a cab to take him to Bournemouth. From there he caught a train to Waterloo.

And all the time he was on the train, Charles Paris sat and thought.

When he arrived in London, he knew what he had to do, but he felt he needed some bolstering before he did it. Not his customary alcoholic bolstering, though; the situation was far too serious for that. No, he needed human contact. He needed to tell someone what he was about to do.

What he really needed was to talk to Frances. He even got as far as standing in a phone box in Waterloo Station and lifting the receiver.

But he chickened out. Frances would be at school. She could be extremely frosty and headmistressy when he rang her at school. Anyway, the memory of Sunday night's shame was still with him. No, he should wait to ring Frances until he felt cleansed and virtuous, until he felt worthy of ringing her. He had a nasty sense that that feeling could be a long time coming. Reluctantly, he put the phone down.

Then he looked at the departures board for the next train to Richmond.

No killing time before this visit. He asked the taxi driver to take him straight to the cottage and watched as the cab drove away.

The black Beetle was parked outside. He knocked on the door, and it was opened by W. T. Wintergreen.

She looked strained, and her eyes were pinkish from recent tears. But she carried herself with a kind of calm dignity.

'Ah,' she said, 'I had expected you might come.' She stood back to let him into the tiny sitting room. 'Can I offer you a cup of tea or coffee, perhaps?'

There was something incongruous, given the circumstances, about these genteel observances. Charles refused the offer of refreshment with matching gentility.

He sat edgily on the chair his hostess had indicated. Reading his mood, she said, 'You don't need to feel any anxiety, Mr. Paris. It's all over now.'

He sensed that she was telling the truth and relaxed partially.

'So I suppose it's just confession time,' said W. T. Wintergreen with a sigh.

'I suppose it is.'

She nodded slowly. 'It is my intention to make a full confession to the police. However, Mr. Paris, I am quite happy to run through the details for you if you so wish.'

'I would be most grateful,' he said, amazed at how easily he was dropping into her own, slightly formal, style of speech.

'Yes. You see, I have not been unaware of your interest in this little...series of murders.'

'Oh?'

'And I congratulate you on finding out as much as you have. As someone who has spent much of her life bending her mind round the problems of detective fiction, I can recognise a brain which works in a similar fashion.'

'Oh, thank you.' Charles really appreciated such a professional compliment, but once again he couldn't help being struck by the incongruity of this conversational square dance.

'I suppose,' said W. T. Wintergreen in a manner that was almost languorous, 'it is the fiction that is to blame for everything that has happened. I don't mean because it was crime fiction that I wrote. That is irrelevant. What you have been investigating have not been the actions of an unhinged old lady who can no longer distinguish fictional crime from real crime. No...'

She was silent. The faded eyes were unfocused behind their spectacles.

But she pulled herself together before Charles had to prompt her. 'No, I suppose you might say that I have been protecting my creations.'

'Stanislas Braid? Christina? Sergeant Clump?'

She nodded slowly. 'Yes, yes, that is exactly it. When you were last here, Mr. Paris, I remember our discussing the creative process, discussing how involved writers become with their characters.'

'How much of themselves they put into those characters,' Charles suggested gently.

'As an actor, of course you would understand. Well, most writers can cope with the problem. They get deeply involved with their characters while they're writing the books, but then they...have a break, go on holiday, they...get back to normal. I suppose it depends really on how much else they have in their lives. In my case, there hasn't been much else in my life.'

'Looking after your father till he died?'

'Yes.'

'Not, I gather, the easiest of men.'

'No, not the easiest. Very jealous and – He was jealous of my writing. He was the reason why I stopped writing.'

'So, as your own life became more circumscribed, more claustrophobic – looking after your father, looking after your sister – you retreated more and more into the world you had created in your fiction.'

'Yes.' She let out a brittle little laugh. 'I gather the American enthusiasts of the crime-fiction genre have now designated a special category of the "cozy" British mystery. And I suppose it is a "cozy" world. Everything looked after, everything tied up. All emotions neatly cut off at the ends, not fraying and tangling like real emotions. A sense of justice, the knowledge that Right will triumph, reinforced, of course, in the days when I was writing, by the existence of the Death Penalty. At the end of the book the criminal would be unmasked, and the reader could sleep easy in the confidence that the murderer was meeting his Final Retribution.'

'And then, of course, there was the character of Stanislas Braid himself, wasn't there, Winifred?'

'I cannot deny that he had a certain appeal for me.'

'A lot easier to deal with than most of the real men you had encountered.'

W. T. Wintergreen allowed herself a little smile. 'More containable, certainly.'

'A lot easier to deal with than your father?'

Her mood changed abruptly. 'These murders,' she said, 'this series of murders. I expect you have gathered most of what happened, but I'll spell it out for you.

'First,' she continued briskly, 'that dreadful actress. I'm afraid I had been in a very emotional state ever since the idea of the television series was mooted. It had been a long time since I wrote the last Stanislas Braid book, and all this new interest brought back a lot of things I thought I had forgotten. I was unhappy with many of the ideas that the television company proposed. The actors and actresses did not look as I had visualised the characters, though I may say you, Mr. Paris,' she conceded, 'were not physically inappropriate for the part of Sergeant Clump.'

'Oh, thank you,' said Charles.

'But the girl...the girl who was meant to be Christina...In all the books her fair hair and blue eyes are described. Suddenly for me to see this...swarthy Mediterranean type...was a profound shock. And she was so far from the *soul* of the character.'

Charles had wondered how long it would take before souls came up again.

'Actually killing her,' said W. T. Wintergreen, 'was an impulse, hardly a decision. That morning, at the end of the break, I saw her walking out of the studio. I was near the study set. I took the candlestick, hit her with it in that little room, pulled the shelves down on top of her, and returned the murder weapon. The whole sequence of events took...less than a minute, I would think. Afterwards I could hardly believe it had happened, it was all over so quickly.'

Charles looked thoughtful. 'For someone who has devoted so much of her life to devising devious and ingenious methods of killing people, your own first attempt at murder was a bit amateur.'

'I agree. As I say, it wasn't a rational choice, just the impulse of a moment of insanity.'

'Yes.'

'But it seemed to achieve the right effect. The dreadful girl was gone, and suddenly the new Christina is everything she should be. She looks right, and she has this wonderful ethereal quality of childish innocence.'

Charles cleared his throat, recollecting the real character of Joanne Rhymer.

'So I did not feel guilty about the murder. It seemed to have been right.

Everyone seemed happier. And though I was slightly shocked that I could have been capable of something like that, I was able to put it from my mind.'

'You had no intention at that stage of committing further murders?'

'Good heavens, no.'

'So what did Tony Rees do to make you change your mind?'

'Ah.' She was silent for a moment. 'Well, you may recall during the recording of the second episode that there was an unfortunate exhibition in the studio?'

'When Ben Docherty banned you from the premises.'

'Yes. Extremely regrettable. And for me devastating. Because, although much of what was happening to *Stanislas Braid* caused me deep disquiet, I was obsessed by the series. I still felt a need to watch everything that happened, every rehearsal, every piece of filming. I felt it was...my baby.'

She used this phrase as if she had just coined it and nobody in the history of the world had ever used it before. A tear glistened in her eye. She reached up under her glasses and brushed it clumsily away before going on. 'I was devastated by the prospect of being excluded from my own series, so I had to find some way to keep in touch.'

'And Tony Rees saw you out of the studio,' Charles suddenly recalled.

'Exactly. When we reached the Reception of W.E.T. House, I asked him whether, for a financial consideration, he would keep us in touch with the production schedule.'

'You chose the right person. For a financial consideration Tony Rees would have done anything.'

'He certainly didn't need too much persuading. But at least we now had a way of keeping vaguely in touch with what was going on. Of course, we were not allowed in the studios, but they couldn't keep us away from the filming.'

'So you and Louisa were down at Swanage from the start?'

W. T. Wintergreen nodded, and in Charles's mind a whole new set of ideas tumbled into place. 'In fact, you were in that pub I went into on the Sunday evening. You were sitting in the alcove with Tony – you had your backs to the door – and he only came up to me in such a friendly way because he didn't want me to see you.'

'Yes.'

'And the reason he spilled his drink over me was only to distract my attention while you two went out of the pub.'

'That is what happened, yes.'

'I've just realised something else,' Charles continued in a burst of excitement. 'You and Louisa were in the crowd, all wrapped up in anoraks, when we were filming in Corfe Castle. And that was why Tony Rees wanted to borrow Mort Verdon's schedule for the next episode. He gave it to you up at the castle that afternoon.'

A nod confirmed this.

'So why did he have to be killed?' asked Charles quietly.

'He said he had actually witnessed the murder of Sippy Stokes.'

'I see.' Charles was pleased to have another of his conjectures proved right.
'And he wanted a large price for his silence?'

'A much larger price than I could afford to pay.'

'So you pushed him out of the window in the castle ruins?'

'It was not intentional murder. Again, I wasn't thinking straight. I was angry. There was a scuffle. He fell. I didn't know at the time that he had died.'

'Convenient that he had, though.'

'Oh, yes. Very convenient.'

'Which brings us,' said Charles, 'to Russell Bentley.'

'Russell Bentley…' W. T. Wintergreen looked drained; the emotional strain of her confession was beginning to tell.

'Let me say what I think happened, Winifred. You tell me if I'm right.'
She nodded acquiescence.

'It wasn't what he was doing to the Stanislas Braid character that worried you so much as what he was doing to the Stanislas/Christina relationship. His constant desire to play down the emotion between the two of them upset you. That relationship was for you one of the most important parts of the books, and he was trying to kill it. Then, during the filming in Corfe Castle, you heard Russell arguing that one of your favourite scenes, the avowal of Stanislas and Christina's love for each other when their lives were threatened, should be rewritten. You found the rewrite in Will Parton's room, with the note on it saying that it was all Russell's idea, and from that moment Russell Bentley was your next target. Am I right?'

'You are right,' she conceded graciously. 'This morning I hid myself near where you were filming and when my opportunity came, I shot him. My third murder.'

'No,' said Charles.

'No?'

'You missed. Russell Bentley isn't dead.'

W. T. Wintergreen slumped with a little sigh against her chair. 'Thank God.'

There was a long silence in the tiny sitting room. Finally, Charles asked, 'Where's Louisa?'

'Upstairs,' W. T. Wintergreen replied softly. 'Upstairs. I will go to prison. I will not be able to look after her anymore. Louisa needs someone to look after her.'

'Yes.' Charles smiled grimly. 'Can I see her, Winifred?'

The bedroom was on a scale with the rest of the cottage. It was decorated in the subtlest of pastel shades. The wallpaper was almost white, with a tiny motif of a pale yellow flower. Under an eiderdown of the palest pink, her head propped up on a pillow of the same colour, lay Louisa Railton.

Her hair was neatly brushed and laid out across the pillow. Her eyes were closed, and her body was completely relaxed. There was no movement.

Charles looked across at the old crime writer. Down Winifred Railton's lined cheeks tears flowed unchecked.

'There,' she said, 'Mr. Paris. The last in my series of murders.'

Chapter Seventeen

'NO,' SAID Charles Paris. 'It's the first.'

'What do you mean?'

'I mean that you have never murdered anyone outside your fiction. Until today. And this' – he indicated the body on the bed – 'I think would qualify as a mercy killing rather than a murder.'

'I did kill them,' W. T. Wintergreen asserted. 'I did.'

Charles shook his head.

'Why don't you believe me, Mr. Paris?'

'I don't believe you partly because of your personality. You say you committed the murders in fits of irrationality, but you aren't the sort of person to suffer from fits of irrationality. Your head is far too firmly screwed on for you to behave as you claim to have done. Yes, the *Stanislas Braid* books are very close to your heart. And yes, you were upset by some of the things W.E.T. was doing to your property, but you wouldn't have committed murder – not for something like that.'

'You don't know. You don't know me that well,' she objected defiantly.

'Another give-away,' Charles went on, 'was your reaction just now when I told you Russell Bentley hadn't been hurt this morning. If you were the crazed, irrational creature you claim to be, you would have been disappointed because the latest in your series of murders had failed. But no, you were relieved, deeply relieved that another life had not been wantonly lost.'

There was a silence. Then she announced firmly, 'I'm going to the police, and I'm going to tell them exactly what I've told you.'

'Yes, I'm sure you are,' said Charles. 'And maybe they'll believe you, and maybe they won't. I should think, if someone like me can see through your story, professional police investigators won't have much difficulty in doing the same.'

'But I –'

'The reason you're going to the police is because the police have been in touch with you, isn't it?'

She nodded. 'The police in Dorset talked to us yesterday after Tony Rees's death. Then, in the evening, we had a call from Scotland Yard, the people who have been investigating the actress's death. They said they wanted to talk to us. Either we could fix a time, or if we hadn't made contact within twenty-four hours, they would come and find us.'

Charles looked at his watch. 'And your twenty-four hours is nearly up.'

'Yes.'

'Which is why you killed Louisa.'

'As I said, she couldn't cope with my being away.' W. T. Wintergreen frowned, as if in pain. 'I don't like you talking about my killing her. She didn't feel a thing. I often put her to bed with her sleeping draft, but this time I just gave her a larger dose. She's all right now. She won't have to know about any of this, any of the unpleasantness.'

'You've always protected her from unpleasantness, haven't you?'

'She was never very strong. She found life...difficult.'

'So do most of us. But very few are lucky enough to have someone like you to keep the world at bay.'

He moved across to Louisa Railton's girlish dressing table and picked up a silver-framed photograph. The picture showed a beautiful girl in her early teens. But for the anachronism of the haircut and the collar of the dress that showed at her neck, it could have been Joanne Rhymer. 'I can see why you were so pleased when the part was recast.' He turned to face W. T. Wintergreen. 'Louisa was Christina, wasn't she?'

'I don't know what you mean.'

'Oh, I think you do. I think you wrote the books partly for her.'

'Well, perhaps partly. We were very close.' The old bespectacled eyes strayed across to the bed, as if hoping that its occupant would suddenly come back to life.

'As you said, the books were "cozy". They dressed up unpalatable things in a palatable form. Murder, the ultimate crime, is dressed up as an intellectual game. Other crimes – equally offensive crimes – were also dressed up and sanitised.'

'I don't understand what you're talking about, Mr. Paris.'

'Yes, you do. Stanislas Braid was your father, Miss Railton.'

'No, he wasn't. As I said, our father was a very difficult man, and Stanislas is –'

'I mean that Stanislas Braid was how you dressed up your father. Just as you dressed up your sister as Christina. And the idealised relationship between the two of them was how you dressed up the rather less attractive reality of the relationship between your father and your sister.'

She let out a little gasp, staggered slightly, found her way to a bedside chair.

'I'm right, aren't I?' murmured Charles.

Very slowly, the old head nodded. 'In those days such things weren't talked about. You didn't have them blazoned across every newspaper and television programme. But yes, after our mother died, our father did' – she swallowed – 'start to touch Louisa.'

'And she never really recovered from the trauma?'

'No, I suppose not. I don't fully understand these things, but certainly...in some ways my sister never grew up. She couldn't cope with life.'

'So it went on for some years?'

'For some years, yes. In a way, I don't think Louisa realised there was anything wrong. She loved him, you see, and she thought love made everything all right. So long as he was alive, she was strange, maybe immature, not fully grown-up, but it was after he died that she really broke down.'

'And from then on you had a full-time job looking after her. Which is why you never had time to start writing again.' W. T. Wintergreen acknowledged the truth of this with an almost imperceptible nod. 'And was it after your father's death that Louisa started to become obsessed by the *Stanislas Braid* books?'

'Yes. She'd always liked them, been amused by them, but after our father died…yes, she became obsessed by them.'

'So she was the one whose whole identity was threatened by the changes that W.E.T. was making to the books, particularly changes to the character of Christina or Christina's relationship with her father.'

W. T. Wintergreen made only a token gesture of dissent at this.

'I think, Miss Railton, that almost everything you told me downstairs about how the murders were committed was true, so long as you cast Louisa in the role for which you cast yourself. She was the one who saw Sippy Stokes in the studio and was seized by the impulse to pick up that candlestick.'

'She – my sister was not well. She had times when she was not herself.'

'Yes, and you nursed her through all of them. But she had never committed murder before, had she?'

W. T. Wintergreen shook her head.

'And then she told you what she'd done. Told you, I would imagine, with pride. And that news put you in such an emotional state that you weren't up to going into the studio the following day.

'But you managed to put it from your mind. The death seemed to be accepted as an accident, the new Christina was wonderful, the chances for success of the series seemed greatly improved. As you said, you could almost believe that the crime hadn't happened.'

'Yes.'

'Until the murder of Tony Rees. With that one I don't think what you said downstairs was quite accurate. When you claimed that you had killed him, you said it was an accident. But Louisa murdered him quite deliberately, didn't she?'

There was no response.

'And when I saw you on Durlston Head this morning, the reason you looked so bewildered was not because you had just shot at Russell Bentley but because you had just snatched the gun from Louisa after she had shot at him.'

The old lady was silent. She no longer made any attempt to deny the truth of what he said.

The silence in the childlike bedroom extended for a long minute. Then, with an effort, W. T. Wintergreen clamped her hands on to the arms of the chair and heaved herself wearily upright. 'Well, I think I'd better get to see the police now. Don't want to put them to the trouble of coming out to fetch me.'

'When you do see them,' Charles Paris asked, 'will you tell them the truth? Or will you continue to do what you've spent all your life doing: protect your sister?'

'That,' W. T. Wintergreen replied with dignity, 'is my decision.' And with something that was almost a grin, she continued: 'The one inalienable right of crime writers in their own stories is to choose whodunit.'

Chapter Eighteen

OUTSIDE FOR THE first time that year, June had decided to blaze, but no dribble of sunlight percolated through the grimy windows of the St. John Chrysostom Mission for Vagrants Lesser Hall. The only effect of the change in the weather had been to reheat the trapped, moted air inside to a new staleness.

It was the first day of rehearsal for the last episode of *Stanislas Braid*, '*The Mashie Niblick Murder*.' There had been much discussion about this title. Though that was what the original W. T. Wintergreen book had been called, Ben Docherty had been of the opinion – with some justification – that the average member of the I.T.V. audience hadn't a clue what a mashie niblick was. Will Parton, taking a perverse liking to the title, had argued that golf was a very popular television sport. The producer had countered that though golf was indeed popular, clubs were now referred to by numbers and not by exotic names.

'We must definitely change the title,' he had said firmly.

'No, we mustn't,' Will Parton had said equally firmly. 'The original book was called *The Mashie Niblick Murder*.'

'Oh, come on,' Ben Docherty had objected. 'You've changed everything else. Why this sudden conscience about the title?'

The argument had gone back and forth for some time, until the Producer pulled rank and said he was in charge of the series, he would make that kind of decision. And his irrevocable decision was that the title should be changed.

This conversation, however, had taken place in the morning. Later in the day, when Ben Docherty, the alcohol dying in him, was at the nadir of his mid-afternoon listlessness, Will Parton had simply handed his typescript over to the P.A. with instructions for her to type it up as it was, title and all. By the time the producer noticed what had happened, '*The Mashie Niblick Murder*' had appeared on too many forms and schedules for it to be worth the effort of alteration.

With the progress of the series, listlessness had become Ben Docherty's dominant mood, and from him the rot seeped through to everyone else involved in the production. The gradual realisation came that as a television series *Stanislas Braid* was actually not very good. W. T. Wintergreen's books were dull and dated, and in spite of Will Parton's valiant efforts, the scripts never quite escaped being dull and dated, too. A charismatic central performance might perhaps have lifted the whole venture, but as the series went on, Russell Bentley's limitations became increasingly apparent. He was basically a very wooden actor.

No one ever actually said the series was going to be a disaster. Indeed, to use the word disaster would have been overstating the case. The programmes would go out, and be dutifully watched with half an eye in those millions of households where the control was never moved from I.T.V., but they would never rise above the gently slopping surface of customary television mediocrity.

In the early days of the production much had been said about prime placings, about the series 'spearheading the autumn schedules', but gradually such talk died away, to be replaced by rumours of *Stanislas Braid* being 'held over', even rumblings of that worst of all fates, 'being held over till next summer'. The summer schedules, everyone knew, were the Sahara of television, in which programmes slowly dehydrated and perished, unseen and unmourned.

In the same way, the talk of a second series, which had been rife during the first month of recording, trickled away to nothing. The second-series options on the artistes, so carefully agreed by their agents and the W.E.T. casting directors, were destined never to be taken up.

No one commented on these changes. They had all been in the business long enough to have experienced plenty of previous dashed hopes. The only positive reaction came from Jimmy Sheet. Finally realising the true quality of the vehicle in which he had been intended to make his mark as an actor and remembering who had recommended it to him, he sacked his agent. Then, deciding that he still hadn't wrung all there was to be wrung out of the music business, he started organising a final international concert tour. He also made a killing on property deals in Miami and started buying up office blocks in Rio de Janeiro.

Other less organised members of the *Stanislas Braid* production team also started to make plans for what to do at the end of their contracts.

Russell Bentley was already committed to a national tour of a venerable stage thriller, which a new producer was convinced could follow the path of other venerable stage thrillers through the provinces and into the West End. So the star, who had by now lost interest in his performance as Stanislas Braid, was much exercised in going through the play script, deciding which lines would have to be changed before he could fully realise his customary performance as Russell Bentley.

Joanne Rhymer, by diligently working her way through all of the straight men involved in *Stanislas Braid*, had by the end of the series achieved full Blue Nun status. This was confirmed by the arbiter of such distinctions, Mort Verdon. She was, needless to say, going straight on to another job. Ben Docherty had introduced her to a London Weekend Television producer, who, impressed by the range of Joanne's talents, had booked her instantly for the role of the hero's girlfriend (and who knew what else) in his forthcoming series.

Her mother – surprisingly, given the usual duration of her liaisons – was still with Ben Docherty. As soon as recording on *Stanislas Braid* was completed, the producer was going to take Gwen Rhymer on a gastronomic tour of France. Assuming he survived the alcoholic and physical demands of that, he would then return to W.E.T. to supervise the remaining post-production work on *Stanislas Braid* and to start work on 'an exciting new project'. The exciting new project was a drama series about adolescent problems for schools. Though this assignment might be seen by outsiders as a demotion from the mainstream of television drama, Ben Docherty's boss had assured him that it was 'a key appointment in a pivotal area'. What this meant was that the commercial television franchises were shortly going to be up for renewal, and W.E.T. was making one of its periodic assertions of concern in the area of public-service programme-making.

Rick Landor, having directed the penultimate episode of *Stanislas Braid*, had some editing and sound dubbing to do on the series and then would be moving on to direct a game show for Thames Television. His ambition of a feature film remained as far off as ever.

Will Parton's ambition was a major serious stage play. He had had the idea for years; it was just a matter of finding the time to write it; and throughout the series he had been promising himself that he would settle down to the play, ignoring all other distractions, the minute his work on *Stanislas Braid* was finished.

But then he had had an offer from Yorkshire Television to script a series they were doing about nineteenth-century medical pioneers. Only take about three months.

Well, four or five months with the rewrites. And the money was, once again, very good. Will spent a whole evening with Charles Paris in the W.E.T. bar, agonising over his dilemma, before making the inevitable decision. After all, he reasoned, it was only five months maximum. And the extra money would give him even more of a cushion when he got down to writing what he really should be writing. So the major serious stage play, a project of which he was growing increasingly terrified, was deferred yet again.

Charles Paris himself had, needless to say, not made any plans for what to do when his W.E.T. contract expired. Presumably, the following week would see him once again signing up at Lisson Grove Unemployment Office, just around the corner from W.E.T. House. It was ironic, really. While he was working there, he had no need to take advantage of that accident of geography, but the minute his employment ceased, he would have to start making the trek over again.

He'd feel the draft a bit when he was back to just the giro cheque. He had had no difficulty in accustoming himself to the regular W.E.T. money. Or in spending it with equal regularity. Come the end of the final recording in less than a fortnight's time, it would all be gone. And, of course, on such earnings there would be tax to pay...Still, that was next year's problem.

He looked around the St. John Chrysostom Mission for Vagrants Lesser Hall and thought how thoroughly W. T. Wintergreen had been forgotten. No one in the rehearsal room, except for Charles Paris, was aware of her own small crime and her sister Louisa's greater crimes. No one was aware that she had made a confession to the police and been arrested. Nor that in prison, awaiting a trial that must surely have released her, she had quietly died, her life perhaps without purpose after her sister's death.

Charles Paris had been the only person from *Stanislas Braid* to attend the quiet cremation. Had it been one of the actors on the series who had died or a member of the production team, W.E.T. would have been effusive in representation and flowers, but then no one really knew about W. T. Wintergreen's death. And, after all, she had been only a writer.

The scene in the rehearsal room was predictable. As foretold by Maurice Skellern, read-throughs had been abandoned, and rehearsals now began straightaway, with blocking movements around the taped-out sets on the floor. Russell Bentley was arguing over some line that he felt was out of character. Ben Docherty was saying it might need changing. Will Parton was remonstrating violently that he wasn't going to do any more bloody rewrites. Joanne Rhymer was coolly eyeing the young actor who was that episode's murder victim.

In other words, it was business as usual on *Stanislas Braid*. Charles Paris's eyelids were heavy. Maybe he could doze off a little of the previous night's excess before they got to the first Little Breckington Police Station scene.

Must start looking around for some work, he thought lazily as he drifted off. Not a good time of year, though. Very quiet, the beginning of the summer, as Maurice Skellern always said. Mind you, Maurice Skellern always said every other time of year was very quiet, too.

There was something else, though, wasn't there? Something else niggled in Charles's mind. Something he'd been intending to do for six weeks or so. What was it?

Oh, yes. Of course. It was Charles Paris's last thought as sleep took over: Must ring Frances.

CORPORATE BODIES

To Roger and Hilary

Chapter One

ON OF THE reasons why I became an actor, Charles Paris reflected wryly as he swung the wheel of the forklift truck, was to avoid tedious jobs like this. To avoid any job in fact with a predictability about it, any job for which you had to turn up at the same predictable hour every day, in which you had to climb a predictable career structure, in anticipation of a predictable retirement age and a predictable pension.

Actually, when he came to think about it, he wouldn't have minded the predictable pension. Or the predictable salary, come to that. He'd survived more than thirty years of the actor's fluctuating fortunes – long periods of 'signing on' enlivened by occasional bouts of work – but it was a kind of insecurity into which he'd never quite relaxed. As he got older, he did fantasise increasingly, with a slight wistfulness, about the idea of a regular income. This shaming thought was not one that he'd have mentioned to a fellow-actor, but it was there, lurking.

Maybe if he'd had a regular job, he conjectured, with regular hours, a regular salary and regular promotion, his life might have had more shape. Maybe his marriage might even have stayed together. Though it was difficult to envisage Frances in the role of a corporate wife. Everything might have been better, though. It was hard to be sure.

On the other hand, it was extremely easy to be sure that any employment of that kind would have driven him mad with boredom.

Charles Paris was an actor, like it or not. Even when, as in some years, his earnings were too low to qualify for taxation; even when, as in slightly better years, the taxman had the nerve to hound him for a slice of the little he had; even when directors, blind to his obvious genius, callously turned him down for parts; even when critics advised him to take up market gardening (as *The Financial Times* once had); whatever disasters arose, Charles Paris's mind couldn't cope with the idea of being in any other profession.

And driving a forklift truck in the Delmoleen warehouse for a morning was quite fun. It was only the idea of having to do it every morning – and every afternoon, come to that – that was insufferably tedious.

He looked across at Trevor, who actually did have to do it every day. The operator looked sullen. His bad temper, however, was not caused by the eternal tedium of his job, but by the fact that that particular morning Charles Paris was doing it.

The trouble was that that morning the job involved *speaking* and, while Trevor was a dab hand at forklifts, capable of performing pirouettes on a man-up orderpicker, or turning a narrow-aisle swivel-head reach-truck on a 5p piece to bring down a palletised ton's load stored twenty feet above his head, when it came to *speaking* he wasn't so hot. Which was why the company had brought in an actor to do the speaking for him.

Delmoleen was making a video to show at trade fairs, encourage recruitment and generally bolster company solidarity. Charles Paris had become involved in exactly the same way that he got most of his jobs – through a friend.

Charles did have an agent, but it often seemed that getting work for his clients was against Maurice Skellern's religion. Taking 15 per cent on the work they got for themselves was, however, quite within the Commandments, and Charles, who had set up the Delmoleen job direct, was anxious lest his agent should find out about it.

The friend who had introduced him to his first corporate video was called Will Parton, a writer whom Charles Paris had encountered on the *Stanislas Braid* television series. Will's destiny in life, as he kept telling anyone and everyone who would listen, was to write a major serious stage play. He'd had the idea for years, just a matter of carving out enough time actually to get the thing written.

But the creation of the *magnum opus* kept getting deferred by television work. 'Well, you have to pay the bills,' as Will kept saying with an apologetic shrug. In fact, for Will Parton, as a single man in a highly-paid profession living in a two-bedroom flat, the bills were not too daunting. He could easily have afforded a six-month sabbatical to get the play written – had he really had the will to do so.

But he found television work so lucrative and – once he'd taken on board the fact that it involved more *re*writing than writing – so comparatively easy, that the serious stage play, like the horizon, constantly receded. Writing a corporate video for Delmoleen was, in spite of the way Will kept talking about 'taking on a new challenge' and 'broadening my range', simply another way of staving off the evil moment when he'd have to find out if his play idea really was any good.

But he wasn't involved just as writer. Will Parton, perhaps in reaction to the countless years he had spent being ordered around by countless directors, had recently gone into production. He had formed a company called *Parton Parcel*, through which he hoped to dip his own ladle into the corporate gravy train. Though its impressive letterhead featured the names of various friends to give a bit of *gravitas*, the organisation was in fact a one-man band. Will reckoned to bring in other staff as and when required. When he got a production, he would hire in freelance directors, cameramen, soundmen and so on. There was no shortage of such skilled personnel around; the recession in television was biting everywhere.

The Delmoleen contract was the first that *Parton Parcel* had secured. Will had followed up a contact in the company, who had introduced him to the Delmoleen Marketing Director just at the moment when the Managing Director had expressed the need for a morale-boosting video. Will Parton had had a meeting with the Marketing Director, who knew nothing of that particular world, and produced the requisite bullshit, as a result of which the *Parton Parcel* tender, suitably modest for such a relatively new set-up, had been accepted.

Charles Paris had had no compunction about accepting Will's offer to put him up for the video. The writer had rung one evening and said, 'The Delmoleen people'll take you on my say-so, no problem. They don't know anything about actors.'

Deciding, as he usually did on such occasions, not to take offence at the inadvertent slight, Charles had responded enthusiastically. The previous few months had been, in Maurice Skellern's favourite phrase, 'quiet, very quiet'. In fact, the previous year had been almost totally silent, one of the worst of Charles's career. The rumbles of approaching recession had led to cutbacks in the theatre and advertising and, as the commercial companies began the ritual circling which precedes the award of new franchises, television opportunities had also become very limited. Things were always bad in his profession, but Charles had never known them quite this bad.

'What is Delmoleen?' he asked after Will had confirmed an interview time for the following day.

'Bedtime drink...'

'Well, yes, Delmoleen "Bedtime" is the best known product in this country, but they manufacture a whole bundle of other stuff. All food products. You'd be amazed at the diversity, and the places they export to. I tell you, Charles, I've had to read so much guff on Delmoleen that I'm now one of the world's experts. I could bore you for hours on the subject.'

'Don't bother.'

'No, I'll leave that to the Delmoleen executives. God, they take it all so seriously. Make Muslim Fundamentalists look insipid...Ooh, that is a thought. One thing, Charles...'

'Yes?'

'You have to take it seriously too. No giggling.'

His voice took on a tone of injured innocence. 'Would I?'

'Won't even answer that. No, please, whatever crap they talk – and I can guarantee you they will talk plenty of crap – straight face, OK? And don't you dare catch my eye.'

'I will be as demure as a Jane Austen heroine.'

'Hm.' The writer didn't sound convinced.

'Oh, Will, what should I wear?'

'For the interview?'

'Right. In my experience of commercials and things, if you don't turn up in the right gear, you don't get the part.'

'Yes, it'll be just the same with this lot. They haven't got the imagination to realise that an actor's capable of wearing different clothes.' Will dropped into the drawl of a theatrical pseud. 'OK, love, the major role you are being considered for in my new oeuvre is that of...a forklift truck driver.'

'A forklift truck driver?' Charles echoed in his best Lady Bracknell. 'I don't believe I am familiar with the customary garb of forklift truck drivers.'

'Well, if you follow the sartorial style of Trevor, who is one of the real ones on-site, you'll go for a tasteful Status Quo T-shirt, a pair of appropriately understated tracksuit bottoms and rather grubby trainers.'

Charles moved into his Victorian actor-manager voice. 'I will obtain the requisite wardrobe. And vocally...? I dare say a person in such employment would favour the vowels of the proletariat...'

'Yes, better be a bit "off".'

'It shall be done.'

'OK, Charles, see you tomorrow. Train to Bedford, change there on to the branch line to Stenley Curton. Factory's just opposite the station. Go to main reception, ask for Ken Colebourne's office.'

'Right. Thanks for puffing my name up.'

'No problem. But remember – don't giggle!'

The audition – no, he must stop saying that, it gave away how long he'd been in the business, no actor younger than Charles Paris ever used the word 'audition', they all talked about 'interviews' these days – the interview for the Delmoleen job was not the most artistically taxing that he had ever undergone.

As any actor should, he had of course prepared for the encounter to come, trying out voices and expressions in front of his mirror, and taking on the character with its tracksuit, T-shirt and trainers. (It was a mild May. He didn't need any kind of topcoat.)

For the train to Bedford, he had even gone to the extent of buying a copy of the *Sun* rather than his customary *Times*. Unfortunately, having read every word of the paper twice before the train drew out of St Pancras, he was reduced to looking out of the window for the rest of his journey. Still, he comforted himself, that is probably what a forklift truck driver would have done, so, boring though it might be, he was at least continuing to get into character.

He reflected that, to go the whole hog, he should really have got into a 'Smoking' compartment and lit up a Players Number Six, but there were some things, even for his art, Charles Paris could not bring himself to do.

Will Parton's directions had been precise and Charles found his way to the Delmoleen site without any hitches. The view from the exit to Stenley Curton railway station was dominated by a long two-storey brick building directly opposite. Probably late nineteenth century, it had been built for some unspecified and discontinued industrial purpose, but now unmistakably belonged to Delmoleen. The company logo arched hugely over the main gates, and reappeared on the new fascia that had been grafted on to the reception area.

When Charles asked for Ken Colebourne, he was directed out of the main building to the township of low modern rectangles behind. Though these looked boring and functional from the outside, the interior of the office into which he was ushered was anonymously graceful, with black wood and smoked glass, low tables, charcoal sofas and armchairs. Expensively photographed and discreetly framed Delmoleen products looked down from the walls.

Will was already there, and introduced the other two men. The writer was dressed in a voluminous suit and exotic tie, a marked contrast from his customary uniform of denim shirt and jeans. 'They don't listen to you if you're not wearing a suit,' he had confided. 'Always got to go for the gravitas in this business, you know, Charles.'

Charles was invited to sink into one of the sofas. Coffee was produced. He sat there, waiting to be asked to do his bit, but Ken Colebourne, the Marketing Director, and Robin Pritchard, the Product Manager for Biscuits and Cereals, showed no interest at all in his artistic abilities.

This was probably just as well. On the phone the night before, Charles and Will Parton had spun some childish fantasies about suitable audition pieces for the meaty role under consideration.

Charles had opened the bidding rather feebly with 'To lift or not to lift, that is the question'. Then Will had gone all Keatsian with a reference to 'bursting Joy's grape against his pallet fine'. Charles had countered by 'Once more unto the reach-truck, friends, once more/ Or fill the shelves up with unwanted stock'; after which their conversation had degenerated into a series of variations on the word 'fork', until Charles ended things by saying that such jokes were terribly vulgar and 'the kind of thing with which he would no longer have any truck'.

The result of all this was that, if he had been asked to read anything, the giggle-risk-factor might have become unacceptably high. Being in costume and character, as always, reduced the danger, but didn't eliminate it completely. Still, so long as he didn't catch Will's eye, Charles found he could look appropriately and soberly impressed while Ken Colebourne expatiated on the many virtues of the Delmoleen company and products.

'I mean, we are very big. And when I say big, I mean big. Isn't that right, Robin?'

'Oh yes, Ken. Delmoleen is big.'

'I mean, still an independent corporation, we haven't been swallowed up into one of the multinationals, but the fact remains that our outreach is big.'

'Global,' Robin Pritchard confirmed, 'global.'

'Ah. Right. Good,' said Charles, in his enthusiastic but slightly noncommittal 'off' voice. Actually, it was the one he had used in *The Birthday Party* at Bury St Edmunds ('Charles Paris's performance seemed nearer to Panto than Pinter' – *Eastern Daily Press*).

'But, though we're big,' Ken Colebourne went on, 'we are still a caring company. Caring for the environment, obviously...Isn't that right, Robin?'

'Right, Ken.'

'But also caring for our employees. And that's what this video's about. It's to show that everyone the company employs is part of the Delmoleen family, and that "big" doesn't automatically mean impersonal.'

The pause extended. Charles, reminding himself he wasn't back in *The Birthday Party*, broke the silence with a 'Right'.

'This is something that's a big priority with B.T..'

'Right,' said Charles again, wondering mildly what British Telecom had to do with food products.

'He's very much behind the whole concept.'

Clocking the fact that 'B.T.' was a person, Charles threw in a 'Good' by way of variety.

'Isn't that right, Robin?'

'Oh, certainly, Ken. The whole thing's really Brian's baby.'

So that sorted out the 'B' of 'B.T.' Brian who? Clearly someone of considerable importance in the hierarchy. Charles nodded thoughtfully, deciding that, given the awe with which the name had been mentioned, it would be inappropriate to ask who 'B.T.' or 'Brian' was.

He wondered if the difference in the way the two men spoke of their superior was another reflection of the difference in their styles. 'B.T.' had a dated and distanced feel to it, while the 'Brian' implied not only a more informal approach, but also greater intimacy in the Product Manager's relationship.

'And you've always been the midwife to Brian's babies, haven't you, Ken?'

As Robin Pritchard said this, Charles was aware of an undercurrent in the younger man's voice. It was nothing as positive as insolence, but the intonation implied some kind of challenge. And a flicker in the Marketing Director's expression showed that he was aware of that challenge.

They were a contrasted pair; Ken Colebourne short and thick-set, grey-haired but with eyebrows and moustache still black. The suit was bluish with close white stripes: the tie, red, blue and white bands of different widths that didn't quite amount to anything regimental. Ken's voice had a Midland roughness. He gave the impression of a tough pragmatist who had worked up the hard way. Not a man with a great sense of humour. Certainly not a man to cross.

The Product Manager for Biscuits and Cereals was at least twenty years younger, and had more obvious educational gloss. University certainly, possibly business school as well. The brown suit on his long frame was more fashionably floppy than Ken Colebourne's, the tie looked like a detail from some twentieth-century abstract painting. Robin Pritchard wore round tortoiseshell glasses, and had either a weak mouth or a permanently sardonic expression. Or possibly both.

Suddenly Charles identified the quality in the younger man's voice. Robin Pritchard was, ever so slightly, sending up Ken Colebourne. His older colleague was fully aware of this, and didn't like it. Ken was the one who was meant to be running the interview, but Robin very subtly implied that it was taking place by his licence.

'The reason we wanted to see you, Mr Paris...' the Marketing Director went on. 'I mean, obviously we respect Will's advice and his recommendation of you as an actor...but we had to check that you look right.'

'Right,' Charles echoed reasonably.

'You see, this video will be seen all over the place. I mean, in-house, as induction to new employees...quite possibly for recruitment purposes...probably at trade fairs...It is going to cover the whole international scope of the Delmoleen operation – and that is big, as I may have said.'

Yes, thought Charles, you have said it. A few times.

'So, it's important that we don't have anyone in the video who looks wrong for the Delmoleen image.'

'No, we do have a global profile to maintain, after all, don't we, Ken?' Now that Charles had identified the element of mockery in Robin Pritchard's manner, it seemed more overt.

As intended, the Marketing Director was a little flustered. 'Yes, yes, of course. So, really, Mr Paris, we've called you in just to have a look at you, see how you fit in to the Delmoleen picture.'

'Well, here I am,' said Charles, spreading his arms wide in an ingenuous shrug.

'Yes...yes...' said Ken Colebourne, focusing on the actor as if for the first time, as though he hadn't been able to form any visual impressions while he'd been talking. After a moment's scrutiny, there was another thoughtful 'Yes'; then another; then 'I'm not really too sure.'

'Oh, for heaven's sake, Ken. You're not at a cattle market.' Robin Pritchard turned to Charles with confidential bonhomie. 'I do apologise for my colleague's bad manners, Mr Paris.'

'No problem.' And it wasn't. Compared to the diplomatic skills demonstrated by some television directors, this was the height of good manners.

Robin Pritchard's words were a problem for Ken Colebourne, however. Again, the Marketing Director had winced, biting back some angry riposte. He knew that, in a verbal contest, the younger man would be the more nimble and only make him look clumsy.

'To be quite frank, Robin, I'm a bit worried about the age factor...'

Charles tried not to show that the barb had been hurtful. Like all actors, he always tried to look younger than his real age. This was not – or at least not wholly – for the reasons of vanity that drive some women to such deceptions; it was a matter of simple survival. There are few enough parts around, anyway; no actor wants to disqualify himself from any of them by being too old. Whenever Charles was asked at an audition – sorry, interview – the direct question, 'How old are you?', his automatic reply was, 'Forty-eight, but play younger.' Which wasn't the exact truth, but near enough for an actor.

Ken Colebourne expanded his point. 'I mean, remember, what B.T.'s keen to do is to project the overall image of Delmoleen. Is that going to be helped by having a forklift truck driver on the verge of retirement?'

Ouch! Now that one really did hurt.

Will Parton came to his friend's rescue. 'The point is, Ken, that we want to project the whole company...you know, like an extended family. So we've got to have a spread of ages. I mean, the kid who's going to be in the office for this warehouse sequence, Dayna, is only about eighteen...but we need the other end of the spectrum too. In an extended family, you've got kids...and you've got grandfathers...'

How dare you, Will? Even though he was a grandfather three times over, Charles Paris wasn't enjoying the direction of the conversation one bit.

'I'm still not sure...'

Will came in with the clincher. 'Brian was very keen on this when I talked to him. I mentioned the "extended family" idea and he liked it a lot.'

'Oh. Oh well, that's fine then. Consider yourself hired, Mr Paris.' Ken Colebourne reached a stubby hand across his desk. Robin Pritchard seemed to find something infinitely amusing in a vortex at the end of his tie. Will Parton looked innocently up to the ceiling. Charles Paris tried to avoid his friend's eye.

And that's how he got the job of being a forklift truck driver.

Chapter Two

'NO, NO, NO, NO!' said Trevor. 'You got to swing the wheel round with more power than that.'

'Well, I don't want to go crashing into –' Charles began.

'I thought that looked fine, actually,' the Director, Griff Merricks, interposed in a conciliatory tone. Not difficult for him; conciliatory was the only tone he possessed.

Now over sixty, Griff's main claim to fame in the business was his 'unflappability'. Charles suspected that this quality, which at times verged on torpor, arose from the fact that the director had no interest whatsoever in any of the work he did. He was a competent framer of shots, unimpeded by imagination, who had pottered along amiably enough in the BBC until he reached retirement age, and was therefore now ideally qualified to direct corporate videos.

Will Parton, having worked with Griff on a few projects and knowing him to be 'safe' to the point of tedium, had offered him the Delmoleen job on behalf of *Parton Parcel*. Glad once again to be in work, Griff Merricks continued as he always had done, resolutely safeguarding apple-carts from the risk of upset.

Trevor the forklift truck driver, however, seemed bent on a rampage of apple-cart upsetting. At the beginning of the morning he had been most amenable, keen to show off his forklifting skills and demonstrating a lively interest in the camera that was being used for the filming ('Like, a bit of a hobby of mine, video, like...'

In fact, he had been perfectly docile until he discovered what Charles's role was to be in the proceedings. From that moment, he had made as much trouble as he could. And was clearly not about to change his behaviour.

'It didn't bloody look fine!' he protested. 'Listen, I've done the tricky bit on the truck, haven't I? I actually brought the pallet down from the shelves, didn't I?'

'Yes,' Griff Merricks conceded soothingly. 'But when we filmed that, we did it in longshot. What we're doing now is cuffing to Charles in close-up to say the lines. All we need to see from him on the truck is the final turn of the steering wheel.'

'But what I'm saying is that the people watching this video's going to think that he and me're the same person.'

'Yes, that's the idea.'

'That's why you've put us in these bleeding overalls, isn't it?'

Trevor pulled disparagingly at the pristine blue fabric. Charles looked down at his overalls, thinking of all the wasted effort he'd put into matching Trevor's usual costume. He caught the eye of Will Parton, who was clearly thinking the same thing. The writer smugly preened in his neat suit and tie. Charles looked abruptly away. If he started giggling now, the aggrieved Trevor was quite likely to assume the laughter was at his expense and become even more belligerent.

'Well, it's partly that, Trevor,' Griff Merricks was agreeing tactfully, '– so that you and Charles look alike – but it's also because the overalls have got the Delmoleen logo on them, and throughout the film Ken's very keen to build up the corporate identity, so that whenever we see one of the workers – I mean, a Delmoleen employee other than a management executive – we see them wearing these overalls.'

'But nobody in the company actually does wear them.'

'No, Trevor, but for the video they do.'

'Huh. Right load of cobblers this video's going to be then, isn't it?'

'We-ell...'

Charles's gaze wandered round the warehouse. It was a massive space, divided into sections by high walls of shelving loaded with pallets of Delmoleen products. Other yellow forklift trucks lay idle in the narrow aisles. The shutters of the loading bays along one wall were open, showing the maws of empty lorries. At one end of the space were offices, two prefabricated structures, stacked on top of each other like shoe boxes against the wall.

It felt strange to be working there. Not that Charles hadn't worked in stranger settings, but that had always been for drama, when all the resources of the location had been dedicated to the production. In this case, the priorities were different, and the film crew was clearly a positive hindrance to the main business of the warehouse.

Still, Trevor seemed impervious to the resentment of his work-mates and was in no mood to expedite the morning's shoot. 'Point I'm making is, if you have him' – a contemptuous finger was jerked towards Charles – 'turning the wheel of the truck like a wanker, people who see it're going to think I'm a wanker, aren't they?'

'It's a point of view...' Griff Merricks looked nonplussed. Maybe conciliation wasn't going to be enough in this particular case; unfortunately it was the only weapon his armoury contained.

Charles stepped into the breach. 'Look, Trevor, perhaps you could show me again how to do it,' he humbly suggested, vacating the driver's seat. 'You do it so well, and I know I'm making a real pig's breakfast of it.'

'You can bloody say that again,' Trevor concurred. But the simple psychology had worked; it had brought a grin – albeit a patronising one – to the driver's face. He sprang into the truck's seat with insulting ease.

'Look, can we make it quick, please...?' This wingeing voice belonged to Alan Hibbert, the Warehouse Manager, who had been hovering around uneasily all morning, trying time and again to move the proceedings along.

He had received assurances from Ken Colebourne that the filming would only take a couple of hours and would cause minimum disruption. Unversed in the ways of television and film – where everything always takes immeasurably longer than it's meant to and where the words 'minimum disruption' always mean 'maximum disruption' – Alan Hibbert had actually believed the Marketing Director's words. And was now, to his cost, finding out the truth.

Ken Colebourne had kept saying that they were only using one aisle for the filming and that the work of the rest of the warehouse could continue uninterrupted, but every time Alan Hibbert tried to get one of the other forklifts going, it either became entangled in the spaghetti of cables spawned by the cameras and lights or was ordered to stop because it was making too much noise during a take.

The marriage between show business and the industrial process was not getting off to a very good start.

'Look, it's dead simple. Bloody child of three could do it.'

Charles grinned weakly, prepared to suffer Trevor's scorn in the cause of speed.

'First you switch on the ignition – right?'

Charles, nodding like an idiot, watched the key turned, as if the operation were a complex feat of microsurgery. 'Right.'

'And then you simply push this lever on the left of the steering wheel forward and you're in gear – right?'

Charles watched this manoeuvre completed with the ardour of Galahad being given a sneak preview of the Holy Grail. 'Right. You don't use the clutch?' he asked breathlessly.

'Can do, but don't have to,' Trevor assured him. 'And look – you're moving.'

'So you are,' agreed Charles, amazed by the miracle of the forklift truck slowly edging forwards.

'And then you give it a touch of the accelerator to go faster.'

'Just like a car, really.'

This thought did not seem to have struck Trevor before. 'Well, yeah, I suppose, if you like. Bit like a car.'

On reflection, he decided this comparison might diminish the mystery of his calling. 'Different from a car, though.'

'Yes, of course.'

'I mean, driving a forklift...well, it's a specialised skill.'

'I'll say.'

Trevor flashed a look at Charles, suspecting mockery. Unable to decide whether or not there had been any, he went on, 'Anyway, what you got to do is swing the wheel like so.' He matched the action to his words. 'With a bit of bloody beef, though. If people are going to think it's me, I don't want to come across as a bleeding fairy, do I?'

This prompted a laugh from somewhere over behind the stacks. Trevor turned sharply at the sound but could not identify its source.

'No. Right,' said Charles, long accustomed to the fact that 50 per cent of the population thought all actors were 'bleeding fairies'. Presumably, it had been one of that 50 per cent who had just laughed.

'Reckon you can do that then?' Trevor asked, his voice again heavy with sarcasm.

'Think so.' Charles judiciously mixed humility into the confidence of his reply.

Trevor didn't look convinced. He nonchalantly swung the wheel of the forklift again and brought the truck to rest exactly where it had started.

'That's terrific,' said Griff Merricks. 'Thank you very much, Trevor. Right, Charles, could we run it?'

But the real operator wasn't going to relinquish his seat to any thespian surrogate quite so easily. 'You don't smoke, do you?' he asked Charles accusingly.

'No, I don't.'

'Oh.' Trevor couldn't keep the disappointment out of his voice. 'Only you mustn't smoke round one of these.'

'Well, I wouldn't, because I don't.'

'And the whole warehouse is a "No smoking" area, anyway, Trevor,' Alan Hibbert pointed out testily.

But the operator was not to be deflected from his narrative. 'Point is,' he continued, eyeing Charles beadily, 'some of these trucks run on Calor gas, and there's a risk of a leak and if you get a naked flame from a cigarette –'

'Yes, well, since, as I say, I don't smoke, and since this one I'm working on is actually powered by electricity, I don't see –'

'Bloke in a warehouse over Northampton,' Trevor continued inexorably, 'he had a crafty fag while he was driving one of the Calor ones...Whole thing went "woomph"...they was picking bits of him off the shelves for months.'

'Well, that sounds –'

'What you have to watch with the electrical ones,' Trevor went on, 'is that you don't leave them with the engine running. Flattens the batteries. Have to be recharged every night, you see. If there's one way to get yourself unpopular in a warehouse, it's to leave your engine running and flatten your battery.'

'Well, I'll certainly be careful not to –'

'And this machine's got a "Quick Release" button, and all...'

'Has it?'

'It's got a guard over it, so's you can't push it by mistake...' Trevor appraised Charles disdainfully, 'well, unless you're a complete wanker. It's meant for lowering the forks quick when you've unloaded but, if you press it when you got a pallet up, whole sodding lot comes smashing down.'

'Ah,' said Charles, bewildered as to the cause of this sudden verbal diarrhoea. Maybe it was just intimidation, or perhaps the operator, affronted at the assumption that he wasn't up to the task of speaking, wanted to assert his credentials in that department.

Griff Merricks seemed to take the second view, or at least to reckon that it was Trevor's exclusion from a more active role in the filming that was making him so uncooperative. 'Um...' he proposed, 'I was wondering whether you would mind doing something else for me in the video...'

'Oh?' The speed of reaction showed that the director had judged his subject right. There was a glint of enthusiasm in Trevor's grudging acquiescence. 'I suppose I could, if you insist – since my day's work's bloody shot to pieces, anyway.'

'Well, what I'd like you to do, Trevor, is to be seen chatting with the secretary who comes out of the warehouse office.'

'What do I say to her then?'

'It actually doesn't matter what you say. We won't hear it, just see you talking – OK?'

Trevor nodded magnanimously. 'Sure, I'll help you out.' He got down from the seat of the forklift. Granted another role in the proceedings, he no longer needed to continue asserting his dominance over Charles.

'So what I'd like to do now...' the Director illustrated his intentions with wide arm movements, 'is pick up from the end of the manoeuvre you just did for us, Trevor. We've got you bringing the pallet down at the end of the aisle – that's in the can. Then I want to sweep across the warehouse...'

'What, do a pan, like?' asked Trevor, keen to assert his mastery of video jargon.

'That's right – pan across the warehouse...and if you're walking towards the office, just as the secretary comes out...I'll linger for a moment on the two of you chatting...then come across to the end of the aisle...just as you're emerging on the forklift, Charles, and...' A thought crossed the Director's mind. 'Is this going to be all right with you, Will?'

The writer, thus deferred to, shrugged his agreement. Serene in his suit, he was leaning against a pallet of Delmoleen 'Bedtime (Lite)' and being very accommodating about whatever changes to his script happened to be suggested. Like the video's director, he had no creative interest at all in the filming. So long as *Parton Parcel* was being paid, so long as *Parton Parcel* paid him, and so long as nobody demanded any rewrites, he was quite content.

Even if he hadn't been a representative of the production company, the writer would still have been there for the shoot, maintaining at least the illusion of interest. And, Charles thought cynically, Will's attendance at Stenley Curton had the additional advantage of keeping him away from home. Stuck in his flat, he really would have no alternative but to start writing the definitive play.

'Then, Charles,' Griff went on, 'you say your bit and –'

'But how will I know when to walk and when to talk?' asked Trevor.

'I'll give you a cue.'

'A cue? What do I want a bleeding cue for?' The blank look on the operator's face suggested that he was thinking in terms of snooker. Perhaps interpreters, fluent in show business jargon, would be required.

'I'll give you a wave,' Griff Merricks hastily amended.

'Oh, right. So...what, you give Heather a wave and all, so's she knows when to come out.'

'Yes. Though in fact it won't be Heather who gets the wave.'

'Why not? Heather's the only secretary round the warehouse. Runs the Dispatch Office – and don't we all know it? Real Miss Bossyboots, she is.'

'Yes, it's just we, um, we thought it might be better if we had someone else as the secretary.'

'Not bringing in another bleeding actor, are you? Actress, I should say.' Maliciously he added, 'If you can tell the difference.'

'No. No, it's someone from the company...Ah, here she is.'

The Director turned to greet a young woman who had just entered the warehouse. Nature had made her pretty, and artifice had been enlisted to make her even prettier. Probably still only in her late teens, she had short blonde hair and big blue eyes emphasised by mascara-spiked lashes. A trim figure was outlined by her tight navy business suit. The skirt, fashionably short, and the heels, fashionably high, showed her legs to advantage. The perfect picture was marred only by a discontented tightness round her thin lips.

'Ah, Dayna...' said Griff Merricks. 'Perfect timing. We were just getting to your bit. Dayna, this is Charles Paris.'

'Good morning, Dayna.'

'Hello.' She had the local accent, but there was a lethargic sexiness about her voice.

'And I don't know if you've met Trevor...'

It was clear from Trevor's expression, if not from Dayna's, that they certainly had met. In fact, the girl's arrival had reduced the operator to confusion. She offered him a cool grin, but he could only redden and stutter in response.

Suddenly further participation in the video seemed to have lost its appeal. 'Yeah, well, I think, actually, maybe I won't stick around. I'm on early dinners, so I think I'll, you know, be off...' And he walked out of the warehouse.

The girl watched him go without emotion, then turned the beam of her blue eyes on to Charles. A half-smile haunted her lips, waiting for a response from him. If he grinned, she would be prepared to laugh at the departing Trevor; if he gave her no encouragement, she wouldn't.

Charles gave nothing. The half-smile faded from her lips.

'Well, don't worry,' said Griff Merricks. 'I'm sure we can get one of the other operators to do that for us, can't we, Alan?'

'I'm sure we can,' the Warehouse Manager agreed sourly, 'particularly since they've been stopped all morning from doing bugger-all else.'

Another forklift truck operator was enlisted and issued with a new set of gleaming blue overalls. Charles sat in his truck and ran through the lines in his head. He tested out the machine, switching on the ignition and pushing forward the gear lever, which was very loose and engaged easily. The truck edged forward. Charles gave a little kick of acceleration and swung the steering wheel with what he hoped Trevor would consider sufficient beef.

The truck jerked sideways and the load on its fork crashed into a shelved pallet of Delmoleen 'Oat Nuggets'. Considering how relatively slowly he had been moving, the impact had caused quite a lot of damage, ripping the polythene covering and digging deep into the stacked cartons.

He looked around sheepishly, hoping no one had noticed, but was met by the unforgiving eye of Alan Hibbert. Charles tried a smile. 'Quite a powerful machine, isn't it?'

'Yes,' said the Warehouse Manager, tersely unamused. 'You just be bloody careful with it.'

'I will be.'

'And make sure it's bloody switched off when you've finished farting around with it.'

'Of course.'

Infinitely gentle, Charles reversed his truck away from the disaster and switched off the ignition. Trying to avoid Alan Hibbert's eye, he looked across to the ground-level office, inside which Griff Merricks was instructing Dayna on her first acting role. Behind them stood a dowdy woman of uncertain age. While Charles watched, she turned on her heel and went out of sight into another room. He wondered idly if the woman was Heather, the 'Miss Bossyboots' who ran the Dispatch Office.

The lines were no problem, but a few takes were needed before Charles Paris could co-ordinate them perfectly with the movements of his forklift truck. Finally, on the fourth attempt, the timing worked.

As directed by Griff Merricks, the cameraman panned across the office end of the warehouse. On her cue, Dayna picked up an invoice from a desk and came out of the office, moving as if she hoped to be talent-spotted for a part in *Emanuelle XII*. The forklift truck operator who had replaced Trevor walked forward on his cue to meet her. They stopped and engaged in fascinated discussion about some detail of the invoice.

The camera panned across to the entrance of the aisle up which Charles Paris was gingerly coaxing his forklift truck. With aplomb, panache and – yes – beef, Charles swung the steering wheel round so that he was facing the camera, disengaged the gear lever, and launched into his speech. Will Parton's prose in this instance wasn't perhaps up to Pinter, but *The Birthday Party* voice still seemed to work fine.

'This is where many of the Delmoleen range of products get loaded to be transported to the four corners of the world. My job's an important part of the distribution process, and I get a lot of satisfaction from being a link in a global chain.' As instructed by Griff Merricks, Charles grinned and gave a little toss of his head. 'It's a good feeling to know that I'm a member of the Delmoleen family.'

Each time he said these words, Charles was again struck by the incongruity of a family which has to book in actors to play its members, but he didn't let this thought put him off the task for which he was being paid. Again following instructions, he engaged the gear lever, swung the steering wheel round (with plenty of beef), and drove the forklift truck sedately out of shot.

Charles was surprised to hear a single pair of hands clapping. As he looked round to the source of the noise, it was quickly joined by the clapping of other hands.

By the entrance to the warehouse was a little knot of people. Ken Colebourne stood on one side, with Robin Pritchard on the other, flanking a couple in the middle. The man, tall and fiftyish with a craggy face, wore a dark suit and plain red tie; the woman, of about the same age, was dressed in a pale blue suit, with co-ordinated dark blue hat, shoes and handbag.

The craggy-faced man had been the first to clap. The sycophantic speed with which the others had joined him, and the nervous sheen on Ken Colebourne's forehead, left Charles in no doubt that the newcomer was 'B.T.' or, as the more relaxed Robin Pritchard would call him, 'Brian'.

Chapter Three

HIS NAME was Brian Tressider, and he was the Managing Director. The lady in pale blue was, predictably enough, his wife. She was called Brenda.

It was no surprise that their arrival caused a stir, but Charles felt the reaction was more than just one of awe. Brian Tressider was automatically impressive by virtue of his position, but he seemed also to command a great deal of affection amongst his work-force.

The warehouse staff gathered round him and he had a cheerful word and a Christian name for most of them. This wasn't just the researched 'common touch' of a politician; there seemed to be a genuine feeling among the employees that their MD was 'one of them'. Charles got the impression that Brian Tressider had worked his way up from the shop floor and was respected for it. The uneroded Midland twang in his voice supported that supposition.

His wife hadn't quite the same natural manner. Though she was punctiliously amiable and interested in everyone, Brenda Tressider's bonhomie showed signs of hard work – if not of calculation, then at least of application. Her vowels betrayed a more privileged upbringing than her husband's; she had the kind of upper-class voice which implies patronage and condescension even when they aren't there.

She must once have been beautiful and had since then been very well maintained. Her face now was lined beneath the skilful make-up and her hair had had an assisted passage towards blondeness, but the grey-blue eyes still packed a powerful punch. Charles also approved the suppleness of her well-exercised body. Quite classy.

He was introduced to both of them by an anxiously obsequious Ken Colebourne. The Marketing Director's cautious deference implied a less affable, steelier side to Brian Tressider, an insistence on high standards and a readiness to bawl out anyone who didn't match up to those standards.

Robin Pritchard was also watchful in his boss's presence. Though his manner was characteristically more laid-back than Ken's, the Product Manager was nonetheless on his best behaviour, ready to respond instantly to any switch in Brian's mood.

But that mood was currently sunny and looked set fair to remain so. Brian Tressider chatted easily to the people involved in the video, asking for technical explanations from Griff Merricks and his crew, joking with Will and

Charles. If this was like a visit from royalty, it was a very relaxed one.

His wife's conversation, however, conformed to the more traditional royal style. 'Charles Paris? Yes, now of course I know the name. Tell me, what would I have seen you in recently?'

As ever, when asked this question, Charles's mind went a complete blank. Given the progress of his career during the previous year, a complete blank was entirely appropriate.

'Ah. Well, erm...'

'Of course, if it's theatre, we may not know as much about it as we should. Brian and I don't get to the theatre as often as we'd like these days. Do tend to get involved in quite a lot of evening functions.'

'Yes. Erm...' Suddenly, from the recesses of his memory, he dragged out a recollection of once having worked. 'I was in a television series that was on a couple of years back. Detective thing...*Stanislas Braid*...don't know if you, er...'

'Of course!' said Brenda Tressider. 'Of course, I knew I recognised the face.' This was phrased in such a way that she didn't have to admit whether or not she'd seen any of the series. 'Charles Paris – *Stanislas Braid*.'

She repeated the names, as if satisfied at having made a forgotten connection, but Charles reckoned it was also a way of entering the information into her mental filing system. He felt certain that, if they ever met again, she would greet him with 'Charles Paris, yes, of course. You were in that *Stanislas Braid* series, weren't you?'

It was a good skill to have, though, that kind of social memory, an essential skill for a busy hostess. Charles just wished he couldn't see the wheels turning quite so obviously as the machinery clicked into action.

Brian Tressider's manner may have been as studied as his wife's, but it seemed more spontaneous. He found a friendly word for everyone. Heather from the Dispatch Office had emerged to greet the boss, and coloured winsomely at some remark he threw at her.

Then he clapped an arm round Alan Hibbert's shoulder. 'Yes, don't tell me, Alan – this video's throwing all your scheduling to buggery.'

'Well, I'm afraid it is, B.T.. We've got to get the regular Wednesday deliveries off and we can't wait around too long for –'

'Don't worry about it. You'll make up the time.'

'I can't see why we –'

'No, really, Alan, the video's important. I wouldn't have agreed to our doing it if I didn't think so. And if you lose half a day here in the warehouse, or if we lose a day's production even, it's not the end of the world.'

'Never thought I'd hear you talk like that, B.T..'

'Priorities change. Of course I want to maximise production, but keeping everyone's nose to the grindstone every second of the day may not be the best way of achieving that. Making everyone feel they belong to the company could be more effective in the long run. A contented work-force is an efficient work-force, Alan.'

The Warehouse Manager looked at his boss with a blatant scepticism that suggested their relationship went back a long way. 'Sounds like you've been reading another of those management books, Brian.'

The Managing Director let out a short laugh. 'Maybe I have.' He laughed again and turned to Griff Merricks. 'Tell me, how much more you've you got to do here?'

'Couple more set-ups of Charles on the forklift. Just cutaways, really, for editing purposes.'

'How long do you reckon?'

'Half an hour top weight.'

'And how long to clear up?'

'Another half-hour?'

'And then you'll be out of Alan's hair?'

'No problem.'

'That's it then.' Brian Tressider turned back to his Warehouse Manager. 'Break all your staff now for early lunch – OK? Get them all back at two, and you'll be able to work through the afternoon with no interruptions.'

'All right.' Alan Hibbert went off to communicate this decision to his operators. They needed no second bidding to leave the warehouse, and had all vanished within seconds.

'Oh, and Griff...' the Managing Director went on, 'if you want to bring your boys up to the Executive dining room for a drink and some lunch when you're through, please feel invited.'

This was the best suggestion Charles Paris had heard all morning. 'That's very kind,' said the Director. 'What, all of them?' This question did not encompass as many as it would have done on a proper television OB. Union regulations do not apply for the making of non-broadcast material, so Griff's technical support comprised only a lighting cameraman and sound recordist.

'Well, all the ones who're wearing ties,' said Brian Tressider over his shoulder, as he took his wife's arm and led her towards the warehouse door.

Charles Paris caught the flicker of glee in Will Parton's eye. But he was distracted from melancholy thoughts of his tielessness by a little scene which was taking place the other side of the warehouse. The girl Dayna stood by the door as Brian and Brenda Tressider approached, with Ken Colebourne and Robin Pritchard close behind them. When they were almost level with her, Dayna leant against the doorframe in a frankly voluptuous pose, and winked.

What was surprising about the gesture was its lack of subtlety. Almost as if she was parodying a vamp. It was the performance of someone either highly sophisticated or deeply naive.

The Managing Director stopped in his stride for a moment, as if about to say something, but then thought better of it, and steered his wife out of the warehouse.

It had only lasted a second, and very few people had noticed the incident, but it did seem bizarre.

'Right,' said Griff Merricks, 'let's get these last few shots done quick as we can.'

'Sure,' said Will Parton. 'Then off to the Executive dining room for "a drink and some lunch", eh?' He grinned at Charles. 'That is – those of us who're wearing ties.'

Charles grimaced long-sufferingly back at him.

'Don't worry,' said Will in a voice heavy with mock-solicitude. 'I'm told the Rissoles and Spotted Dick in the staff canteen are out of this world.'

'Thank you very much.'

The writer shook his head sadly. 'Such a pity it's not licensed.'

It's remarkable how quickly television people can work when they've got a proper incentive. The last few shots of Charles on the forklift truck were in the can within ten minutes and almost before he'd got out of his seat, the cables were all unplugged and coiled up, ready to be packed away. Within another half-minute, Will Parton, Griff Merricks, his cameraman and sound recordist had all disappeared in search of the Executive dining room.

Blatant discrimination, thought Charles. Meant to be living in an egalitarian society, and yet there's still this massive undercurrent of prejudice against people who don't wear ties. Huh.

He looked disconsolately round the empty warehouse. Through the windows of the ground-level office he could see Dayna and Heather involved in inaudible conversation.

A childish temptation gnawed at him. He moved back to the forklift truck and sat in it. Loaded shelves meant that he was out of sight of the office.

Really would be fun to make the lift work, wouldn't it? Raise and lower a pallet...? Even see if he could pick one up perhaps...

He turned the key in the ignition. The engine started. He reached for the lifting controls.

But no. That was being stupid. Could easily cause a lot of damage. Press that 'Quick Release' button by mistake and you could send a whole pallet's load smashing down. Be your age, Charles Paris. ('Forty-eight, but play younger.')

Reluctantly, he switched the ignition off and got down from the truck.

Just as well, really. The girl Dayna was coming out of the office. If she saw what he was up to, she'd think he was out of his mind.

She didn't seem aware of his presence, but stood irresolute by the door. The room inside was empty. Heather must have retreated to her inner office.

Not wishing to draw attention to himself, Charles moved silently out of the warehouse, in search of the staff canteen.

Outside, he met Trevor who, with his habitual surliness, directed Charles Paris towards the delights of Rissoles and Spotted Dick.

Chapter Four

IN THE EVENT, he went for the Steak Pie and Jam Roly-Poly, impassively served from behind heated counters by hard-faced women in pale blue housecoats. The vegetables suffered from that sogginess endemic to British institutional food (and rather too much British restaurant food), but otherwise the meal tasted all right. And the prices were amazingly low. Delmoleen subsidised its employees' eating generously.

Any sneaking hope he had had that the canteen might be licensed was quickly dispelled, and, to his amazement, Charles found himself ordering a cup of tea with his lunch. It must have been the influence of the environment, and perhaps his costume, as his actor's instinct slotted him instantly into the role he was playing. Cup of tea, dollop of gelatinous custard...it made him feel as if he was back in one of those early sixties plays of social realism, something like Wesker's *Chips with Everything* ('The effeteness of Charles Paris's performance left me suspecting that the RAF would have turned him down on medical grounds' – *The Huddersfield Examiner*).

Still, he thought piously, good thing not to be drinking at lunchtime – although the righteous sensation of having satisfactorily finished his day's work deserved the reward of a quick one.

But no, it was good. Too few lunchtimes passed these days unassisted by drink. To have abstinence forced on him like this gave Charles the reassuring feeling that he wasn't an alcoholic. He could take it or leave it...

He would rather *take* it, obviously, but at least he wasn't chemically dependant...

Or probably wasn't.

He tried to put from his mind the image of Will Parton and Griff Merricks downing glasses of wine in the Executive dining room, and comforted himself with the promise of a large Bell's when he got back to his bedsitter in Hereford Road.

The canteen offered him the same measure of conviviality as it did of alcohol. Since he didn't know anyone there, he had hardly expected a hearty welcome and cheery hands waving him over to join tables, but he was surprised by the positive antipathy that exuded from the Delmoleen employees.

He was recognised as an outsider – probably the unfamiliar overalls didn't help – and as such he was suspect. While he looked around for a seat, he was first briefly scrutinised by the other diners and then pointedly ignored. Finally finding an empty table piled high with the detritus of earlier lunches, he sat down and ate his meal as quickly as possible.

He had finished inside ten minutes and it still wasn't one o'clock. He wandered outside the canteen. Knots of Delmoleen workers stood around smoking and chatting. Over on a bit of open ground an improvised game of football was under way. The only acknowledgement Charles's presence received was the odd deterrent stare.

He wondered at first if they could recognise him as an actor and were showing the traditional reaction to 'bleeding fairies'. But there was no way anyone could know his profession. Maybe they suspected him of being a management spy, a time and motion consultant. But that too was nonsense. No, he finally decided that he was incurring resentment simply because he was unfamiliar.

It wasn't a pleasant sensation, though. Charles felt tempted just to leave, catch a train, go home. Griff Merricks had said he only needed the few extra shots for editing and those were done.

On the other hand, in the pre-lunch confusion, Charles hadn't actually been granted an official release. And directors were notorious for changing their minds after a couple of drinks. Charles had been booked for the full day and his professionalism told him that he shouldn't leave until Griff Merricks gave him formal permission. The daily rate he was being paid was quite impressive, and Charles didn't want to screw up the chances of further work in this lucrative area by being absent when needed.

He contemplated finding a local pub to pass the next hour. But he hadn't seen any when he arrived at the station, and no doubt if there was one around, it would be just another outpost of the Delmoleen resentment of strangers.

Disconsolately, but vigorously, as if his movement had some purpose, Charles strode back towards the warehouse. He'd left his raincoat there, apart from anything else. And in his raincoat pocket was a potential lifesaver. Not, he reflected virtuously – if a little wistfully – a half-bottle of Bell's, but something much more wholesome – a copy of *Persuasion*. He did find rereading Jane Austen every few years wonderfully therapeutic.

As he entered the warehouse, the huge space was very still.

But it was not completely silent. From somewhere in the distant stacks Charles could hear the hum of an electric motor.

He moved towards the source of the sound.

It was in the aisle they had used for the filming. Where he had left his forklift truck, a pile of loose cartons, fallen from a shelf above, lay scattered on the ground. The truck itself had moved forward and was embedded into the pile of empty pallets which stood against the wall at the end of the aisle. Its engine still protested as it pressed against the slowly splintering wood.

Charles tried to work out what could have happened. If the ignition had been left switched on and the motor running, it was just possible, given the looseness of the gear lever, that one of the falling cartons could have knocked it and engaged the engine. Then the truck would have moved forward.

But that did assume that the motor had been left running.

And Charles knew he had switched the ignition off.

It was as he had this thought that he heard the other sound.

Lower than the mechanical hum of the forklift engine, and more human.

He moved forward, suddenly panicked.

Yes, through the slats of the pallets, slumped against the foot of the wall, he could see a human shape.

The moaning was ominously low and feeble.

Charles Paris leapt into the seat of the forklift and pulled the gear lever into reverse. The truck jerked back, dragging some of the pallets with it. Others toppled noisily to the ground.

Charles disengaged the gear and switched off the ignition.

Then he tugged at the heavy pile of pallets to clear them from the wall. His hands snagged on the rough wood. He was aware of splinters digging in, but felt no pain.

As he pulled back the last obstruction, the moaning was interrupted by a little gasp, almost a sigh of pain.

Charles looked down into the space he had cleared.

The limbs lay at odd angles, unnaturally compacted against the wall.

The shallow rasp of breathing could still just be heard from the crushed body, but blood trickled from the nose and mouth, indicating severe internal injury.

It was the girl, Dayna.

Chapter Five

HE LOOKED around for help, but there was no one else in the warehouse. The girl was unconscious and looked ghastly, but vague recollections of the basic principles of first aid told Charles he shouldn't move an injured person. He'd just have to leave her and go for help.

He hurried up the aisle to the office at the back. There was no one in the outer room. He knocked on the interconnecting door and moved through into the inner office.

Brian Tressider and Heather looked up with surprise at his entrance, but without embarrassment. Nothing untoward had been going on, and indeed looking at the two of them – he wirily elegant, she frankly frumpy – it was an unlikely thought that anything might have been. She sat at her desk, an opened but untouched packet of sandwiches in front of her. He stood at the other side of the room.

The Managing Director cocked an interrogative eyebrow at Charles.

'There's been an accident. It's dreadful. In the warehouse. We need an ambulance.'

'What's happened? Who's been hurt?'

'Dayna.'

It seemed to Charles that, at the mention of the name, Heather searched Brian Tressider's face for some reaction. What she was expecting was hard to judge, but, whatever it was, the craggy face remained impassive.

'Get on to Security, Heather. And Personnel. They'll have a contact for her parents or next-of-kin. And find Alan Hibbert – quickly!'

'Yes, Brian.'

'I think you should call an ambulance first.'

Charles's suggestion was rewarded by a flash of anger from the Managing Director's grey eyes. 'Security will do that.' Brian Tressider didn't take kindly to being told how to run his company.

Just as she reached for the receiver, the telephone on Heather's desk rang. She picked it up. 'Oh, Mother, what is it *now*? Well, it is a bad moment. We've got an emergency on and...'

Brian indicated the door. 'Show me,' he commanded.

Charles Paris ushered him through the offices to the warehouse, and down the aisle to where the girl lay. Her breathing seemed even weaker. The pool of blood from mouth and nostrils was spreading ominously.

Brian Tressider showed no emotion. 'Did the pallets fall on her?'

'No, the forklift had somehow started and pushed them against her. I moved the truck back.'

The Managing Director gave a curt nod. 'Industrial accidents are buggers. Last thing you want in a place like this.' He looked back up the aisle to the scattered cartons. 'Those must've fallen and knocked the truck into gear.'

'Does that really seem likely?' asked Charles.

The flinty grey stare was turned on him. 'Well, I can't think what else happened, can you?'

'Just seems a coincidence. Anyway, somebody must've left the truck switched on.'

Brian Tressider shrugged. 'Happens all the time. Trucks keep having to be recharged when they shouldn't because some idiot's left them running. Dozy lot of buggers you get in a place like this.'

'But presumably you will investigate to find out who did leave it switched on?'

'Yes, we'll investigate.' His voice didn't express much confidence in the efficacy of the procedure. 'They'll all deny they were the last ones to touch it.'

'I think *I* was the last one to touch it. You know, in the filming.' This prompted another sharp stare. 'Then I'd bloody well keep quiet about it, if I were you.'

'But I know I left it switched off.'

'Yes, I'm sure you did.' The scepticism in the tone was undisguised. Though he might not have used the expression 'bleeding fairies', Brian Tressider clearly shared the common prejudice against the theatrical profession.

He looked down at the injured girl and pursed his lips with annoyance. 'Why people can't just do what they're meant to do I'll never understand. Most industrial accidents occur because people are where they shouldn't be, or doing what they're not meant to be doing.'

'Well, what do you think she was doing behind the pallets?'

This got another shrug. Such speculation apparently held no interest for Brian Tressider.

They heard hurried footsteps and turned to see Alan Hibbert approaching. The Warehouse Manager took in the scene instantly.

'Shit,' he said softly.

'Yes. Shit,' Brian concurred. 'Is the nurse on her way from Surgery.'

A nod. 'And they've called an ambulance. She's still alive, isn't she?'

'At the moment. Not looking too good, though. Maybe we should put a blanket over her or something?'

The Warehouse Manager found a blanket and gently covered the still form. 'Silly girl. She was a right little mixer, B.T.. Always poking her nose into things that weren't her business.'

Again the Managing Director didn't seem interested. The girl's behaviour was irrelevant. It was the inconvenience of the accident that seemed to preoccupy him. 'Have to do a full report, Alan, won't we...'

The Warehouse Manager caught the slight interrogative inflection at the end of this. 'Sorry. No way round it. I must get on the blower to the Environmental Health Department straight away.'

'I'd hold fire till she's been moved to the hospital, if I were you,' said Brian Tressider.

Alan Hibbert looked at his boss in some surprise. Despite the softness of tone in which they had been spoken, the words had been not a suggestion, but an order.

The warehouse staff who'd been involved in the video and the film crew who had made it were assembled in Heather's back office an hour later for a debriefing from their Managing Director.

'Listen, we're all obviously very upset about what's happened and I hope it's reinforced to the lot of you working in this warehouse just how seriously the safety regulations have to be followed. Now of course we're going to have an internal investigation to find out exactly how the accident came about and to make sure that this kind of thing can't happen again...isn't that right, Alan?'

The Warehouse Manager nodded. He was completely solid with his boss. Both of them knew that an investigation had to take place; neither of them wanted that investigation to make any waves. All they did want was for Delmoleen to return to business-as-usual as soon as possible.

Already, Charles had noticed with some shock, the site of the accident had been cleared up, sawdust scattered and swept away, disinfectant sprinkled. Along the other aisles of the warehouse forklifts and stockpickers plied their trade, as the waiting lorries slowly filled with Delmoleen products. Whatever kind of investigation did ensue, it wasn't going to have much to go on from the forensic point of view.

'And it's quite likely,' Brian continued, 'that we could be the subject of an external investigation too. In fact, it's pretty well certain that the boys from the Environmental Health Department will be along soon.

'I'm going to be in London and abroad for the next few weeks, so I want to say to all of you now, that if their inspectors do come round to talk to you, please co-operate. Answer any questions they ask you, but – and this is an important "but" – don't tell them more than they ask. OK? No speculation, no comments about the poor kid's character – none of that stuff, all right?'

The assembled group nodded agreement. Ken Colebourne caught Robin Pritchard's eye and shook his head wryly.

'Isn't it possible,' Charles hazarded gently, 'that the police might also make some kind of investigation?'

A roomful of cold eyes focused on him.

'I wouldn't have thought that would be necessary,' said Brian Tressider. 'We are talking about an *accident* here.'

'Yes, but –'

The Managing Director's voice continued on a level note. He was not used to being interrupted. 'I would also have thought that a police investigation was something that you particularly would wish to avoid, Mr Paris – as the last person to leave the warehouse before the accident, *and* the last person to touch the forklift that caused it.'

'I'm fairly sure I wasn't the last person,' Charles persisted. 'I'm also positive that I switched the engine off when I left the truck.'

'I'd doubt that.' Now Trevor had joined in the argument. 'Did any of you see the way he was farting around on that forklift this morning – bloody hopeless? Hardly knew if it was in "forward" or "reverse". Can't expect a bloody actor to remember whether he's left it switched on or not.'

Without this aggression, Charles probably wouldn't have made a public accusation, but he was stung and spoke before he could stop himself. 'I know I switched it off,' he announced firmly, 'and I'm pretty sure that someone else switched it back on again. In fact, as I left the warehouse, I saw someone going in.'

Trevor sensed he was about to be named and came in quickly with his admission. 'All right, I was going in there, don't deny it. Left me fags. Just nipped in to get them.'

The operator blushed defiantly, judging that the pro-cover-up mood of the meeting would probably preclude further questions.

But he'd underestimated his Managing Director. Brian Tressider wanted the investigations to be concluded as quickly as possible, but he wasn't going to ignore this new information. 'Why didn't you mention this before, Trevor?'

The blush grew deeper. 'Like I said...I just nipped in. I, er...I...'

He looked acutely uncomfortable, but salvation came from an unexpected source.

They all looked round as Heather spoke. 'That's right. I saw Trevor as he came into the warehouse. Then he came into my office for a chat. You remember, because my mother rang while you were here, didn't she, Trevor?'

There was an infinitesimal pause before the operator replied, 'Yes, Heather, that's right.'

Charles was convinced they were lying. 'So how long was Trevor with you?'

'Till about one, I suppose.'

Nearly all the time that Charles had been absent from the warehouse. He'd seen Trevor on the way out, gone to the canteen to eat his Steak Pie and Jam Roly-Poly, and apparently just missed Trevor on his return. What on earth had Heather and the forklift operator talked about for so long?

'Yes, it would have been one o'clock,' Heather went on, 'because that's when you came in, Brian. Trevor had just gone out *there*' – she indicated the door that led to the exterior – 'when you came in from the warehouse, Brian.'

The Managing Director eyed the actor sardonically. 'Well, I think we seem to have sorted out Trevor's movements, anyway, Mr Paris.'

Charles wasn't satisfied. Nor could he provide a logical motive for Heather's rescue of Trevor. Perhaps it was done simply in the cause of company solidarity. Or maybe she nursed a secret passion for the operator. Heather must have been in her early fifties. She didn't look the sort of woman in whose life romance had featured much; so it was in theory possible that she might have a love object as unprepossessing as Trevor.

But whatever her motivation, Charles still didn't believe the alibi she had provided. 'Look, it still seems to me –'

He was interrupted by the ringing of the telephone on Heather's desk. She answered it. 'Yes. Oh, hello, Mrs Tressider. Yes, he's here. Brian.' The phone was handed across.

'Yes, darling? Mr and Mrs Richman? Oh, right. Well, say all the appropriate things. Yes, I'll come over and talk to them straight away. See you shortly.'

He handed the phone back to Heather, and sighed. 'Brenda's at the hospital, with the girl's parents. I'm afraid Dayna's just died.'

There were mixed reactions of shock and other sentiments appropriate to the announcement of a death.

Only Brian Tressider showed nothing.

And once again Charles was aware of Heather staring into her boss's face, looking for some reaction.

But what reaction she was expecting it was again impossible to tell.

Chapter Six

NEEDLESS to say, there wasn't a bar on the local service from Stenley Curton, nor were Charles Paris and Will Parton lucky enough to catch a properly equipped train from Bedford, so it was St Pancras before they could get a drink. And they needed it so much that they hardly noticed the unappealing surroundings of the station buffet. (Actually, to be truthful, environment never impinged that much on Charles's consciousness when he was drinking.)

They had hardly spoken on the journey, both shocked into silence and locked in their own thoughts. The first large Bell's went down without words, hardly touching the sides, but the second opened the floodgates.

'Do you know anything at all about the girl, Will?'

The writer shrugged. 'Not a lot. My in-depth study of the Delmoleen operation didn't get as far as the typing pool.'

'That's what she was – just a typist?'

'Come on, she was only about nineteen. She was hardly going to be Sales Manager, was she?'

'No. And you don't know anything else about her?'

'Just that she tended to be around a lot.'

'How do you mean?'

'Well, I've been over at Stenley Curton a good few times in the last months and, whoever I had a meeting with, I always seemed to see Dayna Richman at some point. It was as if she was pushing herself forward all the time.'

'What does that suggest – that she had fallen madly in love with you?'

Will shook his head wearily. 'No, Charles. It suggests that she had fallen madly in love with the idea of being on camera.'

'Ah. She saw appearing in a corporate video as the first step on the ladder to stardom? Hoping some major film director would spot her talent and catapult her to Hollywood?'

'Maybe something on those lines. Or maybe she just saw it as a way of getting noticed within the company. She was pretty ambitious, I gather. As you saw, liked attention. Hardly a shrinking violet.'

'Hardly. And presumably she worked in the Dispatch Office?'

'No, she didn't. I think she was in Personnel, some department like that. Though apparently she was always applying for other jobs. Really, Charles, I hardly know any more about her than you do.'

'You must at least know how she came to be in the video?'

Will Parton spread his hands wide. 'Think of what she looked like. You're doing a video to boost the in-house image of the company...so who do you show in the Dispatch Office – the frump or the vamp? Heather or Dayna?'

'See what you mean. So you reckon Dayna kept puffing herself forward with just that outcome in mind?'

'I'd have thought so, Charles. And it worked, didn't it? She got the job.'

'Yes. And who would have given her that job – I mean, who actually said, "All right, Dayna, you do it"?'

'Be Ken Colebourne, I suppose. He's sort of in charge of the video from the Delmoleen end – he's the one I have to check everything with. So if he suggested Dayna to Griff...well, Griff's hardly the kind of guy who's going to argue, is he?'

'No. Did you actually hear that exchange take place – I mean, hear the moment when Ken suggested Dayna should be in the video?'

Will screwed up his face as he tried to remember. 'Ye-es. Yes, I did. It was only a couple of weeks back. Griff just said fine. He was getting paid, he didn't care what was suggested.'

'No.'

Their glasses had unaccountably emptied themselves once again. Will went to the bar to remedy this defect. Charles looked thoughtful. His mind was buzzing with potential motivations. Taking the proffered refill from Will, he mused, 'Heather must've been pretty miffed.'

'Hm?'

'Heather – the one who runs the Dispatch Office. I mean, she doesn't look the sort of woman whose life has been full of excitements. For her to have been aced out of the video by some dolly bird who doesn't even work in the department must've been pretty galling.'

'Apparently not. No, according to Ken Colebourne, Heather was delighted.'

'Why?'

'Maybe hard for you, as an actor, to believe it, Charles, but there are people in this world who don't like showing off, people for whom the idea of being under public scrutiny is absolutely terrifying. It seems that Heather is one of those. Ken had asked her to be in the video, but the prospect appalled her. She kept begging him to find someone else, and when Dayna was suggested, Heather was over the moon.'

'Oh,' said Charles, disappointedly watching that particular conjecture crumble away. He moved on to another one. 'There had clearly been something going on between Dayna and Trevor, hadn't there?'

The writer lifted his shoulders dismissively. 'Could've been.'

'Oh, come on, Will. It was obvious. Did you see the way he reacted when she arrived? Up until that moment, he'd been all keen to do more in the video, then suddenly he goes cold on the whole idea. They must've been having an affair, or just've broken off an affair or...'

'Charles,' said Will with deliberately infuriating condescension, 'there are other motivations in life apart from sex.'

'Maybe, but –'

'Just because you're obsessed with the subject, and just because, as a dirty old man, you can't look at a pretty young girl without immediately wondering who's bonking her, it doesn't mean that everyone is the same.' He affected the drawl of intellectual pretension. '*As a writer*, of course, I have a much deeper understanding of the multifarious nature of human motivations.'

Will had given too good a cue to the counter-attack for Charles to ignore it. 'And, *as a writer*, do tell me – what are you going to be working on next? Can it be that you're finally about to start on the new play we've all heard so much about?'

The barb found its target. Will Parton coloured. 'No. That'll have to wait. I've still got quite a lot to do on the Delmoleen front, as it happens.'

'What, more out at Stenley Curton?'

'Uhuh. Few more bits showing what a united company it is. Bijou scenettes in some of the offices, shots of the actual manufacturing process, staff relaxing in the canteen, high jinks in the firm's social club, all that. And then, if I play my cards right, I might secure *Parton Parcel* the contract for the Delmoleen sales conference in Brighton at the end of September.'

'I see. This one could run and run.'

'With a bit of luck, yes.'

'Well, if any of those bijou scenettes might involve a forklift truck operator capable of speech, do let me know.'

'Now taking bookings, are you, Charles?'

'Well, I do actually have a few free days...Just the odd one or two...Well, any time, really...Any date you care to mention, between now and my death...And, if it's a really good part, I won't let a little thing like that stop me.'

'So I just get in touch with your agent, do I?'

'Don't you dare! Keep Maurice out of this. No, anything corporate, do it direct.'

'OK.' Will dropped the bantering tone. 'Actually, there could be a bit in the canteen sequence. Need someone to talk there.'

'I'll happily expatiate on the virtues of the Jam Roly-Poly for you.'

'May well take you up on that. I'll let you know.'

'I've heard that line before somewhere...can't think where. Still, it would be great if there is anything.' Charles grimaced thoughtfully. 'No, I'd really like to get back to Stenley Curton.'

'What, for –?' Will looked at his friend despairingly. 'Oh, Charles, *no*.'

Charles looked the picture of aggrieved innocence. 'What are you on about?'

'This is like on the *Stanislas Braid* series, isn't it? You see this as the start of an investigation. You just don't believe in the philosophical concept of an *accident*. You think that girl Dayna Richman was murdered, don't you?'

'Yes, I do,' said Charles.

Will Parton groaned. Charles Paris went to refill their glasses.

* * *

'Frances, it's me.'

'Ah,' said his wife's voice from the other end of the phone.

'Charles.'

'Yes, Charles, I do know who you mean. My "Ah" was not an "Ah" of incomprehension, but an "Ah" of "Ah. That is my husband on the phone."'

'Is that a good sort of "Ah"?' he asked hopefully.

'I wouldn't plan your retirement on it.'

'Ah.' There was a silence. 'I just rang because –'

'"You just rang because I had almost reached a state of equanimity about our marriage.'

'What?'

'You have an uncanny sense of timing, Charles.'

'Oh?' To an actor that had to be a compliment.

'Every time I reconcile myself to the fact that we really are finished, and that I won't ever hear from you again, and it's just as well, and now thank God I can get on with the rest of my life…you ring up.'

'Ah.'

'Always at exactly that precise moment.'

He let out a little, tentative laugh. 'Well, that must say something, mustn't it?'

'Huh. I don't think you'd like it if I spelled out what it *does* say, Charles.'

'No, no, fine. Well, leave that as read,' he said hastily.

'So…to what do I owe the pleasure of this call? You've missed my birthday, it's not Christmas yet, so what is it – some mutual form, some documentary relic left over from the days of our marriage, that needs countersigning?'

'No, Frances. No, it's just, er…I wanted to talk to you.'

'Why suddenly now? What is so different about today, as opposed to any other day in the last four months when you could have wanted to talk to me?'

'Oh, surely it's not as long as –'

'Four months,' she said implacably.

'Well, I…' He opted for vulnerability. 'Well, I've been feeling a bit low and…'

It was a bad choice. 'Everyone feels low from time to time, Charles.'

'Yes…'

'It's just that some of us don't go on about it all the time.'

'No, of course. I just –'

'Charles, why are you ringing?'

'Well, it was kind of to make contact and –'

'You've made contact. If you have anything else to say, say it. I've got someone here.'

He was shocked by how much her words hurt. Recovering himself, he said, 'I was wondering if we could get together…'

'What for?' she demanded brusquely.

'Well, for a…you know, for a drink…for a meal…just to see each other…'

'Hm.'

'I mean, that's what other married couples do, isn't it?'

'I wouldn't use the "other married couples" line with me, Charles, if I were you. It doesn't go down very well.'

'No. Well...I...As I say, just be nice to see you.'

All this got was another 'Hm'.

'As I say, just for a drink or...'

'I'd rather it wasn't just for a drink, Charles.'

'What do you mean?'

'I've served my time hanging round grotty pubs and wine bars, waiting for you to turn up...'

'I wouldn't be late. I'd –'

'No, if you want to see me, you invite me somewhere nice.'

'Nice?'

'Yes. You think of something nice, that I – not *you* – but *I* would like to do, and when you've thought of it, you ring me up and invite me to it.'

'Ah.'

'And then, if I like the sound of it, and if I happen to be free on the relevant date...then I'll accept the invitation.'

'Right. Erm, but, Frances –'

'Bye, Charles.'

He stayed by the pay phone on the Hereford Road landing after he had put the receiver down, still smarting. It was ridiculous to feel like this. Surely he'd long since abrogated any right to feel jealous of Frances.

Why should he imagine that she would always be on her own when he called? Given the amount he was contributing to it, he could hardly criticise her for the way she chose to conduct her own social life.

And, anyway, 'someone here' could mean anything. A fellow-schoolmistress. Any one of her many women friends. An elderly neighbour. A Jehovah's Witness.

He was being stupid and he knew it.

But he was still surprised at how much it hurt.

In an attempt to shift his thoughts, he dialled another number.

'Maurice Skellern Artistes.'

'Maurice – it's Charles.'

'Oh yes, how're things? Got any work?'

Charles found himself blushing as he replied, 'No. Surely that's a question an actor should ask his agent rather than the other way round?'

'Oh, I don't know, Charles. Hear so many cases these days of clients getting work behind their agents' backs and not even telling them.'

'Ah. Do you?' Charles laughed uneasily. 'So, anyway, you heard of anything coming up?'

The reply was so familiar he could have joined in. 'Not a dicky bird, Charles. Things are very quiet at the moment, very quiet.'

'Not a good time right now...you know, with the summer coming up.'

'Sure, and then it'll be the autumn coming up, won't it, Maurice? And that won't help.'

'You're right there, Charles. And then we'll be on to the winter, and nobody makes any decisions when there's Christmas just round the corner, do they?'

'No. So we'll just have to wait till the spring, won't we?'

'Yes...' There was a pause. 'Mind you, that's never a lot better either, is it?'

As he put the phone down, Charles wondered why on earth he had imagined that a call to his agent might possibly cheer him up. As always, it just left him more depressed than ever.

And on this occasion – infuriatingly – because of the work he'd been doing for Delmoleen, it also left him feeling slightly guilty.

Chapter Seven

WITHIN A couple of weeks Charles Paris once again found himself doing work his agent didn't know about. Will had managed to swing it that one of the 'bijou scenettes' in the canteen did involve a forklift operator capable of speech, so once again Charles was to don the pristine Delmoleen overalls and give his impression of Trevor.

It was a bit like being a stuntman, he reflected, though whereas stuntmen did physical tricks for people who could act, he was doing acting tricks for someone who could manage the physical stuff with no assistance.

This time he wasn't the only actor involved. When he met Will Parton at St Pancras, the writer introduced a tall figure by his side. 'Charles Paris – this is Seb Ormond.'

It transpired on the train journey that Seb Ormond was one of those actors who specialised in corporate work. Indeed, it was a long time since he had set foot on a stage or performed in a film or television production that was seen by the general public. But his conversation left no doubt that he made a very good living from his 'in-house' career.

To Charles it was a constant source of amazement how many specialities there were within his profession, and the broad range of work that being an actor could encompass. He often suspected that the ones who specialised were the shrewd ones. As in any other area of entrepreneurial life, what such actors had to do was to carve out little niches for themselves, maintain the standards of their work, build up goodwill and, hopefully, make themselves indispensable. Charles knew actors who did that in commercial voice-overs, Victorian music hall, cruise ships entertainment and many other unlikely areas.

Sometimes he regretted that he had never carved out such a niche for himself, but always came back to the view that doing the same thing all the time must get very boring. Doing nothing all the time – which was the pattern that his life seemed to be following these days – was also boring, but at least he could dream of potential employment in every branch of show business (even though so few jobs in any branch actually materialised).

Seb Ormond was one of the names on the *Parton Parcel* letterhead. He wasn't actually a partner, but had an agreement with the company whereby, when Will needed an impressively-suited figure for a business meeting, Seb would turn up. For a substantial fee. *Gravitas* didn't come cheap.

He was also, of course, available for ordinary work as a corporate actor.

Which was how he had been booked for that day at Stenley Curton. Again for a substantial fee. Considerably more than Charles Paris was being paid.

Seb Ormond was dressed in a dark suit with a discreet stripe, a shirt with an even more discreet stripe, and a tie the discretion of whose stripe would have qualified it for the Diplomatic Service. On the station platform he melted into the crowd – just another executive commuter. Only the fact that he was catching a morning train *out* of St Pancras rather than arriving on one coming *in* might have raised any suspicion about his identity.

'Seb's Management today,' Will Parton explained unnecessarily. 'Ken Colebourne's decided that he wants to demonstrate Delmoleen's egalitarianism, so we're going to have an executive mucking in with the riff-raff in the canteen.'

'And none of the real executives'd do it?' asked Charles.

'Good heavens, no. None of them'd be seen dead in the canteen. Anyway, this executive has to *talk*.'

'Aren't the Delmoleen employees who see this video going to think it odd that they don't recognise any of the people in it?'

'Not that odd. It's quite a big company. Stenley Curton's not the only site. Anyway, I sometimes wonder whether anyone ever will see the video.'

'Why?'

'Well, Ken Colebourne seems pretty ambivalent about it – don't know that he ever thought it was that great an idea. Reading between the lines, I reckon it's something Brian Tressider foisted on to him and now Brian's abroad, not breathing down his neck all the time, Ken's losing interest. He's of the old school..."never had videos in our time and it didn't do us any harm..." you know the sort.'

Charles nodded. 'But they're not going to cancel the production?'

'Oh no, contract with *Parton Parcel*'s all sewn up. The thing'll get *made* – they're committed to that. Just may never get *shown*.'

'Ah.'

'Still, that hardly matters to any of us, does it?'

They all agreed that, so long as they got paid, it couldn't have mattered less.

Seb Ormond was happy to share his experience of corporate work with Charles – indeed, it would have been hard to prevent him from doing so.

'Thing you've got to do is get the clothes right, Charles. Go up for an interview in the wrong kit and you may as well forget it.'

'Yes, I'd heard that.'

'So you got to be sure you've been properly briefed. I went up for one where they were looking for an Estate Manager, and my bloody agent told me it was an Estate Agent. As you can imagine – total disaster!'

'Do you do most of this stuff through your agent?' asked Charles, once again feeling rather guilty.

'No, I fix the bulk of it myself, but because I do so much, the agent does get enquiries.'

Charles felt marginally less guilty.

'So you've got to sort out the basic wardrobe.' Seb Ormond looked across at Charles who, although fairly confident he would once again be given the overalls, had dressed in his 'Trevor' costume. 'Of course, I don't do many blue collar roles...'

'No. Well, obviously...' And it was obvious. Seb Ormond's patrician features and greying hair had 'Management' stamped all over them.

'So the basic wardrobe I have is what I think of as the Managing Director's suit, the Sales Manager's suit, the Bank Manager's suit, and the Ad Agency suit.'

'And these are all different?'

'You better believe it, Charles.'

'Can I ask which suit you're wearing today...?'

'Today's Sales Manager.'

'Oh. Right.'

'Back in the old days I got most of my basic wardrobe off tellies I did.'

'What, buying them at the end of the series?'

Seb Ormond nodded. The practice they referred to was common among actors. At the beginning of a television series, running characters would be taken shopping by the Wardrobe Department to kit out the part they were playing, and at the end there was an arrangement whereby these clothes, frequently much more costly than the actor could have run to in normal circumstances, were sold to him at a very reduced rate.

Charles could identify the productions which had dressed a lot of his actor friends, particularly in really expensive items like leather jackets. And of course actresses playing characters with designer tastes had a field day.

Charles himself had done less well out of this system than others in his profession. This was partly because he rarely got running parts and, when he did, they tended not to be people who dressed in his style. Recent forays into television would have netted him the blazer and trousers of a golf club barman or the uniform of a 1930s police sergeant, neither of which he felt was quite 'Charles Paris'.

'*Now*, of course,' Seb went on, 'I buy my own clothes.' He responded to Charles's quizzical look. 'Well, it is quite a while since I did ordinary telly. And fashions do change, you know. Can't turn up as an MD in a suit whose cut's five years out of date, can you?'

'Ah, no,' agreed Charles Paris, whose one suit had recently celebrated its Silver Jubilee. He avoided the sardonic eye of Will Parton who had seen the garment in question.

What Seb Ormond was saying gave Charles a strange sense of *déja vu*. It reminded him of old actor-laddies he had heard reminiscing about repertory theatre in the twenties and thirties. 'In those days, of course,' they would ramble on, 'you had to have your own basic costumes. Dinner suit was essential, and a grey pinstripe, and tweeds as well. Otherwise you didn't get the job. No Wardrobe Department to provide that sort of stuff in those days.

And, my God, the hours you'd work! Be playing one show at night, rehearsing the next following morning, learning lines for a third...

He was brought back to the present by the unsurprising fact that Seb Ormond was still talking. 'Some characters you get asked to do, of course, need a touch of fine tuning on the costume front. I mean, easy enough to choose the right suit, but shirt and tie may need a bit of thought. I did a GP last week.'

'Oh, really?'

'Basic Bank Manager's suit, shirt with slightly frayed collar and hospital tie that was just a little bit greasy. Worked a treat. Shall I tell you how well it worked?'

'Go on,' Charles fed obligingly.

'The Medical Advisor on the film, who really was a GP, turned up in the identical costume.'

'I say. Well done.'

'Wasn't bad, though I say it myself.' Seb Ormond smiled with modest self-congratulation. 'Buggers, medical ones, though.'

'Oh?'

'Well, a good few of them are for drug companies. You have to remember these great long names of chemical formulas and what-have-you. Real killers, some of those. Investment and insurance aren't much fun, either – lot of that stuff reads like absolute garbage. Just have to learn it by rote, as you would a foreign language, and hope to God you've got the pronunciation right. I must say, learning Beckett or Stoppard's a doddle compared to some of the scripts you get given on the corporates.'

'Haven't given you anything difficult today,' said Will Parton smugly.

'Oh no, today's a real treat from the script point of view. Do it standing on my head. Nice words, Will.'

The writer, whose great play remained resolutely unwritten, preened himself at this compliment on his Delmoleen dialogue.

Seb Ormond evidently enjoyed the centre stage position and held on to it. 'Actually, funny thing on that medical video the other week. As I say, I was meant to be a GP and it was actually shot in a real GP's surgery. The way it goes...I have a patient in there, I have to go to a filing cabinet, get out his records and say, "Well, I'm sorry, Mr Whatever, the current treatment doesn't seem to be working. What I recommend..." etc. Get halfway through it, look down at the file and see the notes have DIED printed across them in large letters. Now I never corpse, but I'm afraid that just got to me – pissing myself with laughter I was.

'OK, I sober up, go for Take Two – pick up another file – exactly the same thing. DIED it says. I break up again. Turns out the entire cabinet was full of files of dead people. Couldn't have live ones, you see – breach of medical confidentiality.'

'Ah,' said Charles. 'Right.'

'You done a lot of corporate stuff, have you?' Seb Ormond asked magnanimously, maybe opening up the conversation for Charles to bring in a few anecdotes of his own.

'No. Lot of theatre, of course.'

'Oh, *that*,' said Seb Ormond dismissively.

The camera caused quite a stir in the canteen. *The Parton Parcel* crew had started work early, catching the last of the breakfast and the first of the tea-break trade, but nonetheless their presence prompted a lot of jockeying for position at adjacent tables by staff who wanted to be in shot.

Charles was yet again amazed at the potency of television and its ability to cloud the judgement. The chance of appearing on a screen, in whatever context, could turn the heads of people who in every other respect seemed to be completely sane. What else could explain the recurrent phenomenon of ordinary members of the public actually *volunteering* for the ritual humiliation of television game shows?

This thought also prompted Charles to wonder how much taking part in the Delmoleen video had meant to the late Dayna Richman; and how much she would have been prepared to do to ensure that she did get into it.

The morning's filming was straightforward, and the atmosphere more relaxed than it had been in the warehouse. Work on the video was not disrupting production in any way, and the impassive women dispensing tea and coffee from their urns showed no signs of resentment (or of anything else, come to that). No officious Canteen Manager was on hand to monitor the shooting, and Ken Colebourne, who was vaguely keeping an eye on things, seemed to be in a genial mood.

Charles and Seb Ormond delivered their lines with professional exactness, and Griff Merricks, exuding his customary negative charisma, was easily satisfied with what they did. The whole shoot was wrapped by noon, just as the canteen started to fill with early lunchers.

Will Parton looked at his watch. 'Executive dining room then, is it, Ken?'

'Well, yes, sure.'

The writer grinned smugly across at his friend. 'Oh dear, not improperly dressed again, are we, Charles?'

'Surely I'll be all right? If I keep the overalls on. These overalls are a darned sight smarter than any suit I possess.'

'That, Charles, is a comment on your suits rather than on the overalls.'

'Ha, bloody ha, Will.' Charles appealed to the Marketing Director. 'It doesn't really matter whether I'm in a suit or not for the Executive dining room, does it?'

But he had underestimated the hieratic structure of a company like Delmoleen. Ken Colebourne grimaced awkwardly. 'I'm afraid it isn't really possible, Charles. I mean, obviously, nothing personal, but there might be other people having lunch there who thought you were actually on the work-force and getting some kind of extra privilege. Wouldn't look good.'

'Oh,' said Charles, crestfallen.

Will gave him a patronising pat on the arm. 'Never mind. Who's the lucky boy? I notice the canteen's got Irish Stew on the menu today.'

'Thanks a bundle.'

Ken Colebourne didn't know how seriously to take this banter, but recognised a potential social problem. 'Erm, sorry. It's not that I want to appear inhospitable or anything...'

'Doesn't matter. Don't worry about it.

But the Marketing Director did worry about it. This challenge to his diplomatic skills had taken on a disproportionate importance for him. He coloured and looked awkward. 'I really am sorry, Charles.'

'Don't be. It's no problem.'

'No, but I...Look...' A solution presented itself. 'Tell you what, rest of you go off to the Executive dining room – I'll stay here and have lunch with Charles.'

'You don't have to. I'm fine.'

But, having satisfactorily negotiated his way out of the awkwardness, Ken Colebourne would brook no opposition to his plans. He went to one of the internal phones to ensure the video party's welcome in the Executive dining room, and then joined Charles in the queue for canteen lunch.

Resisting the seductions of the Irish Stew, Charles opted for Steak and Kidney Pie. To follow, he once again went for the Jam Roly-Poly, a delicacy that wasn't often on offer in the pubs and restaurants he frequented. As his portion – a whorl of sponge veined with vermilion jam – was dolloped into a bowl, he was forcibly reminded of the dish's schoolboy nickname, 'Dead Man's Leg'.

'As a matter of fact,' said Ken Colebourne when they had found a free formica-topped table and embarked on their first course, 'I find it quite a relief to eat in here sometimes. You can only take so much of posh, I reckon.'

Though this was undoubtedly said in part to alleviate the pain of Charles's exclusion from executive dining, the Marketing Director did sound as if he meant what he said.

'So you come in here often, do you?'

'Every now and then.'

'Oh, you should have been in the video – an authentic member of Management who actually eats in here. Could have done Seb Ormond out of a job.'

Ken Colebourne recoiled at the idea. 'No, thank you. Do anything rather than stand up and talk more than I have to. Sales conference is nearly four months away and already I wake up nights sweating about the presentation I got to do them. I know it's part of modern management – communicating, packaging yourself, packaging your ideas – but I must say I wouldn't mind winding the clock back a few years on all that stuff. I mean, the Sales Manager I used to work for in the sixties, only communication technique he used was telling us all to get our bloody fingers out. And it worked.'

'So you started as a salesman, did you?'

'Well, no, got promoted to salesman. Out of school I was a runner in the warehouse.'

'On the forklifts?'

'Didn't have many of those when I started. Used trolleys. Scurried back and forth along the stacks, picking up the stock by hand, then loading it on to the lorries.'

'Was it fun?'

'Well, the work was bloody boring, but then most work is, isn't it? Good bunch of lads, though, we had some laughs. Spent all our spare time playing football – that's all we thought about, really. That and the birds, of course.'

'You sound as if you'd like to be back there.'

'Well...' The Marketing Director sighed. 'Lot of ways things were much simpler then. Minute you walked out of the building you stopped thinking about work – didn't think about it much while you was doing it, come to that.'

'Whereas now...'

'Yeah. Whereas now...' The simple repetition adequately expressed his change of circumstances.

'Responsibilities...' Charles prompted.

'You can say that again. And new management techniques, and training programmes, and brainstorming sessions, and management consultants, and bloody videos and...'

'It sometimes seems to me,' Charles suggested cautiously, 'that there's a kind of connection between how badly business is going and the amount of training that gets done.'

'Too right. These days, when the product isn't selling, they don't put more effort into selling it, just more effort into training people how to sell it.'

'And are Delmoleen products not selling?'

Ken Colebourne shrugged. 'It's tough everywhere. Country's on the edge of recession, if it hasn't actually already tipped over. No, it's always been tough – just the way people try to deal with the problem changes.'

His tone left little doubt that he preferred the old solutions to those currently being offered.

'And I don't care much for the new style of management that's come in,' he continued. 'Back in the old days you knew people, you had friends, you thrashed things out over a few beers. Now it's all so impersonal...Sit there at endless meetings sipping Perrier, listening to all this jargon and bullshit... I feel like a fish out of water most of the time. Not really my scene, modern management.'

'Still, you've done all right,' said Charles reassuringly. 'Warehouse runner to Marketing Director – that's a pretty good progression, isn't it?'

'Oh yeah,' Ken Colebourne agreed wearily. 'Always the way in business – only way up is to move away from what you're good at. I've been in my current job seven years. That's a long time for this kind of work. Don't know how much longer I'll keep it.'

'Are you under threat then?'

'Everyone's under threat these days. Marketing's the sort of department that can easily get clobbered. You know, management changes...'

'Mm.' Charles had a sudden thought. 'Did Brian Tressider come up the same way as you?'

'What makes you ask that?'

'I don't know. The way you and he behave together...sort of suggests you go back a long way.'

'Well, you're right. We were at school together, here in Stanley Curton. Both joined Delmoleen on the same day. Alan Hibbert came in round that time too. Of course, Brian was the one who was always going on to great things.'

'You've done all right yourself.' Charles repeated the reassurance.

'Yes. He looks after his own, Brian.'

There were volumes of subtext in this sentence. Charles read in it Ken Colebourne's basic insecurity, his distrust of his own abilities, his fear that he had risen through the ranks of Delmoleen on the coat-tails of his more successful friend.

'Doesn't strike me as the kind of person who'd let sentiment stand in his way if he didn't think someone was pulling their weight.'

'No. No, I suppose not.' But Ken Colebourne didn't sound as if he believed it, more as if he was trying to convince himself.

'Unusual these days, isn't it, for a company to have many in management like you two, who've come up through the ranks...?'

'Very unusual. And getting more unusual by the day. The business school graduates are taking over everywhere.' He grimaced his opinion of this development. 'No, Delmoleen is unusual. Lot of people still here I've known virtually since I started.'

'What about Trevor?' Charles asked casually. 'He been here long?'

For the first time in their conversation, Ken Colebourne looked guarded. 'Quite a while. Since he left school.'

'Just like you.'

'Yes. Mind you, he's twenty years younger than me.'

'Mm.' Charles spread the congealing duvet of custard over his Dead Man's Leg. 'Was there something between him and that girl Dayna?'

A shutter of caution came down over Ken Colebourne's eyes. 'I don't know what you're talking about.'

'An affair.'

'An affair between Dayna and *Trevor*?' He seemed genuinely astonished by the idea. 'But there was no way that...'

He thought better of finishing the sentence.

'There was something going on,' Charles persisted. 'Trevor behaved very strangely when Dayna came into the warehouse that morning...you know, the day she died.'

The shutter stayed down. 'I didn't notice anything odd.'

'Well, it was odd, you take my word for it.'

The Marketing Director became engrossed in his Lemon Meringue Pie. 'Big place like this, a lot of relationships start up, break up...Goes on all the time. And then a lot of totally unfounded rumours of relationships start up and get gossiped about. I make a point of not listening to any of it, and you'd do well to do the same.'

'But surely you –'

'It's not actually part of my job to know precisely who's bonking who at any given moment.'

'No, obviously it's not. I'm just asking you if you happen to know whether Trevor and Dayna had ever gone around together.'

Ken Colebourne concentrated on severing the end from his wedge of Lemon Meringue Pie.

'I've no idea,' he said.

But Charles Paris was left in no doubt that the Marketing Director was lying.

Chapter Eight

KEN COLEBOURNE downed the last of his Lemon Meringue Pie quickly, suddenly remembering someone he had to see about some artwork. He rattled out another quick apology about the Executive dining room, made a perfunctory goodbye, and was gone.

Thereby raising Charles Paris's suspicions even more.

Why should his question have proved such a source of embarrassment? Had Charles been asking about some connection between Dayna and the Marketing Director himself, then the reaction might have been justified.

If he really had nothing to hide, Ken Colebourne could have answered a simple 'Yes' or 'No' – or even a bluff 'Mind your own bloody business' to the enquiry about Dayna and Trevor's relationship. By behaving as he did, he had raised the spectre of his own involvement with one or both of them.

It was a matter on which Charles would have to find out more.

Because the passage of time did not dilute his conviction that Dayna Richman had been murdered.

Charles knew he had left the forklift's ignition switched off. Sometimes, he was aware, especially when he had been drinking, recollections of his actions were hazy, but on that occasion he hadn't touched a drop all morning (not even the quick pre-teeth-cleaning snort of Bell's which was becoming a regrettable habit these days). He had even been particularly abstemious the night before, not wishing to screw up his first foray into a new and potentially lucrative area of work. No, he'd left the ignition switched off all right.

So, at the very least, somebody had entered the deserted warehouse to switch it on again. And there would have been no point in doing that, unless the somebody in question had wanted to use the truck. The forklift certainly hadn't been used to shift any stock, but it had been used to crush the girl.

What had Dayna been doing there, anyway? Why on earth should a girl dressed up to look her best on camera go scrabbling behind a pile of dirty pallets?

Charles decided that, while he was on Delmoleen premises, he should try to have a little look round the warehouse, see if there was anything hidden between the pallets and the wall that Dayna might have been searching for.

Though anything that had been there would probably have been tidied up in the course of the investigations into her death.

These investigations, Charles had gathered that morning from Ken Colebourne, had now been completed. The in-house enquiry had come up with recommendations that Delmoleen staff restrict their movements to the works areas where they had business to be – which was tantamount to saying that, if Dayna hadn't been where she shouldn't have been, the accident wouldn't have happened. Or, in other words, that her death had been her own fault.

There had also been an investigation from the Environmental Health Department, whose findings had been quoted at the girl's inquest. They echoed the strictures of the in-house enquiry, and made other specific safety recommendations for application in the warehouse.

The police had not been involved, but then, in a case of industrial accident, why should they be?

Charles wondered if the situation would have been different had the girl been killed outright. If he had discovered a corpse rather than a fatally injured person, maybe the police would have been summoned.

But somehow he doubted it. The whole business gave off a smell of cover-up. Within the Delmoleen site, the company seemed to do its own policing. The 'accident' having happened, it had been dealt with quickly and efficiently, in a way that caused minimum publicity and minimum disruption to company business. If anyone other than Charles Paris had had a suspicion of murder, he got the feeling they would have suppressed it – or perhaps been persuaded to suppress it – in the cause of Delmoleen.

Or was he getting paranoid?

'That one's the actor, is it?' he heard a loud, crackly voice say as he was leaving the canteen.

Half-turning to the source of the noise, he saw an elderly woman in a fur-collared overcoat sitting at a table with Heather from the Dispatch Office. The elderly woman's lips moved continuously, softly smacking against each other, as if she was talking all the time.

If the similarity in the set of the two women's eyes had not informed him, then Heather's reaction would have given away the fact that the older woman was her mother. There is a distinctive, atavistic, excruciating form of embarrassment that only parents can engender, and evidence of it glowed on Heather's cheeks. 'There's no need to be so loud. He'll hear you,' she hissed.

Her mother was not a whit perturbed. Seeing Charles looking in their direction, she immediately addressed him. 'Hello. My daughter says you're in this film they're making.'

He admitted that he was. Heather blushed even deeper as her mother said, 'Would you like to sit down with us? There's still tea in the pot.'

He was unsure whether the pain in Heather's eyes would be aggravated more by his acceptance or by his refusal, but, seeing a possible opening for further investigation, he drifted across to join them.

'Get the gentleman a cup.'

Heather seemed relieved to have somewhere to take her blushes and moved obediently across to the beverage counter.

'My name's Charles Paris.' He proffered his hand.

The old woman shook it. Hers was dry and scaly. 'Mrs Routledge. I'm Heather's mother.'

'I thought you must be.'

'She's a good girl, my daughter. Every Wednesday she gives me lunch here in the canteen. Gets me out of the house, you know, gives me a chance to see people a bit.'

'Yes.'

Heather returned wordlessly and put a Pyrex cup and saucer down in front of Charles. Mrs Routledge, as was appropriate, acted as 'Mother' and poured in milk and tea. She had the sugar-shaker poised before he managed to stop her.

'I was just telling Mr Paris what a good daughter you are to me, Heather.'

The younger woman almost imperceptibly cringed. Mrs Routledge was using that distinctive kind of parental commendation which is infinitely more diminishing than insults. 'I'm such a lucky old lady to have a daughter who looks after me so well. We live together, you know...'

Charles just managed to interpose an 'Ah' into this stream of consciousness.

'Always have done. I encouraged Heather to get away when she was younger, but she never seemed to have the will really, did you, love?' It was clear that most of Mrs Routledge's questions were rhetorical, as she steamrollered on, 'So it's just the two of us. Heather's father died...ooh, how many years ago is it now, Heather?' But again she supplied her own answer. 'Twenty-seven, it is. Twenty-seven years ago. And since then there's just been the two of us. You're an actor, you say?'

Assuming that, despite this sudden change of direction, Mrs Routledge's conversational method would not alter, Charles said nothing.

His tactics were proved to be correct. 'Yes, Heather said you were. And you've been here working on this film they're making all about Delmoleen, isn't that right? I thought so. You know, they wanted Heather to be in the film. Yes, they did. They wanted to film her in her office. She didn't have to say anything, just sit there and be filmed. But she didn't want to. I said she was being silly. I said, there's no harm in just sitting there, the camera won't bite you, it's silly to be so shy. I've always said she should push herself forward a bit more. But you wouldn't do it, would you, Heather?'

In the course of this monologue, Charles caught its subject's eye. Beneath Heather's embarrassment gleamed an undercurrent of sheer blind anger. He gave her a half-smile; she responded with a wry tightening of her lips.

Now he looked closely at her, he saw that Heather Routledge was not an unattractive woman. The grey eyes were flecked with blue, and her skin had a tactile sheen. It was only the anonymous dowdiness of her clothes and awkwardness of her stance that created the image of ugliness. Illuminated by a little self-confidence, she would actually have been rather attractive.

'Still, there's no way I'm criticising my daughter. Oh no, I'm very lucky, and I'm not one of those old ladies who doesn't appreciate her good fortune.

I'm extremely grateful for everything my daughter does for me. Do you know, Mr Paris, except for Wednesdays when she invites me in here, Heather rings me from work every single lunchtime.'

He managed to slip in an appreciative nod at this point.

'Yes, I'm very lucky. Every lunchtime. And she talks for a long time.'

Given Mrs Routledge's taste for monologue, this sounded unlikely, but neither of them questioned it. Years of experience had dissuaded Heather from taking issue with anything her mother said, and Charles found that he was subsiding into the same mesmerised acceptance.

'Every lunchtime,' Mrs Routledge repeated. Then, confident of the total subjugation of her audience, she allowed herself a slurp of tea. 'Ooh, this is getting very stewed. Go and get us some more hot water, Heather love.'

Her daughter, an obedient automaton, went back to the beverage counter and tried to attract the attention of one of the impassive women in pale blue housecoats.

Charles may have been sinking under the hypnosis of Mrs Routledge's endless talk, but he had enough will left to recognise an opening for his investigation. 'You say Heather rings you every lunchtime?'

'Every lunchtime, without fail.'

'So I dare say she's told you a bit about the video we've been doing?'

'Oh yes, all the details.'

'And I expect she rang you the day we were filming in the warehouse a few weeks back...'

'Oh yes, she did. She was on for a long time. I remember the day, because it was later that I heard about the dreadful accident to the poor girl who was in the film. Do you know, she was playing the part Heather would have been doing?'

'Well, yes, I –'

'And I kept thinking afterwards, if Heather had actually been doing it, then she would have been the one who had the accident.'

'I'm not sure that –'

'But wasn't it dreadful for that girl? A lot of that machinery they use isn't properly tested, you know. They've had other accidents here. There was a young man in one of the hoppers who...'

Heather had made contact with an impassive woman in a pale blue housecoat. The hot water was being procured. Charles hadn't got long.

'That day, Mrs Routledge,' he interrupted firmly, '– the day of the accident – do you remember what time Heather rang you?'

The old woman was so unused to being asked direct questions that she replied instinctively. 'Yes, I do. It was just before half-past twelve. I know, because I'd been listening to *You and Yours* on Radio Four – it's a good programme, that – and then they'd started with one of these new shows they keep trying to do with young comedians and bad language, and I don't hold with that – there's enough muck in the world without putting it on the wireless – and just after I'd switched off, Heather phoned.'

'And how long were you on the phone?'

The direct questioning really seemed to be working. Mrs Routledge replied, 'Oh, a good half-hour, because they'd just done the news headlines at one when I switched the wireless back on again.'

'And did Heather say whether there was anyone with her while she was talking to you?'

'Anyone with her?'

'Anyone else in the office?'

'Well, Brian – that's Mr Tressider – he came in, about one it must've been, because Heather said he'd come in and that's why she had to ring off. We've known Brian a long time, you know. He used to work here in Stenley Curton and at one time I hoped –'

Heather was moving back towards them with a pot of hot water, so Charles cut short Mrs Routledge's reminiscence. 'But Heather didn't say there was anyone there during the rest of the conversation?'

'No, no, of course not.' The old woman was only momentarily puzzled by this. Sensing a silence to be filled, she launched off again into her monologue. 'No, we've known Brian Tressider since he was a boy. He went to a school near here which...'

Heather looked at Charles curiously as she put the pot down. He looked equally curiously back at her.

What she was thinking he couldn't know. What he was thinking changed the whole premise of his investigation.

Mrs Routledge may have confirmed her daughter's alibi for the time of the murder, but she had virtually destroyed Trevor's. Heather had said the operator had been in her office at the relevant time, but surely he wouldn't have stood there for half an hour listening to Heather's minimal reactions to her mother maundering on.

So, if Trevor hadn't been in her office, where had he been? And, more importantly, why had she said he was there?

What possible motive could Heather Routledge have for lying to protect Trevor?

Chapter Nine

CHARLES felt heavily ballasted with Jam Roly-Poly as he walked out of the canteen. Spending much time round Delmoleen, he realised, would have a devastating effect on his waistline (though, actually, these days it was more a general area than a precise line). Presumably, most of the people who used the canteen were manual workers who'd burn it all off pretty quickly; for actors the task might be more difficult.

Of course he didn't have to eat so substantially. Among the bays of the food counter there had been a salad bar, but, though Charles enjoyed salad as a garnish to a meal, he'd never been able to think of it as a meal in itself. Though capable of going without food for long periods if necessary – as, for instance, during the innumerable technical runs of plays that his career had encompassed – if given the chance to eat, Charles Paris liked to have a proper meal. And for him a meal didn't feel proper unless there was a slab of meat in the middle of it. Ideally, it should also have alcoholic accompaniment, though, if indulged at lunchtime, that did tend to make him a little dozy in the afternoon.

The Delmoleen canteen had deprived him of alcohol, but he doubted whether anything would have subdued his excitement that afternoon.

The information he had gathered from Mrs Routledge represented a big breakthrough in the murder investigation. With Trevor's alibi shot to pieces, the possible scenario which had led up to Dayna Richman's death had altered radically. Putting on one side for a moment the reasons for Heather's behaviour, Charles Paris now had to find out more about the forklift operator's actions that fateful lunchtime.

And that meant paying another visit to the warehouse.

On his way across from the canteen, Charles met a very excited Will Parton. The excitement was in part due to the fact that the Delmoleen Executive dining room – unlike the canteen – did include alcohol amongst its privileges, but it had a second, more important, cause.

'Got another job, Charles,' the writer said gleefully.

'Oh yes?'

'Met Robin Pritchard in the Executive dining room.'

'You know all the stars, don't you?'

'Anyway, Biscuits and Cereals are launching a new product – very exciting, going to be very *big*...'

'With *global* outreach, no doubt?'

'You said it, Charles. It's going to be launched to the sales force at the sales conference in September, and he wants me to organise the presentation.'

'Just you as a writer, or is this a *Parton Parcel* job?'

'*Parton Parcel*. I mean, obviously I will write everything, but I get to direct it as well, if I want to – or bring in an outside director or...well, the possibilities are infinite.'

'This going to be another video job?'

'Could be. I'm having a meeting with Robin to sort out the nitty-gritty next week. At the moment we're thinking about a live kind of revue format, possibly with a slide presentation backing it up...we might add a video element, though...details to be sorted out, as I say. But it's a big, solid job – keep me busy for quite a while.'

'So the play gets deferred yet again?'

Will Parton looked pained. 'Got to go where the work is, Charles love.'

'Oh yes. You don't have to tell me that.'

'No.'

'And of course, if there is a role in the presentation for a speaking forklift truck operator...or indeed anything else...I'm a very versatile actor, you know...Forty-eight, but play younger...?'

'I'll bear it in mind, see if there is anything,' said Will loftily. He was rather enjoying the impresario role. His dismissiveness of Charles was revenge for years and years of working as a journeyman in television, endlessly rewriting, doing exactly what directors told him all the time. Through his involvement in *Parton Parcel* and the corporate videos, Will Parton was achieving a taste of that magic possession so rarely granted to writers – power.

'Are you going to the station, Charles?'

'Will be shortly. When's the next train?'

The writer, in his new hyper-efficient producer mode, had such facts at his fingertips. 'Two thirty-seven.'

'Oh, well, we've got a bit of time. Just someone I want to have a word with, so...see you on the platform?'

Will Parton looked at his friend wryly. 'You're not still off on this murder investigation routine, are you?'

'Well...' Charles shrugged awkwardly and made a hasty change of subject. 'What is this new product Robin Pritchard's launching?'

'Oh, couldn't tell you that, Charles. Bound to secrecy.' Will dropped into the earnest tones of the Product Manager. 'But I can tell you it's going to be very *big*.'

'Look, I'm not going to pass it on to anyone. No one I know gives a damn about new departures in the wonderful world of foodstuffs.'

'Ah, you may think that, Charles, but can't be too careful.'

'What you're actually saying, Will, is that you don't know what it is yet, do you?'

The writer was only momentarily discomfitted. 'That I'm afraid I can't reveal. But if the information had been kept from me, there would be good reasons for it.' He looked around elaborately and hissed, 'Industrial espionage – their spies are everywhere.'

'Come off it.'

'True. Lot of other companies desperate to increase their market share. If they found out about the new launch at this stage, it'd give them time to develop their own rival products.'

'Does it really work like that?'

'You betcha.' Will Parton winked conspiratorially. 'Biscuits and Cereals is a crumby business, Charles.'

The forklifts in the warehouse were plying their endless trade, loading up with pallets from the shelves and carrying them across to the insatiable lorries.

No one seemed to notice Charles's entrance. The Delmoleen overalls had been shed, so perhaps his 'Trevor' costume helped him melt into the scenery. More likely, the operators on their trucks were concentrating too hard on their work to see the newcomer.

He cast a quick glance at the outer office, but it was empty. Heather was either in the back room or, more likely, still suffering her mother's monody of irrelevancies.

The aisle where Dayna had died was empty. At its end once again there was a pile of empty pallets, though probably the original stack had been removed and another accumulated in the weeks since the incident.

Charles moved softly down the aisle. He knew it was ridiculous to hope that anything might still remain in the cavity between the pallets and the wall, but he was now fully psyched up and had to prove it by the evidence of his own eyes.

The hum of the forklifts and the occasional raucous shout from their operators sounded very distant.

He came to the end of the aisle and, with a quick look to either side, moved forward to the pallets.

'What the hell are you doing?'

Charles whirled round and found himself face to face with Trevor, who had just emerged from the end of the adjacent aisle. Whether he had been monitoring Charles's progress since the actor came into the warehouse or had just appeared at that moment by coincidence was impossible to know.

But the operator looked very mean. From his hand dangled one of the crowbars that was used for raising the lids of crates.

Charles said nothing as Trevor advanced towards him.

'Why're you snooping around?'

'We're here doing some more work on the video,' Charles's dry mouth managed to reply.

'That's in the canteen. No reason why you should be in here.'

'No. I just wanted to have a look around.'

Trevor tapped the crowbar on his open palm. 'Well, nobody wants people like you looking around.'

Charles tried to brazen it out. 'Perhaps not, but I want to do it. I still want to know what happened to Dayna Richman.'

'She died. There was an accident with a forklift truck and she died. If you hadn't left the truck switched on, she'd still be alive.'

'I didn't leave the truck switched on.'

'Don't try and be clever with me.' Trevor moved closer, close enough for Charles to smell the stale cigarette smoke on his breath. 'Just mind your own bloody business and get out of here – otherwise you're going to get hurt.' The crowbar was menacingly half-raised.

'You wouldn't dare hurt me in here. I'd shout. Someone'd hear me.'

Trevor let out a short bark of laughter. He jerked his head back towards the other forklifts. 'Everyone here's a mate of mine. None of them have got much time for bleeding wankers like actors. If I want to hurt you, nobody's going to stop me.'

'Listen,' said Charles, sounding calmer than he felt, 'I want some information from you.'

'Oh yes? And what makes you think I'm going to give you any information?'

'To clear your name.'

'My name doesn't need clearing. Dayna's death was an accident, unfortunate combination of circumstances, the enquiry said. No individual to blame.'

'But the enquiry was just a cover-up.'

Trevor shrugged. 'Prove it.'

'Listen,' Charles said again, trying to assert himself, 'I don't think Dayna's death was an accident.'

'Oh no? What was it then?'

'Murder.'

'Really? Well, as I just said – you just try and prove it.'

'What's more,' Charles went on recklessly, 'I think you are the one who killed her.'

The attack came so quickly he had no time to defend himself. He felt the neck of his T-shirt grabbed so that the collar closed round his neck like a noose. At the same moment Trevor's knee smashed up into Charles's balls.

He supposed he should have been grateful that the crowbar hadn't been used, but, in the eye-watering agony of that moment, he thought he would have preferred it.

Trevor's smoky breath was right up against Charles's face as the voice hissed, 'Don't you dare ever say that again! You repeat that and there will be a murder done! And you'll be the one whose body never gets found! You breathe another word about –'

'Trevor,' said an authoritative voice from behind Charles, 'what the hell do you think you're doing?'

* * *

Charles had forgotten just how much a knee in the balls could hurt. His life, though shadowed by alcohol, had included surprisingly little drunken brawling, and he had to think back to playground fights of his schooldays for comparable injuries. But he had no problem in recognising the pain.

The trouble was, the way it made him walk instantly identified the cause of his problem, and he'd found the short trip from the warehouse to the office of his saviour, Ken Colebourne, extremely embarrassing. Delmoleen workers – both male and, to his surprise and mortification, female – provided a range of ready, if unoriginal, witticisms as he passed.

In the office – thank God – the Marketing Director kept a secret supply of liquor, and a couple of medicinal brandies slightly dulled the grinding agony in Charles's testicles – so long as he didn't try to do anything clever, like moving. He felt a sudden, totally irrational desire to sneeze, and prayed that he would be able to control it.

On the other side of the desk, Ken Colebourne looked serious. 'I'm extremely sorry about what's happened, Charles, but I'd really be grateful if you could keep quiet about it.'

Yes, of course. The Delmoleen name mustn't be tarnished by any adverse publicity. The company must be kept smelling of roses, just as it had been after Dayna's death.

As it happened, Charles didn't want any enquiries into what he had been doing to provoke Trevor's attack, so he had no intention of making a fuss. He told Ken as much.

The Marketing Director didn't look totally reassured. 'It really is very important that this is kept quiet.'

'Don't worry. It will be.'

'Good.' But a note of doubt remained in his voice. 'Why did you want to talk to Trevor?'

'I didn't. I was just down there, and he started talking to me.'

'I'd keep well away from him if I were you. He's a nasty piece of work. Can be quite violent.'

Charles made the mistake of moving. 'You don't have to tell me,' he agreed through gritted teeth.

'No.' Ken still seemed uncertain, as if there was something else, some further reassurance, he wanted from Charles. 'If you had been thinking of having any dealings with Trevor,' he went on awkwardly, 'I'd give up the idea. It won't do you any good. You won't get anything out of him. He's trouble, you know.'

'I do know.'

'Hm.' But the Marketing Director couldn't leave the subject alone. 'You weren't asking him about what he and Dayna got up to, were you?'

'No. As I say, he just came up to me and started getting aggressive. I think he was probably still miffed that I was substituted for him in the video.'

Ken Colebourne nodded, not believing the explanation any more than Charles did. 'Yes, that was probably it. Anyway, as I say, Charles, I'd leave it. Difficult for an outsider to understand quite how things work in a place like Delmoleen. I'd just steer clear of Trevor and forget the whole business, if I were you.'

Charles nodded. That was unwise; the movement jolted right through his body and ripples of pain lapped outwards from his groin.

The Marketing Director looked at his watch. 'You going to be all right to get back on the train? I could lay on a car for you if you like.'

'Oh, I'll be fine.' Then Charles thought of the gleeful pleasantries with which Will Parton was likely to greet his affliction. The prospect of the writer's wit working overtime all the way to St Pancras was more than he could face. He winced. 'Well, actually, if you wouldn't mind...'

Ken Colebourne got on the phone to his secretary and organised transport. He proffered more brandy. Charles was at first inclined to refuse, but then thought, what the hell, I'm not going to be in any state to do anything else today, may as well succumb. He allowed his glass to be generously filled, without worrying about the fact that he'd almost definitely move on to the whisky when he got back to Hereford Road. He'd cross that hangover when he came to it.

'So I have your word that you won't mention this to anyone?' Ken insisted.

'No problem. Forgotten all about it already.'

Charles was intrigued by the man's over-reaction. Again it suggested some involvement in the affairs of Trevor and Dayna, and stimulated rather than allayed suspicion.

What the Marketing Director said next stimulated it even more. 'And if there's any favour I can do for you that'll help you forget the whole business, well, you only have to say the word...'

This was so unexpected that it took Charles a moment to realise he was being offered a bribe. 'Favour?' he echoed stupidly.

'Yes.' Ken Colebourne wasn't finding these negotiations particularly easy, but he was managing without total embarrassment, which suggested it wasn't the first time he'd made such offers.

'I wasn't talking money, of course, though it might be possible for some kind of arrangement to be made on those lines. But I was thinking more of...well, maybe some kind of event you'd like to attend...?'

'Event?'

'I have a lot of dealings with public relations companies. Most things can be arranged these days. The unobtainable has become very obtainable if you know who to ask.'

'What kind of unobtainable?'

'Well, concerts, theatre, opera tickets, those'd be no problem, whatever show you wanted to see. I can pick up that phone now and get you seats for tonight at the hottest show in the West End.'

'Oh?'

'Or, of course, if it's sport that interests you...well, you name it. Test matches, rugby internationals, Ascot, golf, Wimbledon, Henley, whatever you fancy...And I'm not just talking tickets here, I'm talking executive hospitality – you know, the full package. A really good day out.'

'Ah.' Charles, so unused to being courted in this way, was lost for the right response.

'I mean, what I'm saying is that I do very much appreciate the way you've taken this incident...' Ken Colebourne spelled out the deal, 'you know, saying you'll forget all about it, not take it any further...so I'd like to say a little thank-you to you in some appropriate way. Bit of a quid pro quo if you like .

'I see.'

'So what do you say? Anything in the little lot I've mentioned that might maybe appeal to you...?'

Charles had never had to ask himself before whether or not he was corruptible. By custom, the subjects of bribery are people who wield power and influence. There's never been much percentage in trying to corrupt a predominantly out-of-work actor.

So the ethical dilemma that faced him was unfamiliar.

He certainly had no intention of abandoning his murder investigation. But Ken Colebourne had talked in such veiled terms that it wasn't at all certain that that was what was being asked.

On balance, Charles decided that accepting one of the offers would not be compromising himself at all. At the very least, he deserved some compensation for his bruised testicles.

And, besides, there was one entertainment on Ken's list that did appeal a great deal.

It didn't actually appeal much to Charles Paris himself.

But he knew someone it really would appeal to.

He asked Ken Colebourne to make the arrangements.

Chapter Ten

'FRANCES, it's me.'

'Ah.'

'We're getting predictable.'

'What do you mean?'

'I keep ringing up and saying "Frances, it's me" and you keep saying "Ah".'

'So?'

'So nothing. I just mention it in passing.'

'Ah.'

'There's another one.'

'Mm. How are you then? All right?'

'Well, I am suffering a bit because someone kneed me in the balls.'

'Perhaps that'll teach you to stop chasing young girls.'

'It wasn't anything like that. It was...oh, never mind. Look, Frances, you remember when we last spoke...'

'How could I forget it? You rang up and said "Frances, it's me" and I said "Ah".'

'Yes. But on that occasion we also agreed that when I next rang up it should be with an invitation to something nice that you might like to do.'

'I'm not sure that we agreed it. I said it'd be nice. I don't recall you being that enthusiastic.'

'Well, be that as it may. The thing is, I am now ringing to invite you out to something nice that I think you'll enjoy.'

'Oh yes? When?'

'Saturday week.'

'What time?'

'Late morning till early evening.'

'Ah.'

'That's another "Ah", Frances. And, you know, the intonation of your "Ahs" is getting increasingly deterrent.'

'Yes. The thing is, Charles, that that Saturday is the middle Saturday of Wimbledon.'

'I know.'

'Well, if you know that, then you should also know that I get totally hooked during the Wimbledon fortnight and spend every spare moment glued to the television.'

'I do know that. That's the point.'

'What's the point?'

'The point is that I want to drag you away from watching Wimbledon on the television...'

'But it's one of the things I really enjoy!'

'...and take you to watch Wimbledon in the flesh.'

'Where?'

'At Wimbledon.'

'Oh. Charles, you're not suggesting that you and I, at our age, drag ourselves over to Wimbledon in the early morning and queue for hours to –?'

'No, Frances, I am saying I have two tickets to an executive hospitality suite at Wimbledon for that Saturday, and I am asking whether you would do me the honour of accompanying me there as my guest?'

'Ah.'

'Now that's a much nicer "Ah", Frances.'

'Charles, bit of a crisis.'

'What kind of crisis, Will?'

'Got a meeting with Robin Pritchard at eleven-thirty tomorrow morning. About this new product. With him and the account executive from the ad agency. Thing is, Seb Ormond was going to go along with me.'

'Why?'

'As set-dressing, really. Told you I don't want them to get the impression that *Parton Parcel* is just a one-man band.'

'But it is just a one-man band, isn't it?'

'Of course it is, but that's not the point. Having Seb sitting there looking dourly executive in his suit gives the set-up a bit of...I don't know...'

'*Gravitas*.'

'The very word. Anyway, Seb's cried off. Bugger's going to Manila for a new washing machine.'

'Seems a long way to go for a washing machine.'

'Don't be deliberately obtuse, Charles. He's presenting the launch of a new washing machine out there... you know, standing up, reading from an autocue and getting paid a fortune for his pains.'

'All right for some.'

'Anyway, thing is, it puts me in a bit of a spot.'

'Lack of *gravitas*, you mean?'

'That's it. You see, I want my set-up to look like a heavy-duty, solid company, so I can't turn up to a big meeting on my own.'

'I don't quite see why.'

'You take my word for it, I can't. I know these people. Numbers count with them. So, Charles, reason I'm ringing is I wondered if you might be free to come along with me tomorrow...'

'Oh. Well, Will, I'm very flattered that I'm the person you first thought of.'

'Of course you're not the person I first thought of! Nobody else was free.'

'Oh.'

'Come on, will you do it?'

'*I* might not be free,' said Charles loftily.

'Don't be ridiculous, Charles. You're always free. Come on, help me out of a spot.' There was a silence. 'If you do, I'll see that there's something for you at the sales conference in Brighton...'

The bribe of work had its usual, instantaneous effect. Charles agreed to go to the meeting.

'But what will I have to do?'

'Nothing.'

'Nothing?'

'No, just sit there holding a briefcase and look like you're making a mental note of everything that's being said.'

'Why?'

'It'll intimidate them a bit. Always a good idea to have one person at a meeting who doesn't say anything – it makes all the others terribly self-conscious about what *they're* saying. And raises the *gravitas* quotient.'

'Ah. Right. But isn't Robin Pritchard going to think it's odd, me being there? I mean, he last saw me as a forklift truck operator. I don't think forklift truck operators have a particularly high *gravitas* quotient.'

'Don't worry. He'll be seeing you in a different context. I'll tell him you're part of the *Parton Parcel* set-up and that that's why you did the first job. It won't be a problem.'

'If you say so. What voice shall I use?'

Charles rather fancied using the one he'd developed for Thomas Cromwell for *A Man For All Seasons* at Worthing ('This play is as well-made as a mahogany sideboard, and the acting was matchingly wooden' – *West Sussex Gazette*). Or possibly his Sir Benjamin Backbite from that Cheltenham *School for Scandal* ('The only scandal about this dire production was that Arts Council money helped to fund it' – *Gloucester Citizen*).

But such speculation was quickly curbed by Will. 'I told you, you don't say anything.'

'But –'

'And if you do have to say anything, you use your own voice.'

'Oh. OK.' He couldn't pretend he wasn't a little disappointed.

'And, again, no giggling.'

'Promise.'

'One other thing, Charles...'

'Yes.'

'Suit.'

'Ah.' Then, hopefully, 'You don't think the suit I've got could be –'

'Charles...' The intonation said it all.

'No. I see. Right.'

'Point is, actually, if you're going to be doing much more corporate work...'

'Yes?'

'Which you do want to, don't you...'

'Oh, yes, yes, sure.' The reply was instinctive. It wasn't particularly corporate work he wanted to do, just work.

'Well, it really is about time you started building up your wardrobe. I mean, for every time you're asked to do a forklift truck operator, you're going to be offered ten executives.'

'Hm. So what you're saying, Will, is that I'm going to have to buy a suit?'

'That's exactly what I'm saying.'

'And before this meeting?'

'Right.'

Charles was torn. Buying a suit was unbelievably low on his list of priorities. On the other hand, if that investment was the necessary key to a whole new field of lucrative work...'OK, Will, I'll buy one in the morning. Where is the meeting? Out at Stenley Curton?'

'No, it's in London. But, Charles, we must meet before the meeting.'

'What, you need to brief me?'

'Good heavens, no. But you don't think I trust you to buy a suit on your own, do you?'

They met, as arranged, at Oxford Circus. Charles was a bit vague about where to go from there. 'John Lewis pretty safe, isn't it? Or Marks & Spencers sell suits these days, don't they?'

He thought he was doing rather well, given how long it had been since he made a comparable purchase. Two ideas for where to go straight away – not bad. But the expression on Will Parton's face told him that he was not doing well at all.

'For heaven's sake, Charles, we're dressing an up-to-the-minute executive here, not a Leader of the Labour Party.'

'What do you mean?'

'We're after something with a bit of *style*.'

'Oh, come on, a suit's a suit, isn't it?'

'No, it isn't.' Will slid into his 'affected artist' voice. 'A suit's like a theatrical performance, love – it can look as if it's been totally grafted on from the outside, or it can flow from within so that one cannot tell where the personality stops and the suit begins.'

'Oh, my God.' Charles was reminded of an occasion in the sixties. He had been in Stratford, wearing a former suit, an ancient voluminous garment in fuzzy charcoal tweed inherited from his father, and had met an actor wearing a collarless Beatle-style number in identical fabric.

'Look,' Charles had said, holding his sleeve against the other actor's, 'same material.'

'Yes,' the actor had responded waspishly, 'but I had a *suit* made out of mine.'

Will hailed a cab and took Charles to Covent Garden. There he led him into a long narrow shop. The graphics over the door were so trendily minimalist that Charles couldn't read what the place was called. Once inside, Will showed a determination to kit his friend out as a minor *mafioso*.

'Surely this is too big,' whispered Charles, as he shambled out of the changing booth in a slightly shiny striped ensemble, which hung off him like the skin of an elephant six weeks into a crash diet.

'He thinks it's too big,' said Will, gleefully cruel.

'It is the *style*,' said the razor-thin shop assistant, with a waspishness which raised the possibility that his father might have worked at Stratford in the sixties.

'Feels quite lightweight, too,' Charles persisted. 'I like a suit with a bit of bulk. You know, for the winter. Got to keep warm.'

'It's summer,' said the young man, with a contemptuous flick of his pony-tail.

'Yes, but got to think ahead.'

'And since most offices these days are air-conditioned, today's executive tends to favour the lighter fabric.'

'Oh.'

'And have a topcoat to wear outside when the weather's cold.'

'Ah.'

'We do have an extensive range of topcoats if you –'

'Ah, er, no, thank you,' said Charles, who had just caught a glimpse of the price ticket on the suit. He looked across at Will and flapped his arms like an apologetic penguin. 'What do you think?'

'Hm. It's a bit *sober*, isn't it?'

'*Sober*?'

The writer turned maliciously to a hanging suit in pale flecked tweed, whose effect was of home-made cream of mushroom soup with croutons in it. 'This makes a bit more of a statement, doesn't it?'

Charles scotched that idea very quickly. 'Yes, but it's a statement from which I would firmly wish to dissociate myself, thank you very much.'

They ummed and erred. The young man wondered whether the gentleman would look better in a light brown herringbone (but in a defeated tone which implied he didn't really think the gentleman would look better in anything).

Charles took another look at himself in the mirror. He pulled the looseness of the double-breasted jacket away from his stomach. 'At least this is quite flattering to the fuller figure,' he chuckled.

'No, actually, sir,' said the young man, 'the style does look rather better on someone with a proper figure.'

'Oh well, perhaps I should be shopping for a new figure rather than a new suit,' Charles suggested, with a grin.

'Wouldn't be a bad idea,' the young man murmured, fingering one of his earrings.

'That one's a good fit,' said Will. 'Gives you a bit of edge, certainly.'

'Is "edge" what we're looking for?' asked Charles cautiously.

Will glanced at his watch. 'We haven't got too long to piss about. I think we should go for it, Charles.'

'Well, If you're sure –'

'Yes, we'll have it.'

'If that's your decision,' sighed the young man, in the manner of someone whose recommendation that Caesar stay at home on the Ides of March has just been overruled.

'Right, you'd better keep it on, Charles. Oh no, first you need a shirt and tie.'

'I'm wearing a shirt and tie.'

Protest was vain. He was dragged over to another display and kitted out with a soft cotton shirt whose sleeves were puffy enough to play Hamlet in, and a silk tie with a design that Braque might have knocked up and rejected while prostrated by flu. The tie, he noticed, cost as much as the last suit he had bought.

Paying was a problem. Charles had just achieved the unachievable and, following an ugly sequence of threatening letters, managed to pay off the debts on both his credit cards. At that unaccustomed moment of solvency, he had resolved to impose on himself a rigid regime of economy. That this intention was serious can be judged from the fact that he even – briefly – contemplated counting, and if necessary rationing, the number of bottles of Bell's whisky he bought.

Still, the road to hell is paved with plastic. He drew out the card and once again plunged deep, deep into debt.

He tried to convince himself that the clothes were a valuable investment for his career, but natural cynicism made such casuistry impossible.

While he changed into the shirt and tie, the shop assistant bundled his old clothes into a plastic carrier, which he placed on the floor behind the counter.

'Could I have those, please?' asked Charles, as he was about to leave.

'Good heavens,' murmured the young man, lifting his eyes to heaven. 'You mean you want to *keep* them?'

Chapter Eleven

CHARLES PARIS felt an absolute prune as he walked into the Delmoleen Knightsbridge offices. The shiny material of his new suit flapped irritatingly around him. Surely, not since the days of Demobilisation, had anyone walked around in clothes so patently the wrong size.

He was reassured, however, in the conference room where they met, to discover that Robin Pritchard and the agency man were dressed in almost identical garb, suits hanging in folds around them, bright silk ties progressing uneasily from Cubism to Surrealism. And when he actually came to look at Will, he saw that the writer was wearing much the same uniform. So, though Charles Paris still felt a prune, he was at least at a convention of prunes.

Certainly Robin Pritchard made no indication of their having met before, even though Charles was introduced by the same name. This was probably just professional discretion on the Product Manager's part, though Charles couldn't help wondering whether the suit transformed him so totally that it expunged all memory of his former forklift operator persona.

Robin Pritchard started by saying how very *big* the new product was going to be, how *huge* its launch campaign would be, how *global* its likely outreach, and how *massively* it was going to increase Delmoleen's brand share in that particular market.

Charles Paris sat through all this looking properly executive, the neat briefcase Will had supplied beside him, trying to give the impression that its contents were something of more significance than his old clothes. But his mind was wandering.

He took in the expensive sparseness of the conference room, which was of a piece with the rest of the Delmoleen Head Office. The reception area and corridors were all light grey, with flecked grey carpets. Desks were of darker grey, while low sofas and armchairs were delicately pink, like the underside of a trout. A few discreetly expensive abstract paintings hung on the walls.

There was nothing about the place that obviously said Delmoleen. Compared to the Stenley Curton site with its huge logos, or Ken Colebourne's office decorated with product pictures, the Knightsbridge premises were reticently anonymous. Only a small steel plate on their portico mentioned the Delmoleen name. They could have been the headquarters of an insurance company, an advertising agency, a merchant bank, a hotel chain, anything.

Presumably it was here that Brian Tressider had his office and spent most of his time. Charles wondered idly whether the Delmoleen video would include shooting at the London end. There wasn't much chance of his being required if it did. The London-based executives were probably quite capable of speaking for themselves and, though he did now possess the right suit for a managerial role, his facial similarity to the speaking forklift operator might not pass undetected.

His mind came back to Dayna Richman's murder – came back rather guiltily, it must be said. He had been trying not to think about it for the last few weeks. It wasn't the memory of Trevor's knee in his crutch that put him off, nor was he deferring in response to Ken Colebourne's bribery – it was just that he didn't know how to proceed on the case. Without any good reason to return to Stenley Curton, it was hard to continue the investigation.

And, in a way, the investigation was complete. Charles Paris was convinced that Trevor had killed Dayna, though he couldn't precisely define the man's motive. Presumably, sex was at the bottom of it somewhere. It usually was when a man and a woman were involved. A lovers' tiff, something along those lines...Anyway, the prospect of finding any proof of what had actually happened seemed ever more remote.

'And the really important, revolutionary, mould-breaking thing about the product is that it's *green*.'

Robin Pritchard's pronouncement brought Charles back to the present with a jolt. The Product Manager looked triumphant. The agency man, who already knew what the product was, shook his head in benign amazement at the boldness of its concept. Will Parton, who didn't yet know what the product was, looked as impressed as only someone pitching for a lucrative contract can.

They all turned to Charles Paris for his reaction. He decided that an expression of awestruck reverence would be appropriate and, since they all looked away with satisfaction, presumably he had got it right.

'Now when I say *green*,' Robin Pritchard continued, 'obviously I'm using the word in the environmental sense...'

'Obviously,' Will Parton agreed.

'So all the ingredients will have been organically grown, and not only will they – the ingredients – be listed on the wrapper, but their provenance will also be detailed – you know, to show that they have been processed in a way that has done the minimum harm to the environment...'

Will, who Charles had heard on many occasions say that he didn't give a damn about the environment so long as he had a fridge that worked, nodded enthusiastic endorsement of Robin Pritchard's words.

'What is more, the wrapper will be made from wholly recycled paper and be coloured by pigments that are totally biodegradable. Not only that, but, for every unit sold, a sum of money will be donated to an environmental charity – you know, to replace some of the rainforest, do something for the ozone layer, whatever...'

'How much?'

'How much?'

'Yes, how much will be given to the environmental charity?'

Will's question seemed to fluster the Product Manager. 'Well, the precise, er...the precise details are yet to be worked out. I mean, we are talking a percentage here, and inevitably a fairly small percentage –'

'But the purchasers needn't know that,' the agency man chipped in smugly. 'The campaign will emphasise the *fact* of the donation rather than the precise *amount*.'

'Exactly,' said Robin, 'but, nonetheless, given the number of product units we are hoping to shift, we are talking a very considerable sum of money.'

'Certainly, certainly,' the agency man conceded magnanimously. 'And the environmental value of the product will obviously be stressed at every point of the campaign.'

'And so,' said Will, 'every unit that's sold, for the rest of time, will be raising money for the environment.'

'Well, no, not *for the rest of time*,' said Robin Pritchard cautiously. 'I mean, we do obviously have to think of our profit margins. No, the donations will be made only over the initial three-month period of the launch.'

'And then they'll stop?'

'Yes, in effect they will. I mean, you can't go on doing that kind of thing for ever. Delmoleen's not a charity, you know.'

'Of course not.'

'But again,' the agency man chipped in, 'while our campaign will stress the donation element over the launch period, it would not be of interest to anyone for us to make too much of a song and dance about the moment when that element is dropped.'

'No, of course not,' Will Parton concurred.

'So, as you'll have gathered, this thing is going to be really big. What do you say, Will?'

'Certainly sounds *big*, Robin. And very exciting.'

'Charles?'

He didn't quite know the correct response. Will had told him to say nothing, but to do so to a direct question seemed downright rude. So he just shook his head in astonished disbelief and said, '*Big*.'

Robin Pritchard nodded, gratified, but Charles couldn't help adding, 'Sorry, you haven't said what the product is yet...'

'It's the Delmoleen "Green",' the Product Manager announced momentously.

'Ah.' Charles nodded. 'Green what?'

'It's just called the "Green". That's the beauty of the name, its sheer, minimalist simplicity.'

'Yes. Yes, of course. But what is it? Is it a breakfast cereal or a biscuit or a...?'

'Oh, right. With you, Charles.' Robin Pritchard pursed his lips. 'The Delmoleen "Green" is such a revolutionary concept in biscuitry that it's very hard to define. I guess the nearest existing product to what we're talking about here is a muesli bar.'

'A muesli bar?'

'Right. The Delmoleen "Green" has all the virtues of the traditional muesli bar...' (Charles found it difficult to imagine that muesli bars had been around long enough to have their own traditions) '...and those of the current "State of the Art" muesli bar – I'm talking 100 per cent natural ingredients, high wholegrain dietary fibre content, low sugar, low saturated fat, the obvious stuff...The Delmoleen "Green" has all that and a bit more – but it also has the special feature which is going to take it rocketing to the top of the Crunchy Bar and Snack Biscuit Brand Share.'

'What's that?' asked Will Parton, dead on cue.

'It's green,' Robin Pritchard whispered reverentially.

'Green?'

'Yes, 100 per cent green.'

Charles Paris, confused, couldn't stop himself from saying, 'But you said that. You said it was green. It's called the Delmoleen "Green" –'

'And it's green.'

'Ah.' That still didn't clarify things much for Charles.

But the Product Manager's next words did. 'It is green in colour. Green like Nature, green like little green apples, green like the leaves of spring, green like...' He ran out of poetic inspiration, 'green like – green. Coloured, of course, from natural dyes, the Delmoleen "Green" will be the only product in the entire *global* muesli bar range that is actually coloured green.'

An impressed silence ensued.

Then, tentatively and sycophantically, Will Parton asked, 'You don't mean that the wrapper will be green in colour too?'

'You said it,' a complacent Robin Pritchard confirmed. 'Now, is that marketing or is that marketing?'

Will Parton shook his head in slow, stunned amazement. 'I'd say that's marketing.'

The Product Manager smiled the kind of smile Tamburlaine might have allowed himself when he entered the vanquished Persepolis. He looked at his watch. 'Now we have a table booked for lunch to get down to the nuts and bolts of the launch, but before that I have a little surprise for you.'

'Oh?' they all said, elaborately wondering what it could be.

Silently Robin Pritchard pressed down the key of an intercom and murmured, 'Ready, Janice.'

The door opened and a smartly-suited secretary entered. She carried a silver salver. On it lay three rectangles of what looked like green fibre matting.

'No? It isn't?' asked Will (overacting a bit, in Charles's estimation).

'Yes, it is. You three will be the only people outside Delmoleen ever to have tasted a Delmoleen "Green".'

Appropriately honoured noises were made, as the girl handed around the sacred batons.

Among the many, many foodstuffs that Charles Paris enjoyed, muesli bars did not figure at any level. And a green muesli bar would, under normal circumstances, be something to be consigned instantly to the dustbin.

The idea of eating a green muesli bar immediately before lunch was even more disgusting.

But he, like Will Parton and the agency man, lifted one of the rectangles off the salver as if handling a Dead Sea Scroll.

And he, like the others, looked to Robin Pritchard for the inestimable gift of permission, which was conceded by a gracious nod of the head.

Charles Paris, Will Parton and the agency man lifted their Delmoleen 'Green' to their mouths in unison. Together, they took the first bite. Together, they shook their heads discreetly from side to side as they tried to dislodge a chunk from the sticky whole. Together, they munched.

'Ah,' they all said together, 'wonderful.'

Or that was probably what they said. It was difficult to be sure because their teeth were a bit glued together.

The lunch did not hold much interest for Charles. The food was fine, good trattoria fare, but his enjoyment of it was marred by all the bits of green oats, nuts and other fibre stuck between his teeth.

Then there was the drinking problem.

'Now, what are we going to have to drink?' Robin Pritchard had asked bonhomously on arrival.

Charles's mouth was half-open before he caught the steel in Will Parton's eye. 'Mineral water for me,' said the writer firmly.

'Me too,' said the agency man.

'Charles?'

'Yes, mineral water. Sounds terrific.'

Ooh, it hurt. Not only because he'd really been promising himself a few nice glasses of nice wine, but because he so deeply hated mineral water. Charles Paris was not a party to the Perrier conspiracy. When he wanted water – and even he, occasionally, particularly if he woke parched in the middle of the night, did want water – he found the tap perfectly adequate to his needs. The idea of paying bubbled-up prices for bubbled-up water appalled him. Apart from anything else mineral water at lunchtime meant that all afternoon his stomach would rumble like a demented washing machine going into its final spin.

He thought wistfully of the business world Ken Colebourne had referred to with such nostalgia, when deals were thrashed out between friends over a few beers.

Still, Charles Paris was there solely to help Will secure the contract for *Parton Parcel*. Just as he had swallowed down every last crumb – and there did seem to be a lot of them – of the Delmoleen 'Green', so he would swallow down the mineral water. He was playing a part, after all. That thought, a direct appeal to his own professionalism, did bring a kind of comfort.

It wasn't difficult for him to maintain his pose of silence during the meal. Robin Pritchard went on and on about the brilliance of his product, the agency man went on and on about the brilliance of his ideas for its launch campaign, and Will Parton went on and on about the brilliant, though as yet unspecified, way in which he would present the Delmoleen 'Green' to the sales force at the Brighton conference in September.

Charles, trying to imagine how Seb Ormond would play his part, looked grave and deep and nodded thoughtfully a lot.

There was only one moment when the conversation caught his interest. Will was setting out his stall, expatiating on how brilliantly he had scripted the Delmoleen video, which brought up the subject of the day's shooting in the warehouse.

'Oh yes,' said Robin Pritchard. 'That was when the factory bike got crushed.'

'Factory bike?' queried Charles, as if he had never heard the expression.

'Used to describe a young lady who's – what shall we say? – generous with her favours?'

'Oh. So Dayna Richman had that reputation, did she?'

'Quite justified, from all accounts. Cut a swathe through the warehouse lads like the First World War, I gather.'

'Was Trevor one of the victims?'

'Trevor with the forklift?'

'Mm.'

'Good heavens, no. Trevor's gay.'

'Oh?' That was unexpected. On the other hand, it did explain the unidentified laugh which had greeted Trevor's reference to Charles as a 'bleeding fairy'.

Charles couldn't resist the follow-up question. 'You don't happen to know if she was going around with any of the other lads at the time she died, do you?'

'Wouldn't have thought so. Having tested out her basic skills and found everything in working order, I think young Dayna was aiming a bit more up-market.'

'What? Are you talking about anyone in particular or –?'

'*Charles…*' Will Parton hissed with a veiled look of fury. 'Robin, about the actual sales conference...'

Charles felt guilty. He mustn't screw up the deal for *Parton Parcel*. No, his murder investigation would have to go on hold yet again.

He would have to be content for the moment with the tiny fragment Robin Pritchard had given him.

The new information did put an intriguing new light on the situation, though.

Chapter Twelve

'MY GOD, Charles, what on earth are you wearing?' Frances stood aghast at the door of her flat.

'It is possible for me to look smart, you know, Frances.'

'Smart? Is that smart? Have you got a part in *Godfather IV* or what?'

'I am just dressed as the young executive dresses these days.'

'Since when have you been a young executive? I've heard of mutton-dressed-as-lamb, but...My God, Charles, what's that smell? It's not mint sauce, is it?'

'It's after-shave,' he confessed sheepishly (or mutton-dressed-as-lambishly). Will had tipped him the wink that some kind of 'man's fragrance' really was required to complete the executive image.

'Good heavens.'

'Come on. The car's waiting.'

Ken Colebourne had done them proud. Car to pick up Charles in Bayswater, on to Highgate to collect Frances, and then down through the traffic to Wimbledon.

'This is very exciting,' Frances said. 'Haven't actually been to Wimbledon for about ten years. Always used to queue up and go in my teens, but in later life being in charge of school parties rather took the gilt off the experience. Spent all the time watching my charges rather than the tennis, seeing they weren't being picked up by randy young men or rubbed up by dirty old men. No, this really is wonderful.'

She looked terrific that morning. With age, Frances had managed to stay elegantly thin rather than turning stringy. She was neatly dressed in a generously-skirted navy suit and cream blouse with a big collar, an ensemble Charles hadn't seen before.

It was still a shock that he no longer knew his wife's wardrobe inside out, but that was one of the many rights he had given up by walking out on her all those years ago. Unreasonable though he knew the desire was, some part of Charles still felt she should consult him about the clothes she bought.

Though he wanted the freedom to vanish off her landscape for months on end, he couldn't quite reconcile himself to the idea of Frances leading a life of her own. Though he knew he was being a dog in the manger, a jealous arrogance kept telling him he really was the love of her life and, so long as he was alive, she'd never be truly independent.

Increasingly, though, the evidence was turning against him. Charles was hoist with his own petard. He had left Frances in the hope of attaining his own independence, but over the years she had proved much more adept at making a life of her own than he had.

He liked to think the mutual ties remained so strong, that, in spite of detours and diversions, the relationship was still central to both of them. And even that one day they'd get back together again.

But he was decreasingly convinced that Frances felt the same. The coolness that she had at first affected as a defence against him now seemed more instinctive.

'Juliet was so jealous when I told her where we were going. She still loves her tennis.'

'Oh. Right.' Charles had always intended to do more things, like play tennis, with his daughter while she was growing up, but he had been away a lot, and then of course he'd moved out, and suddenly she had been grown up and married and a mother three times over, and he had realised that his chance was gone and that Frances had been responsible for every aspect of Juliet's upbringing.

'I must get in touch with her,' he said contritely.

'Yes, you must,' Frances agreed with some asperity.

He looked sideways at her as the car negotiated the heavy traffic of Wimbledon High Street, and felt an ache of longing. He really must make a proper effort to get her back. Frances was too good to lose.

He knew he had had such intentions many times before, but they had always been diluted by lethargy or diverted by skirmishes with other women. When he was actually with Frances, it seemed inconceivable that he could ever fancy anyone else. But he recognised the volatility of the masculine character, that resurgent and shameful inability to meet any woman without thoughts of sex intruding; and he knew that, given the right circumstances, with Frances off the scene and someone else attractive to him on it, the whole process would start all over again.

But this time he really must put all irrelevant thoughts to one side, and work to regain Frances's affection. He felt a sudden stab of lust as he looked at her.

Greatly daring, Charles Paris put his hand on his wife's knee.

She didn't remove it. She looked straight into his eyes and smiled a warm smile of complicity.

That had to be a good sign.

It was rather a good feeling to be whisked past the endless, patient lines of tennis fans to one of the main gates. Their driver sorted out a time and pick-up point for the end of the day's play, and gave them a phone number to call if any change was required to these arrangements. Their tickets were checked at the gate and, following the map in the neat information pack which Ken Colebourne had sent Charles, they made their way to the Delmoleen marquee.

As they walked through the crowds, Frances commented on how the atmosphere had changed since she'd last been there. 'There weren't all these booths and shops. There wasn't nearly so much for sale, I'm sure.'

Charles stopped by a display of clothes, indicating a green and purple track suit with 'The Championships – Wimbledon' logo. 'Like me to buy you one of these?'

'Not quite my style, Charles. But don't let me stop you getting one for yourself.'

'Don't think it's quite my style either.'

'I don't know, love. Now I've seen that suit, nothing you wear's going to surprise me.'

She put her arm in his. And she had called him 'love'. It was nice having a wife.

He felt this even more when they reached the Delmoleen marquee. Following the map, they had turned into an alley of corporate entertainment. There were rows of marquees on either side, fronted by neatly fenced-off areas with white chairs and round tables shaded by beach umbrellas. Men in suits and smartly dressed ladies stood sipping champagne in the various pens.

From the small signs on the entrances Charles recognised among the corporate entertainers a major bank, an insurance company and the BBC. On the forecourt of the BBC marquee stood various well-known television faces, pretending they weren't aware that everyone recognised them.

The Delmoleen marquee's number was clearly marked on the map and its entrance discreetly signposted by the company logo. Charles was glad he had Frances with him. Much easier to make an entrance into a crowd of strangers as a couple. There really was a lot to be said for marriage. Good system.

As it turned out, there were some faces he recognised. Brian and Brenda Tressider were there, so was Ken Colebourne, but he looked in vain for Robin Pritchard. Charles had rather hoped to see the Product Manager again and follow up on their last, incomplete conversation. However, it looked as though the murder investigation would have to remain on hold.

The other guests were smartly anonymous, presumably substantial customers or suppliers having their relationships with Delmoleen cemented and massaged by a corporate freebie. Charles had been a little worried than Brian Tressider might question his right to be there, wondering what possible benefit could accrue to the company from scratching the back of an unemployed actor – even one supposed to have some ill-defined connection with the *Parton Parcel* production company. But of course the Managing Director, whatever his true feelings on the matter, was far too urbane to let them show.

Well-rehearsed on the guest-list, he effusively welcomed Charles and Frances, telling her that her husband had done excellent work on the video they were making.

Brenda Tressider was equally punctilious, and her social filing system did not let her down. 'Yes, of course, Charles Paris, how delightful to see you again. You entertained us so much in that splendid *Stanislas Braid* series. It must be really strange seeing your husband on the television screen so often, Mrs Paris.'

'Well, it's not *that* often,' said Frances – rather traitorously, to Charles's mind.

'Oh, but much more than the average wife. I mean, I've seen Brian interviewed once or twice on business programmes and it always gives me a very odd feeling. But I suppose, like most things, you get used to it.' A uniformed waitress with a tray of champagne materialised at her elbow. 'Now do help yourself to a drink, and let me introduce you to some people...'

They were impeccably introduced to everyone and Charles found, as he usually did on these occasions, that the names went straight in one ear and out the other. So did all the useful background detail that Brenda Tressider supplied for her guests. She was doing her job wonderfully, presenting innumerable prompts to conversation; it wasn't her fault that Charles Paris seemed incapable of retaining the information.

Frances was much better at this sort of thing than he was. She plunged instantly into conversation with one of the women about the latest American infant tennis sensation, and was quickly whirled away, leaving her husband stranded.

Charles stood grinning fatuously round a group of three couples, whose names and companies he had instantly forgotten. He sipped at his champagne, then took a longer swig. The waitress manifested herself once again beside him. He put down his empty glass and picked up a full one.

'What a lovely day for the tennis,' he said, opting to keep his remarks uncontroversial.

The three couples agreed it was a lovely day for the tennis.

'Yes, lovely day for the tennis,' Charles confirmed.

He had a sense of *déjà vu*. For a moment he couldn't place it, then recalled that he had spoken exactly that dialogue in one of those fifties french-window comedies about a publisher. (They had all been about publishers; to the dramatists of the time, publishing represented a lucrative profession whose demands were in no danger of impinging on anyone's private life.) Now what had the play been called...? Oh yes, *Service Not Included*, he remembered it now.

He also, unfortunately, remembered the review the *Halifax Evening Courier* had given his performance. 'Charles Paris wanders dementedly through the play, like Van Gogh trying to decide which ear to cut off.'

He saw Ken Colebourne grinning and waving, and excused himself from further reaffirmation with the three couples of how good a day it was for tennis.

'All the arrangements went all right, did they?'

'Fine, Ken. Yes, very grateful to you for setting the whole thing up. My wife's absolutely delighted to be here. I must introduce you.'

'Well, first let me introduce you to my wife. Patricia dear, this is Charles Paris.'

The sight of Patricia Colebourne was quite a shock. He had hardly noticed her, lost in the shadows under one of the umbrellas. She was agonisingly thin; the beige linen dress hung slackly from the angularity of her shoulders; and her skin had a waxy pallor. Two sticks were hooked from the lip of the table.

She was clearly a very sick woman, and yet the formalities of introduction do not traditionally include a medical bulletin, so Charles could only shake the hand that felt like a bunch of dry twigs and say, 'Pleasure to meet you.'

'Patricia's a great lover of the tennis,' said her husband. 'Been watching it all day this week, haven't you, love?'

His manner towards her combined embarrassment with a kind of defensive pride.

'Yes. And I hope to see that young Yugoslav playing this afternoon. She's amazing. Supposed to be on court at two, I think.' She looked at the watch that dangled loosely from a skeletal wrist. 'Probably better start walking over there now. I'm afraid I move very slowly these days, Mr Paris.'

She was joking, but the mention of her disability served to clear the atmosphere.

'Oh, you're not that bad, love. Anyway, we've got lunch to eat first. I'm sure you'll enjoy that.'

As if on cue, Brian Tressider raised his hands, gesturing towards the interior of the marquee. 'Going through for a spot of lunch now – set us up for the excitements of the afternoon, eh?'

There were three round tables each seating six inside the marquee (a structure, incidentally, of greater permanence than the word usually implies). Frances, who was proving a great hit with her new friends, was whisked away to sit with them. 'Unless you'd rather sit with your husband...?'

'Good heavens, no,' she replied with a sweet grin to Charles. 'We see quite enough of each other.'

He didn't quite know how to take this. Inside a normal, cohabiting marriage, such a remark would be a sign of strength, of a couple so secure in their mutual affection that they didn't need to spend every minute in each other's pockets. Given the unusual circumstances of Charles and Frances's marriage, though, the interpretation was potentially different. Did Frances really mean that their three or four meetings during the last year had been quite sufficient? Or was she just making a joke at his expense?

Charles inclined to the second view, though not with that total confidence which would make him feel secure. Frances was definitely playing games with him, but he couldn't be certain how serious those games were. She had been hurt too many times to allow the progress towards any possible reconciliation to be easy for him.

So there was Frances's table, which she seemed effortlessly to dominate; and the table towards which Brian Tressider had firmly ushered his pre-selected guests; and there was the third table, which was definitely lowest in the hierarchy. Charles Paris sat at the third table.

On one side of him was a young man with sleeked-back hair and a suit and tie even sharper than Charles's; on the other, a girl with carefully frizzed blonde hair, whose trim figure was enhanced by a navy leather suit that teetered between sexiness and tartness.

It soon became apparent that they were married. The young man took Charles's hand firmly in his and announced, rather as if presenting a business card, 'Daryl Fletcher, and that's my wife Shelley.'

'Hello. My name's Charles Paris.'

'We're here because it's part of Daryl's bonus.' The girl had one of those Cockney voices that sound as if the owner's just going down with a sore throat.

'Well, it's not exactly part of the bonus, just a kind of pat on the back. I got Top Salesman,' he confided to Charles.

'Oh. Oh, well done.'

'Yes. I'm North-West Area. Quite something for a North-West salesman to beat all those jammy bastards in the South.'

'I should think it is,' Charles agreed sagely.

'Don't know they're born, half of that lot. I got Runner-up last year, but this year I really pulled out the stops.'

'Well done.'

'Means me and Shelley get a weekend for two in Paris.'

'And the car, Daryl.'

'Yeah, and the car. Get presented with that at the sales conference. I'll trade it in, mind. Just some little Fiesta. Not my sort of motor. But the money'll be handy.'

'Yeah, except you'll just spend it on your other car.'

'All right, what if I do, Shelley? I'll see you get a bit of naughty lingerie, and all.'

This seemed to strike her as disproportionately funny.

'I got a pretty nice motor, you see,' Daryl confided to Charles. 'I don't mean the company car – no, I drive round day by day in a Ford Sierra, but I got this car back home with a bit of character.'

'Oh,' said Charles, to whom all cars had the same character.

'Cortina,' said Daryl airily.

'Oh,' said Charles, reassured. He had been afraid of being blinded by car talk, but this was all right. He had heard of the Cortina. Reliable, long-running Ford model, now out of production and a bit boring, really. But at least, he comforted himself, there's not a lot you can say about a Cortina.

Charles couldn't have been more wrong.

'It's the old Mk I,' Daryl confided.

'Oh yes?'

'Picked it up at a scrap-yard four years back. Saw its potential straight off.'

Charles couldn't conceive what possible potential a car from a scrap-yard might have.

'Basically in good nick, but I had to do a lot of body and chassis work.'

'Ah.'

'Built a full roll cage inside.'

'Did you?'

'Yeah, and then while I got the body off, I give it a four-inch chop. Pleased with the way that worked, I was. Lovely job, though I say it myself.'

He looked up for approbation, but Charles wasn't quite quick enough to replace the bewilderment in his expression with something more congratulatory.

'You do know what I mean by a "chop" don't you, Charles?'

'Er, well...'

'Tell you for free,' Shelley chipped in. 'It's nothing to do with a chopper!' This again struck her as extravagantly funny.

'We are talking "custom" here,' Daryl explained generously. '"Chop" means you take the roof down a few inches.'

'Ah. Why?'

'Well, gives you a bit of style, doesn't it?'

'Does it?'

Daryl's social training told him perhaps he ought to open the conversation out a bit. 'What do you drive then, Charles?'

A chuckle. 'Well, er, taxis, if anything.'

'You a taxi-driver?' asked Shelley.

'No.'

'What are you then?' asked Daryl.

'An actor.'

The answer struck both of them dumb. They wracked their brains for things that might be said to an actor, but nothing offered itself.

Charles filled the silence. 'What I meant was that the only cars I really travel in these days are taxis. I use the tube most of the time, but if I do go in a car, it tends to be a taxi.'

'You mean you haven't got a motor?' asked Daryl in softly awestruck tones.

'No, I haven't. Used to, when I was living with my...' He caught a glimpse of Frances entertaining her new friends at the adjacent table, 'some time back,' he concluded lamely.

'Blimey,' said Daryl quietly. 'Haven't got a motor.'

'No.'

But not for nothing had Daryl Fletcher been nominated Top Salesman. It was a salesman's job to keep talking, and he wasn't going to let anything – even a shock on the scale that he had just received – deter him from his duty.

'You know, when I took the engine on the Mk I apart, I found the cylinders was still well within specs, so what I done was...'

After about two millennia of this monologue, during which Charles, almost without noticing, consumed smoked salmon, *boeufe-en-croûte* and meringue *glacé*, together with a lot of red wine, he became aware of a general movement around him.

Frances caught his eye and waved. She pointed at her watch. 'Two o'clock. Match starting on the Centre Court.'

'Oh yes, right.'

Charles started to stand up, but Frances's words had stopped Daryl in mid-description of how he'd recalibrated the gauges from an old Cortina GT. The Top Salesman rose to his feet, 'Great, I want to see this. Dishy pair of birds playing.'

Charles sank back into his chair. The risk of ending up sitting next to this cataract of Custom Car arcana was too great. 'I'll just have a cup of coffee and be right along, Frances.'

His wife shrugged and nodded. She wasn't exactly unused to Charles making his own timetable.

The marquee did not empty completely, though most of the guests went off to watch the tennis. Ken Colebourne had gone some twenty minutes earlier, gallantly escorting his fragile wife, and Brian Tressider had led his party off soon after. But a few lingered over the last of their coffee, wine or brandy.

Shelley Fletcher, Charles observed, had made no attempt to move.

'I'll go along in a bit,' she said. 'Only women on Centre Court this match.' She giggled. 'I'll wait till the hunks get out there.'

'Ah.'

'Daryl's very fond of his Cortina,' she explained, unnecessarily.

'Yes,' said Charles Paris. 'Yes, he is, isn't he?'

Chapter Thirteen

OUT OF THE corner of his eye, Charles kept catching movement on a television screen high in the corner of the marquee. White figures moved against a green background. The volume had been turned down low; applause sounded like distant sea-wash. But the picture was still distracting. He moved his chair round a little so that the screen was out of his eyeline.

This had the unintended effect of bringing him closer to Shelley. She raised her eyebrows in a quizzical, half-mocking challenge.

'I'm sorry. It's just, er, that monitor, sort of putting me off my stroke.'

'Ooh. Can't have that, can we, Charles?'

She had an engaging way of saying his name. In her husky Cockney, it came out as 'Chowss'.

'Look, I didn't mean –'

'Don't worry. I've never complained about fellers getting too close to me.'

'Ah. Ah,' said Charles. He wasn't used to this kind of heavy innuendo, certainly not from someone presumably in her mid-twenties. He adopted the traditional British method of taking the heat out of any situation. 'Lovely day, isn't it?'

She agreed that it was a lovely day. 'Nice to be down here, and all.'

'Yes. You're a Londoner, aren't you?'

'Mm. Mind you, one of the disadvantages of being married to the Top Salesman in the North-West Area is you have to live up there.' She grimaced. 'We're in Preston.'

'Is it that bad?'

'No, the people's quite friendly and that, but all my mates is really down here.' She put on a pious expression. 'Still, the little woman has to go wherever Hubby goes. And do whatever Hubby tells her to, and all, doesn't she?'

Shelley even managed to imbue this with a sexual overtone.

'I didn't think women thought like that nowadays. Thought you were all more liberated.'

'Oh, don't worry, Chowss, me and Daryl are a very *liberated* couple.'

He somehow didn't think they were both using the word 'liberated' in the same sense.

'And the thing is, a "liberated" couple can always find people of similar interests wherever they are. Even up in Preston. Quite a lot of "liberated" people we've met up there, you know.'

Charles nodded casually, not quite sure that he was hearing right. Shelley seemed to be saying that she and Daryl were into some kind of partner-swapping. In fact, her whole conversation could have come straight out of a soft-porn magazine. He had a sudden vision of the bookshelves in the Fletcher sitting-room – rows of Custom Car magazines, interleaved with *Penthouses* and *Escorts*.

'So are you going to be stuck up there long?' he asked uncontroversially. 'I don't know a lot about Daryl's kind of work. Is it the sort of job where you move around a lot?'

'Yeah. Lot of salesmen do. Daryl's been with Delmoleen for a long time, working his way up, like, but now he's got Top Salesman, it's probably as far as he can go in the company. You know, he's not Sales Manager material – well, not yet, anyway – so he'll probably start looking for something else soon.'

'Something down South?'

'Hopefully, yeah.'

One of the discreet uniformed waitresses appeared beside them. 'Would you like some more wine? Madam? Sir?'

'Could probably force myself,' said Charles expansively.

Another full bottle of red wine was placed on the table between them. He gestured with it towards Shelley's empty glass.

'Why not? Neither of us got to drive. The chauffeur car's part of the day.'

'For me too.'

'Yeah. Hope you don't mind my asking, Chowss, but why are you here? Funny place for an actor to be, isn't it?'

It was a question he had been fearing, but he managed to fudge together some kind of answer about *Parton Parcel* and the filming that he had done at Stenley Curton.

'Oh yeah, how is the old place?' asked Shelley.

Charles's detective antennae started twitching. 'Why, did you ever work there?'

'Yeah, I started there as a typist straight out of school. 'Swhere I met Daryl. He was doing Midlands Area then. We got together and...' She shrugged, 'Rest is history, innit?'

'Yes.' He took a nonchalant sip from his glass. 'I don't know if you heard, but there was a dreadful accident that day we were filming in the warehouse...'

'Course we heard. Dayna, wasn't it?'

'That's right.'

'People been saying for a long time she was going to get her comeuppance. No one thought it'd come that way, though.'

A casual 'Oh?' proved to be quite sufficient prompting for more information.

'Well, Dayna really was a bit of a scrubber. I mean, she, like, *used* sex.'

A high moral tone had come into Shelley's voice. Clearly she regarded Dayna's behaviour as very different from her own. What was done within the confines of marriage – or, as it seemed from what she'd said, a series of marriages – was unimpeachably respectable, compared to *using* sex.

'How do you mean, exactly?'

'Well, Dayna, like, used her body to get things out of men. You know, early days she'd go out with blokes for nice meals and that. She thought the meal was OK, she'd give the bloke what he wanted. Meal not up to scratch, he didn't get nothing.'

'Not the first time that kind of transaction's happened.'

'No, right, I agree, but Dayna went on from there…you know, wanted "little presents" from blokes she went out with.'

'What kind of presents?'

'Jewellery, hi-fi, that kind of stuff.'

'Money?'

'Don't think so. Not directly. No, I think she reckoned if it was just for money, then she might as well be a prostitute. Didn't like that idea. Oh no, our Dayna had her standards – just they was a lot lower than most other people's.'

'Ah.'

'Funny thing was, I don't think she really liked sex that much.'

'Oh?'

'Well, back in the old days, you know, before me and Daryl got married, there used to be some fairly wild parties around the place.' She looked straight into his eyes, daring him to be shocked and flinch away. 'You know, lot of couples, go to someone's house, all the bedrooms is open, play some games…maybe with forfeits – you have to take off this, take off that, girl has to go off with this bloke, bloke has to go off with that girl – you know the kind of thing I'm talking about…'

Charles nodded, as if his social life was one endless round of such parties.

'It was only fun, you know. We all had a laugh. Anyway, Dayna come along to one or two of these parties, but seemed like it wasn't her scene.'

'You don't mean she was shocked?'

'No, no, take more than that to shock Dayna. No, she joined in all right first couple of times, but then she kind of lost interest. No percentage in it for her, you see.'

'What do you mean exactly?'

'Well, like I said, she used sex to get something out of blokes. Our kind of scene, you know, where we just did it for fun…well, nothing in it for her.'

'Right. I see.'

Shelley giggled at some recollection. 'Coo, we used to get up to some daft stuff, though…'

If she started expanding too much on what they got up to, Charles was afraid he might not be able to keep up his unshocked eye contact, so he said, 'A girl who behaves like that's going to be very popular – in one sense – but she's also going to make herself pretty unpopular too, isn't she?'

'With the blokes she's dumped, you mean?'

'Yes.'

'You'd think so, wouldn't you? Funny, though, I mean a lot of the girls at Delmoleen's badmouthed her all the time...you know, what a slut she was and all that, but the blokes on the whole, certainly the blokes she'd been with – I mean, the ones who you'd expect to be really pissed off– I very rarely heard them say anything against her.'

'That's strange.'

'Yeah, it is actually, isn't it? Never really thought about it before, but it is strange. Like she had some hold over them or something.'

'Any idea what that hold could have been?'

Shelley shrugged. 'Why you asking all this about her, anyway?'

Charles finally broke the eye contact. 'Just interest, I suppose. You know, having been there on the day she died, and...well...'

'Mm.' Shelley stretched and looked up at the television screen. 'Looks like the ladies is coming to an end. Must go and get my seat before the hunks come on.'

'Yes,' said Charles hastily. 'Just something about one other person I met out at Stenley Curton...bloke called Trevor...'

'Trevor?' she echoed blankly.

'Drives a forklift in the warehouse.'

'Oh, *Trevor*, right.'

'He been working there a long time?'

'Well, certainly there when I started, so that's got to be five years back.'

'Yes. Was he ever involved in any of the parties you were talking about?'

'Trevor?' She let out a husky bark of laughter. 'Trevor wouldn't have fitted in to that scene at all. He'd have stuck out like a...' She chuckled throatily. 'Well, he wouldn't have stuck out at all. Ladies are not Trevor's thing.'

'Ah.' At least he'd got confirmation of Robin Pritchard's information.

'So he had nothing to do with you lot at all?'

'No, his social scene was *very* different from ours.' She paused. 'Only contact we had with him, we might borrow some stuff now and then.'

'What sort of stuff?'

'Video. Trevor was very into video. I mean, now everyone's got a camcorder, but five years ago...none of us was that well off for a start...but, you know, some of the blokes – well, and the girls, let's be fair – was quite keen to have themselves, like, recorded...you know, while they was at it...and then play it back and get turned on all over again. You ever done that, Chowss?'

Again her mocking blue eyes were very directly fixed on his. At one level, Charles didn't take her brazenness seriously. It was a game she was playing, more for her benefit than his. At another level, though, he couldn't help being titillated by it.

He laughed what he hoped was a man-of-the-world laugh, implying infinite confident experience of every known sexual permutation.

Shelley's grin suggested that she didn't believe the implication. 'So, anyway,' he said, clearing his throat, 'you used to borrow Trevor's equipment?'

Shelley roared with laughter. 'No, like I said, that wouldn't have been any use to us at all. We borrowed his *video*.'

'Yes, yes. You knew what I meant.'

'Maybe I did, maybe I didn't.'

'Did he just lend it, like that?'

'Oh, I'm sure one of the lads bunged him a flyer. Only happened a few times. Then one of the other salesmen got a promotion and he bought his own camcorder and that was it.'

She went off into another of her giggles. 'Do you know, Daryl once rigged it up in a bedroom and filmed this couple who didn't know it was there. Then they come round to dinner couple of weeks later and he puts the cassette in the video and plays it to them. Ooh, it was funny. They was dead embarrassed. Got a really evil sense of humour, my husband,' she concluded with some pride.

That kind of practical joking didn't come under Charles's definition of 'sense of humour', but he let it pass.

'Just going back on what we were saying...you were never aware of any relationship between Trevor and Dayna, were you?'

'Relationship? Trevor and Dayna? Well, from what I've said about their interests, I can't see it, can you? She was only after rich men and he wasn't after women of any kind – doesn't sound like True Romance to me. No, if they did have any kind of relationship, you can bet your bottom dollar it was financial.'

'Hm. You say Dayna was after rich men?'

'Rich...powerful...comes to the same thing, really, dunnit? No, what Dayna wanted to do was sleep her way right to the top.'

They heard a throat clearing and turned to see Brian Tressider looking at them. Behind him was Ken Colebourne who instantly and protectively steered his Managing Director away to chat to one of their major distributors who was working his way down a brandy bottle.

But Charles had seen an unexpected look in Brian Tressider's eyes. He felt sure that the Managing Director had heard Shelley's last words.

And that they had had a particular relevance for him.

Charles had been about to go and watch some tennis, but Daryl had reappeared to claim Shelley for the 'hunks' match, and the risk of accompanying them to the Centre Court was still too great. To give the Custom Car danger time to recede, Charles had another glass of wine.

Then Ken Colebourne joined him. Patricia, he announced, was quite happy watching the tennis. In fact, she was sitting with Frances and they seemed to be getting on very well. 'Still, I've never been much of a one for tennis – just knocking the ball back and forth over the net all the time, so far as I can see. Grand Prix racing, now that's the sport I like to watch.'

Charles groaned inwardly. It would be too dreadful to have jumped out of the Custom Car frying-pan straight into the Formula One fire.

But, fortunately, the Marketing Director seemed to have no desire to expatiate on his hobby. Instead, he was in a mood to tell jokes and, after a few glasses of wine, Charles was prepared to indulge the mood. Even to join in it. So the two of them, fuelled by yet more wine, played that traditional pastime of mutual joke-telling which for centuries has kept men from talking about anything that matters, and given them the illusion of conviviality without any real contact.

At one point Charles did try to get the conversation on to Brian Tressider, but Ken Colebourne alertly deflected the subject. Charles was once again struck by the care with which the Marketing Director protected his boss.

And so the afternoon passed. Other Delmoleen guests drifted in and out of the marquee, tea and cakes were served at some point. Drinks were available as long as anyone wanted them, and Charles had a bonhomous sense of having chattered amiably with a great many really nice people.

They were a splendid lot, he decided, really, *really* nice people. All that nonsense that was talked about people in industry and the arts being different...People, when you came down to it, people were people – that's what mattered. Not where they came from or what they did, but the fact that they were people. People.

He was saying this with some force to the major distributor who was working his way down a second brandy bottle and finding that, though his new friend was agreeing with him, it was still a point that needed repeating, when he became aware of a cleared throat behind him.

He turned round to see Frances. She still looked lovely in the navy suit. He told her how lovely she looked. Then, in case she hadn't got the message, he told her again.

'Yes, Charles,' she said – somewhat coldly, he thought. 'It's time we went to meet our car.'

'Oh, really? Feels like we've only just arrived.' He rose to his feet. The marquee wobbled rather endearingly around him. 'Must just have a pee.'

When he came back, Frances was thanking the Managing Director for Delmoleen's hospitality. Brenda Tressider stood by her husband's side, smiling graciously.

Charles joined in the thanks. It really had been a splendid day.

Brian Tressider was delighted he had enjoyed it.

Oh yes, it really had been a splendid day, Charles confirmed.

Brenda Tressider looked forward to seeing him on the television again soon. Were there going to be any more of that delightful *Stanislas Braid* series?

Well, no, there weren't, actually, but there was still no denying that it had been a splendid day.

Frances led him away.

He told her how lovely she looked.

'Yes, all right, Charles, you've said that.'

'Have I? Well, it's still true. I –'

'I hope you didn't make Ken Colebourne drink too much.'

'What do you mean – make him? I –'

'I was talking to his wife, Patricia. She's very worried about the amount he drinks.'

'Oh, come on, he's Marketing Director. In that kind of job, I should think the drinking goes with the territory.'

'Well, Patricia worries about it. She's very dependent on him, you know.'

What a perfect cue, thought Charles. He took his wife's arm. 'And I'm very dependent on you, you know.'

Frances firmly disengaged her arm. 'Ah, there's the car over there.'

They got in the back. 'Where to first?' asked the driver.

'Ah,' said Charles. 'Well, look, Frances, why don't we go back to your flat? Then we can have a drink, and I'll take you out for dinner and –'

'Hereford Road first, please,' said Frances. 'My companion will be getting off there.'

Charles felt he should argue, but he was really too tired. As he stretched back into the comfortable upholstery, he looked through half-closed lids at Frances. Her mouth was a tight, tense line.

Oh dear, what *had* he done wrong this time? He reached across to put his hand on her knee.

Frances removed it.

Well, what had he done wrong? It had been a splendid day. A splendid day.

It was only as he slipped into sleep that Charles realised he hadn't seen any tennis.

Chapter Fourteen

'I MEAN, if you like,' said Will Parton, 'we could do the presentation as a song-and-dance routine.'

'I think that could be terrific,' Robin Pritchard enthused. 'Really give the salesmen and their wives a bit of entertainment. Get across how exciting and up-to-the-minute the Delmoleen "Green" is going to be.'

'Look, we don't want things to get out of hand.' This voice of restraint was Ken Colebourne's. He had overall charge of the Brighton sales conference and for him the whole undertaking was already quite complicated enough. The Ambassador Hotel and Conference Suites had been long booked, but there were still many details of the programme to be arranged. Song-and-dance routines sounded like potential trouble. 'I mean, the salesmen and their wives are going to get a full professional cabaret after the Thursday evening banquet. They don't want any more of that kind of stuff. Let's keep the presentations simple.'

The Product Manager for Beverages agreed. Paul Taggart was a pugnacious little Scot, clearly suspicious of Robin Pritchard's empire-building. 'All we need to do is tell the salesmen the facts. Bring them up to date on existing products, tell them the state of play on the new products, show them the packaging, commercials if they're ready, and leave it at that.'

'But the Delmoleen "Green" is such a new concept, we want to communicate the excitement we all feel about it.'

'Robin, it is no more a new concept than Delmoleen "Surge", which I will be introducing in Brighton.'

'Of course it is, Paul. "Surge" is nothing more than a repackaging job. It's just your basic Delmoleen "Bedtime" in a different jar.'

Knocking his product was hitting a Product Manager where it hurt, and Paul Taggart responded angrily, 'It is not. The sugar content has been reduced to almost zero, the glucose content boosted, and a whole bunch of different vitamins added.'

'But it will still be perceived by the public as a simple bedtime drink.'

'No, it will not!' Paul Taggart was almost beside himself. 'That is the whole point. "Surge" is the first Delmoleen product to get away from that "bedtime" tag. It's an "any time you feel like it" beverage. "Surge" is being marketed as a health drink – not a relaxant, but a stimulant.'

'Mind you,' said Ken Colebourne judiciously, 'that is the way the basic

Delmoleen drink is marketed round the world. In every other country it's sold for its stimulating and energy-giving qualities. Britain's the only place where it sells on its relaxing qualities.'

'Why is that?' Will managed to chip in curiously.

'Something to do with national character, I think,' said the Marketing Director.

Charles Paris was enjoying himself. He and Will were out at Stenley Curton to attend the first 'nuts and bolts' planning session for the Brighton sales conference. It was an evening meeting in Ken Colebourne's office. Lavish salvers of sandwiches lay on the green baize cover of the table in front of them. There were also liberal supplies of coffee and mineral water (but unfortunately nothing else).

Charles had anticipated a fairly boring session and was cheered by this entertaining conflict between the Product Managers.

'So,' Paul Taggart went on, 'the marketing of "Surge" is going to be a whole new concept for the salesmen.'

'So's the marketing of "Green".'

'But, in the long term, "Surge" is going to be the more important product. The Beverage market is much steadier. Confectionery's very volatile, always subject to changes of fashion.'

'That's nonsense,' blustered Robin Pritchard. 'And, anyway, the Delmoleen "Green" is not Confectionery. If it were, it'd attract VAT, apart from anything else, and wreak havoc with our pricing strategy. There is no way it's going to be marketed as Confectionery.'

'Well, people are hardly going to pick up a muesli bar from the Cereals display, are they?'

'The Delmoleen "Green" is a bit more than just an ordinary muesli bar, Paul. Anyway, it's not being marketed as Cereals – it's being marketed as a Snack.'

'Huh. The Snack market's even more volatile than Confectionery.'

Ken Colebourne decided it was time for mediation in the war of Cereals and Biscuits against Beverages. 'Please, please, we've got a lot to get through. But I would like to endorse Paul's point. Given all the other entertainment the sales force're going to get, I think we want to keep our presentations at the conference as simple as we can.'

The Product Manager for Beverages smiled complacently. 'Thanks, Ken. Always the voice of sanity. What entertainment are they going to get, by the way?'

'All the usual stuff'll be laid on for the wives. Then at the Thursday banquet there's a dance band and, of course, the cabaret.'

'Who've you got?'

'Not absolutely finalised, but looks likely to be...' He mentioned the name of an American girl singer who'd been big in the charts in the early seventies.

'What, is she here doing a tour?'

'No, we're flying her over just for this.'

'That's going to cost you.'

Ken Colebourne nodded grimly. 'Got to go bigger and better than Torquay last year. Don't want any more of the salesmen thinking of moving.'

'Suppose not.'

'And then the comedy cabaret – assuming we get the contract sorted out OK – is going to be Nicky Rules.'

They were all impressed by the name. Nicky Rules was one of the country's top comedians, a television game-show host known chiefly for the viciousness with which he insulted its contestants and the glee with which the contestants lapped up his abuse.

Charles was possibly more impressed than anyone else present – not because either of the names mentioned were favourites of his, but because, being in the business, he had some idea of the kind of fees they could command. It had never occurred to him that a company like Delmoleen would be prepared to pay that sort of money just to entertain its sales force.

Robin Pritchard had been silent for the last few minutes, but not because he had conceded defeat on the presentation of his product. He had been merely biding his time, and now came back forcibly to the attack.

'I still want to put across the Delmoleen "Green" with a bit of razzmatazz. I want the salesmen to see a presentation they're going to remember.'

'They'll remember it perfectly well if it's done straight,' said Ken Colebourne coldly.

'No, they won't. They'll just doze off, as ever. Look, the presentation's in the afternoon – thanks to someone else getting the morning slot for their product...'

The Product Manager for Cereals and Biscuits looked daggers at the Product Manager for Beverages, who grinned smugly.

'And we all know what that means – the salesmen will have had a few too many at lunchtime and, if they just get a straight presentation, they'll see it as a good excuse for a kip.'

'You're out of date, Robin,' said Ken Colebourne. 'That old hard-drinking image of the salesman has changed. They're much more responsible and accountable these days.'

He had chosen the wrong line of attack. 'Out of date?' Robin Pritchard echoed contemptuously. 'Out of date? *You* have the nerve to call *me* out of date?'

'Well –'

'For one thing, I don't believe that salesmen ever really change. For another, this company is going to do nothing for its image if it keeps using presentation methods out of the Ark.'

'Look –'

'I want the Delmoleen "Green" presented to the sales force in an exciting way, not just a talking head and slides.'

'Talking head and slides has worked perfectly well in the past.' As ever, when pressured, Ken Colebourne summoned the name of his hero as evidence. 'B.T. doesn't even bother with the slides.'

'No, but Brian's a charismatic speaker. People'd listen to him, whatever the circumstances, whatever he was talking about. Other people need more help.' Robin Pritchard looked at the Marketing Director with an expression that fell little short of insolence. 'Will you be doing your usual marketing overview?'

'Yes,' said Ken Colebourne, trying not to sound defensive. 'End of the afternoon, just before B.T. speaks.'

'With slides, as ever?'

The Marketing Director's lips were tight across his teeth. 'Yes.'

'Hm. You haven't ever thought of getting someone else to do that, have you?'

'Who else? I'm Marketing Director. It seems pretty ridiculous to have anyone else talking about marketing.'

'I meant an actor.'

'What do we want bloody actors in our sales conference for?'

'Just to make the presentation look more professional.'

This gibe really got to the Marketing Director. 'Listen, I am going to do that overview, because I am the person who knows most about the subject! And if I'm not professional enough, well, that's bad luck!'

Having heard Ken's views on the subject of speaking in public, Charles was a little surprised at how vehemently the Marketing Director defended his right to do it. But then, of course, this was office politics. The argument was not primarily about who presented the marketing overview, it was just another manifestation of the protracted conflict between the two executives.

'Very well,' said Robin Pritchard lightly. 'On your own head be it, Ken…as usual. But since we have Will here, do you mind…' his voice was heavy with sarcasm, 'if I just ask him for his professional advice…'

'No. No, go ahead.'

'OK, Will, if we could somehow persuade the dinosaurs of Delmoleen that we don't have to present "Green" to the sales force by the old sleeping-pill methods…would you have some alternative suggestions…?'

'You bet,' said the writer gleefully. 'I have thought through quite a lot of potential scenarios…'

Charles knew this was a complete lie. Will Parton had given the subject no thought at all. He was busking, but – it had to be admitted – busking quite convincingly.

'We could go up the comedy sketch path, of course – plenty of ideas there, which I'd be happy to spell out for you – but I think a more fruitful approach could be song-and-dance…you know, glitzy, bit of showbiz, get in some dancers, a choreographer and –' he announced, offering the spur-of-the-moment thought as if it was something he'd been mulling over for months, 'we could have all the dancers dressed in green.'

'This I *like*,' said Robin Pritchard, while his two colleagues looked sourly on.

'The important thing, though, Robin, is to get the right song for the presentation. I was thinking it should be something with "green" in the title.'

'An existing song, you mean?'

'Exactly.'

'But we're never actually going to find a song that's about muesli bars,' the Product Manager objected. 'Least of all green muesli bars.'

'No, of course we're not. But we take an existing song and we parody the lyrics.'

'Don't you get copyright problems if you do that?' asked Charles.

'Ah, you would if it was for public performance. Because it's in-house, no one's ever going to know about it. There are really no rules in the corporate world. Writers' Guild regulations don't apply. Nor do Equity, nor Musicians' Union. It's a free for all.'

'Do you have any songs in mind?' asked Robin Pritchard.

'Well, yes, there are a few obvious ones.' Will's mouth opened and closed as he wracked his brains for a single relevant title.

'*Greensleeves...?*' Charles offered helpfully.

'Yes, yes, good. Or, um...*Mountain Greenery*....or...' The writer started to get into his stride. '*Green Tambourine...The Green Leaves of Summer...*'

'*Green Grow the Rashes, O!*' Charles contributed.

'Yes.'

'And that has the advantage of being out of copyright, so there couldn't possibly be any problem.'

'No. And it could go...' Will paused, still improvising like mad, then started to sing, '*I'll sing you one, O!*'

Charles intoned the chorus. '*Green grow the rashes, O!*'

'*What is your one, O?*'

'*Green grow the rashes, O!*' the actor repeated, leaving the writer with the difficult bit.

A momentary light of panic crept into Will Parton's eye, but he recovered himself. '*One is green, completely green, and ever more shall be so!*'

'I think we really could be on to something here,' said Robin Pritchard earnestly.

'*I'll sing you two, O!*' Charles sang, trying to avoid Will's eye.

'*Green grow the rashes, O!*'

'*What is your two, O?*'

'*Green grow the rashes, O!*'

Charles suddenly realised that he had lumbered himself with the creative bit. 'Erm...erm...

'*Two, two the muesli bars,*

'*Wrapped up all in green, ho! ho!*' he pronounced with triumph.

'*One is green, completely green, and ever more shall be so!*' Will completed the chorus lustily.

They pressed on but Charles's control had gone. His eyes streamed and he could hardly get the words out through suppressed giggles. Will was managing better, but even his voice trembled on the edge of hysteria.

The killer came when Will supplied the line for 'three':

'*Three – beats all ri-i-i-i-vals!*'

Charles was finished; he could only wheeze helplessly.

'This won't do,' said Robin Pritchard suddenly.

'I'm sorry,' Charles gasped. 'It just struck me as terribly –'

'No, this song – *Green Grow the Rashes, O*! It could have very unfortunate associations. It might give potential customers the idea that the Delmoleen "Green" would bring them out in a rash.'

'Oh dear, hadn't thought of that,' said Will, his voice heavy with concern. He turned sardonic eyes on his friend and the corner of his mouth twitched as he asked, 'Had you, Charles?'

'I, er...I, er...' Charles rose desperately to his feet, fighting down the hysterics. He rushed to the door of the office. 'I'm sorry,' he cried, as he sped helplessly off down the corridor. 'Asthma! Asthma!'

Chapter Fifteen

CHARLES regained sufficient control to return to Ken Colebourne's office and nod soberly through the rest of the meeting. The office politics and power games continued, and it was interesting to see how Robin Pritchard slowly gained the ascendancy. Maybe he was demonstrating techniques he had learnt at business school, though Charles suspected that it was just the fact of his having been there that weakened his opponents. Ken Colebourne and Paul Taggart had both risen through the ranks. In the past this would have given them confidence over any mere graduate; but in the paranoid climate of a threatened recession nobody knew anything any more, and the concept of 'management training' had taken on a new mysterious potency.

The Product Manager for Cereals and Biscuits' positive gain from the meeting was the agreement to let *Parton Parcel* develop creative ideas for the presentation of the Delmoleen 'Green' at the Brighton sales conference. The Marketing Director and the Product Manager for Beverages remained uneasy, but there was no doubt that Robin Pritchard had won the round.

The meeting broke up at half-past nine, but as Charles and Will were about to leave, Ken Colebourne called the writer aside. Could they have a few words about the budget...?

Since this was clearly money talk, no doubt a bit of haggling about how much *Parton Parcel* would be paid for the additional work, Charles discreetly withdrew. Will's timetable showed that the next – and indeed the last – train back to Bedford was at ten twenty-seven, so they agreed to meet at Stanley Curton Station.

Charles emerged into a warm, moonless night. The two Product Managers had hurried off to their executive cars (and no doubt their executive homes and their executive wives). The whole Delmoleen site was very still. A few lights gleamed from the main building, presumably somewhere security officers patrolled, but Charles felt as if he was completely alone.

He looked at his watch. Leaving time to get to the station, he still had half an hour to play with. He tried to persuade himself that what he wanted to do with that half-hour was make another search for the pub that must exist in the vicinity. It wasn't difficult. The prospect of a drink was always a strong persuader to Charles Paris and, in order to look convincingly executive at that evening's meeting, he hadn't touched a drop all day.

But, in spite of the seductive image of a pub, he knew – inexorably though unwillingly – that that wasn't where he was going to go. In his suit there was something which confirmed what he had intended to do from the moment he left his bedsit that morning.

His hand closed round the small torch in his jacket pocket, and he moved cautiously towards the warehouse in which Dayna had met her death.

The main doors of the warehouse were firmly locked. Charles circled the building to the loading bays at the side. He climbed up on to the concrete platform the lorries backed up against, and moved along, dashing a spurt of torch-light at the bottom of each rolling shutter, but here too the padlocks were secure.

Maybe he should have secreted a crowbar about his person as well as the torch. Nobody would have noticed; the suit was voluminous enough to hide a platoon of Royal Engineers.

He sidled round to the end of the warehouse where the offices were. His eyes had by now accommodated to the meagre light and he could see quite clearly. He cast cautious looks along the alleys between other buildings, but there was no one in sight.

The door to the back office was locked, and he turned his attention to the windows. Delmoleen's warehouses didn't run to air-conditioning, so there was a possibility someone might have left a latch unfastened.

Charles felt along the frames and was rewarded by the rattle of metal on metal. A loose fanlight. He hooked his little finger under the metal ridge, then the next finger and the next. He pulled the fanlight outwards and fixed it in the open position.

He looked around again, but the darkness was unpeopled. As he reached his arm inside, the sudden thought of security alarms came to him. He withdrew his hand and ran the torchlight round the adjoining frames. There were no signs of wiring or contact-breakers.

It was still a risk, but one that he had to take. On a big enclosed site like the Delmoleen one, he told himself, most of the security devices would be on the outer perimeter fence; there were unlikely to be alarms on individual buildings.

Whether this reasoning was correct or not, no warning bell sounded as he reached through the fanlight, firmly grasped the handle of the abutting window, raised it and pushed the pane outwards.

Breathing heavily, Charles Paris heaved himself up on to the sill and pulled his body through. It was more of an effort than he had expected, but, after some ungainly kicking, he landed in a heap on the floor. He hoped the suit hadn't got torn; still, it felt all right as he patted himself down.

He closed the window and the fanlight. Security men were bound to be patrolling at some point, and there was no need to leave a calling card for them.

Keeping the beam low, he flashed the torch round the room and then extinguished it. As expected, he was in the office where he had reported Dayna Richman's death to Brian Tressider. Oh yes, and Heather had been there too on that occasion. Charles had a sudden vision of the secretary sitting at home at that very moment, listening to her mother's continuing monologue of disparagement.

The door connecting the two offices was unlocked and he moved onwards. Through the windows ahead of him, the emptiness of the warehouse loomed.

With the interconnecting door closed, Charles Paris felt confident to leave his torch switched on. A sweep round the office revealed nothing untoward. Sheaves of invoices and dockets hung from clips on the walls. A planner chart listed staff holidays. On a calendar, gift from a haulage company, under a quaint Dickensian print of drayhorses, days had been diagonally scored through right up to the current date. Everything was neat and orderly. Heather ran a tight ship.

Charles stepped through into the body of the warehouse. The beam of his torch could not reach its ceiling, nor to the end of the long narrow aisles. His light ran questing along past huge boxes of Delmoleen 'Bedtime', Delmoleen 'Nutty Flakes', Delmoleen 'Oat Nuggets', Delmoleen 'Bran Bannocks', as it sought out the aisle in which Dayna had met her death.

At the office end of the warehouse forklift trucks stood in orderly rows, linked to the wall by their recharging cables, still, like tethered animals.

The stock had changed, but Charles counted his way along to be certain that he had found the right place. Then, with torch modestly lowered to illuminate only where he took his next step, he moved down the aisle.

The setting seemed different in the softly enveloping darkness, but once again there was a pile of used pallets against the far wall. When he reached them, Charles directed the torch across the jumble of slatted wood.

He wasn't certain what he had been looking for, but when his beam outlined the shape of a small door through the planks, he felt confident that he had found it.

It was impossible to move the pallets and hold his torch at the same time and, since there was nowhere he could prop it to shed any useful light, he flicked the switch off and dropped the torch into his pocket.

Charles's hands gripped at the roughly finished wood as he tugged the first pallet away from the wall. He tried to manoeuvre it silently, but hadn't been prepared for quite how heavy it was. The sweat trickled on his temples and down the small of his back as he struggled.

Suddenly the obstruction worked itself free. Charles sprawled backwards and the pallet crashed on to the floor, just missing his legs.

The impact was grotesquely loud in the cavernous emptiness.

But no other sound followed. Apparently there was no one in the warehouse to be disturbed.

Encouraged, Charles picked himself up and felt for the outline of the next pallet. This one he jerked and worried free, tipping it out of the way with noisy abandon.

The others shifted more easily, clattering aside as more of the wall was exposed. In a matter of moments Charles had unimpeded access to the small door.

He retrieved the torch from his pocket and focused it on the metal rectangle. Battered and dusty, the door had once had a handle, but now only a small circular hole remained. Charles hooked a finger inside and pulled. The hinges creaked, as the door reluctantly moved towards him.

He shone the torch inside. The space was about two-foot square. On the facing wall was some kind of electrical equipment, old ceramic-collared sockets, thick cables snaking to brittle plastic junction boxes, a black ribbed metal box inset with a large rectangular switch.

Maybe the set-up was some kind of recharging unit for earlier designs of forklift trucks. Whatever it had been, though, it was clearly long disused. Thick dust coated the components and an uneven carpet of fluff lay on the floor.

The torch beam flicked around the grubby walls. At first Charles could see nothing of interest, but on a second examination, he noticed something on top of the switching unit.

Black and dust-covered like the rest of the box, at first they looked like part of the structure, but now he could distinguish two flat rectangular shapes.

Charles Paris leant into the cupboard to blow away some of the dust, then gingerly reached for the top rectangle.

He sat back on his heels and trained the torch on to what he was holding.

It was a VHS cassette in a black cardboard case.

His mind just had time to register this fact, before a sudden crash of pain on the back of his neck seared fire across his eyes.

And then everything went black.

He probably wasn't out that long.

Maybe it was the hum of the electric motor that brought him round. Or the crunch of splintering wood.

He looked up to see two low headlights slowly approaching.

He was also aware of a lesser light source near him on the ground. It must be his torch, still switched on.

He reached for the floor, but something obstructed him. Wood. Planks of wood. He was lying on something slatted.

A pallet.

As his hand closed round the torch, he tried to lift himself up, but the movement resurrected the agonising pain at the top of his spine. He was almost blinded by it, and knew that for the time being he was immobilised.

He pointed the pathetic beam of his torch between the oncoming headlights.

The silver maker's logo gleamed against the yellow front of a forklift truck.

Raised higher, the torch beam cavernously shadowed the clenched face of the truck's driver.

Trevor.

And Charles Paris felt convinced that he was seeing the last thing Dayna Richman saw before she died.

Chapter Sixteen

HE BRACED himself for the pressure of wood against his body, but it didn't come. His fuddled senses pieced together the fact that there was nothing between him and the truck. He was not going to be crushed against the wall by a pile of pallets.

So at least, though Charles Paris's end might be the same as Dayna Richman's, the route by which he reached it was going to be different.

As the pallet jolted and shuddered beneath him, he suddenly understood what that route was to be.

Slowly he felt the wooden platform lift from the ground, and slowly, infinitely slowly, he felt it rise up through the darkness. Charles Paris had become an item of palletised stock.

And as he rose higher and higher, he remembered, with sickening clarity, the truck's 'Quick-Release' control.

Being dropped from twenty feet on a pallet would ensure that Charles Paris never gave his definitive King Lear. Even a more-than-usually-deformed Richard III looked unlikely.

In fact, the end of his acting life was in sight. And not just his acting life. If the fall didn't finish him off, a couple more pallets dropped on to his broken body should do the trick.

Or, of course, the descent of a pallet loaded with stock would leave nothing to chance.

What a way to go. Crushed by hundreds of packs of Delmoleen 'Bedtime'. The drink was marketed (at least in the British Isles) on its soporific qualities, but surely its manufacturers never intended it to impose quite so permanent a quietus.

Slowly and inexorably, Charles Paris's pallet, his proposed funeral bier, rose through the gloom.

He tried desperately to concentrate, to make his stunned mind work.

There must be something he had going for him. By the law of averages.

A quick review of his options suggested that the law of averages didn't operate in this situation.

How long had he got? Logic told him that Trevor would lift the pallet as high as possible before dropping him. And how high was that?

A little light from the headlights percolated upwards, showing the outlines of shelving on either side at the end of the aisle. The pallet was nearly level with the top shelf.

And that must be the limit of its range. The shelving was designed to use the machine's maximum reach. In a matter of seconds, Trevor would flick the 'Quick-Release'.

Charles only had once chance and it was a slim one. The platform on which he lay swayed some three or four feet from the corner of the nearest shelf. He wasn't good at heights and it wasn't a leap he would have relished in full daylight. To attempt it in the semi-darkness was probably suicidal.

On the other hand, to wait for Trevor to drop him was certainly suicidal, and if he was going to die, Charles preferred a method that at least gave him the illusion of self-determination.

He dragged himself into a crouching position on the pallet. The pain in the back of his neck intensified, dizzying him for a second. The upright on the corner of the shelving rippled before his eyes in the uncertain light.

Still, he had no other hope. With a silent prayer to the God who got so shamefully neglected except at such moments of crisis, Charles Paris unsteadily took up the position of a starting sprinter and, kicking off with his feet, launched himself into the void.

As he did so, he felt the wood of the pallet disappear beneath him like the trapdoor under a hanging man. The impact of his body slamming and wrapping itself round the upright of the shelves compounded with the crash of the falling pallet to shake the whole warehouse.

Every part of Charles's body trembled with shock. The pain in his neck peaked, threatening unconsciousness. Life surged and flickered in him like the power of a fading generator.

But his wrenched arms still clasped the perforated steel of the shelf support.

He was still alive.

He scrabbled around with his feet, and found the reassuring solidity of the plastic-wrapped stock on the shelf below. He tensed one foot on its surface, then the other, and allowed his legs to share the weight with his strained arms.

From the darkness beneath, he heard a confused oath from Trevor, then the sound of the forklift truck being put into neutral. It could only be a moment before the operator realised what had happened.

And when he did, Charles's prospects weren't going to improve that much. The forks of the truck could all too easily knock him off his perch, or bring down any pallet of stock on which he found refuge.

Still, he'd be safer inside the shelves than dangling from their edge. Easier to lower himself to the second shelf than pull himself up to the top. Cautiously feeling his way with his feet and moving his hands from hole to hole along the metal spar, Charles slid into the gap between two loaded pallets. Holding his body up with aching arms braced on the stock, he felt gingerly with his foot for the bottom of the shelf.

At first his shoe dangled hopelessly in a void, but then his shin brushed against an upright, on which he managed to find a precarious toehold.

'You won't get away, you bastard! I'm coming to get you!'

Trevor's voice was chillingly sudden in the empty warehouse. Charles tried to squeeze himself back into the depths of the shelves, but the boxes of stock he pushed against gave way.

The webbing and plastic wrapping of that particular load must have been damaged in transit, because the cartons were loose.

Charles found himself falling forwards as the stock was dislodged.

For a second all he felt was rushing emptiness.

Then, with the impact of a car crash, the ridged metal edge of the shelf slammed into his chest, forcing the breath from his body, but at least breaking his fall – though, from the way he felt, it might have broken a few other things in the process.

But at the moment of his own crash, Charles was aware of an answering thunder from below, the clatter of falling cartons, the change of engine note of a forklift truck going into gear.

And a human cry, which was suddenly cut off.

Chapter Seventeen

AT LEAST it proved that Dayna Richman's death could have been accidental. One of the cartons had fallen on to the lever of the forklift truck, pushing it into gear, and the machine was once again pressing urgently against the pile of pallets.

On the other hand, for the cartons to have fallen by chance, without the agency of a human hand, remained too much of a coincidence.

But such thoughts were only allowed a fleeting passage through Charles's mind. The greater urgency was to find out what had happened to Trevor. As fast as he could, but with extreme caution and a great deal of pain, he felt his way down the end of the shelving to the warehouse floor.

As he did so, the image of Dayna's death kept flashing through his mind. It would be a tragic irony if her murderer had been trapped by the same unlikely means.

Charles leapt into the forklift's seat and pulled the lever into reverse. With a protesting grind of gears, the machine backed off. He switched off the ignition and dropped down to the floor, then peered through the confusion of pallets to the wall.

There was no sign of Trevor.

Charles reached into the debris of splintered wood and picked up his torch, which lay exactly where he had dropped it. He swung the beam round over the chaos of dented cartons.

Trevor's legs struck out from under a mound of Delmoleen 'Oat Nuggets'. Charles pulled the cartons away to expose the silent operator.

Trevor lay still, but he was breathing. There was a scratch on his temple from the edge of one of the boxes, and already the skin beneath was swelling into an egg. His right leg was bent awkwardly under his left.

He moaned gently as the last carton was removed. The sound wasn't a moan of agony, more the mumbling of someone asleep. Charles decided that the man was not badly injured, just temporarily knocked out.

Help must be summoned. Charles was in two minds as to whether he should be on the premises when that help came. An anonymous call to Delmoleen security and a discreet exit before they arrived might save a lot of awkward questions.

But there was something else that had to be done. With another quick check to see that Trevor could be left for a moment, Charles went across to the pallets and moved enough back to expose the small cupboard.

He opened it and swept his torch beam round the inside.

Just one video cassette this time.

He picked it up and pushed it into one of his jacket's voluminous pockets.

Trevor's moaning was now more articulate. Words became distinguishable as consciousness returned. Charles moved across.

The operator blinked in the light of the torch. 'What the hell's going on?' Recollection returned when he saw Charles's face. "Why, you bastard!'

He made to rise, but winced in agony as he put weight on his right leg. 'Shit! My leg – it's bloody broken!'

'I'll get help,' said Charles.

Trevor looked up, still furious through his pain. 'I wanted to kill you,' he said. 'I should have killed you!'

'Why?' asked Charles coolly.

'Because you said I killed Dayna. I can't have people going around saying that kind of thing. If that kind of rumour ever got to the police...'

'Well, did you kill her?'

'No, of course I bloody didn't!'

'I saw you coming into the warehouse just before she died.'

'Ah, but –'

'And don't bring up the alibi that Heather so conveniently provided for you. That's shot to pieces now.'

Trevor didn't try to argue with this.

'Incidentally, why did Heather suddenly cover up for you?'

'God knows. I was as surprised as anyone. Mind you, wasn't going to look a gift horse in the mouth. Got me out of a nasty spot and no mistake.'

'But she's not a particular friend of yours?'

Trevor shook his head. The movement reactivated the pain in his leg and he grimaced.

'I don't know,' he said when he'd recovered himself. 'Heather's devoted to Delmoleen. 'Well, devoted to Brian Tressider, anyway. I think she probably just saw a moment of danger to the company, and said the first thing she could think of that would stop an outside investigation.'

'And you were happy enough to go along with it?'

'Sure.' Another spasm of pain crossed Trevor's face. 'Look, I need an ambulance. Have some pity, for Christ's sake.'

'Why?' asked Charles, atypically cruel. 'You were trying to kill me. Why should I show any pity to you?'

'Because my leg bloody well hurts!'

'I'll get help in a minute. I just want you to answer a couple of questions first.'

Trevor didn't argue. 'What are they?'

'First – did you kill Dayna?'

'No, I didn't! I told you – it was an accident. I didn't intend it to work out like that.'

'But you did go into the warehouse, didn't you?'

'Yes.'

'And it was you who switched on the ignition of the forklift?'

'Yes. Yes.'

'Why?'

'Because I was bloody angry.'

'Who with?'

'You!'

'Me? What had I done?'

'You'd just got up my nose all that morning. I was angry that they thought I couldn't do my own job, that they had to bring in a bloody actor to do it for me!'

'That wasn't my fault.'

'Maybe not, but it got me livid. You didn't know a thing about forklifts.'

'No, but –'

'So I reckoned if they saw that you'd left the truck running all lunch-hour, flattening the battery, they'd realise how bloody useless you were.'

'So you switched the truck on just for that?'

'Yes.'

'But you didn't leave it in gear?'

'No, I bloody didn't!'

'Did you see Dayna come into the warehouse?'

'No. Look, all I did was I left it running...Then the cartons fell, pushed it into gear and unfortunately she was behind the pallets. It was an accident.'

Charles looked sceptical. 'Sounds pretty unlikely to me. I do know, incidentally, why Dayna was behind the pallets. She knew where you kept the videos, didn't she?'

Trevor looked even more truculent. 'So?'

'What were those videos, Trevor?'

'Oh, just some rubbish I used to sell round the factory. Porno stuff.'

'Films you'd made yourself?'

'No. No, these were things I'd copied. Could usually find a few of the blokes here who'd buy them. Anything was more exciting than their bloody wives, in most cases.'

'Did any of the videos feature Dayna?'

'No. Like I said, they was just stuff that'd been pirated.'

'But your video camera has been used for filming couples on the job,' said Charles, remembering what Shelley Fletcher had told him.

Trevor looked defiant. 'I've lent it to people. What they did with it was up to them.'

'Did Dayna ever ask you if she could borrow it?' Trevor looked up sharply at the question, so Charles pursued his intuition further. 'Did she ever ask you to film her in a sexual situation?'

'She asked. I said no.'

'So you didn't even lend her the camera?'

'Well...Yes, I did.'

'Why?'

'There was...Well, there was something she knew which...I didn't want anyone else to know.'

'Something about your sex-life?'

'You could say that.'

'Surely not just that you're gay?'

Trevor looked up sharply. 'How did you know? Did she tell you?'

'No, of course not. I worked it out for myself,' Charles lied. 'But surely that doesn't matter. It's no big deal these days.'

'Maybe it isn't in the bloody theatre. Place like this it's still a big deal. Have to be very careful...particularly if you're interested in someone else in the company...'

'And are you? Is there someone else in the company?'

Trevor looked almost tearful, weary, glad to confide his troubles. 'There's a boy in the Post Room. I'm pretty sure he's interested, but...Oh, it's difficult. That's why I was here tonight. Supposed to be meeting him here. Little bugger never showed, did he?'

'And did Dayna know about this boy? Was that the hold she had over you?'

'No, wasn't that. This little bastard's only just joined the company. No, Dayna knew about... something else.'

Charles had a sudden intuition. 'Was it something to do with minors? Under-age boys?'

Panic flared in the operator's eye. 'Did she talk to you? What did she say?'

'Nothing, nothing,' Charles soothed. 'I was just guessing.'

'Really?'

'Yes. Did Dayna say she'd got evidence against you?'

'Claimed she had. Claimed she'd photographed me outside a place... It's a gents' lavatory where...well...'

'Did you ever see the photographs?'

'No. But the place she mentioned was right, and the time she said she'd seen me.'

'Hm. And that's why you reacted against Dayna that morning when we were filming here?'

Trevor gave the smallest of nods.

'So she was blackmailing you...?' This too was confirmed. 'Just as she blackmailed other people round Delmoleen...?'

'I don't know that for sure. But I think so. I'm fairly certain that's why she wanted to borrow the camera – to set it up so she could film herself on the job.'

"With whom, though, Trevor? Who did she want to be filmed with?"

'I don't know. Really don't.'

It sounded like the truth. 'Would explain why the men she'd been with didn't criticise her too much afterwards...' Charles mused. 'She was an ambitious girl by all accounts, Dayna, wasn't she?'

'Yes. She wanted to get to the London office. Had applied for a post there just before she...you know, before she died.'

'Really? That's interesting. Do you know if she got the job?'

'Not certain. Think she probably did, yes.'

'Hm. I've heard people say she wanted to screw her way right to the top of the company...'

"Wouldn't have been out of character.'

'But you can't give me any names...'

Trevor gave a decided – but incautious – shake of his head. He winced as the pain from his leg tore through him.

'I'll call an ambulance,' said Charles. 'And, actually, I don't think I'll be around when it comes.'

'Probably just as well.'

'Another industrial accident. Likely to get as detailed an investigation as the last one.'

'I should think so.'

The atmosphere between the two men had changed. It was never going to become one of complicity or even friendship, but at least the overt hostility was gone.

'By the way,' said Charles graciously, 'I'm prepared to forget the fact that you tried to kill me.'

He got a gruff 'thank you' for that. 'I'm sorry, but I couldn't have you going round saying I'd murdered Dayna. I mean, that was bound to open up a whole can of worms about...you know, other things...'

'Don't worry. I won't make the accusation again.'

'Right. Good. So that means you know I didn't kill her.'

'Sure,' Charles agreed. 'All you did was switch on the forklift's ignition.'

And he was very close to being convinced that that really was all Trevor had done.

But he'd reserve judgement until he'd watched the video cassette that nestled in his jacket pocket.

For the call to security that announced an accident in the warehouse, Charles used the voice he had perfected for *Gaslight* ('Charles Paris was about as sinister as a teddy-bear with a bow round its neck' – *Leicester Mercury*). The security guard didn't sound very frightened by it either, nor particularly interested, but he said someone would be over there soon.

Charles made good his escape by the same route that he'd entered the warehouse and, to his amazement, got to Stenley Curton Station in time to join Will on the ten twenty-seven train to Bedford.

'What the hell's happened to your suit?' the writer asked.

Charles looked down. A pocket flapped, torn down one side. Two of the double-breasted buttons had gone. The fabric was scored with furrows of black dirt.

'Oh, er, I fell over,' he replied feebly.

On their journey back he told Will Parton nothing of what had happened. Nor did he mention what he was carrying in his suit's surviving pocket. This was partly because secrecy seemed essential until he'd got a few more details sorted out. And partly because he gave in to the healing sleep that his battered body cried out for.

At St Pancras, still muzzy and confused, Charles hailed a cab and gave the address of the only discreet person he could think of who owned a video.

'What the hell's happened to your suit?' Frances asked.

She stood in the doorway of her flat in a dressing-gown, face puffy with sleep. Someone who always hated being woken up in the middle of the night, she did at least have the restraint not to say, 'Do you know what time it is?'

'Take a long time to explain,' said Charles. 'Look, for reasons which would also take too long to explain. I need to borrow your VCR.'

Frances looked at her watch and raised her eyebrows. 'I see.'

The tape was a commercial hard-core pornographic film. The antics of the cast demonstrated a bored mechanical professionalism. There was no soundtrack, but the looks of the participants suggested a German or Scandinavian origin. None of them was recognisable from Delmoleen.

Charles looked at the screen with a mixture of cheap arousal and fascination. Incredible to think that these people belonged to the same profession as he did. Or did they? Was it necessary to have an Equity card for this kind of work? Did such performers have their own professional directory, he conjectured, like the more traditional actors' *Spotlight*? And, if they did, what kind of photographs did they put in it? And what physical characteristics did they list? It was mind-boggling.

After four or five minutes of the film, Frances said shortly, 'I'm going back to bed.'

Charles had planned an appealing, dog-like look, followed by a request for permission to sleep on her sofa. There was always a chance of graduating from sofa to bed. Or of taking Frances a cup of early morning tea...which could always lead to a nice little restorative cuddle...and a nice little restorative cuddle could always lead to...He composed the appealing, dog-like look and turned its full power on his wife.

'I'm sorry, Frances, I do have to watch this all the way through.'

'Yes, I'm sure you do, Charles,' she said drily.

'But I was wondering if I could –'

'Let yourself out when you've finished,' said Frances, and closed the door.

Chapter Eighteen

'THEN I awake and look around me
At the other muesli bars that surround me,
And I realise...I realise that I was only dreaming.
'Cause there's only one of true calibre,
Full of vitamins and fibre.
Oh, there's none can touch
The green – "Green" – Del – mo – leen.'

The singer stopped with arms outstretched and the four dancers froze in an unsteady tableau around him. The pianist folded his arms, face expressionless, mentally off-duty until next summoned to do something.

'Yes,' said Robin Pritchard, 'yes. I think that's beginning to come together.'

'We'll be running it a few more times,' Will Parton assured him. 'You know, to get it really crisp. And, of course, it'll look different when we've got the prop.'

Robin Pritchard pursed his lips. 'It's a real bugger that wasn't here for this run-through.'

The prop to which they referred was a six-foot-long model of a Delmoleen 'Green', which was to feature prominently in the dancers' routine. The yard-broom which was deputising in the rehearsal didn't really give the same impression.

'I know,' Will concurred. 'God, I'll never use that company again. I've been on the bloody phone to them every day for the past fortnight. They swore it'd be here for today. It's just not good enough – particularly when you consider what they're charging to make the thing.'

'Well, they won't get paid, that's for certain,' said the Marketing Director with the grim satisfaction of the man who was controlling the sales conference budget.

Robin Pritchard took another critical look at the stage. 'The actual bar is going to make a big difference to the look of the thing. But I think there's no question the presentation's going to wake the sales force up. They're never going to have seen anything like that before.'

'You're certainly right there, Robin.' Ken Colebourne's expression was sardonic. He hadn't been keen on the song-and-dance idea at the outset, and nothing in its subsequent development had made him change his mind. The benefits of such presentation remained dubious, and the complications it introduced – organising accommodation for the performers, arranging the presence of a piano, having costumes and props made – were the last thing he needed at his busiest time of the year.

The strain seemed to be getting through to the Marketing Director. Charles thought he looked frazzled, and on one or two occasions when things had gone wrong in the run-through, Ken's temper had proved to be very short. Still, putting on a major sales conference must be a stressful business. Or then again, Ken Colebourne might have problems at home. Perhaps Patricia's health was deteriorating further. One could never really know the pressures inside a marriage like that.

'I wonder if you want me to make it a bit more Tom Jones-like?' the singer asked.

He was an identikit club singer, spreading to fat, with hair dyed black to give him an ersatz Mediterranean look. Though currently in pastel golfer's leisurewear, he was the kind of performer, Charles felt sure, whose stage suit was a shiny midnight-blue tuxedo worn over ruffled shirt and corset-like cummerbund.

'How do you mean exactly?' asked Will.

"Well, I could do a bit more…you know, gyration of the hips. Make it more obviously Tom Jones. I mean, I'm doing his voice, so a lot of them are going to get it all right, but we want them all to recognise that it is Tom Jones I'm doing, don't we?'

'Most of them won't even know who Tom Jones is,' muttered Daryl Fletcher truculently. He had been dragged down to the conference hall because Ken Colebourne insisted that they should rehearse the presentation of his car, and Daryl really didn't think his presence was necessary. He'd rather have been up in the Panorama Bar on the eighth floor, knocking back a few drinks and lording it over the other salesmen whose annual figures hadn't been as good as his.

Actually, Charles agreed with Daryl's reservation. Although he had shared Will's excitement when they decided to parody *The Green, Green Grass of Home* for the launch, and shared the hilarity with which they had adapted the lyrics, he had always had a sneaking suspicion there was something wrong about the choice. A 1966 hit for a singer who'd since virtually given up the British scene for the lucrative American cabaret circuit was not calculated to strike many chords in the hearts of salesmen in their twenties.

'No, I think what you're doing's probably enough, erm...' Will Parton had completely forgotten the singer's name, 'love,' he concluded safely.

Actually, the 'love' was a bit more than just a cop-out. Now Will was directing, he had become frightfully showbiz. It must have been all those patient years of being a television writer – agreeing with directors' increasingly illogical suggestions, meekly rewriting and rewriting until his original concepts vanished in a welter of words – that made him so relish the role. Here, in the unobserved environment of the Brighton Ambassador Hotel and Conference Suite, he could indulge his show business fantasies and gain a private, but sweet, revenge on every director he had ever worked with.

'Now have you tried on the cozzies yet?' he continued, directorially bossy.

'When?' asked one of the bored female dancers. 'We was called for two o'clock, we've been here since two o'clock. It's now eight o'clock. When are we supposed to have had time to try on costumes, eh?'

They had been kept busy all that time. There were two men and two women, though the one who rather grandly designated himself 'Dance Captain' kept referring to them as 'boys and girls'. He had kept them at it, learning the very basic choreography of their number and the necessary manipulations of the yard-broom, on the stage when it was free and at the back of the hall when it wasn't. The rehearsal they had just done had been the first full one, with music and singer. Clearly more work was needed, but Ken Colebourne kept looking anxiously at his watch. They were overrunning their scheduled time, and there was still a lot to be run through.

'We got to move this on, Will,' he said.

'Yes, of course. Time for one more run of the song.'

'No.'

'Oh, come on, it's not up to standard yet,' Robin Pritchard protested.

'That is your problem, not mine,' said Ken Colebourne, with a degree of satisfaction. 'If you'd kept the presentation simple, we'd be finished by now.'

The Product Manager for Biscuits and Cereals argued, but for once he didn't get his own way. Despite the stresses of what he was doing, Ken Colebourne had great experience of organising sales conferences, and there was no doubt that he was in charge. Robin Pritchard accepted defeat, and went off with his grumbling singer and dancers for a dress parade. The singer was to wear a green tuxedo, the 'boys' green waistcoats and trousers, and the 'girls' green catsuits.

'OK. Next I want to run my marketing overview sequence,' said Ken. Then he noticed someone hovering at the back of the hall, trying to attract his attention. 'Yes, Heather, what is it?'

Charles turned to see the secretary from the warehouse step forward. He was not surprised to see her. Apparently the two days of the sales conference was a kind of bonus granted the more senior Delmoleen office administration staff. According to the nudging information of Daryl Fletcher, most of them used this as an annual licence for a bit of extramarital hanky-panky. As Heather Routledge coughed diffidently before speaking, Charles could not somehow imagine her to be involved in any such goings on.

'There was a message for you, Ken. Could you ring Nicky Rules?'

'Oh, God, he's not going to cancel on me, is he?' The Marketing Director had so much on his plate at that moment that the thought of having to find a new cabaret for the following night's banquet was more than he could contemplate.

'No, it's all right. Just a couple of things he wants to check about the company.'

'Oh, all right. I'll ring him when we're through here. Thanks, Heather.'

She walked awkwardly back out of the hall. She wasn't actually ungainly,

Charles decided, just lacking in confidence. Her movements had the self-defeating clumsiness of someone desperately unwilling to draw attention to herself.

'I don't know,' said Ken to Will. 'That Nicky Rules does go on. Prides himself on tailoring his material to his audience. Likes to make in-jokes about people in the company. So he's on the blower to me about three times a day. And I gather he's been talking to other management people too. Suppose I should be grateful that he bothers, but, God, it all takes time.'

He moved towards the stage. 'Right, I'll do my presentation. Just to check that the script's coming up right and the slides are in the right order.'

'Oh, look, when do we get to my bit?' Daryl Fletcher complained, seeing more valuable drinking time slip away.

'My piece runs straight into the video that introduces B.T. – that's all clips of him from television...on *The Money Programme*, interviewed at the CBI conference, in that environmental series, all that stuff. Once we've played the video, B.T. comes on, does his talk and finishes up presenting you with the car.'

'Well, is he going to be here for the rehearsal?'

'No, he's hosting a reception upstairs.'

'Look, if Brian Tressider isn't bloody here, I don't see why I should have to bloody –'

'Daryl!'

Ken Colebourne's authority was unmistakable. The Top Salesman subsided into ungracious silence.

'Right, I'll make this as quick as I can.' The Marketing Director strode on to the stage and spoke into a microphone. 'Are you ready in the box? Marketing Director's Report – OK? Got the script lined up?'

'Yes. It's there on the autocue,' a disembodied voice replied over the talkback. 'Who's operating the slides?'

'I am.' Ken Colebourne picked up the control from a lectern. 'That way there's no chance of them getting out of synch.'

He launched into his spiel. He was a workmanlike but not a charismatic speaker, reading with level intonation from the autocue on the transparent lectern in front of him, and punching up the relevant slides at the relevant moments. Packshots of products appeared on the screen behind him, graphs of sales figures, pie-charts of market shares. It was all competent, and rather dull.

Charles felt bored. He had done his bit. Will had fulfilled his promise to find something in the sales conference for Charles Paris. Early thoughts of including him in the Delmoleen 'Green' presentation had fortunately been abandoned. Although Charles had served his time in musicals, singing was not one of his strong points, and his dancing had cut a swathe of despair through battalions of choreographers. Indeed, the *Walton and Weybridge Informer* had once reviewed his performance in *My Fair Lady* in the following uncharitable terms: 'Charles Paris's Professor Higgins is the best argument I've ever seen against turning *Pygmalion* into a musical.'

But a convenient non-singing, non-dancing role in the Delmoleen sales conference had been found for him. The Product Manager for Confectionery, though very effective at his job, suffered from a mild stutter which was exacerbated by the strains of public speaking, so Charles had been delegated to present the current state of the confectionery market. It was not the most complex role he had ever been faced with, but his reading of it in rehearsal had apparently satisfied the Delmoleen audience.

Even though he'd done his bit, Charles didn't really feel he could leave the conference hall. He was also there in his *Parton Parcel* capacity, and was even wearing his suit to prove it. (The suit, incidentally, had been cleaned and had had its pocket invisibly mended. The effect of these ministrations had been to rob it of its designer shapelessness. Now it just looked shapeless.) So he thought he'd have to sit out the full term of the rehearsal, although he could feel painfully the allure of bars and receptions in the hotel above him. Once again, as in all the Delmoleen 'shirtsleeve' sessions, lavish salvers of sandwiches had been produced. And, once again – to Charles's considerable disappointment – no liquid stronger than mineral water.

He sneaked a look at his watch. Half-past eight now. Oh, he really could murder a large Bell's.

He half-heard the drone of Ken Colebourne's presentation. 'And we still stand by the principles which made the company successful when it started. We take pride in those principles. Everyone who works for Delmoleen knows that all our products are made by the most modern manufacturing methods...'

Ken Colebourne clicked the control in his hand. A slide of a factory interior full of gleaming machinery, tended by immaculate workers in white overalls, was shown.

'They know the same high quality Delmoleen goods are sold all over the world...'

On the screen, in front of a rusty corrugated iron hut, next to a broken-down tractor, two grinning Caribbean children held up a pack of Delmoleen 'Bran Bannocks'.

'They know what the public think of Delmoleen. They know that the public trust the guarantee of hygiene that only comes from Delmoleen – and not from other companies I could mention.'

The screen filled with newspaper headlines about a scandal from earlier in the year which had crippled one of Delmoleen's main rivals. '"THEY'RE RUBBISH! I'LL NEVER TOUCH ANYTHING THEY MANUFACTURE AGAIN!" SAYS BOTULISM BOY'S HEARTBREAK MOTHER.' (This slide was guaranteed to produce a big laugh from its salesmen audience.)

'And they know that Delmoleen goods are sold at a price that's more than competitive...'

Another click of the control produced a slide showing a dull semicircle of rival bedtime drinks, all marked with their inflated prices. In the foreground, brightly lit, stood a carton of Delmoleen 'Bedtime', almost eclipsed by a huge price label of '98p'.

'So they begin to understand what being a part of the Delmoleen family is really worth. And, in these environmentally-conscious times, they know that Delmoleen products are only made from the freshest of organically-grown natural ingredients...'

A still life of expensively photographed vegetables appeared on the screen.

'Yes, Delmoleen cares. Delmoleen is like a family. And I want to show you what sort of people are part of the Delmoleen family...'

A slide appeared of half a dozen workers grouped under the arch of the company logo. There were a couple in shining blue overalls, a couple in white, a man and a woman in business suits. They were carefully selected to show a mix of ages and ethnic origins. All wore gleaming smiles.

'Next,' said Ken Colebourne, 'you're going to be addressed by the man who keeps that family atmosphere and that family success going – our Managing Director, Brian Tressider. But, first, let's see some of the occasions when he's been in the public eye during the last year. And, seeing this, you'll ask yourself how he manages to fit everything in to just twenty-four hours a day. He seems to be at it all the time!'

This was the cue for the video. The slide of smiling workers disappeared, and instantly the screen filled.

But what filled it was not a compilation of Brian Tressider's media appearances during the previous year.

Instead, two naked bodies thrashed against each other in the steamy heat of a sexual encounter.

Daryl, whose expression suggested he knew of the substitution, sniggered, and Charles, suddenly seeing the aptness of Ken Colebourne's introductory words, could not hold back his own laughter. Will Parton also started giggling.

The Marketing Director was looking out front, puzzled, and it took him a moment to turn and face the source of their amusement.

When he did, his reaction was instantaneous and furious. 'Where the hell did you get that from? Stop it!' he screamed into the microphone. 'Stop it! We mustn't see any more! B.T.'d go mad if he knew about it! He thinks it's been destroyed. Stop that bloody tape!'

The unseen operator at the back of the hall, either from genuine incompetence or because he was enjoying the joke, took a while to obey this command, which gave the audience time to see more of the action.

And what Charles saw told him that this was just another commercial pornographic tape. The participants had nothing to do with Delmoleen. Certainly the man was totally unlike Brian Tressider. What was interesting, though, was not the tape itself, but Ken Colebourne's reaction to it. Or rather his over-reaction. He had panicked completely. And, though he could soon recognise that his Managing Director didn't feature, what Ken had said suggested that it wouldn't have surprised him to see Brian Tressider in such compromising circumstances.

Chapter Nineteen

'NAH, IT WAS just a laugh,' said Shelley. 'Daryl's always doing stuff like that. His sense of humour's bleeding mental.'

'So he wasn't making any point by getting the video shown?'

'No, Chowss, he doesn't work like that. Daryl was just miffed that he had to go and sit through hours of rehearsal when all he was going to have to do was say "Thank you very much for my car". So he thought "What can I do to liven things up a bit? I know, bung the bloke in the control box a flyer – get him to show a smutty video." That's how his mind works. It's only a joke – that's Daryl all over.'

She looked affectionately across the bar to where her husband was drinking and swapping either scatological jokes or custom car minutiae with a bunch of fellow salesmen.

Charles was inclined to believe her. It would have been in character for Daryl to stage that kind of meaningless prank. And there was no reason to believe that the Top Salesman had any suspicions about Dayna Richman's death, so he really had no other motive for doing it.

For Charles, on the other hand, the video – or rather Ken Colebourne's reaction to it – had triggered an avalanche of new thoughts.

The Marketing Director's first response, before he saw what was actually being shown, was the one that mattered. He had panicked, thinking what was on the screen was not a commercial product, but a secretly-filmed video of a man and a woman making love.

Charles only knew of one person in the Delmoleen set-up who had ever been into that kind of stuff. Dayna.

She had tried to persuade Trevor to film her with a sexual partner, and blackmail seemed to be a speciality of hers. Even though the forklift operator said he'd refused her request, it was quite possible that she'd found someone else more ready to co-operate. Or indeed she could have set up the apparatus herself. It wouldn't have been a problem; camcorders were getting easier to use all the time.

Assuming then that such a blackmailing tape existed – and Ken Colebourne's reaction suggested he knew it did – the question arose as to who was Dayna's co-star.

And Charles didn't reckon he had to look far for the answer. Dayna Richman had made no secret of her intention to screw her way to the top. She had confronted Brian Tressider in an unequivocally sexy way in the warehouse on the day she died. And, what was more, he had been on the premises at the time when her 'accident' happened. The scandal her disclosure of their relationship might cause to a man in his position was quite sufficient motive for murder.

All the evidence suddenly seemed to be pointing in the same direction.

"Well, all that looks bloody boring.'

Shelley's words brought him back to the present. She was looking disparagingly at a printed sheet of paper.

'What's that?'

'"The Wives' Programme."' Her voice was heavy with irony. 'Always at these conferences they set up some exciting things for the little ladies to do while the men are stuck in meetings.' She held the paper out. 'Look – "Visit to the Royal Pavilion and tour of its kitchens; Shopping in the Lanes; Lunch; then a Tour of a Local Winery, followed by Cream Tea"...Well, stuff that for a game of soldiers!'

'Doesn't appeal?'

'No, bleeding boring. Got all the other wives to cope with, apart from anything else. Dreary load of old bags most of them are. And dear Brenda Tressider leading us on, like some bleeding Chief Guide or Brown Owl. Won't catch me doing any of that, I can tell you.'

'So how're you proposing to spend tomorrow?' asked Charles.

Shelley grinned a rather mischievous little grin. 'Thought I might look for some entertainment here.'

'Here? What, at the conference, you mean?'

'Nah. Upstairs in my room is what I mean. Do I make myself clear?'

She certainly did. Charles was once again struck by how very attractive she was. Shelley Fletcher had that overt sexiness which can always override masculine better judgement.

She chuckled throatily. 'Might you be free then during the day tomorrow, Chowss?'

He was hooked instantly. 'Well, yes. I've got to do the Confectionery presentation, but that's first thing in the morning, so, say, after eleven... yes, I am pretty well free.'

She turned the full beam of her blue eyes on to his. 'Good. Good.'

'Good,' Charles echoed.

''Cause Daryl and some of the lads'll be able to sneak out from the odd session, I'm sure.'

'Oh?' said Charles.

'And some of the secretaries, and some of the wives 'n' all – there are a few who swing a bit and wouldn't be that keen on the Royal Pavilion, if someone suggested the right alternative...'

'Ah.'

'No, I think we could have a nice time tomorrow, Chowss,' she purred.

'Tomorrow. Oh, *tomorrow*. Oh, Damn,' he said, preparing to lie. 'I've suddenly remembered Will Parton, my partner in this business, is insisting that I should sit in on as many of the conference sessions as possible tomorrow.'

He'd had no alternative. He knew it was a hopelessly old-fashioned reaction, but – much though he would have relished an individual encounter with Shelley Fletcher – Charles Paris had never been able to come to terms with the idea of sex as a community activity.

Perhaps because his day's drinking had started so late, Charles did find he was rather making up for lost time. Or it may have been the company. The Delmoleen salesmen and their wives seemed determined to enjoy their employers' hospitality to the full, and round of drinks followed round with astonishing fluency.

It was only when he crossed the hotel's reception area to find a Gents and felt a blast of cold air from outside, that Charles realised how drunk he was. Must slow down, he thought. Mustn't cock up the Confectionery presentation in the morning. A speech delivered by someone with a really bad hangover wouldn't be much improvement over one delivered by a man with a stutter.

'Excuse me,' asked a voice from the reception desk, 'are you Mr Paris?'

'What? Oh. Yes.'

'There was a telephone message for you. Could you ring Mr Skellern as soon as possible, please?'

'Right. Thanks,' said Charles, as he stumbled on towards the Gents.

Very unusual, he thought as he peed copiously, for Maurice to be ringing him. But he didn't have the warm feeling that an actor traditionally gets from a message to ring his agent. His first thought was not that the National Theatre had suddenly decided they wanted him to do his Hamlet. Nor that Hollywood had finally made a decision in his favour about who the new James Bond was to be. No, his first thought was that Maurice had somehow found out that his client was working without telling him.

Yes, Charles would return the call. But 'as soon as possible' might not be very soon.

Thinking of phone calls, he must ring Frances too. Been a bit unfortunate, their last encounter. Well, their last two encounters, come to that. The day at Wimbledon hadn't been a major social triumph. No, little bit of minor fence-mending might be needed there. Must ring Frances and sort things out with her. Soon.

But not tonight. Always better to be sober when attempting reconciliation with his wife.

One more drink, he thought as he re-entered the bar. Just one, then I'll stop. Need a clear head for the morning.

But with the number of such good intentions he had formulated in his life, Charles could have laid out a five-lane motorway to hell. The one drink became four, and those escalated into Room Service bottles of whisky in his bedroom with Will Parton and a bunch of salesmen whose precise names Charles couldn't recall but whom he knew all to be very good chaps.

Rendered incautious by alcohol, Charles and Will started saying what they really thought about the corporate world. All the giggling they had been carefully holding in for the last weeks burst out, and Charles found the salesmen an easy and indulgent audience for his impression of Robin Pritchard.

'It's so big,' he was saying. 'I mean, *big* on a *global* scale. You know, we're talking *cosmic outreach* here. I mean, on a scale of one to ten, the concept scores a cool hundred. We are not talking ordinary muesli bar here, we are talking *galactic* muesli bar.'

The salesmen roared their appreciation, encouraging him to continue.

'And the revolutionary thing about this new muesli bar – I mean, the, like, *globally*, *cosmically* different element in its concept – is that the new Delmoleen "Green" tastes exactly like a pan-scourer!'

The salesmen loved this too. They roared again. In fact, the hilarity was so general and so raucous that none of them heard the door open.

'Could you keep the noise down, please!'

In the doorway, with a face like a glacier, stood Brenda Tressider.

Chapter Twenty

EVERYONE was suddenly sober. With mumbled apologies and subdued good nights, Charles's guests filed past Brenda back to their own rooms. When they had all gone, she shrugged apologetically. 'I'm sorry. Ken Colebourne's got the suite above you here. I don't want him disturbed. His wife Patricia's not at all well.'

'No, *I*'m sorry,' said Charles. 'Just all got a bit out of hand.'

'Yes.' He had expected her to turn on her heels and leave immediately. To his surprise, she lingered, as if undecided.

He gestured to the debris of abandoned glasses. 'Can I offer you a drink or something?'

She came forward determinedly and sat down in an armchair. 'Do you have any mineral water?'

'Tap.'

'All right.'

He took a glass into the bathroom, swilled it out and filled it. Brenda Tressider thanked him as profusely as if he had handed her a glass of Dom Perignon. As ever, her manners were impeccable. And, as ever, she was impeccably costumed – on this occasion in the little black dress she had worn for the evening's reception.

Instinctively, he found himself draining the remains of a whisky bottle into his own glass before sitting on the edge of the bed opposite her. But his head felt clear, his mind sharp.

'You shouldn't do that kind of thing when the salesmen are around,' Brenda Tressider announced.

'What kind of thing?'

'Knocking the product. Knocking Delmoleen.'

'Oh, it was just a joke. It was –'

She overrode him. 'You still shouldn't do it. It's hard enough to motivate the sales force at the best of times. If they start thinking it's all right to make fun of the company, they stop believing in it.'

'I'm sorry.'

'It's easy enough for you. You come in from outside, you have no loyalty to Delmoleen, no doubt the whole business is just a laugh for you –'

'No, I wouldn't say –'

'For the people in the company, it's their lives, it's their jobs. It's important that they believe in it...'

Charles Paris was properly chastened. He nodded abjectly. 'I'm sorry.'

To his surprise, he saw the shadow of a smile on Brenda Tressider's lips, '...even in the teeth of the evidence.'

'What do you mean?'

'I mean that faith in Delmoleen is like any other faith. You have to limit knowledge for it to grow.' She responded to his quizzical expression. 'If you start actually analysing the company, analysing what it's doing, how it works, all that...well, you couldn't possibly sustain your belief in it. So you have to close your mind to the detail, and just hold on to the faith for its own sake.'

'And exercises like this sales conference take place to reinforce that faith?'

'Exactly. Just like a Revivalist Meeting. All this tub-thumping, all this talk of "the Delmoleen family", the video you've been involved in....it's all there for the same purpose. You may not actually be able to make the sales force believe in the company, but at least you can get them to suspend their disbelief in it.'

Charles hadn't expected her to be the kind of woman who quoted Coleridge. 'And impersonations of Robin Pritchard make it more difficult for the disbelief to be suspended?'

'Yes, they do...' She smiled before the compliment, 'However accurate those impersonations may be.'

'And what about you, Mrs Tressider? Do you believe in Delmoleen?'

'It's my job to believe in Delmoleen,' she replied drily. 'Or my job to believe in Brian, which comes to the same thing.'

'And do you ever have problems suspending *your* disbelief?'

She sighed. 'It doesn't really matter whether I do or don't. I have a function to perform in the company, just as he does. I have to ensure that Brian can operate at his maximum efficiency, I have to see that the home runs smoothly, I have to be on hand for business entertaining...'

'You have to make small talk and sound interested in the conversation of all kinds of boring people...?'

'I didn't say that, Mr Paris. You did.'

'You're very discreet.'

'Something which you, it appears, could not be accused of.'

'No. I'm sorry. You've had much more practice at it than I have.'

'That is certainly true.'

'So...your life must run on a pretty tight timetable?'

'That is also true.'

'It must sometimes have been hard reconciling the demands of your home and the company.'

'Sometimes.'

'Particularly when you had young children around.'

'Brian and I have no children, so that problem never arose.'

'Ah.' He wasn't sure whether or not he should say he was sorry. There had been no self-pity or other discernible emotion in her words.

'No, I have great respect for women who manage the demands of a family as well as everything else.'

'So you see your role in life exclusively as looking after Brian?'

'Yes.'

'There are some people nowadays…' he began cautiously '– some women, certainly – who would think that was rather an old-fashioned view of a wife's role.'

'They can think what they like. I have no doubt at all that I work extremely hard to fulfil a very necessary function. I don't see myself as subservient to Brian. I think my contribution to the success of Delmoleen is quite equal to his – and, if you asked him, I think Brian would say the same.'

'Ah. Well. Good.' Charles took a swig of his whisky. He was playing for time. He needed to move the conversation on to a more controversial tack, and he wasn't certain of the most tactful way to do it. In fact, he rather wondered whether there was a tactful way of accusing someone's husband of murder.

'Mrs Tressider…' he hazarded, 'presumably someone in Brian's position has to be very careful not to become involved in any scandal…'

'Naturally. Any public figure is aware of that danger. The press these days are all too ready to pillory people.'

'Yes…' He hesitated again. 'In a set-up that has as many employees as Delmoleen, you're inevitably going to get a few bad apples, people who might bring the company name into disrepute…'

'You run that risk, yes, obviously. But you try to minimise it by careful recruitment and quick dismissal when you realise you've made a mistake.'

Charles nodded, wondering if Brenda Tressider's professional poise ever broke down. She was so in control, he felt an unworthy desire to see her crack just once, to see the vulnerable female beneath the carapace. But maybe there wasn't one.

He decided he'd have to cast caution to the winds and plunge in. 'Mrs Tressider, you remember the young girl who was killed in the warehouse accident the day we were making the video there…'

Her filing system was as infallible as ever. 'Of course. Dayna Richman.'

'I've heard rumours about the place that she was into a bit of blackmail…'

'Oh?' The monosyllable was almost without intonation.

'Rumours that she used sex to blackmail men in the company. Rumours in fact that video tapes existed of her with senior members – or at least a video tape of her with a senior member – of the Delmoleen management...'

'Ah.' This monosyllable contained more. In fact, it contained a lot – an acceptance of a revised situation and the need for a new approach to cope with that situation. But still Brenda Tressider showed no untoward emotion. 'Brian had hoped that no one else knew about that. He thought the information had been contained. It will distress him considerably to know that it's common gossip round the company.'

'It's certainly not that,' Charles hastened to assure her. 'I had to make fairly detailed investigations to find out about it.'

'Good. So are you the only person who knows about the existence of the tape?'

'Possibly, yes. Except for the other participant, I assume. It seems reasonable to suppose that Dayna had told him about the tape, had asked for money in exchange for it...'

'Yes. She had,' Brenda confirmed. 'And now you're doing the same, are you? How much do you want?'

'No, it's not that.'

'Don't play games with me, Mr Paris. You can't have any other reason for raising the matter. Come on, tell me your price. I'm sure Brian won't have any difficulty raising the money – so long as you're not asking something ridiculous.'

'Mrs Tressider, I am not asking for money – honestly I'm not.'

'Then why are you talking about the tape?'

'Because I'm trying to find out what happened to Dayna Richman.'

"We know what happened to Dayna Richman. She was killed in an accident in the warehouse at Stenley Curton.'

She said this in such an unarguable, matter-of-fact way that Charles was convinced she really did have no suspicions about the death. Though Brenda Tressider could apparently accept with equanimity her husband's infidelity, the idea that his offence might be more serious did not enter her head.

'Listen, Mrs Tressider, the timing of Dayna's death was, to say the least, coincidental.'

'What do you mean?'

'There are various traditional methods of stopping the demands of blackmailers. One is by paying them off – though the victim can never under those circumstances feel quite secure that the demands won't recur...'

'They won't recur if the incriminating evidence has been handed over in exchange for the money.'

Charles grimaced. 'Depends. What we're talking about here is a video tape. Very easy thing to copy these days, Mrs Tressider.'

'Yes. I hadn't thought of that.'

'Anyway, as I was about to say, there is another, more permanent, way of putting an end to the demands of a blackmailer.'

The idea was so alien to her that, for a moment, she did not understand him. But, as light dawned, he was rewarded by Brenda Tressider's first uncontrolled reaction – one of shock. 'Are you suggesting that the girl was murdered?'

'Yes.'

She quickly had command of herself again. 'That's ridiculous.'

'I don't think so. Look, the girl had somehow arranged to video herself in bed with him, she lets him know she's got the tape, she names her price. But he doesn't feel certain that he'll be buying her permanent silence by paying the demand...so he decides on a more reliable method of keeping her quiet.'

'But I just can't believe it of him. He's the gentlest of men. I mean, I know he has a rough diamond exterior, but, deep down, he wouldn't hurt a fly. You only have to see him with –'

'I'm afraid, Mrs Tressider, that maybe you don't know your husband as well as you think you do.'

He had been hoping for more reaction, and he was certainly rewarded this time. Her face became a mask of amazement. 'My *husband*?'

'Yes, Mrs Tressider. Your husband, Brian.'

'You mean you thought the video was of Dayna Richman and Brian?'

'Yes.'

She shook her head in disbelief. 'Well, I can assure you it wasn't, Mr Paris.'

'You can't be so sure. I know it's sometimes hard for a wife to imagine that her husband –'

'Mr Paris, Brian and I have no sex-life at all. We haven't had for nearly thirty years. That's why we haven't got any children.'

'I'm sorry to have to say this, but it is possible that, flattered by the attentions of a younger woman –'

'No, Mr Paris!' She was almost shouting now. 'It is not possible. Will you please give me the credit for knowing my own husband's medical condition? Brian was involved in a car crash when he was twenty-five, just after we were married. He escaped, fortunately, with what they described as "minor injuries". *Un*fortunately, one of those "minor injuries" put paid to our sex-life. And not just *our* sex-life – Brian's sex-life with anyone else. So, Mr Paris, you can forget your fantasies of my husband frolicking between the sheets with Dayna Richman. I am sorry to say that, though he's very powerful in every other department of his life, down there nothing works at all!'

This time he got all the reaction he had hoped for. Tears poured down Brenda Tressider's face, furrowing through the expertly-applied make-up.

Charles Paris felt a complete heel.

Of course she wouldn't give him any more information. She left his room as soon as she'd recovered from this unseemly breakdown of control. And she recovered very quickly. She'd had a lot of practice at that sort of thing through the long charade of her marriage.

But she'd told Charles enough. If it wasn't Brian Tressider whom Dayna had been blackmailing, there was only one other person it could be.

Chapter Twenty-One

IN SPITE of the volume of whisky he'd consumed, Charles only slept fleetingly. He didn't feel drunk, but his mind was very full. If he did doze off for a few minutes, he would quickly reawake with a new link of logic connecting in his brain.

It all fell into place now. Most of the sequence of solution had been complete when he had cast Brian Tressider as murderer. With a new actor in that role, it all worked even better. The logic was tighter, the conclusion more secure.

He woke for the last time around quarter to six. His head didn't quite ache, but felt scraped and empty with tiredness. He went down to breakfast early, thinking his quarry might do the same, but was out of luck.

Never mind. Time enough. The murderer didn't know that suspicions were homing in on him. It was unlikely that Brenda Tressider would have tipped him off, so Charles need not feel in any danger. He could bide his time, and make the confrontation whenever a convenient moment arose.

Charles Paris ate a large breakfast and did his Confectionery presentation very professionally. Modem conference technology actually made it difficult to do otherwise. The script was on a roller, its speed controlled by an operator in the glass box at the back of the hall. This was relayed to a television monitor concealed on the floor behind the lectern, whence it was projected up on to an angled screen of special glass, where the words were visible to the reader but transparent to the audience. And for the Confectionery presentation, unlike Ken Colebourne's, the slides were also controlled from the box.

So, so long as the speaker had had a run-through and knew the contents of his text, it was pretty hard to go wrong. Particularly if, like Charles Paris, that speaker had spent much of his life reading scripts.

This conference was the first time he had used such apparatus and, seeing how easy the system was, Charles vowed in future to be even more sceptical of the oratory of politicians. It was now possible for any fool to look sincere or appear to struggle for the apposite *bon mot* with a script rolling comfortingly in front of him, unseen by his audience.

After Confectionery, there was a coffee-break and then Paul Taggart did Beverages. His approach was totally businesslike and functional; he supported his argument with slides and did not allow the presentation to be sullied by humour. The eyes of the massed rows of salesmen in floppy suits and Post-Surrealist ties glazed over in the final extended agony of last night's hangover before the blessed resuscitation of a lunchtime drink.

There was no sign of Daryl Fletcher, and a few of the other seats were empty. Charles wondered idly how many Shelley had recruited to join in her day's entertainment.

He also wondered how the glazed salesmen would react to the more upbeat presentation of the Delmoleen 'Green', which was to begin the afternoon's proceedings.

Will Parton was optimistic as they joined the rush for the bars the minute Paul Taggart had delivered his final statistic. 'Going to be great, Charles,' he enthused. 'After that lot, the Tom Jones routine'll really knock 'em dead.'

Charles was less certain, but, God, he felt better for a drink. Couple of beers first, just to irrigate the hangover. Then maybe a Bell's. And a bit of wine with lunch. That should sort him out.

Across the melée of salesmen, who were all drinking as if alcohol was an endangered species, he could see his quarry. But the murderer was surrounded and preoccupied. The confrontation would have to wait.

It finally occurred in the afternoon tea-break, after the Biscuits and Cereals presentation.

Difficult to say exactly how well this extravaganza had gone. Robin Pritchard's initial remark had been predictable, and lulled those of the audience who'd managed to get back after lunch into the somnolent assurance that the rest of the programme would be equally bland. Legs were stretched out under the chairs in front, and eyelids drooped as the salesmen saw an opportunity to catch up on the sleep they had lost the night before and the sleep they would undoubtedly lose after the forthcoming banquet.

The outlining of the proposed ad campaign for the new Delmoleen muesli bar raised a flicker of interest, but none of the salesmen was prepared for the sudden change of gear from commerce to showbiz that followed.

Robin Pritchard made the most of the occasion. Suddenly raising his voice and adding to it a phoney ringmaster's razzmatazz, he shouted, 'But don't take my word for it! No, for the latest, mind-stretching news about the Delmoleen "Green", let me hand you over to – THE GREEN MACHINE!'

The appearance of a thickening green-bow-tied night-club singer in a green tuxedo, escorted by two male dancers in green waistcoats and two female dancers in green catsuits, certainly had the effect of waking the audience up, if only because it was such an unfamiliar sight at a Delmoleen sales conference.

But whether what ensued had the effect of exciting the salesmen about the new product they would shortly have to sell was less certain.

It undoubtedly excited them to laughter.

The performers had put in more rehearsal during the day and were now quite slick. The singer had added a few more sexy hip-gyrations in what he imagined to be the style of Tom Jones, but these elicited only coarse comments from the predominantly male audience.

This ribaldry was exacerbated by the actions of the female dancers. The prop they had been missing on the previous evening – the six-foot green-wrapped giant muesli bar – was held upright by the 'boys' at one point in the routine and caressed lovingly by the two 'girls'. Though the intention of these movements had not been erotic, the effect undoubtedly was. The Delmoleen sales force was an audience highly attuned to the detection of innuendo, and the phallic implications were not lost on them.

'Ooh, lovely! Do it some more!' came a throaty cry from the auditorium at the height of the female dancers' ministrations. This unfortunately got the girls themselves giggling and so, while the singer struggled gamely on, thrusting out his hips and extolling the '*Green* – "*Green*" – *Del* – *mo* – *leen*', the chorus behind him had degenerated into something of a shambles.

Whether or not the sales force got the message about all the virtues of the Delmoleen 'Green', there was certainly no danger that they would forget the name of the product.

So maybe the exercise hadn't been wasted, after all.

At the tea-break, Charles was in the Ambassador Hotel's reception area when he saw his quarry, on his own, going through into one of the lounges. At the bank of telephones in the recesses of the hall, Heather Routledge was hunched over a receiver, her tense body language leaving no doubt that she was once again talking to her mother.

'Oh, Mr Paris,' called the receptionist. 'There was another call from that Mr Skellern.'

'Thank you,' said Charles.

But he was not to be diverted, least of all by a call from Maurice. He went through into the lounge and sat in an armchair opposite his quarry, who was bent over the Top Table seating plan for the evening's banquet.

'Afternoon, Ken.'

The Marketing Director looked up. 'Oh, Charles,' he acknowledged mildly, then grinned. 'Well, I remain to be convinced that Delmoleen sales conferences need to be converted into *The Black and White Minstrel Show*. Though, actually, on this afternoon's showing, it seemed more like *Oh! Calcutta!*'

Charles nodded. Ken Colebourne seemed fairly relaxed, or at least as relaxed as the responsibilities of the sales conference allowed him to be. It would be churlish to add another anxiety to his load at such a moment.

On the other hand, a human life had been taken. And, though, from what he'd heard of her character, he didn't have much respect for Dayna Richman, Charles Paris still had to find out the truth of what had happened to her.

'I want to talk about something a bit awkward, Ken...' he began gruffly.

'Oh yes? Problems?'

'You could say that. It's about Dayna.'

The name caught Ken Colebourne like a blow to the solar plexus. He gaped at his accuser, winded.

'I know about you having slept with her.'

'What!' The Marketing Director half-rose to his feet. 'For Christ's sake keep quiet about that! If Pat found out, it'd kill her!'

'I wasn't proposing to tell Pat.'

'Then what do you want? Are you after money too?'

Ken Colebourne's words satisfyingly confirmed Charles's conjecture. There had been an instant recognition of the subject under discussion, and no attempt at denial.

'No, I'm not after money.'

'Then what do you want? If you're offering moral judgement, I can do without it, thank you. I've punished myself quite enough for what happened. God, if you only knew how much I've regretted it, from the moment I did it – even while I was doing it. But things haven't been easy, with Pat being ill. I'm a normal man – God damn me for it – perhaps a bit over-sexed, I don't know – and that Dayna was a right little vamp. She knew what a man wants all right and –'

'I'm not blaming you for going to bed with her, Ken. I'm blaming you for what happened afterwards.'

'You should blame her for that, not me! I wasn't the one who taped the whole sordid business. I wasn't the one who introduced blackmail into the proceedings.'

'Did you ever get the tape, Ken?'

'No. I'm still not sure that it existed. She may have invented it, just to make her blackmail demands more forceful. Didn't really matter whether there was a tape or not. The threat of her telling Pat was quite sufficient. I'd have paid anything, I'd have done anything, to stop that happening.

'You don't know what it's been like for me with Pat these last few years...to watch someone you love, wasting away...all their life trickling through your fingers. And there's nothing you can do to stop it, nothing you can offer. Except love. So you go on telling them you love them, and then eventually that's all they've got. And the thought that some little tart could have threatened that love...Dayna seduced me when I was at a low ebb. It was nothing, just physical. But it would have killed Pat if she'd found out.'

'So you had to ensure that Pat never did find out?'

'I had to think of ways of doing that, yes.'

'And you confided in Brian Tressider?'

Ken nodded. That, thought Charles, made sense of some of the things Brenda had said the night before.

'Yes, I told Brian. We've always been mates, right from the start. I thought he might see some way out.'

'And did he?'

'Well, he...he offered to help me with the money. Otherwise, he didn't really have any suggestions.'

'So you had to work out what to do on your own?'

The Marketing Director nodded. 'Yes. All kind of solutions went through my head. I hadn't really decided which one to go along with, when suddenly I had the most amazing piece of good luck...'

But Charles was never to find out what that piece of good luck had been.

'Ken!' a controlled but tense voice hissed.

They looked up to see Brenda Tressider standing in the doorway. She was pale.

'Ken, Pat passed out while we were going round the winery.'

He was instantly on his feet. 'Oh, my God! Where is she now?'

'In your suite. I brought her back. She's conscious. She says she's fine. The hotel's organising a doctor.'

'I'll go straight up.' He turned to Charles. 'We'll finish this conversation some other time.'

In his face there was an expression of naked pleading. Do what you like, it seemed to say, do whatever's necessary, but please don't let Pat find out what happened.

After Ken had gone, the expression Brenda Tressider turned on Charles was very different. She had sensed what they'd been talking about.

And she despised Charles Paris for having been so insensitive as to raise the subject.

He felt frustrated as, a few minutes later, he wandered back towards the main hall. To have been so near to a confession from Ken Colebourne and yet not to have got all the details...

A weariness filled him. What was the point, after all? Assuming what now seemed almost certain – that the Marketing Director had arranged the accident that killed Dayna Richman – what possible good would be served by bringing the man to justice for his crime?

All that that could achieve would be to deprive his dying wife of the comfort of a loving husband's presence during her last months.

And, weighing the moral claims of Patricia Colebourne against those of the late Dayna Richman...well, there wasn't much contest, really.

Charles felt low and depressed. He needed to talk to someone to reassure him. Frances? He glanced across towards the telephones. But no, it was term-time. Frances would still be at school, being responsible and headmistressly.

He caught the eye of Heather Routledge, who was still glued to the receiver. She raised her eyebrows in a despairing mime of the impossibility of getting off the phone.

'Charles. We need your help.'

It was Brian Tressider, tall, vigorous, reassuring. No one seeing him could have suspected the tragic deficiency that had blighted his married life.

'Yes? What can I do for you?'

'Look, Ken Colebourne's wife's ill –'

'I know. I heard from Brenda.'

'Right. Well, he's got to stay with her for the moment. But the thing is...'
The Managing Director consulted his watch. 'Ken was about to do his
marketing spiel for the sales force...'

'Oh. Yes.'

'You know how to use that autocue, don't you, Charles?'

The bulk of the presentation went fine. Charles hadn't been concentrating
when Ken had rehearsed the day before, but he was enough of a professional
to read a script unseen with a fair degree of competence.

And, though this time he was operating the slides himself, their cues were
all clearly marked on the script that appeared magically on his invisible
lectern. He held the control in his right hand and just clicked its button at the
appropriate moment. He could see each new slide reflected in the glass of the
control box at the back of the conference auditorium, and thereby check that
he wasn't going out of sequence.

Of course, he didn't get much reaction, but then he hadn't expected much.
Ken Colebourne's script didn't contain many jokes and, after the hilarity of
the 'Green' song-and-dance act, the sales force were saving their laughter for
Nicky Rules' cabaret later on.

It was very near the end of the presentation, when Charles was beginning to
feel confident – perhaps even a little careless – that things started to come
unstuck.

'And we still stand by the principles which made the company successful
when it started,' he read from the autocue. 'We take pride in those principles.
Everyone who works for Delmoleen knows that all our products are made by
the most modern manufacturing methods...'

Nonchalantly, Charles pressed the control in his hand. It didn't seem to click.
Hastily he pressed it again, and was surprised by a huge laugh from the audience.

He tried covertly to turn round. On the screen he could see the slide of the
children in front of their rusty Caribbean hut and broken-down tractor. It
didn't give the impression of 'the most modern manufacturing methods'. He
had managed to get himself one slide out of synch.

Oh God, no. He could feel sweat trickling down his back as he pressed on
through the script, desperately trying to regain control.

'They know the same high quality Delmoleen goods are sold all over the
world...They know what the public think of Delmoleen.'

In the panic, his thumb slipped on the button. It clicked again. Reflected in
the glass of the control box, he could see the screen with its screaming
newspaper headline: "'THEY'RE RUBBISH! I'LL NEVER TOUCH
ANYTHING THEY MANUFACTURE AGAIN!" SAYS BOTULISM
BOY'S HEARTBREAK MOTHER.'

Once again the audience roared. They thought the 'Green' presentation was all
they were going to get in the way of laughs that afternoon. This was a bonus.

Sweat prickled at Charles's temples. 'They know,' he floundered doggedly on, 'that the public trust the guarantee of hygiene that only comes from Delmoleen – and not from other companies I could mention. And they know that Delmoleen goods are sold at a price that's more than competitive. So they begin to understand what being a part of the Delmoleen family is really worth.'

Again his finger slipped on the control. The slide of bedtime drinks appeared, but all the cartons seemed to recede into background behind the huge sign reading '98p'. The audience's hilarity grew.

Head down and run for the line, thought Charles. Just get through it as quickly as possible.

'And, in these environmentally-conscious times,' he gabbled, 'they know that Delmoleen products are only made from the freshest of organically-grown natural ingredients. Yes, Delmoleen cares. Delmoleen is like a family. And I want to show you what sort of people are part of the Delmoleen family.'

Surely that was the final cue, wasn't it? He gave a despairing click on the control.

The screen behind him filled with a picture of vegetables.

The massed salesmen roared in uncontrollable hysteria.

Nicky Rules' cabaret was going to have to be bloody good to be funnier than this lot.

Chapter Twenty-Two

OF COURSE Brian Tressider brought them round. He was a natural communicator, and he even managed to give the impression that the farce of Charles Paris's presentation had been in some way deliberate. He charmed the sales force into a circle of complicity. He motivated them. He made them feel excited – and even privileged – to work for Delmoleen. It was a great performance.

At the end he presented Daryl Fletcher with his Fiesta, which stood in gleaming splendour on a podium at the back of the stage. The Top Salesman, grinning hugely, made some derisively disparaging remarks about his rivals, before taking the keys and posing for cameras in the driving seat of his prize, with his Managing Director standing paternally beside him.

Daryl looked triumphant, but a little weary. Maybe his participation in his wife's plans for the day had taken it out of him.

And from the pride with which he surveyed his Fiesta, no one would have guessed he intended to trade it in as soon as possible and spend the money on more cosmetic surgery for his precious Cortina.

Charles had not expected to encounter Ken Colebourne again that evening, and was surprised to see the Marketing Director hurrying through the crowded bar towards him just before the banquet started. Ken was neatly dressed in dinner suit and black tie. That was the rule for the Top Table, though the assembled salesmen were expected to wear what invitations, for some reason, always call 'lounge suits'.

'How's Patricia?' asked Charles.

'Better, thank you. She's even insisting on coming to the banquet.'

'That's good news, isn't it?'

Ken Colebourne looked uncertain. 'I hope so. She says she feels fine, but it's always difficult to know with her. She might just be doing it out of loyalty. Anyway, she's not going to sit on the Top Table. She'll be on a side one near the door, so if she does have to leave, she can do so with the minimum of fuss.'

'Oh. Right.'

The Marketing Director hesitated. 'About what we were discussing earlier...'

'Yes?'

'You got to keep quiet about it.'

'I will. I said I would.'

Charles suddenly felt the voluminous lapels of his jacket seized as Ken Colebourne's face was thrust close to his. He could smell the staleness of whisky on the man's breath. 'You'd better!' the voice hissed. 'If I find out you've breathed a word about it to anyone, I'll bloody well kill you!'

Charles Paris realised, with a little shiver, that such a threat, from someone who'd done what Ken Colebourne had done, had to be taken seriously.

The banquet was more fun than he'd anticipated. The food was the predictable cardboard, but there was plenty of wine and the company was good. Charles sat with Will Parton, the Fletchers and a group of other rowdy salesmen and wives.

Since they had now discharged their obligations to the conference, the *Parton Parcel* team felt justified in getting quite drunk. Their contribution had been a success...well, probably a success. True, there was a slight question mark over the '*Green, "Green" – Del – mo – leen*' routine, but... No, it had been good, really good...

The more drinks they had, the more good they convinced themselves it had been, and they started to spin lucrative fantasies of all the new assignments *Parton Parcel* would take on, as the company rapidly cornered the market in corporate work.

Daryl and Shelley Fletcher also gave good value. He was flushed with success and alcohol, and she was flushed with something, too. Mercifully, Daryl was kept off the subject of custom cars as he engaged with his colleagues in a ribald exchange of jokes, to which Shelley contributed with many a throaty chuckle. She was a fine example for the success of the Equal Opportunity campaign, demonstrating a mind at least as filthy as any of the men's.

The atmosphere of the evening had about it a blokeishness of the kind Charles usually despised, but, well...once in a while it didn't hurt...

He looked round the crowded banqueting hall. At one of the side tables he could see Heather Routledge sitting beside Alan Hibbert. Neither seemed to be enjoying their perk of being invited to the sales conference that much. They exchanged the odd word, but maybe they had exhausted all their mutual topics of conversation, working day by day in the warehouse at Stenley Curton.

At another side table, Charles could see Patricia Colebourne. She had been sat with a suitably mature group of salesmen and wives, but conversation didn't seem to be flowing there either. Nor was she eating, just pushing the food round her plate with a fork.

She looked ghastly. Now almost transparently thin, her skin had an unearthly sheen and her body swayed slightly as if she might faint again at any moment.

Only the dogged set of her mouth showed the strength of will that was holding her together. She was determined to support her man. However ill she felt, she would not allow anything to keep her away from Ken's big night.

Charles glanced up at her husband on the raised Top Table. He looked stressed and sweaty, as he tried to concentrate on what the satin-tuxedoed smoothie beside him was saying.

This character Charles recognised to be Nicky Rules. Though the game-show that had made this minor comedian into a national figure was not the kind of programme Charles watched, the man's profile was now so high that it was impossible not to recognise him. The sharp nose and beady eyes were a regular fixture on hoardings and magazine covers all over the country.

Nicky Rules was *big*. It was quite a feather in Ken Colebourne's cap to have booked him for the conference – however much Delmoleen had had to pay for the privilege. And, having heard the scale of money that even minor celebrities commanded for corporate appearances, Charles knew that Nicky Rules' fee would have been astronomical – certainly more for that one night than most of the salesmen present earned in a year.

Still, he was the right name to get. Daryl and Shelley Fletcher were very impressed. They loved his show. 'He's so rude, Chowss,' Shelley kept saying gleefully, 'so bloody rude to everyone. I wonder who he's going to get his knife into tonight...?'

Nicky Rules had certainly done his homework.

He prided himself on tailoring his material to his audience. It wasn't that he came up with new jokes. By no means. Most of his jokes that night were of pensionable age, but each had been very carefully adapted to the Delmoleen set-up.

He started predictably enough. 'I was just talking to Brian, your Managing Director, about this conference. I asked him how many salesmen worked for Delmoleen. He said, "About half of them."'

The insulted salesmen roared their appreciation, confirming the old truth that audiences like jokes they recognise.

'Not of course that Brian himself has a problem about working. Never does anything else, does he? You know, he puts in such long hours in the office that on the rare occasions when he does get home, Brenda doesn't recognise him. Last time he walked into his house – and we're talking only six months ago – she called the police, said she got a prowler.'

This wasn't particularly funny, but it got the laughs. There was a kind of sycophantic recognition that the famous comedian had taken the trouble to find out about Delmoleen.

Nicky Rules knew how far he could go. Jokes about Brian Tressider being a workaholic were fine – in fact quite flattering. They bolstered his image, at the same time showing how sportingly he could take a joke against himself. But the comedian didn't risk any lines of a more personal nature against the Managing Director, certainly nothing that might hold him up to ridicule.

With other members of the management he was less charitable. He seemed to know who the safe butts were.

He homed in on the ethnic origins of the Product Manager for Beverages. 'Paul Taggart's not really mean, you know. Mind you, couple of years back, he won a fortnight's holiday for two in the Seychelles. Left his wife at home and went by himself – twice!'

The Product Manager for Biscuits and Cereals did not escape unscathed either. 'Of course, Robin Pritchard went to business school, didn't he? Doesn't actually make him any more efficient, but at least he understands *why* he's inefficient!'

The butt of the joke smiled indulgently at this joshing.

'Did you know that he came to Delmoleen from an electrical goods company? Very high up the management he was there – used to go round selling vacuum cleaners!'

Robin Pritchard looked less amused by this.

'Went round to one lady's house, threw some dirt on the floor, said, "I have so much faith in my product that, if it doesn't clean up every speck of that dirt, I'll eat it off the carpet myself." Woman says, "Here's a spoon. We haven't got any electricity!"'

The audience found this very funny. Robin Pritchard smiled sourly, trying but failing to look as if he found it very funny too.

'And then, of course,' said Nicky Rules, 'there's your Marketing Director, Ken Colebourne...'

The comedian smiled his evil smile. 'Actually, you know, it's not the first time old Ken's been down to Brighton. Was here with his secretary a few weeks back to set the whole thing up – at least that was his story. When he got back to Stenley Curton, he said to his secretary, "Can you ever forget that lovely weekend we had in Brighton?"'

'"Maybe," she said. "What's it worth?"'

The salesmen enjoyed this old joke, too. Ken Colebourne looked uneasy. But worse was to come.

'Of course, Ken's always had an eye for the young girls, hasn't he? When his wife got to forty, he said he wanted to change her for two twenties.'

Where Nicky Rules had got his information from, Charles didn't know. But what he said seemed to be striking a chord with the audience, so maybe Ken did have that kind of reputation round Delmoleen.

The comedian continued inexorably, 'Actually, Ken went up to one of the girls in the typing pool at Stenley Curton – said to her, "I dreamt about you last night." "Did you?" she said. "No," he replied, "you wouldn't let me."

'Then someone walked past his office and heard old Ken and one of the typists talking. "What are you trying to tell me?" she's saying. "I don't know," says Ken. "I'm groping for words." "Well," she says, "you won't find them down there."

'Story I heard about Ken taking on a new secretary. Really likes the look of her, he does. Says, "I'd like you to take the job. How much are you going to want to be paid?" "Hundred and fifty a week," she says. "Great," says Ken,

"I'll give you that with pleasure." "Oh no," she says. "With pleasure it'll be two hundred and fifty!"'

How much longer Nicky Rules would have gone on in this vein, how much bluer he would have got, they never found out. Ken Colebourne had taken all he could take. He rose to his feet, kicked his chair back and strode off to the nearest exit.

Nicky Rules watched him go with a quizzical expression, then turned back to his audience.

'Apologies from the Marketing Director,' he said. 'Suddenly been taken randy.'

The audience roared and roared.

The mocking laughter rang in Charles's ears as he hurried off after Ken.

The banqueting suite was in the basement of the Ambassador Hotel. Charles hurried out into the lobby and saw Ken Colebourne standing by the lifts, waiting impatiently.

The Marketing Director blazed a look of concentrated hatred at him.

'I didn't say a word,' Charles protested. 'I don't know what made him start off on all that stuff.'

'I can never face Pat again. Not after that.'

'Ken...'

Charles stepped forward, but Ken Colebourne was not to be comforted. He turned away, giving up hopes of the lift and pushing through the double doors that led to the stairs. As he turned, Charles caught the glint of a tear in his eye.

Charles followed through the doors, but his quarry was already out of sight. Must have been running flat out to get away so quickly. Charles emerged by the reception area and hurried out through the hotel's main doors. There was no sign of Ken Colebourne on the rain-swept sea front.

Most likely gone up to his suite. Charles went back inside, had a cursory look in the lounges and bars of the ground floor, then walked up to Reception.

'Could you try Mr Colebourne's suite, please?'

'I think Mr Colebourne's involved in the Delmoleen banquet downstairs.'

'No, he just came out. Please.'

The girl checked a list and dialled the number. It was while the phone was ringing that Charles heard a commotion outside the front of the hotel.

Sickened by anticipation, he moved slowly towards the main door.

'I'm afraid there's no reply,' the receptionist called after him.

'No,' he murmured. 'There wouldn't be.'

The Ambassador Hotel is eight storeys high. On the eighth is a bar with panoramic views over the sea. It was to that bar, it emerged later, that Ken Colebourne had gone. He had ordered, paid for and quickly downed a large Scotch, then walked through the doors on to the balcony.

Hardly breaking his stride, he had climbed over the parapet, and jumped.

His body lay crumpled on the pavement directly in front of the hotel's main doors.

Chapter Twenty-Three

THE NEWS was smuggled discreetly to Brian Tressider, who, instantly decisive as ever, decreed that no purpose would be served by breaking up the party. So, showing no untoward emotion, he sat through the act of the American girl singer who'd been big in the charts in the early seventies, and then, when the band took over, began the first dance with Brenda in his arms. He subsequently did more public relations work, dancing jovially with the wives of specially favoured salesmen.

The official announcement of his Marketing Director's death would, he had decided, be made in the morning.

Charles Paris did not return to the banqueting suite. Instead, he went wearily to his room and ordered another Room Service bottle of whisky. They didn't have Bell's but he made do.

The death seemed so unnecessary, and he couldn't totally eradicate a feeling of guilt. Though he deserved no blame for the hideous inappropriateness – or perhaps appropriateness – of Nicky Rules' routine, Charles still felt responsible for having hounded the dead man earlier in the day. It wasn't a good feeling.

He didn't know how long he'd been sitting there, but about a third of the whisky had gone, when there was a gentle tap on his door.

'Come in,' he said, too dispirited to move.

It was Brenda Tressider, still immaculate in her ball dress. He shambled to his feet. 'Come in. Can I get you something? More of that tap water?'

'No, thank you.' She closed the door and moved a few steps into the room. 'I just wanted to say that I'm sorry about what happened...'

'Yes.'

'And that you mustn't feel bad about it.'

'Easily said.'

'Ken was devoted to Pat. He really couldn't have lived without her.'

'No, but they'd have got over this. They could have been reconciled.'

Brenda Tressider looked at him in puzzlement. 'What do you mean? They could have got over it? You know that Pat's dead, don't you?'

'What?'

'She felt ill during the banquet and slipped away without any fuss. She managed to get up to their suite, but there...she must have passed out on the floor...maybe just died straight away. Nobody'll ever know for sure. The

Hotel Manager found her after…after they'd found Ken.'

'But –'

'She was very ill. This had been on the cards for a long time. And I'd always been afraid of how Ken would react when the moment finally came.'

'Oh. So what exactly do you think happened?'

'Ken must've noticed she was missing from her table. In the middle of the cabaret. That must be why he left in such a hurry. Then, when he got to their suite, he found her dead and…just couldn't go on.'

'Tell me, was Patricia present for any of Nicky Rules' routine?'

'No. According to the people at her table, she left before the coffee.'

So Patricia Colebourne had never even been aware of the suggestions that her husband was so afraid of her hearing. She had died in full confidence of his undivided love.

Brenda Tressider's reading of events had not been the correct one. But it was, in its own way, tidy.

And it probably made a more satisfactory ending to the tragedy of Ken and Patricia Colebourne than the truth would have done.

Chapter Twenty-Four

CHARLES PARIS felt exhausted as he crossed the hotel's main lobby on the way to breakfast the following morning. The area was full of luggage and salesmen who were making an early start back to their scattered regions, hopefully re-energised by the previous two days, ready to return to the fray, to sell, sell, sell and increase Delmoleen's precious share of the foodstuffs market.

They didn't look very re-energised. 'Bleary' and 'hungover' would have been better descriptions. And the way some of them snapped at their wives suggested tempers had been shortened by the excesses of the night before.

Predictably enough, in the background Heather Routledge was talking on the telephone – or, more accurately, listening to the telephone. She had the receiver tucked under her chin, leaving both hands free to sort through some files which she was packing into a briefcase. Long practice had taught her that, as when listening to the radio, it was possible to do other things while her mother was talking on the telephone.

Charles found Will at breakfast, looking as ropy as he felt. 'How did your evening pan out?' Charles asked, as he sat down.

'Tiring. Ended up with the Top Salesman and his wife.'

'Oh, Daryl and Shelley? Yes, well, that could have been tiring.'

Will groaned. 'Certainly was.'

'Just the three of you? Or others?'

'Oh, bunch of other people came and went. God, one of the most exhausting nights I've ever spent.'

'Well, you're not getting any younger, Will. Can't go at it in quite the way you used to.'

The writer looked up curiously from his scrambled eggs. 'Go at what?'

'Sex.'

'Sex? There wasn't any sex involved, Charles.'

'Oh. Then what was it that was so exhausting?'

'What was so exhausting was listening to bloody Daryl telling me about all the exciting things he's done to his flaming Cortina!'

'Ah. Yes. Right.'

Charles's coffee arrived. That was welcome. The kipper, however, didn't seem such a good idea as it had when he'd ordered it.

'You heard about Ken Colebourne, Will...?'

'Yes. Bloody tragic.'

'I agree.'

'Well, it means the one authentic Delmoleen contact I've got for *Parton Parcel*'s just gone out of the window.'

Charles winced. That could have been more happily phrased. 'Have to see who the new Marketing Director is, and start the cultivating process all over again.'

'Hm. Still, at least it does mean I've got a solution to my mystery.'

'Mystery?' It took a moment for Will's fuddled mind to catch on. 'Oh, you mean your *murder* mystery. You still harping on that, are you?'

'Oh yes.'

'God, I thought you'd forgotten all about the idea.'

'By no means. No, I now know that a murder definitely took place, I know why, and I know who the murderer was.'

'All right then, surprise me, clever clogs.'

'What do you mean?'

'Well, tell me whodunit.'

'But it's obvious. I thought you'd gathered that.'

'No. I hadn't. Go on then – who're we talking about?'

'Well, obviously – Ken Colebourne.'

'Ken Colebourne.' Will was silent for a moment. 'We are talking about the same murder, aren't we? The girl Dayna in the warehouse...?'

'Yes.'

'Who was crushed by the forklift truck – or rather by the pallets pushed by the forklift truck – during that lunch-break when we were making the video...?'

'Yes.'

'And you think Ken Colebourne did it?'

'I'm certain.'

'Well, you're wrong, Charles.'

'I'm not wrong. I can't be wrong.'

'Oh, everyone can be wrong, Charles. Even you.'

'But –'

Will Parton spelled it out. 'During that lunchtime, you may recall, Griff Merricks and I and the rest of the crew were invited to the Executive dining room. And you weren't, because you were improperly dressed.'

'I'm hardly likely to forget that.'

'No. Well, we were escorted to the Executive dining room by Ken Colebourne. He sat with us right through the meal.'

'But –'

'He only left when he was summoned by a phone call announcing that there had been an accident in the warehouse. I'm sorry, Charles, but your murderer had a perfect alibi for the time of the murder – and I should know, because I am that alibi.'

Charles Paris was totally deflated. In the Deflation Olympics he would have defeated all comers, even pancakes. 'Oh,' he said feebly.

'So sorry to be a spoilsport, love, but I'm afraid you've got to start thinking of another perpetrator for your precious murder.'

And even as Will said the words, Charles did think of another perpetrator. A woman. A woman who was in love with Brian Tressider.

They sat opposite each other in an otherwise empty lounge. She had her coat on, ready to leave the hotel.

'I know exactly what happened that day,' said Charles.

'Oh yes?' She remained cool, unruffled by his accusation. 'Tell me.'

'It was Dayna's boasting that signed her death warrant. She made no secret of her ambitions. She intended to use her sexual charms to make her way up the company. That didn't worry you particularly one way or the other. It was only when she set her sights on Brian that you really saw red.'

'Perhaps.'

'And when you heard that she was going to start working in London.'

That did produce a reaction. A slight indrawing of breath. 'Yes. Yes, that was what did it.'

'Because it was history repeating itself, wasn't it?'

'Yes,' said Heather.

'You'd known Brian from the time you started working at Stenley Curton. He rose up the management ladder and was going to be transferred to London...'

She nodded.

'And at the same time you also had the offer of a job in London...'

'Yes,' she murmured.

'And you were all set to take it, all set to make the break from your family, to start your own independent life, to be near Brian, maybe see how things worked out between you...when your father died.'

'Exactly.'

'I can't imagine your mother was ever an easy woman, Heather...'

'No, she wasn't.'

'But, with your father's death, she started making even greater emotional demands on you.'

'You could say that, yes. In fact, from that moment she trapped me completely. She saw to it that I would never get away from her. Even when she dies, I'll still be trapped. There's not enough of my life left for me to do anything useful with it. Assuming that I had the will to do anything, anyway.'

'So you stayed in Stenley Curton. You monitored Brian's progress from a distance. Then, after a while, you heard he was going to get married.'

'Yes, I cried for weeks when I heard that. I've got reconciled to it, of course. Brenda's the right sort of woman for someone in his position. But, even now, I occasionally have unworthy thoughts about them. Like, for instance, I sometimes get an evil satisfaction from the fact that they don't have children.'

You might be surprised to know what else they don't have, thought Charles.

'But no, it was right. If Brian was going to get to the top, he needed a kind of social leg-up, and that was what Brenda supplied for him. She was at least the right class.'

'Unlike Dayna...'

'Dayna was just a common little scrubber. For her even to think she stood a chance with Brian...well, it was disgusting.'

'Yes. Killing her was a spur-of-the-moment thing, wasn't it, Heather?'

The woman nodded. 'She'd just been in my office, doing all her usual stuff, crowing about the job she'd got in London, crowing about her power over men. That's what I couldn't stand – the way she talked to me about sex... as if it had nothing to do with me...as if I didn't have any kind of sexual identity of my own...'

'Anyway, that got me furious, but I certainly wasn't contemplating murder. And then my mother rang. And I answered the phone and Dayna left the office. But, as she went out, she said something that implied that she had a video tape of her with someone high up in the Delmoleen management...of them, you know, making love...'

'And you thought she meant Brian?'

Heather nodded. Charles could envisage the scene. He was now coming round to the view that Dayna never had had any video of herself with Ken Colebourne. She had seduced him into her bed, yes, but there had been no camera running. That had all been bluff.

Still, she needed something to convince him that it was for real, and thought of Trevor's little cache of pornography. If Ken made any demur about paying her and needed frightening, well, maybe playing him a carefully chosen moment from one of Trevor's tapes might show she meant business.

'I should've realised earlier, Heather, that you've got very adept at doing other things while your mother's talking on the telephone. That day, you left her wittering on, and went through into the warehouse. You hadn't made any plans. Maybe you just intended to reason with Dayna, something like that. But then you saw where she was, scrabbling behind the pallets. And you saw that the forklift engine was running...'

'Yes. I couldn't think why it was.'

'You have Trevor to thank for that...for reasons that aren't important. So it was easy enough to push the truck into gear, pull down some cartons to make it look accidental and...leave things to take their course. Then back into your office, to find your mother continuing her monologue, unaware that you hadn't heard the last few minutes of it.'

'It's not as if I don't know everything she has to say by heart, anyway,' said Heather with sudden viciousness. 'God, she's a cow!'

Charles tended to agree with this assessment, but didn't comment. 'I've been rather slow, actually. I should have realised earlier. Really, from the moment that you gave Trevor an alibi.'

'That was a spur-of-the-moment thing, too. I didn't want there to be any sort of investigation, so I thought, if I got him in the clear, then there wouldn't be.'

'Hm. What, of course, I should have realised was that, once Trevor's alibi was shot to pieces, yours was too. Or your alibi was only your mother at the end of a telephone line.'

Heather smiled. In some strange way, their conversation seemed to have gratified her. 'So, full marks, Charles Paris. You've worked out exactly how the crime was committed.'

'After a few false starts, yes,' he agreed wryly.

'And what do you propose to do about it now?'

'I don't know.'

'Are you going to turn me over to the police?'

'I don't really know what that would achieve.'

'Justice would be seen to be done.'

'Yes, but...Justice in the abstract is a fairly meaningless concept.'

'Not everyone would agree with you on that.'

'Maybe not, but...I don't know. Obviously the death of any human being is a kind of tragedy, but nothing I've heard about Dayna Richman suggests to me that she was any great loss. If I thought your killing her was something rational and premeditated, I'd feel very differently. As it is...I find it odd to hear myself saying this, but her death really doesn't worry me that much.'

'Ah.'

'What about you? Does it worry you?'

'Surprisingly little. In fact, from the moment it happened, I've hardly thought about her death at all.'

An unexpected smile irradiated her face. For a second, she looked almost beautiful. The idea of her as a partner for Brian Tressider did not, at that moment, seem incongruous.

Charles sighed. 'And when I come to think of it, I really don't know what purpose would be served by your going to prison.'

'What do you mean – going to prison?' Heather burst out with sudden venom. 'Don't you understand – I've been in prison for the last twenty-seven years!'

'Yes,' said Charles Paris. 'Yes, I understand.'

There was a silence. Heather toyed for a moment with the handle of her bag. Then she rose to her feet. The brief moment of beauty was past. She looked what she was – an awkward, middle-aged spinster.

'I must go and ring her,' she said.

Chapter Twenty-Five

PARTON PARCEL didn't, as it transpired, corner the market in corporate work. As the recession deepened, corporate budgets were cut back, and the reduced number of contracts that were around went to more established companies.

Anyway, Will Parton got commissioned to write some television scripts about an English detective and an Australian detective doing a year's job-swap. The series was, needless to say, being co-produced with an Australian company, and episodes were to be shot alternately in London and Sydney.

Will cursed his luck, complaining that the commission meant he'd have to put off getting down to his stage play. Still, the bills have to be paid, he said hopelessly, before settling down with relish to begin work on the first script.

For Charles Paris, the work vacuum was not so quickly filled. Indeed, what he'd thought of as his worst year ever looked like being superseded in the badness stakes by the next one. Maurice Skellern said in all his years in the business he'd never known it so quiet.

The agent, incidentally, did find out about the corporate work and was very aggrieved by what he saw as his client 'going behind his back'. Charles, retrospectively and apologetically, paid Maurice 15 per cent of what he'd earned from Delmoleen. What really annoyed him was that while he did so, he actually felt guilty.

Charles kept meaning to contact Frances, but kept putting it off. He thought, after their last encounter, it might be as well to cool things down for a while. Wait until another nice entertainment she'd really like to go to came up. The trouble was, now he'd lost his contacts in the corporate world, invitations to such events seemed to have dried up.

In fact, at times it seemed to Charles Paris that the only lasting thing he'd gained from his corporate experience was the suit. That remained in his Hereford Road bedsitter, on a hanger in the curtained alcove that served as a wardrobe. It hung next to his former suit, the model it had superseded. And with the passage of time, as if by some kind of osmosis of contiguity, it became as defiantly unfashionable as its predecessor.

Delmoleen, under the continuingly vigorous leadership of Brian Tressider, rode the recession better than many of its competitors. His wife, Brenda, continued in her professional role as a tower of strength.

Daryl Fletcher ceased to be a salesman and joined the Marketing

Department of Delmoleen, where he was widely tipped to take over as Marketing Director when the current incumbent, Paul Taggart, retired. Daryl replaced the existing wheels on his Cortina with Firestones on Compomotive 3-piece rims and added some really rad graphics.

His wife Shelley got pregnant. Which was what she'd always wanted to do. She settled down to have lots of babies.

Robin Pritchard got head-hunted and joined another company as Product Manager for a revolutionary new ladies' depilatory, whose outreach was destined to be '*global*'.

Which was just as well, really, because he'd left the company before the failure of the Delmoleen 'Green' launch.

In spite of the findings of test-marketing, the public did not take to the product. For one thing, they were sick to death of muesli bars. For another, they were also sick to death of being told that things they bought were 'environment-friendly'.

Mainly, though, they just didn't like the taste. There was a pretty general consensus that the Delmoleen 'Green' had the flavour and consistency of a table-mat.

Also, the buying public just didn't yet appear to be ready for the concept of a *green* muesli bar. According to retailers, a lot of purchasers had brought their Delmoleen 'Greens' back, complaining they were mouldy.

Lightning Source UK Ltd.
Milton Keynes UK
UKOW041127031212

203110UK00001B/192/A